Sue Townsend, with *The Secret Diary of Adrian Mole Aged 13¾* (1982) and *The Growing Pains of Adrian Mole* (1984), was Britain's bestselling author of the 1980s. Her other hugely successful novels include *Adrian Mole: The Wildnerness Years* (1993), *The Published Confessions of a Middle-Aged Woman (Aged 55¾)* (2001), *Number Ten* (2002) and *Adrian Mole and the Weapons of Mass Destruction* (2004). Most of her books are published by Penguin. She is also well known as a play-wright. She lives in Leicester.

SUE TOWNSEND

Perfect Partners

THE GROWING PAINS OF ADRIAN MOLE

ADRIAN MOLE: THE WILDERNESS YEARS

PENGUIN BOOKS

PENGUIN BOOKS

Published by the Penguin Group
Penguin Books Ltd, 80 Strand, London WC2R ORL, England
Penguin Group (USA) Inc., 375 Hudson Street, New York, New York 10014, USA
Penguin Group (Canada), 90 Eglinton Avenue East, Suite 700, Toronto, Ontario, Canada M4P 2Y3
(a division of Pearson Penguin Canada Inc.)
Penguin Ireland, 25 St Stephen's Green, Dublin 2, Ireland (a division of Penguin Books Ltd)
Penguin Group (Australia), 250 Camberwell Road,
Camberwell, Victoria 3124, Australia (a division of Pearson Australia Group Pty Ltd)
Penguin Books India Pvt Ltd, 11 Community Centre,
Panchsheel Park, New Delhi – 110 017, India
Penguin Group (NZ), cnr Airborne and Rosedale Roads, Albany,
Auckland 1310, New Zealand (a division of Pearson New Zealand Ltd)
Penguin Books (South Africa) (Pty) Ltd, 24 Sturdee Avenue,
Rosebank, Johannesburg 2196, South Africa

Penguin Books Ltd, Registered Offices: 80 Strand, London WC2R ORL, England

www.penguin.com

The Growing Pains of Adrian Mole first published in Great Britain by Methuen 1984
Published in Mandarin Paperbacks 1985
Reprinted in Arrow Books 1998
Published in Penguin Books 2002
Adrian Mole: The Wilderness Years first published in Great Britain by Methuen 1993
Published in Mandarin Paperbacks 1994
Reprinted in Arrow Books 1998
Published in Penguin Books 2003
This combined edition published 2005

1

Copyright © Sue Townsend, 1984, 1993

The moral right of the author has been asserted

Printed in England by Clays Ltd, St Ives plc

ISBN-13: 978-0-141-02738-8
ISBN-10: 0-141-02738-X

THE GROWING PAINS
OF ADRIAN MOLE

To Mum, Dad and the whole family
with love and thanks

'The aristocratic rebel, since he has enough to eat, must have other causes of discontent.'

Bertrand Russell *The History of Western Philosophy*

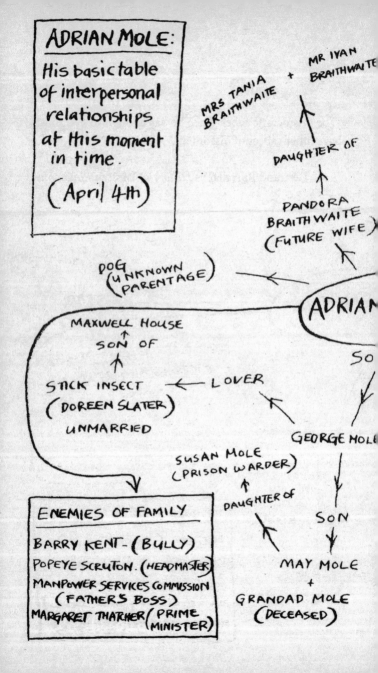

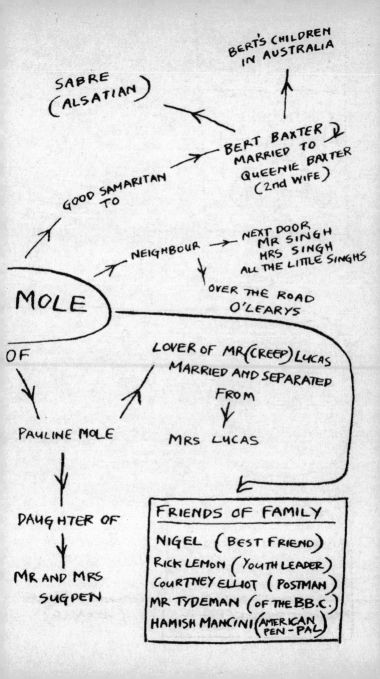

Spring

Sunday April 4th

My father has sent a telegram to the War Office. He wants to take part in the war with Argentina. His telegram read:

QUALIFIED HEATING ENGINEER STOP A1 FITNESS STOP OFFERS HIMSELF IN THE SERVICE OF HIS COUNTRY STOP READY FOR IMMEDIATE MOBIL-IZATION

My mother says that my father will do anything to avoid working for Manpower Services as a canal bank renovator.

At tea-time I was looking at our world map, but I couldn't see the Falkland Islands anywhere. My mother found them; they were hidden under a crumb of fruitcake.

I feel guilty about mentioning a personal anguish at this time of national crisis, but ever since last night when a model aeroplane became stuck fast to my nose with glue, I have suffered torment. My nose has swollen up so much that I am frantic with worry that it might burst and take my brain with it.

I rang the Casualty Department and, after a lot of laughing, the nurse who removed the plane came on the line. She said that I was 'probably allergic to the glue', and that the swelling would go down in a few days. She added, 'Perhaps it will teach you not to sniff glue again.' I tried to explain but she put the phone down.

Pandora has been round but I declined to see her. She would go straight off me if she saw my repulsive nose.

Monday April 5th

Just my luck! It is the first day of the school holidays and I can't go out because of my gigantic swollen nose. Even my mother is a bit worried about it now. She wanted to prick it with a sterilized needle, but I wouldn't let her. She can't sew an accurate patch on a pair of jeans with a needle, let alone do delicate medical procedures with one. I've begged her to take me to a private nose specialist, but she has refused. She says she needs the money for her 'Well Woman' test. She is having her primary and secondary sexual organs checked. Yuk!

The dog is in love with a cocker spaniel called Mitzi. The dog stands no chance, though: (a) it isn't a pedigree, and (b) it doesn't keep itself looking smart like most dogs. I tried to explain these things to the dog, but it just looked sad and mournful and went back to lying outside Mitzi's gate. Being in love is no joke. I have the same problem with Pandora that the dog has with Mitzi. We are both in a lower social class than our loved ones.

Tuesday April 6th

The nation has been told that Britain and Argentina are not at war, we are at conflict.

I am reading *Scoop* by a woman called Evelyn Waugh.

Wednesday April 7th

Wrote and sent Pandora a love letter and a poem. The letter said:

Pandora my love,
Due to an unfortunate physical disability I am unable to see you in person, but every fibre of my being cries out for your immediate physical proximity. Be patient, my love, soon we will laugh again.
    Yours with undying love,
    Adrian
PS. What are your views on the Argentinian conflict, with particular reference to Lord Carrington's resignation?

The Discontented Tuna
I am a Tuna fish,
Swimming in the sea of discontent.
Oh, when, when,
Will I find the spawning ground?

I hope Pandora sees through my poem and realizes the symbolism of 'spawning ground'. I am sick of being the only virgin in our class. Everybody but me is sexually experienced. Barry Kent boasts about how many housewives he makes love to on his father's milkround. He says they are the reason why he is always late for school.

Thursday April 8th
Maundy Thursday. Full Moon

Nose has gone down a bit.

My mother came home from her 'Well Woman' check in a bad mood.

I allowed Pandora to visit me in my darkened bedroom. We had a brilliant kissing session. Pandora was wearing her mother's Janet Reger full-length silk slip under her dress and she allowed me to touch the lace on the hem. I was more interested in the lace near the shoulder straps but Pandora said, 'No darling, we must wait until we've got our "O" levels.'

I pointed out to Pandora that all this sexual frustration is playing havoc with my skin. But she said, 'If you really love me you will wait.'

I said, 'If you really love me you *wouldn't* wait.'

She went then; she had to replace the Janet Reger slip before her mother got back from work.

I have got thirty-eight spots: twenty-eight on my face and the rest on my shoulders.

Friday April 9th
Good Friday

Barry Kent has been spreading malicious rumours that I am addicted to Bostik. His Auntie is a cleaner in the hospital and heard about the nose-stuck-to-model-aeroplane incident. I think it is disgusting that cleaners are allowed to talk about patients' private medical secrets. They should be made to take the Hippocratic oath, like doctors and nurses.

My mother is fed up. She is just sitting around the house smoking and sighing. There was a programme on BBC 2 about French babies being born into swimming pools; it was most interesting (and erotic) but my mother quickly switched over to ITV and watched BERNIE WINTERS!!! When I protested she screamed, 'Why don't you clear off and sulk in your room like other teenagers?'

My father is as baffled as I am as to why my mother is depressed. She's been like it since she came back from the 'Well Woman' clinic.

Perhaps she's not well.

The *Canberra* has gone to the Falklands and taken Barry Kent's older brother, Clive, with it.

Saturday April 10th

Bert has been thrown out of the British Legion club for saying that the Falklands belong to Argentina. Bert doesn't mind, he only used to go to take advantage of their OAP cheap beer offer.

Grandma came round to check our pantry for Argentinian corned beef. We passed the test because our corned beef was made by Brazilian cows.

Grandma has got a funny look in her eyes. My mother says it is called Jingoism, but I think it is more likely to be cataracts forming. We did them in human biology last term, so I speak from knowledge.

Sunday April 11th
Easter Day

The working classes are toiling round the clock to mend Britain's old battleships. Britain is planning to spring a surprise attack on Argentina in six weeks' time.

Grandma made me go to church. The vicar forced us to pray for the Falkland Islanders. He said that they were 'under the tyranny of the jackboot of fascism'. He got dead mad talking about world peace. His sermon went on far too long in my opinion; even Grandma started fidgeting and whispering about getting back to switch her sprouts on.

I have made my mind up to confess to Grandma that I am no longer a Christian believer. She'll just have to find somebody else to help her up the hill to the church. Didn't get an Easter egg: my mother and father said I am too old. Anybody would think there is a law against people of fifteen eating Easter eggs!

Monday April 12th
Easter Monday

I think mother is cracking up; she is behaving even more strangely than usual. She came into my bedroom to change my sheets and when I objected to her dropping cigarette ash on my Falklands Campaign map she said, 'For God's sake, Adrian, this room is like a bloody shrine! Why don't you leave your clothes on the floor like *normal* teenagers?'

I said that I like things to be neat and tidy but she said, 'You're a bloody obsessive,' and went out.

My mother and father are always arguing about their bedroom. My father's side of the room is dead neat, but my mother's side is disgusting: overflowing ashtrays, old yellow *Observers*, books, magazines and puddles of nylon knickers on the floor. *Her* bedside shelves are full of the yukky junk she buys from second-hand shops, one-armed statues, broken vases and stinking old books etc. I pity my father having to share a room with her. All *he's* got on his shelves are his AA book and a photograph of my mother in a wedding dress. She's the only bride I've seen who's got cigarette smoke coming out of her nostrils.

I just can't understand why my father married her.

Tuesday April 13th

After *Crossroads* had finished I asked my father why he had married my mother. Talk about opening the floodgates! Fifteen years of bitterness and resentment spilled out. He said, 'Never make the mistake I made, Adrian. Don't let a woman's body blind you to her character and habits.'

He explained that he met my mother when mini-skirts were in fashion. He said that in those days my mother had superb legs and thighs. He said, 'You must realize that most women looked bloody awful in miniskirts, so your mother had a certain rarity value.'

I was shocked at his sexist attitude and told him that I was in love with Pandora because of her brains and compassion for lesser mortals. My father gave a nasty laugh and said, 'Oh yeah! And if Pandora was as ugly as sin you wouldn't have noticed her bloody IQ and bleeding heart in the first place.'

He ended our first man-to-man talk by saying, 'Look, kiddo, don't even think about getting married until you've spent a few months sharing a bedroom with a bird. If she leaves her knickers on the floor for more than three days running forget it!'

Wednesday April 14th

Mitzi's owner came round to ask my mother to keep our dog away from Mitzi. My mother said that the dog lived in a liberal household and was allowed to go where it pleased.

Mitzi's owner, a Mrs Carmichael, said that if our dog 'continued harassing Mitzi' she would be forced to report our dog to the police. My mother laughed and said, 'Why don't you go the whole hog and take a High Court injunction out?'

Mr Carmichael came round half an hour later. He said that Mitzi was being prepared for Crufts and mustn't suffer any stress. My mother said, 'I've got better things to do than to stand here talking about a romance between a bloody cocker spaniel and a mongrel.' I hoped this would mean she would cook some dinner but no, she went into the kitchen and read the *Guardian* from cover to cover, so I opened a tin of tuna again.

Thursday April 15th

Woke up at 4 a.m. with a toothache. Took six junior aspirins for the pain. At 5 a.m. I woke my mother and father and told them that I was in torment.

My father said, 'It's your own bloody fault for missing your last three dentist's appointments.'

At 5.30 a.m. I asked my father to drive me to the

hospital Casualty Department, but he refused and turned over in bed. It's all right for him: he hasn't got any real teeth. I sat up, racked with agony, and watched the sky get light. The lucky toothless birds started their horrible squawking and I swore that from this day forward I would go to the dentist's four times a year, whether I was in pain or not.

At nine o'clock my mother woke me up to tell me that she'd made me an appointment at the dentist's emergency clinic. I told her that the pain had stopped and instructed her to cancel the appointment.

Friday April 16th
Moon's Last Quarter

Woke up at 3 a.m. in agony with toothache. I tried to suffer in silence but my pain-racked sobs must have filtered through to my parents' bedroom because my father crashed into my room and asked me to be quiet. He showed no sympathy, just moaned on about how he had to work on the canal tomorrow and he needed his sleep. On his way back to bed he slipped on one of my mother's *Cosmopolitans* that she'd left on her side of the bedroom floor. His swearing woke the dog up. Then my mother woke up. Then the lousy birds started. So once again I watched dawn's grey fingers infiltrate the night.

Saturday April 17th

Still in bed with toothache.

My parents are showing me no sympathy, they keep saying, 'You should have gone to the dentist's.'

I have phoned Pandora: she is coming round tomorrow. She asked me if I needed anything; I said a Mars bar would be nice. She said (quite irritably I thought), 'Heavens above, Adrian, aren't your teeth rotten enough?'

The dog has been howling outside Mitzi's gate all day. It is also off its Pedigree Chum and Winalot.

Sunday April 18th
Low Sunday

Pandora has just left my bedroom. I am just about devastated with frustration. I can't go on like this. I have written to Aunt Clara, the Agony Aunt.

Dear Aunt Clara,
I am a fifteen-year-old schoolboy. My grandma tells me that I am attractive and many people have commented on how mature I am for my years. I am the only child of a bad marriage (apart from the dog). My problem is this: I am deeply in love with an older girl (by three months). She is in a class above me (I don't mean in school: we are in the same class at school. I mean that she is a social class above me.) but she claims that this doesn't matter to our

relationship. We have been very happy until recently when I have started to be obsessed by sex. I have fallen to self-manipulation quite a lot lately, and it is OK for a bit but it soon wears off. I know that a proper bout of lovemaking would do me good. It would improve my skin and help my mind to concentrate on my 'O' level studies.

I have tried all sorts of erotic things, but my girl-friend refuses to go the whole hog. She says we are not ready.

I am quite aware of the awesome things about bringing an unwanted baby into the world and I would wear a protective dildo.

Yours in desperation,
Poet of the Midlands

Monday April 19th

We had a dead good debate in Social Studies this morning. It was about the Falklands.

Pandora put the proposition 'That this class is against the use of force to regain the Falkland Islands.'

The standard of debate was quite good for a change. I made a brilliant speech in favour of the motion. I quoted from *Animal Farm* and *The Grapes of Wrath*. I got quite a good round of applause when I sat down.

Barry Kent spoke *against* the proposition. He said, 'Er, I er, fink we should er, you know, like, bomb the coast of Argentina.' He was quoting from his father, yet *he* sat down to a standing ovation!

Dentist's at 2.30, worse luck!

4 p.m. I am now minus a front tooth! The stupid Australian dentist took it *out* instead of repairing it. He even had the nerve to wrap it in a bit of tissue paper and give it to me to take home!

I said, 'But I've got a gap!' He said, 'So has Watford, and if Watford can get used to it so can you.'

I asked him if another tooth would grow in its place. He said, 'Bloody ignorant Poms,' under his breath, but he didn't answer my question.

As I was stumbling out of his surgery clutching my frozen-up jaw he said that he had often seen me walking home from school eating a Mars bar, and it would be entirely my own fault if I was toothless at thirty.

I will walk home another way in future.

Tuesday April 20th

I have now got the kind of face that you see on 'Wanted' posters. I look like a mass murderer. My mother is dead mad with the dentist; she has written him a letter demanding that he makes a false tooth free of charge.

School was terrible; Barry Kent started calling me 'Gappy Mole' and soon everyone was at it; even Pandora was a bit distant. I sent her a note in Physics asking her if she still loved me. She sent a note back saying, 'I will love you for as long as Britain has Gibraltar.'

Wednesday April 21st

It has just been on the news that Spain wants Gibraltar back.

Thursday April 22nd

I couldn't face taking my gap to school this morning so I stayed in bed until 12.45 p.m. I asked my mother for an excuse note. I gave it to Ms Fossington-Gore during afternoon registration. She read it angrily then said, 'At least your mother is honest. It makes a change from the usual lies one has come to expect from most parents.'

She showed me the letter. It said:

Dear Ms Fossington-Gore,
Adrian did not come to school this morning because he didn't get out of bed until 12.45.
Yours faithfully,
Ms Pauline Mole

I will get my father to write my excuse notes in future; he is a born liar.

Friday April 23rd
St George's Day (England). New Moon

Barry Kent came to school in a Union Jack tee-shirt today. Ms Fossington-Gore sent him home to change. Barry Kent shouted, 'I'm celebratin' our patron saint's birthday ain't I?'

Ms Fossington-Gore shouted back, 'You're wearing a symbol of fascism, you nasty NF lout.'

Today is also Shakespeare's birthday. One day I will be a great writer like him. I am well on the way: I have already had two rejection letters from the BBC.

Saturday April 24th

Barry Kent's father is on the front of the local paper tonight. He is pictured holding Barry Kent's Union Jack tee-shirt. The caption underneath his picture says: 'A Patriot mourns loss of National Pride.'

The article said:

Burly World War Two veteran Frederick Kent (45) spoke to our reporter in his homely Council house lounge about his profound feelings of regret that his son Barry (15) was ridiculed and humiliated because he wore a Union Jack tee-shirt to school. Barry is a pupil at Neil Armstrong Comprehensive School. Mrs Kent (35) said, 'My son Barry is a sensitive boy who worships his country and is very fond of St George, so he wore a tee-shirt what had a picture of our great English flag.' Mr Frederick Kent interjected, 'On account of how it was St George's birthday yesterday.'

Mr Kent is refusing to let his son attend school until the teacher concerned, Ms Fossington-Gore (31), makes a public apology.

Mr Reginald Scruton (57), headmaster of the school, said on the telephone today: 'I know the wretched Kent family only too well and I'm sure that we can work something out so that it doesn't make the local rag.' When it was pointed out to Mr Scruton that he was in fact talking to Roger Greenhill, our Education correspondent, Mr Scruton apologized and made the following statement: 'No comment.'

Sunday April 25th
Second after Easter.
Daylight Saving Time begins (USA and Canada)

British troops have recaptured South Georgia. I have adjusted my campaign map accordingly.

Found a strange device in the bathroom this morning. It looked like an egg timer. It said 'Predictor' on the side of the box. I hope my mother is not dabbling with the occult.

Monday April 26th

A mysterious conversation! My mother said, 'George it's positive.' My father said, 'Christ, I can't go through all that three o'clock in the morning stuff again, not at my age.'

It sounds as if my mother is making unreasonable sexual demands on my father.

Tuesday April 27th

Got a letter from Aunt Clara! I read it on the way to school.

Dear Poet of the Midlands,
Well, well, well, you are in a lather aren't you, lovey! Look, you're fifteen, your body's in a whirl, your hormones are in a maelstrom. Your emotions are up and down like a yo-yo.

And of course you want sex. Every lad of your age does. But, my dear, there are people who crave penthouse apartments and exotic holidays. We can't have what we want all the time.

You sound as if you've got a nice sensible lassie; enjoy each other's company. Take up a hobby, keep physically and mentally alert and learn to control your breathing.

Sex is only a small part of life, my dear lad. Enjoy your precious teenage years.

Sincerely,
Aunt Clara

Enjoy my precious teenage years! They are nothing but trouble and misery. I can't wait until I am fully mature and can make urban conversation with intellectuals.

Wednesday April 28th

Stick Insect (alias Doreen Slater) called round to our house today. I haven't seen her since my father and her broke it off.

She was breathing dead quickly and she had a funny look in her eyes. When my father came to the door she didn't say anything, she just opened her coat (she's put a bit of weight on) and said, 'I thought you ought to know, George,' and turned and went down the garden path.

My father didn't say anything. He just leaned against the bannisters sort of weakly.

I said, 'She's looking well isn't she?'

My father muttered, 'Blooming,' then he put his coat on and went to catch her up.

Five minutes later my mother came back from her Jane Fonda's robot class at the neighbourhood centre, she was dead pleased because she had broken the pain barrier.

She shouted, 'George', looked in all the rooms, then asked, 'When did you last see your father?'

I kept quiet, like the kid in the painting. My mother goes berserk if anyone mentions Stick Insect's name.

Thursday April 29th

School is dead brilliant now that Barry Kent's shaved head and ferocious boots are but a bad memory.

Went to the dentist's for an impression. He called me 'Matilda'. I was unable to object because my mouth was full of putty.

Friday April 30th
Moon's First Quarter

My mother and father are getting through a bottle of Vodka a week. Not a minute goes by without one or the other of them bashing the ice tray or slicing a lemon or running to the off-licence for Schweppes.

This is a bad sign. It means something is going to happen.

Saturday May 1st

Grandma rang with her annual gibberish about 'Cast ne'er a clout'. I know it's got something to do with keeping your vest on. But so what? I keep my vest on all the year round anyway.

Britain has bombed Port Stanley airport and put it out of action.

Sunday May 2nd
Third after Easter

Went round to Nigel's and was astounded to hear that his parents are trying to emigrate to Australia! How could any English person want to live abroad? Foreigners can't help living abroad because they were born there, but for an English person to go is ridiculous, especially now that sun-tan lamps are so readily available.

Nigel agrees with me. He asked me if he could stay behind and live at our house. I warned him about the poor standard of living but he said he would bring all his consumer durables with him.

Monday May 3rd
May Day Holiday (UK except Scotland)
Bank Holiday (Scotland)

This morning I spent half an hour in the bathroom studying my nose, after my so-called best friend Nigel asked me last night if I realized I was a Dustin Hoffman look-alike.

I hadn't realized that my nose had grown to such an abnormal size. But the more I looked at it the more I could see that it *is* huge.

My mother bashed on the door and shouted, 'Whatever you're doing in there, stop it at once and come down and eat your breakfast. Your cornflakes are getting soggy!'

When I got downstairs I asked my mother if I reminded her of Dustin Hoffman. She said, 'You should be so lucky, dearie.'

Tuesday May 4th

My mother has stopped wearing a bra. Her bust looks like two poached eggs that have been cooked for too long. I wish she wouldn't wear such tight tee-shirts. It's not dignified in somebody her age (37).

Wednesday May 5th

A strange phone call. The phone rang and I picked it up but before I could say our number a posh woman said: 'Clinic here. You have an appointment with us on Friday at 2 p.m. Will you be able to keep the appointment, Mrs Mole?'

I said, 'Yes,' in a falsetto voice.

'You will be with us for two hours, during that time you will see two doctors and a counsellor who is very experienced in your particular problem,' she said mechanically.

I said, 'Thank you,' in a high-pitched squeak.

She went on, 'Please bring a sample of urine with you, a *small* sample, no full-to-the-brim pickle jars, please.'

'All right,' I croaked.

'Don't upset yourself, Mrs Mole,' the woman said slushily. 'We are here to help, you know.' Then she said, 'Please don't forget our fee. It will be forty-two pounds for your initial consultation.'

'No,' I whispered.

'So Friday at 2 o'clock. Please be punctual.' Then she put the phone down.

What does it all mean? My mother has not said anything about being ill. What is her particular problem? Which 'clinic'?

Thursday May 6th

I heard some very yukky woman talking on Radio Four tonight about how she became a millionairess from writing romantic fiction books. She said that women readers like books about doctors and electronics wizards and people like that. I am going to have a go myself. I could do with a million pounds. The woman said it is important for an author of romantic fiction to have an evocative name, so, after much thought, I have decided to call myself Adrienne Storme. I have already written half the first page:

Longing for Wolverhampton by Adrienne Storme
Jason Westmoreland's copper-flecked eyes glanced cynically around the terrace. He was sick of Capri and longed for Wolverhampton.

He flexed his remaining fingers and examined them

critically. The accident with the chain saw had ended his brilliant career in electronics. His days were now devoid of microchips. There was a yawning chasm in his life. He had tried to fill it with travel and self-gratification but nothing could blot out the memories he had of Gardenia Fetherington, the virginal plastic surgeon at St Bupa's in Wolverhampton.

Jason brooded, blindly blinking back big blurry tears . . .

Friday May 7th

My mother and father were having a discussion about feminism in the car on the way to Sainsbury's this evening. My father said that since my mother's consciousness had been raised he had noticed that she had lost two inches round her bust.

My mother said angrily, 'What have my breasts got to do with anything?' There was a silence then she said, 'But don't you think I have grown as a person, George?'

My father said, 'On the contrary, Pauline, you are much smaller since you stopped wearing high heels.'

Me and my father laughed quite a lot but not for long because my mother gave us one of her powerful glances, then she looked out of the car window. She had a few tears in her eyes.

She looked at me and said, 'If only I had a daughter to talk to.'

My father said, 'We can't take the risk of having another baby like Adrian, Pauline.' Then they began to talk about my babyhood. They made me sound like Damian in the film of *The Omen*.

My mother said, 'It's that bloody Dr Spock's fault that Adrian has turned out like he has.'

I said, 'What *have* I turned out like?'

My mother said, 'You're an anal retentive, aren't you?' and my father said, 'You're tight-fisted, and you've always got your perfectly groomed head in a book.'

I was so shocked I couldn't speak for a bit but, trying to keep my voice light and melodious (not easy when your heart is pierced with the arrows of criticism), I said, 'What sort of son did you want then?'

Their answer took us all around Sainsbury's, through the queue at the checkout, and back to the multi-storey car park.

My father's ideal son was a natural athlete, he was cheerful and outgoing, he was a fluent linguist, he was tall with ruddy unblemished cheeks, he took his hat off to ladies. He went fishing with his father and swapped jokes. He was good with his hands and had a hobby making grandfather clocks. He was good officer material. He would vote Conservative and would marry into a good family. He would set up his own computer business in Guildford.

However, my mother's ideal son would be intense and saturnine. He would go to a school for the Intellectually Precocious. He would fascinate girls and women at an early age, he would enthral visitors with his witty conversation. He would wear his clothes with panache, he would be completely non-sexist, non-ageist, non-racist. (His best friend would be an old African woman.) He would win a scholarship to Oxford, he would take the place by storm and be written about in future biographies. He would turn down offers of safe parliamentary seats in Britain. Instead, he would go to South Africa and lead the blacks into a successful revolution. He would return to England where he would be the first man deemed fit to edit *Spare Rib*. He would move in sparkling social circles. He would take his mother everywhere he went.

When they'd both finished spouting on I said, 'Well I'm sorry if I'm a disappointment to you.'

My mother said, 'It's not your fault, Adrian, it's ours, we should have called you BRETT!!!'

Saturday May 8th
Full Moon

I needed to talk to somebody about my sense of inferiority (which grew even bigger in the night as I lay awake and thought about Brett Mole, the phantom son). So I went to Grandma's. She showed me my baby photos. I must admit that I *was* a bit grotesque: I was completely bald until I was two and I always had a dead fierce expression on my face. Now I know why my mother hasn't got a Technicolor gilt-framed photograph of me on top of our television like other mothers.

But I'm glad I went to Grandma's; she thinks everything about me is brilliant. I told her about Brett Mole, the boy that never was. She said, 'He sounds a right nasty piece of work to me. I'm glad you didn't turn out like *him*.'

Grandma had a bit of arthritis in her shoulder so she took her dress off and I sprayed Ralgex on the pain. Grandma's corset looks like a parachute harness. I asked her how she gets in and out of it. She told me it was all down to self-discipline. She has got a theory that since corsets went out of fashion England has lost its backbone.

Sunday May 9th
4th after Easter. Mother's Day (USA and Canada)

I have just realized that I have never seen a dead body or a real female nipple. This is what comes of living in a cul-de-sac.

Monday May 10th

I asked Pandora to show me one of her nipples but she refused. I tried to explain that it was in the interests of widening my life experience, but she buttoned her cardigan up to the neck and went home.

Tuesday May 11th

We did diabetes in human biology today. Mr Dooher taught us to measure our blood sugar level by testing our wee. This reminded me that I forgot to tell my mother about her appointment at the clinic. Still, I don't suppose it was important.

Wednesday May 12th

I received the following letter from Pandora this morning:

Adrian,

I am writing to terminate our relationship. Our love was once a spiritual thing. We were united in our appreciation of art and literature, but Adrian you have changed. You have become morbidly fixated with my body. Your request to look at my left nipple last night finally convinced me that we must part.

Do not contact me,

Pandora Braithwaite

P.S. If I were you I would seek professional psychiatric help for your hypochondria and your sex mania. Anthony Perkins, who played the maniac in *Psycho*, was in analysis for ten years, so there is no need to be ashamed.

Thursday May 13th

Yesterday before I opened *that* letter I was a normal type of intellectual teenager. Today I know what it is to suffer. I am now an adult. I am no longer young. In fact I have noticed wrinkles forming on my forehead. I wouldn't be surprised if my hair doesn't turn white overnight.

I am in total anguish!
I love her!
I love her!
I love her!
Oh God!
Oh Pandora!

3 a.m. I have used a whole Andrex toilet roll to mop up my tears. I haven't cried so much since the wind blew my candy floss away at Cleethorpes.

4 a.m. I slept fitfully, then got out of bed to watch the dawn break. The world is no longer exciting and colourful. It is grey and full of heartbreak. I thought of doing myself in, but it's not really fair on the people you leave behind. It would upset my mother to come into my room and find my corpse. I shan't bother doing my 'O' levels. I'll be an intellectual road sweeper. I will surprise litter louts by quoting Kafka as they pass me by.

Friday May 14th

Why oh why did I ask Pandora to show me *her* nipple? Anybody's nipple would have done. Nigel says that Sharon Botts will show *everything* for 50p and a pound of grapes.

I have written Pandora a short note.

Pandora Darling,

What can I say? I was crude and clumsy and should have known you would run from me like a startled faun.

Please, at least grant me an audience and let me apologize in person.

Yours with unvanquished love,

Adrian

I think it hits the right note. I got the 'startled faun' bit from one of Grandma's yukky romantic novels. I have sprayed a bit of my mother's 'Tramp' perfume on to the envelope and I will deliver it by hand after dark tonight.

Tramp! Fancy calling a perfume *Tramp*! Ha! Ha! Ha!

Saturday May 15th
Scottish Quarter Day

There were a lot of visitors at Pandora's house. I could hardly get up the drive for Jaguars and Rovers and

Volvos. At first I thought there had been a death in the family because I could see two nuns and a priest eating sausage rolls in the kitchen. Then a gorilla walked in and took a bottle of wine out of the fridge so I realized it must be a fancy dress party. I hid behind the summer house so that I could get a better view: there was a cowboy and a devil talking in one bedroom and a frogman and three gipsies laughing in another. A knight in armour was clanking about in the garden. He was being followed by a cavewoman who was shouting, 'Stand still, Damian. I've found a tin opener!'

Assorted fairies and Kermits and clowns were dancing downstairs, then the gorilla burst in and started dancing with a belly dancer who was wearing a most disgusting flimsy costume which showed her navel and most of her nipples. The belly dancer kept her yashmak on which I thought was hypocritical – as if anybody was interested in looking at her face!

I couldn't see Pandora anywhere, so after about half an hour I ran up to the door and put my letter through the letterbox. As I turned to run back down the drive Toulouse Lautrec shuffled out and was sick in one of the bay tree tubs.

I got home to find Queen Victoria and Prince Albert in our kitchen. Queen Victoria said, 'We're going to the Braithwaites'.' Prince Albert said, 'The dog needs feeding.' Then they swept regally out of the kitchen and up the road to Pandora's. Nobody tells me anything in this house.

Sunday May 16th
Rogation Sunday. Moon's Last Quarter

3 p.m. My mother keeps being sick. It serves her right for staying out until 4 a.m. drinking. My father is still in bed, but he will have to get up soon. He has promised to take Grandma to the garden centre after tea.

7 p.m. Garden centres must be the most boring places on earth, yet adults walk around them with expressions of ecstasy on their faces!

My grandma bought a dozen rose sticks and a bag of fertilizer and a plastic Cupid urn.

My father bought a rose stick called 'Pauline'. He and my mother looked at each other in a sloppy sort of way and held hands over the stick. I left them to it and went and looked at the poisons on the bottom shelves.

I was toying with the idea of buying a bottle when Grandma shouted and asked me to come and carry the fertilizer to the car. Thus my mind was torn from thoughts of death.

Monday May 17th

I was doing my maths homework in the fourth years' cloakroom when I overheard Pandora's confident voice ringing out.

'Yes it *was* a brillo party. But, my dear, I'm rather worried.'

Claire Neilson said, 'Why's that, Pan?'

Pandora said seriously, 'I so *enjoyed* dressing up as a belly dancer, even though it's quite against my feminist principles to exhibit my body.'

Then they moved away down the corridor gassing about Claire Neilson's cat who is expecting kittens.

So, Pandora, who refused to show me *one* of her nipples in the privacy of my bedroom is quite prepared to flaunt *both* nipples at a mixed gathering!!!

Tuesday May 18th

Bumped into Stick Insect in the library. She had her son, Maxwell House, with her. For a thin woman she certainly looked fat.

Maxwell chucked books off the shelves while Stick Insect and I talked about the days when she had been my father's girl-friend. I told her that she had had a lucky escape from my father, but she defended him, saying, 'He is another person when he is on his own with me. He is so sweet and kind.' Yes, and so was Dr Jekyll.

Got *The Condition of the Working Class in England* by Frederick Engels out of the library.

10.30 p.m. I have just realized that Stick Insect used the present tense when she was referring to her relationship with my father. It is absolutely disgraceful. A woman of thirty not knowing the fundamentals of grammar!

Wednesday May 19th

No word from Pandora. When we meet at school she looks through me as if I were the Invisible Man. I have asked Nigel where I can find Sharon Botts. I also went to the greengrocer's to find out how much grapes cost per pound.

Thursday May 20th
Ascension Day

Started reading Fred Engels' book tonight. My father saw me reading it and said, 'I don't want that Commie rubbish in my house.'

I said, 'It's about the class you came from yourself.'

My father said, 'I have worked and slaved and fought to join the middle classes, Adrian, and now I'm here I don't want my son admiring proles and revolutionaries.'

He is deluding himself if he thinks he has joined the middle classes. He still puts HP sauce on his toast.

Friday May 21st

While I was listening to *The Archers* my mother asked me if I minded being an only child. I said on the contrary, I preferred it.

Saturday May 22nd

My father has just asked me if I would like a sister or a brother. I said neither. Why do they keep drivelling on about kids? I hope they aren't thinking about adopting one. They are terrible parents. Look at me, I'm a complete neurotic.

Sunday May 23rd
Sunday after Ascension. New Moon

I couldn't sleep so I got up very early and went for a walk past Pandora's house. I thought about her lying in her Habitat bed wearing her Laura Ashley nightgown and I don't mind admitting that tears sprang to my eyes. However I dashed them away and went to call on old Bert and Queenie.

A wild old woman answered the door, she said, 'What have you got me out of bed for?' It was Queenie with her hair on end and no make-up on.

I apologized and went home to wake my parents up with a cup of tea. Were they grateful? No! My mother said, 'For God's sake, Adrian, it's cockcrow on Sunday morning. Push off and buy the papers or something.'

I bought the papers, read them, then took them up to my parents. I think the central heating must need turning down because my parents were both very red in the face. As I went out I heard my mother say, 'George, we will have to get a lock on that door.'

Monday May 24th
Victoria Day (Canada)

Went to the youth club tonight. Barry Kent was there with his gang worse luck! Rick Lemon was showing a film about potholing in Derbyshire. I was very interested but I found it hard to concentrate on it because Barry Kent kept putting his fingers in front of the projector and making rabbits and giraffes and other animal shapes.

When Barry Kent had gone to the coffee bar to harass the Youth Work student behind the counter I told Rick Lemon about my problems. He said, 'Hey that's bad news, Adrian, but I'm busy tonight. Come and see me at 6 p.m. tomorrow night and we'll have a good rap.'

I think this means that he wants to talk to me at 6 p.m. tomorrow.

Tuesday May 25th

Went to Rick's office in the Youth Club. We had a long talk about my problems. Rick said I was a 'typical product of the petty-bourgeoisie'. He said my problems were the result of my generation's 'alienation from an increasingly urbanized society'. He said my parents were 'morally bankrupt and spiritually dead'. He lit a long, loose herbal cigarette and said, 'Adrian, loosen up. Don't run with the herd. Try and live your life unfettered by convention.' Then he looked at his watch and said, 'Christ I told her I'd be home by seven.'

We walked outside and he got into his wobbly Citroën and said, 'You must come round for supper one night.'

I asked if he was still squatting in the old tyre factory. He said, 'No we've moved into Badger's Copse, the new Barratt housing estate.'

I can't decide if I feel better or worse after talking to Rick. On the whole I think I feel worse.

John Nott has announced on the news that 'one of our ships has been badly damaged.' I hope it is not the *Canberra*. Barry Kent's brother is on it.

Wednesday May 26th

My mother is pregnant! My mother!!!!!!!!!!!!!!!!!
I will be the laughing stock at school. How could

she do this to me? She is three months pregnant already, so in November a baby will be living in this house. I hope they don't expect me to share my room with it. There's no way I'm getting up in the night to give it its bottle.

My parents didn't prepare me or anything. We were all eating spaghetti on toast when my father said casually, 'Oh, by the way, Adrian, congratulations are in order, your mother's three months pregnant.'

Congratulations! What about my 'A' levels in two years' time? How can I study with a toddler smashing the place up around me?

10 p.m. Kissed my poor mother goodnight. She said, 'Are you pleased about the baby, Adrian?' I lied and said 'Yes.'

The ship that went down was the *Coventry*. It is very sad. I am glad that my dad got turned down by the War Office.

Thursday May 27th

Got an airmail letter from Hamish Mancini, the American we met on holiday last year.

1889 West 33rd Street,
New York

Hi there Aid!

Fazed huh! Yeah well, thought I'd communicate. Been feelin kinda unzapped lately, guess mom's divorce to number four kinda unhinged me some. But! Hamish Mancini aint gonna stick around and take no more adult crap, no sir Aid. I'm comin over to visit you some. I got finance. I got documentation, I got nothin keepin me here. Tomorrow I get a flight and wowee I get to see your olde British cottage in the ancient Midlands region.

We'll promenade around ancient ruins. We'll explore Shakespeare land. Huh? I got me some good Lebanon.

See you Saturday buddy.

Hamish Mancini

After reading it and rereading it I think it means that Hamish Mancini is coming to stay with us on Saturday! I wish I hadn't told him that I lived in a thatched cottage.

I haven't told my parents yet. My mother said he ruined her adulterous holiday *avec* Lucas with his constant yapping.

Friday May 28th

Dentist's after school for a false tooth fitting. He took advantage of my weak position in the dentist's chair to make disparaging remarks about British teeth. His assistant is from Malaya so they are both bitter about having lived under the Colonial jungleboot.

I walked home slowly, I was dreading breaking the news about Hamish Mancini's arrival. The dog met me halfway up the cul-de-sac. It was nice to see its happy face.

When I got in I made a big fuss over my poor pregnant mother, I made her a cup of coffee and insisted she put her feet up on the sofa. I put a cushion behind her head and gave her the *Radio Times* to read. I've seen it done in old films (Cary Grant did it to Doris Day).

My mother said, 'It's very kind of you, Adrian, but I can only sit down for a few minutes; I'm playing squash in half an hour.'

But she was in a good mood so I told her about Hamish. She rolled her eyes a bit and pulled her lips tight, but she didn't go mad. So perhaps being with child has improved her temper.

Saturday May 29th
Moon's First Quarter

11.30 p.m. The spare room is prepared, the pantry is full of tinned pumpkin pie, the freezer is bursting with pork grits and corn on the cob and pot roasts. The bathroom has been cleaned to American hygiene standards, the dog has been brushed but Hamish Mancini is not here.

We watched the nine o'clock news but no airliners had crashed into the Atlantic today or any other day this week.

At 11 p.m. my father said, 'Well, I'm not sitting around in my best clothes a minute longer.' So we all took our best clothes off and went to bed.

*

5 a.m. Hamish Mancini is in the spare room. He is playing Appalachian mountain songs on his steel guitar. He got a taxi from Heathrow Airport (130 miles!); the taxi driver found our house all right, but Hamish refused to believe that it was the right address and made the poor bloke drive round our suburb, looking for a thatched cottage. Eventually the taxi driver drove back to our house and got my father out of bed. Hamish paid the worn-out taxi driver with dollar bills.

Sunday May 30th
Whit Sunday

Hamish made a terrible *faux pas* at breakfast. He asked my mother, 'Hey, Pauline, where's that guy, Lucas?'

There was an awful silence, then my father said coldly, 'My wife and Mr Lucas are no longer friends.'

But Hamish went on! 'Gee that's too bad, Mr Lucas was cool y'know? What happened?'

My mother said, 'We don't usually talk about personal matters at breakfast, not in England,' she added.

He said, 'Wow, that great British reserve I've heard about.' He seemed really happy, as if he'd found a whole village full of thatched cottages.

In the afternoon we took him to see Bert and Queenie, he was beside himself with joy. On the way back in the car he kept saying, 'Jee-sus! A genuine Derby [he pronounced it to rhyme with Herbie] and Joan!'

I went to bed at 10 p.m. worn out with his constant enthusiastic exclamations.

Monday May 31st
Spring Holiday (except Scotland)
Bank Holiday (Scotland) Memorial Day (USA)

We took Hamish to the fun fair on our recreation ground. For once Hamish looked a bit subdued. He said, 'I guess Disneyland has kinda given me a false expectation-of-enjoyment level.'

He took my mother on the dodgems and I went on the Flying Whiplash with my father. I was dumbstruck with terror, so was my father; I was OK until I looked down and saw the moron working the machinery. He looked like a Neanderthal man in denims and I had put my life in his clumsy paws!

My father had aged ten years by the time he got off the Flying Whiplash. But when my mother asked him if he had enjoyed himself he said, 'It was grand.'

Our dog has become Hamish's devoted companion; it follows him wherever he goes. Hamish calls our dog 'ol' Blue' and sings it sickly songs about American dogs who sit on their dead masters' graves.

It makes me sick to see how easily the dog's affections are bought.

Tuesday June 1st

Hamish wants to meet Pandora. I told him how things stand between Pandora and me, but Hamish wouldn't listen. He just said, 'But that doesn't stop *me* from meeting her, for Christ's sake.'

Grandma rang up at tea-time and asked if my father would come and collect her but I told her that we'd got an American in the house, so she said she wouldn't bother. She said, 'I'm just too old to cope with Americans, Adrian.' I know how she feels.

Hamish got Pandora's number from our pop-up phone index on the hall table, then he rang her up and invited himself round for supper!

Still, at least the house is peaceful. I am reading *The Quiet American* by Graham Greene, Hughie Greene's brother.

Wednesday June 2nd

Hamish has gone skiing on a dry slope with Pandora. I hope they both break something, preferably their necks.

Thursday June 3rd

I took Hamish to see how an English comprehensive school works today. The only previous knowledge he had of English schools was taken from reading *Tom Brown's Schooldays*, so Hamish was a bit disappointed to find that ritual floggings and roastings had been done away with.

Mr Dock, my English teacher, asked Hamish to give our class a short talk on 'His impressions of England'. Hamish wasn't a bit shy. He went to the front of the class, spat his chewing gum into Mr Dock's wicker basket and said, 'Well, England's great, cute, real fine. Jee-sus it's green! I mean like real green! And I just love your flues [chimneys, translated by Mr Dock]. In the Apple [New York] we don't have flues [chimneys]. I guess the coolest thing, though, is your girls. [Here his eyes met Pandora's.] They may look like icebergs on the surface, but Jee-sus the seven-eighths that's under the surface sure gets a guy warmed up.' He drivelled on for another ten minutes! I was glad when the bell rang.

It is twenty-four days since Pandora spoke to me.

Friday June 4th

Hamish is spending every waking moment at Pandora's house. It is an abuse of our hospitality. A telegram came from America. It was addressed to MANCINI but I opened it, in case his mother had dropped dead or something.

BABY STOP COME HOME TO MOM STOP WE MUST TRY TO INTERACT POSITIVELY STOP HOW THE

BRITS TREATING YOU STOP WIRE ME AND GIVE
ME YOUR ARRIVAL AT KENNEDY STOP I GOT A NEW
SHRINK STOP HE IS PORTUGUESE STOP ETHEL
GLITTENSTEINER SWEARS HE CURED HER
KLEPTOMANIA STOP HOW'S THE WEATHER STOP
IT'S AWFUL HOT HERE STOP BUT IT IS NOT SO
MUCH THE HEAT AS THE HUMIDITY STOP SAY
HELLO TO ADRIAN PAULINE AND MISTER LUCAS
FOR ME STOP I LOVE YOU BABY

I delivered the telegram to Pandora's house. Pandora
took it from me without a word. I turned away without
a word.

Saturday June 5th

Hamish has gone home to Mom. The next time he
runs away from home I hope he goes to Cape Horn
or the Arctic Circle or anywhere I'm not likely to be.

Sunday June 6th
Trinity Sunday, Full Moon

Stayed in my room all day bringing my Falklands
campaign map up to date. I am very aware that I am
living through a historical period and I, Adrian Mole,
predict that the British People will force the government to resign.

Monday June 7th
Holiday (Republic of Ireland)

My mother
Claire Neilson's cat
Mitzi

What have the above all got in common?

The fact that they are all expecting babies, kittens or puppies. The fecundity of this suburb is just amazing. You can't walk down the street without bumping into pregnant women and it has all happened since the council put fluoride in the water.

Tuesday June 8th

Saw Bert Baxter outside the newsagent's. He was sitting in his wheelchair reading the *Morning Star*. We had a long talk about working-class culture. Bert said that if he were a younger man he would infiltrate into the *Sun* newspaper and smash the presses up!

He tried to get me to join the Young Communists. I said I would think about it. I thought about it for five minutes then decided not to. The GCE examiners might get to hear about it.

Wednesday June 9th

It is time I was done with childish things so I have taken all my Enid Blyton books off my bookshelves. I have packed them into an Anchor butter box and put them outside my door. I hope my parents take the hint and stop talking to me as if I were a moron. Anyone who can understand how the International Monetary Fund works (I did it in Maths last week) deserves more respect.

Thursday June 10th

Stick Insect is pregnant!

I saw her in the Co-op this afternoon. Maxwell House was having a tantrum at the checkout so I was spared from speaking to her. The poor woman looked dead miserable. Still it serves her right for being promiscuous. I wonder who the father is?

Friday June 11th

My father is getting fed up with his job as a canal bank renovation supervisor. He says that no sooner do Boz, Baz, Maz, Daz and Gaz, his gang, clear a section of canal than some slob comes along in the night and tips a month's household rubbish on the virgin bank.

The gang are getting a bit disheartened and morale

is low. I offered to set up a vigilante group but my father said that anyone who has carried an old mattress 300 yards in the dark is not going to be put off dumping it by a gaggle of spotty schoolboys.

Saturday June 12th

I have written to Mr Tydeman at the BBC and sent him another poem. I chose Norway as my theme, as I am quite an expert on the Norwegian Leather Industry.

Dear Mr Tydeman,
I had a few moments to spare so I thought I would pen you a letter and also send you my new poem 'Norway'. It (the poem) is in the modernist school of poetry, in other words it isn't about flowers and stuff and it doesn't rhyme. If you can't understand it, could you pass it on to someone who will explain it for you? Any modern poet will do.
Yours faithfully,
Adrian Mole (Aged 15¼)
P.S. If you bump into Terry Wogan in the corridor could you ask him to mention my grandma on the air? Her name is May Mole and she is a seventy-six-year-old diabetic.

Norway
Norway! Land of difficult spelling.
Hiding your beauty behind strange vowels.
Land of long nights, short days and dots over 'O's.
Ruminating majestic reindeers
Tread warily on ice floes

Ever aware of what happened to the
Titanic.
One day I will sojourn to your shores
I live in the middle of England
But!
Norway! My soul resides in your watery ~~fiords fyords~~
~~fiiords~~
Inlets.

Sunday June 13th
First after Trinity

Spent the day at Grandma's reading the *News of the World* and eating proper food for a change. We had roast lamb and mint sauce made from the window box. Grandma is hoping that her next grandchild is a girl. She said, 'You can dress girls nicely.' She has already knitted a purple matinée jacket and half a pair of bootees.

She is using neutral colours 'just in case'. I am dreading the day when there are feet inside the bootees.

Monday June 14th
Moon's Last Quarter

Our usual postman has been replaced by another one called Courtney Elliot. We know his name because he knocked on the door and introduced himself. He is certainly no run-of-the-mill postman, he wears a ruffled shirt and a red-spotted bow tie with his grey uniform.

He invited himself into the kitchen and asked to be introduced to the dog. When the dog had been brought in from the back garden Courtney looked it in the eye and said, 'Hail fellow, well met.' Don't ask me what it means; all I know is that our dog rolled over and let Courtney tickle its belly. Courtney refused a cup of instant coffee, saying that he only drank fresh-ground Brazilian, then he gave my father the letters saying, 'One from the Inland Revenue I fear, Mr Mole,' tipped his hat to my mother and left. The letter was from the tax office. It was to tell my father that they had 'received information' that during the previous tax year he had been running a spice rack construction company business from his premises, but that they had no record of such a business and so could he fill in the enclosed form? My father said, 'Some rotten sod's shopped me to the tax!' I went off to school. On the way I saw Courtney coming out of the Singhs' eating a chapati.

Tuesday June 15th

Today Courtney brought a letter from the Customs and Excise Department. It asked my father (in very curt terms) why he hadn't registered his spice rack business for VAT.

My father shouted at the letter and said, 'Somebody's got it in for me!' My mother and father counted how many enemies they had made in their lives. It came to twenty-seven, not counting relations.

Wednesday June 16th

My father is getting to dread Courtney Elliot's cheerful knock on our door in the morning. This morning it was a letter from Access threatening to cut my father's card in half.

I was hit on the head by a cricket ball today. It was my own fault. When I saw it coming towards me I shut my eyes and ran in the opposite direction. I am at home in bed waiting to see if concussion sets in.

Stick Insect has walked past our house six times.

Thursday June 17th

I have just found a list at the bottom of my mother's shopping bag.

FOR IT	AGAINST IT
Might be a girl	Loss of independence
More family allowance	George doesn't want it
	Months of looking like the side of a house
	Pain during labour
	Adrian bound to be jealous
	Dog might not take to it
	Am I too old at 37?
	Varicose veins
	PAS

Friday June 18th

I pretended to be enthusiastic about the baby at breakfast today. I asked my mother if she had thought of any names yet. My mother said, 'Yes. I'm going to call her Christabel.'

Christabel! It sounds like somebody out of *Peter Pan*. Nobody is called Christabel. The poor kid.

Saturday June 19th

Nigel and I went for a bike ride today. We set out to look for a wild piece of countryside so that we could get back to nature and stuff. We pedalled for miles but all the woods and fields were guarded by barbed wire and 'KEEP OUT' notices, so we could only get near to nature.

On the way back we had a philosophical discussion about war. Nigel is dead keen on it. It is his ambition to join the army. He said, 'It's a good life, and when I come back to civvy street I'll have a trade.'

I thought, 'What, as a contract killer?' But I didn't say anything. Most of the army cadets I know forget that real soldiers have to kill people.

Sunday June 20th
Second after Trinity. Fathers' Day

My father has hogged the television for over a week,
watching the lousy, stinking World Cup. This afternoon when I asked if I could watch a BBC2 documen-
tary about rare Norwegian plants he refused to let me
switch over, and he sat in the dark watching France
versus Kuwait. He was sulking because I forgot it was
Fathers' Day. I made an official protest to my mother
but she refused to arbitrate, so I went up to my room
and brought my Falklands campaign map up to date.
I also checked my Building Society account to see if I
can afford a black-and-white portable. I am sick of
being dependent on my parents' television set.

I went downstairs just in time to see a dead good
pitch invasion led by an Arab bloke in a head-dress. I
don't mind watching an interesting pitch invasion, it's
the football I can't stand.

Monday June 21st
Longest Day. New Moon

Mr Scruton summoned the whole school into the
assembly hall this morning. Even the teachers who are
atheists were forced to attend.

I was dead nervous. It's ages since I broke a school
rule but Scruton makes you feel dead guilty somehow.
When the doors were closed and the whole school was

lined up in rows Scruton nodded to Mrs Figges, who was sitting at the piano, and she started playing 'Hallelujah!'

Some of the fifth years (including Pandora) sang along using different words: 'Hallelujah! What's it to you?' etc. It was quite impressive. Though I thought it was time that the blind piano tuner called again.

When the singing stopped and Mrs Figges was still, Mr Scruton walked up to his lectern, paused, and then said, 'Today is a day that will go down in history.' He paused long enough for a rumour to travel along the rows that he was resigning, then he shouted, 'Quiet!' and continued, 'Today at three minutes to nine a future King of England was born.' All the girls, apart from Pandora (she is a republican), said, 'Ooh! Lady Di's 'ad it!'

Claire Neilson shouted: 'How much did he weigh?'

Mr Scruton smiled and ignored her.

Pandora shouted, 'How much will he *cost*?' and Mr Scruton suddenly developed good hearing and ordered her out of the assembly hall.

Poor Pandora, her face was as red as the Russian flag as she walked along the rows to the exit door, when she passed me I tried to give her a supportive smile, but it must have come out wrong because she whispered, 'Still leering at me, Adrian?'

Mr Scruton dismissed the school after giving us a talk on what a good job the Royal Family do for British exports.

Went to bed early; it had been a long day.

Tuesday June 22nd

The new prince left the hospital today. My father is hoping that he will be called George, after him. My mother said that it's time the Royal Family came up to date and called the Prince Brett or Jason.

Scotland are out of the World Cup. They drew 2–2 with Russia. My father called the Russian team 'those Commie bastards'. He was not a bit gracious in defeat.

Wednesday June 23rd

Pandora has been put into isolation at school. She is working at a desk outside Scruton's office. I left the following note on her peg in the cloakroom:

Pandora,
A short note to say that I admired your spirited stand on Monday.
   From Adrian Mole, your ex-lover
P.S. My mother is with child.

Thursday June 24th
Midsummer Day (Quarter Day)

Found a note on my peg at break this morning.

Adrian,
We were never lovers so it was inaccurate, indeed libellous, of you to sign your note 'ex-lover'. However, I thank you for your note of support.
    Pandora
P.S. I am shocked to learn that your mother is *enceinte*. Tell her to ring the Clinic.

Friday June 25th

My thing is 14cm extended and about 3cm in its unwoken state. I am dead worried. Donkey Dawkins of 5P says his thing comes off the end of a ruler, yet he is only a week older than me.

Saturday June 26th

It was with great pleasure that I saw Mr Roy Hattersley on television tonight. Once again I was struck by his obvious sincerity and good vocabulary. Mr Hattersley was predicting that there will be an early election. He denied that Mr Michael Foot is too scruffy to be the next Prime Minister.

Sunday June 27th
Third after Trinity

I can't go on with this charade of churchgoing every Sunday. I will have to tell Grandma that I have become an agnostic atheist. If there *is* a God then He/She must know that I am a hypocrite. If there isn't a God then, of course, it doesn't matter.

Monday June 28th
Moon's First Quarter

Bert rang me when I got home from school to bellow that Social Services had paid for him to have a phone installed in his pensioner's bungalow. Bert told me that he had already phoned one of his daughters in Melbourne, Australia, and Queenie had phoned her eldest son in Ontario, Canada. They had listened to Dial-a-Disc, the Recipe for the Day, the Weather Forecast, the Cricket News, and they were both looking forward to listening to the GPO's Bedtime Story. I pointed out to Bert that he would have to pay for each phone call he made, but he laughed his wheezy laugh and said, 'I shall probably be a gonner before the bill comes in.' (Bert is nearly ninety.)

Tuesday June 29th

Usual last-minute discussion about where we are going for our summer holiday. My father said, 'It'll probably be our last. This time next year we'll have the nipper.' My mother got dead mad, she said that having a baby was not going to restrict her. She said that if she felt like walking in the Hindu Kush next year, then she would strap the baby on her back and go.

The Hindu Kush! She moans if she has to walk to the bus stop.

I suggested the Lake District. I wanted to see if living there for a bit would help my poetry.

My father suggested Skegness. My mother suggested Greece. Nobody could agree, so we each wrote our choice on a scrap of old till roll and put them into a Tupperware gravy maker. We didn't trust each other to make the draw so my mother went and fetched Mrs Singh.

Mrs Singh and all the little Singhs came and stood in our kitchen. Mrs Singh asked, 'Why are you having this procedure, Mrs Mole? Can't your husband decide?' My mother explained that Mr Mole had no superior status in our house. Mrs Singh looked shocked, but she drew a piece of paper out of the hat. It said 'Skegness'. Worse luck!

Mrs Singh excused herself, saying that she must get back to prepare her husband's meal. As she left I noticed my father glance wistfully at her in her pretty sari and jewelled sandals.

I also noticed him looking sadly at my mother in her overalls and ankle boots. My mother said, 'That poor downtrodden woman.'

My father sighed and said, 'Yes.'

Wednesday June 30th

My mother wants to move. She wants to sell the house that I have lived in all my life. She said that we will need more room 'for the baby'. How stupid can you get? Babies hardly take any space at all. They are only about twenty-one inches long.

Summer

Thursday July 1st
Dominion Day (Canada)

Nigel has arranged for me to have a blind date with Sharon Botts. I am meeting her at the roller-skating rink on Saturday. I am dead nervous. I don't know how to roller-skate – let alone make love.

Friday July 2nd

Borrowed Nigel's disco-skates and practised skating on the pavement in our cul-de-sac. I was OK so long as I had a privet hedge to grab at, but I dreaded skating past the open-plan gardens where there is nothing to hold on to.

I wanted to wear my skates in the house so that I would develop confidence, but my father moaned about the marks the wheels made on the cushion floor in the kitchen.

Saturday July 3rd

12.15 p.m. Got up at 6 a.m. for more roller-skating practice. Mr O'Leary shouted abuse because of the early morning noise, so I went to the little kids' play park and practised there, but I had to give up. There was so much broken glass and dog muck lying about that I feared for the ballbearings in the skates. I waited for the greengrocer's to open, bought a pound of grapes, went home, had a bath, washed my hair and cut my toenails etc. Then I put my entire wardrobe of clothes on to the bed and tried to decide what to wear.

It was a pitiful collection. By the time I had eliminated my school uniform I was left with: three pairs of flared jeans (FLARES! Yuk! Yuk! Nobody wears flares except the worst kind of moron), two shirts, both with long pointed collars (LONG POINTS! Yuk!), four of Grandma's handknitted jumpers (HANDKNITTED! Ugh!). The only possible clothes were my bottle-green elephant cords and my khaki army sweater. But which shoes? I had left my trainers at school and I can't wear my formal wedding shoes to a roller-skating rink, can I?

At 10.30 I rang Nigel and asked him what youths wore at roller-skating rinks. He said, 'They wear red satin side vent running shorts, sleeveless satin vests, white knee socks, Sony Walkman earphones and one gold earring.' I thanked him, put the phone down and went and had another look at my clothes.

The nearest I could get were my black PE shorts, my white string vest and my grey knee socks. I am the only person in the world not to have a Sony Walkman and I haven't had my ears pierced so I couldn't manage those two items, but I hope that Sharon Botts won't mind too much.

Do I go in my shorts etc or do I change when I get to the rink? And how will I know which girl is Sharon Botts? I've only seen her in school uniform and in my experience girls are unrecognizable when they are in civilian clothes.

Must stop, it's time to go.

6 p.m. That's the first and last time I go roller-skating. Sharon Botts is an expert. She went whizzing off at 40 mph, only stopping now and again to do the splits in mid-air.

She sometimes slowed down to say, 'Let go of the barrier, Dumbo,' but she didn't stay long enough for me to divert her into having a longer conversation. When it was time for the under-twelves to monopolize the rink, she sped to the barrier and helped me into the coffee bar. We had a Coke then I clumped off to the cloakroom to get the grapes. When I gave her them she said, 'Why have you bought me grapes? I'm not poorly.' I dropped a hint by looking knowingly at her figure in its lycra body stocking and miniskirt but then the roller disco started and she sped off to do wild disco dancing on her skates. She was soon surrounded by tall skated youths in satin shorts so I staggered off to get changed.

I rang Nigel when I got home. I complained that Sharon Botts was a dead loss. He said that Sharon Botts had already rung him to complain that I had showed her up by dressing in my school PE kit.

Nigel said that he is giving up matchmaking.

Sunday July 4th
Fourth after Trinity. American Independence Day

I was just starting to eat my Sunday dinner when Bert Baxter rang and asked me to go round urgently. I bolted my spaghetti Bolognese down as quickly as I could and ran round to Bert's.

Sabre, the vicious Alsatian, was standing at the door looking worried. As a precaution I gave him a dog choc and hurried into the bungalow. Bert was sitting in the living room in his wheelchair, the television was switched off so I knew something serious had happened. He said, 'Queenie's had a bad turn.' I went into the tiny bedroom. Queenie was lying in the big saggy bed looking gruesome (she hadn't put her artificial cheeks or lips on). She said, 'You're a good lad to come round, Adrian.' I asked her what was wrong. She said, 'I've been having pains like red-hot needles in my chest.'

Bert interrupted, 'You said the pains were like red-hot knives five minutes ago!'

'Needles, knives, who cares?' she said.

I asked Bert if he had called the doctor. He said he hadn't because Queenie was frightened of doctors. I rang my mother and asked for her advice. She said she'd come round.

While we waited for her I made a cup of tea and fed Sabre and made Bert a beetroot sandwich.

My mother and father came and took over. My mother phoned for an ambulance. It was a good job they did because while it was coming Queenie went a bit strange and started talking about ration books and stuff.

Bert held her hand and called her a 'daft old bat'.

The ambulance men were just shutting the doors when Queenie shouted out, 'Fetch me pot of rouge. I'm not going until I've got me rouge.' I ran into the bedroom and looked on the dressing table. The top was covered in pots and hairnets and hairpins and china dishes and lace mats and photos of babies and weddings. I found the rouge in a little drawer and took it to Queenie. My mother went off in the ambulance and me and my father stayed behind to comfort Bert. Two hours later my mother rang from the hospital to say that Queenie had had a stroke and would be in hospital for ages.

Bert said, 'What am I going to do without my girl to help me?'

Girl! Queenie is seventy-eight.

Bert wouldn't come home with us. He is scared that the council will take his bungalow away from him.

Monday July 5th
Independence Day Holiday (USA)

Queenie can't speak. She is sort of awake but she can't move her mouth muscles. My mother has been round at Bert's all day cleaning and cooking. My father is going to call in every day on his way home from the canal. I have promised to take horrible Sabre for his morning and evening walks.

Tuesday July 6th
Full Moon

Bert's social worker, Katie Bell, has been to see Bert. She wants Bert to go back into the Alderman Cooper Sunshine Home temporarily. Bert said he 'would prefer death to that morgue.'

Katie Bell is coming round to see us tomorrow. She is checking Bert's lie that my mother and father and me are providing twenty-four-hour care for him. Queenie is still very poorly.

Wednesday July 7th
Katie Bell is a strange woman. She talks (and looks) a bit like Rick Lemon. She was wearing a donkey jacket and denim jeans and she had long greasy hair parted down the middle. Her nose is long and pointed (from poking into other people's business my father said).

She sat in our lounge rolling a cigarette in one hand and taking notes with the other.

She said Bert was stubborn and suffering from slight senile dementia and that what he needed was to see a consultant psychogeriatrician. My mother got dead mad and shouted, 'What he needs is a day- and a night-nurse.' Katie Bell went red and said, 'Day and night care is prohibitively expensive.'

My father asked how much it would cost to put an old person in an old people's home. Katie Bell said, 'It costs about two hundred pounds a week.'

My father shouted, 'Give me two hundred pounds a week and I'll move in and look after the old bugger.'

Katie Bell said, 'I can't relocate funds, Mr Mole.' As she was going she said, 'Look, I don't like the system any more than you do. I know it stinks, but what can I do?'

My mother said, 'You could wash your hair, dear, you'd feel much better without it straggling around your face.'

Thursday July 8th

I left a note on Pandora's peg today. It said:

Pandora,
Queenie Baxter is in hospital after a stroke. Bert is on his own in the bungalow. I am going round and doing what I can, but it would be nice if you could visit him

for a bit. He is dead sad. Have you got any photos of Blossom?

Yours, as ever,

Adrian

Friday July 9th

A brilliant day today. School broke up for eight fabbo weeks. Then something *even better* happened tonight.

I was in the middle of ironing Bert's giant underpants when Pandora walked into the living room. She was carrying a jar of home-pickled beetroot. I was transfixed. She gets more beautiful every day. Bert cheered up no end. He sent me off to make some tea. I could hardly keep my hands still. I felt as if I'd had an electric shock. I looked yearningly at Pandora as I handed her her tea. And she looked yearningly back at me!!!!!!!!

We sat around looking at photos of Blossom, Pandora's ex-pony. Bert droned on about ponies and horses he had known when he was an ostler.

At 9.30 I washed Bert, sat him on the commode and then put him to bed. We sat by the electric coal fire until he started snoring, then we fell into each other's arms with little sighs and moans. We stayed like that until Bert's clock struck 10 p.m. Sex didn't cross my mind once. I just felt dead calm and comfortable.

On the way home I asked Pandora when she realized that she still loved me. She said, 'When I saw you ironing those horrible underpants. Only a superior type of youth could have done it.'

It has just been on the news that a man has been found in the Queen's bedroom. Radio Four said that the man was an intruder and was previously unknown to the Queen. My father said: 'That's her story.'

Saturday July 10th

My father took Bert to visit Queenie, so I went to Sainsbury's on the bus. My mother gave me thirty pounds and asked me to buy enough food for five days. I remembered our last Domestic Science lesson, in which Mrs Appleyard taught us how to make cheap meals with maximum nourishment, so I bought:

2 lb Lentils
1 lb Dried peas
3 lb Wholemeal flour
1 pkt Yeast
1 lb Castor sugar
2 pints Plain yogurt
20 lb King Edward's
2 lb Brown rice
1 lb Dried apricots
1 Tub cream cheese
½ lb Krona margarine
A large cabbage
2 lb Breast of lamb
A huge Swede

4 lb Parsnips
2 lb Carrots
2 lb Onions

How I dragged it all to the bus stop I'll never know. The bus conductor was no help. He didn't assist me to pick a single potato from off the floor of the bus.

I am going to write and complain to Sainsbury's about their lousy brown carrier bags. They ought to stand up to being dragged half a mile without splitting. My mother didn't thank me when I handed her fifteen pounds change! She whined on and on about forgetting the frozen black forest gâteaux and tinned peas etc.

She went mad when she saw that I had not bought a white thick-sliced loaf. I pointed out that she had all the ingredients with which to make her own bread. She said, 'Correction. *You* have the ingredients!'

Spent all evening bashing dough about, then chucking it into tins. I don't know what went wrong. I opened the oven door and checked it every five minutes but it just wouldn't rise.

Sunday June 11th
Fifth after Trinity

Pandora says I should have kept the oven door shut.

My father refused to eat his breast of lamb stew. He

went to the pub and had a microwave mince and onion pie and crinkle-cut chips.

He is asking for a coronary.

Monday July 12th
Holiday (Northern Ireland)

Brainbox Henderson has started a youth club poetry magazine. I have submitted some of my Juvenilia plus a more recent mature poem called:

Ode to Engels
or
Hymn to the Modern Poor
Engels, you catalogued the misfortunes of the poor in days
    of yore,
Little thinking that the poor would still be with us in
    nearly 1984.
Yet stay! What is this I see in 1983?
'Tis a queue of hungry persons outside the Job Centre.
Though rats and TB be but sad memories
The pushchairs of the modern poor contain pasty babies
    with hacking coughs
Young mothers draw on number six
Young fathers queue to pay fines
Old people watch life pass by the plate-glass windows of
    council homes
Oh Engels that you were still amongst us pen in hand
Your indignation a-quiver
Your fine nose tuned to the bad smells of 1983.

Pandora read it at Bert's. She says that it is a work of genius.

I have sent a copy to Bert Baxter. He is always going on about Engels.

Tuesday July 13th

Brainbox Henderson showed me Barry Kent's pathetic entry for the poetry competition. Kent is convinced he is going to win the first prize of £5. It is called 'Tulips'.

> Nice, red, tall, stiff,
> In a vase,
> On a table,
> In a room,
> In our house.

According to Henderson, Kent's poem shows Japanese cultural influences! How stupid can you get?

The nearest Barry Kent has been to Japanese culture is sitting on the pillion of a stolen Honda.

Wednesday July 14th
Moon's Last Quarter

Every night this week I have been round to Bert's and taken vile Sabre for one of his four-mile walks, but I couldn't face it tonight. I hate the way people cross the road to avoid us. Sabre hasn't bitten anybody for ages, but he always *looks as if he's about to*. Even other Alsatians flatten themselves against walls when they see Sabre approaching. I wish that Queenie would hurry up and get better; she is proud to be seen out with Sabre. She says, 'An Alsatian a day keeps the muggers at bay.'

Thursday July 15th
St Swithin's Day

Pandora's parents took Bert to the hospital to visit Queenie this evening, so Pandora and I spent two brillo hours lying on her parents' bed watching the video of *Rocky I*. I kept my hands strictly away from Pandora's erotic zones. When the film finished we talked about our futures. Pandora said that after University she would like to dig water holes in the Third World countries. She demonstrated how an artesian well is sunk by using her lit cigarette. Unfortunately the cigarette fell out of her hand and burnt a hole in the duvet. Pandora is dead worried; her parents are fanatical non-smokers.

I am reading *Lucky Jim* by a bloke called Kingsley Amis. My father says that Kingsley Amis used to be the editor of the *New Statesman*. It is surprising how much my father knows about literary matters. He never reads books but he is forced to listen to Radio Four on his car radio because the dial has jammed and he can't get Terry Wogan.

Friday July 16th

5.30 p.m. Stick Insect has just rung to ask if my father is back from work yet. I told her that he calls in on Bert Baxter on his way home every night. She said, 'Thank you, I'll ring back later,' in a sad sort of voice. I expect she is regretting her promiscuous behaviour now that her baby is imminent.

I told my mother it was a wrong number; pregnant women should not be upset.

Saturday July 17th

I have just seen my father and Stick Insect walking along the canal towpath arm in arm. I know the path is a bit cobbly but surely Stick Insect could have walked without assistance. It's kind of my father to support Stick Insect in her hour of need but he should be more careful of public opinion. If people see an old-looking man arm in arm with a pregnant woman they are bound to assume that he is the father of the foetus. I hid behind the old bridge until they'd passed out of sight, then went to call for Pandora.

Sunday July 18th
Sixth after Trinity

My father announced at breakfast that he is going to have a vasectomy. I pushed my sausages away untouched.

Monday July 19th

Went to see Grandma after Bert's. She was making her Christmas cake. She let me drop the twenty pence pieces in the mixture and stir it around a bit while I made a wish. I was dead selfish really; I could have wished for world peace or Queenie's quick recovery or for a safe confinement for my mother, but instead I wished that the spots on my shoulders would clear up before my summer holiday. I am dreading baring my back to gawping holiday-makers on Skegness beach.

The Queen's personal detective, Commander Trestrail, has had to resign because the papers have found out that he is a homosexual. I think this is dead unfair. It's not against the law and I bet the Queen doesn't mind. Barry Kent calls *ME* a poofter because I like reading and hate sport. So I understand what it is like to be victimized.

Tuesday July 20th
New Moon

Got a foreign letter, it is addressed to me but it must be a mistake. I don't know any foreigners.

> Norsk rikskringkasting, BERGEN, Norway.

Kjaere Adrian Mole,

John Tydeman viste meg ditt dikt 'Norge' og jeg var dypt rørt av de følelser de uttrykte. Jeg håper du en dag vil besøke vårt land. Det er vakkert og du vil kunne oppleve fjordene og se hvor Ibsen og Grieg levde. Som en intellektuell person burde det interessere deg. Når du besøker oss og snakker med oss vil du oppdage at våre vokaler ikke er så eiendommelige. Husk at vi bare har lange netter og korte dager om vinteren. I juni er det helt motsatt. Så kom om sommeren – vi skal ta imot deg på beste måte.

Til lykke med dine studier av norsk laerindustri.

Hjertelig hilsen

Din,

Knut Johansen

Wednesday July 21st

Only eight days to go before my holiday in Skegness begins. I have asked my father if Pandora can come with us. I can't bear the thought of being alone with my parents for a fortnight. My father said, 'She's welcome to come along providing she stumps up a hundred and twenty quid.'

Thursday July 22nd

When we were round at Bert's doing his cleaning I asked Pandora if she would like to come to Skegness. She said, 'Darling, I would follow you into Hell, but I draw the line at Skegness.'

Bert said, 'Pandora, you're nought but a stuck-up little Madam. It'll do you good to mingle with the proletariat. Life ain't all dry ski slopes and viola lessons you know.' He gave a big sigh and said, 'Personally I'd give me right ball for a week in Skeggy.'

Pandora blushed a lovely pink colour and said, 'I'm awfully sorry, Bert. One tends to forget that one's privileged.'

Bert lit a Woodbine, sighed again and said: 'I shan't 'ave another holiday now, not at my age. No: *death*'s the only rest I've got to look forward to.'

To create a diversion Pandora phoned the hospital and asked how Queenie was. The nurse said, 'Mrs Baxter asked for her pot of rouge today.' Bert cheered up when he heard this news; he said: 'That means the old gel's on the mend.' We put Bert to bed, then I walked Pandora home.

We had a dead good half-French, half-English kiss, then Pandora whispered, 'Adrian, take me to Skegness.' It was the most romantic sentence I have ever heard.

Friday July 23rd

11 a.m. A dirty white cat turned up on our doorstep this morning. It had a tag round its neck which said, 'My name is Roy' but there was no address. It ignored me when I got the milk in so I ignored it back.

6 p.m. My mother and father have had a big row about Roy. My father accused my mother of encouraging Roy to stay by giving him (the cat) a saucer of milk. My mother accused my father of being an animal hater.

The dog looks a bit worried; I expect it feels insecure. Roy spent the day asleep on the toolshed roof, unaware of the trouble it was causing.

Saturday July 24th

Went shopping for holiday clothes today. My mother came with me. I wanted to buy a grey zip-up cardigan from Marks and Spencer (there is a cold wind at Skegness). I tried it on but my mother said it made me look like Frank Bough and refused to pay for it. We had a bit of an argument about my taste in clothes versus her taste in clothes. In fact, looking around, I could see quite a few teenagers were having arguments with their parents.

We walked around the rest of the shops without speaking for a bit until my mother dragged me into a punk shop and tried to interest me in a lime-green leopard-skin-print tee-shirt. I refused to try the taste-less thing on, so she bought it for herself!

The sadistic-looking shop assistant said, 'That's a cool mother you got.' I pretended not to hear him. It wasn't difficult: Sid Vicious was singing a filthy version of 'My Way' on the shop's stereo system. It was so loud that the chain jackets and studded belts were reverberating.

Our next stop was at Mothercare, where my mother went mad buying miniature clothes and stretch-mark cream. I was hoping that she would buy a nice respect-able maternity dress for the dreaded day when her lump starts to show, but she informed me that she was intending to carry on wearing her dungarees. I will be a laughing-stock at school.

Sunday July 25th
Seventh after Trinity

Did a bit of 'O' level revising. I've got the lousy stinking mocks to do when I get back to school. I am doing English, Geography and History at 'O' level and Woodwork and Domestic Science and Biology at CSE.

It's all a big waste of time, though, because intellec-tuals like me don't need qualifications to get jobs or worldly success: it just comes automatically to us. It is because of our rarity value. The only problem is getting influential people to *recognize* that you are an intellectual. So far nobody has recognized it in me, yet I have been using long words like 'multi-structured' in my daily intercourse for ages.

Monday July 26th

Courtney Elliot brought bad news this morning. It was a letter from the Manpower Services Commission telling my father that his canal bank clearance project was 'seriously behind schedule'. My father stormed on and on about, 'What do they expect if they pay slave wages?'

My mother said (quite mildly for her), 'Well you've hardly *worked* like a slave, George. You're always home by four-thirty.'

My father went out and slammed the kitchen door. I ran after him and offered to help him on the canal bank, but he said, 'No, stay at home and help your mother with the holiday packing.'

My mother and Courtney Elliot were doing the *Guardian* crossword together, and the holiday clothes were still in the Ali Baba basket waiting to be washed so I took the dog round to Bert's and watched the Falklands Memorial Service on television.

St Paul's Cathedral was full of widows and bereaved people. I went home and chucked my Falklands campaign map in the bin.

Tuesday July 27th
Moon's First Quarter

My mother had a pompous note from Pandora's father today. He is refusing to give Pandora £120 for Skegness!

The mean git says that he has already forked out four hundred quid for a canoeing holiday down the Wye for his family in September, and Pandora's made-to-measure wet suit was costing forty quid so he was 'unable to stretch his finances further.' So, a fortnight without Pandora looms ahead, unless I can think of a way to make £120 in a hurry. Pandora hasn't got any money of her own; she spends all her pocket money on viola strings.

Wednesday July 28th

My mother's lump started showing today, but she is doing nothing to disguise it. In fact she seems quite *proud* of it. She is showing it to everybody who comes to the house.

I have to go out of the room.

Thursday July 29th

My father has been working flat out on the canal bank for the past three days. He hasn't been getting home until 10 p.m. at night. He is getting dead neurotic about leaving it and going on holiday.

Went to see Queenie in hospital. She is on a ward full of old ladies with sunken-in white faces. It's a good job that Queenie was wearing her rouge, I wouldn't have recognized her without it.

Queenie can't speak properly so it was dead embarrassing trying to work out what she was saying. I left after twenty minutes, worn out with smiling. I tried not to look at the old ladies as I walked back down the ward, but it didn't stop them shouting out to me and waving. One of them asked me to fetch a nice piece of cod for her husband's tea. The tired-looking nurse said that a lot of the old ladies were living in the past. I can't say I really blame them; their present is dead horrible.

Friday July 30th

Our family went to Pandora's house to discuss what was involved in looking after Bert while we are on holiday.

Bert grumbled all the way through the meeting. He's never a bit grateful for anything you do for him. Sometimes I wish he *would* go and live in the Alderman Cooper Sunshine Home.

My mother gave this list to Pandora's mother:

1. He will only drink out of the George V Coronation cup.

2. He takes three heaped spoons of sugar in tea.
3. Don't let him watch *Top of the Pops*; it over-excites him.
4. District Nurse comes on Tuesdays to check for pressure sores.
5. He'll *only* eat beetroot sandwiches, scrambled eggs, Vesta curries and various Dream Toppings. Don't waste your energy in trying to extend his range. I've tried and failed.
6. He moves his bowels at 9.05 a.m. precisely. So please make sure you arrive at his bungalow in plenty of time to arrange the commode.
7. Sabre needs *at least* a four-mile walk *every day*. Any less and he becomes quite impossible.
8. Don't talk to Bert during *Crossroads*.
9. Mrs Singh will cover for you in an emergency, but she *must* be chaperoned.
10. He's OK to be left at night providing he's had his quota of brown ales (THREE BOTTLES).
11. He'll accuse you of fiddling him out of his pension. Ignore him.
12. *The Best of British Luck!*

Saturday July 31st
Rio Grande Boarding House, Skegness

Pandora came round early this morning to say goodbye; normally I would have been in anguish at the prospect of being without her for two weeks, but I was too busy packing my cases and looking for my swimming trunks to break down. Pandora helped me by packing my medical supplies for me. We finally left our cul-de-sac at 6 p.m.

The car broke down at Grantham so we didn't arrive at the Rio Grande until 12.30. The boarding house was locked and in complete darkness. We stood on the steps ringing the bell for ages, eventually a miserable-looking bloke unlocked the door. He said 'Mole Family? Yer late. These doors are locked at 11 p.m. an' there's a 50p fine for latecomers.'

My mother said, 'And whom might you be?'

The man said, 'I'm Bernard Porke, that's whom I am – Proprietor of the Rio Grande.'

My mother said, 'Well, thank you for your effusive welcome, Mr Porke.' She signed the register while I went and helped my father get the cases off the roof rack.

The tarpaulin had disappeared somewhere *en route*, so everything was wet through. I am writing this in my basement room. It overlooks the dustbins. I can hear Mr and Mrs Porke quarrelling in the kitchen next door.

I wish I was back in the Midlands.

Sunday August 1st
Eighth after Trinity. Lammas (Scottish Quarter Day)

I was woken up by Mr Porke shouting, 'Only one piece of bacon per plate, Beryl. Are you trying to ruin me?'

I got dressed quickly and ran up six flights of stairs

to my parents' attic room. Woke them up and told them that breakfast was nearly ready. My father told me to run down to the dining room and bag a decent table. (He is experienced in seaside boarding houses.)

I sat at a table next to the massive picture window and watched my fellow boarders take their places at the tables. For some reason everyone was whispering. Mothers kept telling their children to sit still, sit up straight, etc. Fathers stared at the cruet.

My parents' arrival caused a bit of a stir. My mother never keeps her voice down, so everyone heard her complaining about the nylon sheets, including Mr Porke. I'm sure that's why our table only got two pieces of fried bread.

Monday August 2nd
Bank Holiday (Scotland). Holiday (Republic of Ireland)

My father has gone back to his proletarian roots. He bought a 'Kiss me Quick, Squeeze me Slowly' hat and walked along the promenade swigging out of a can of lager.

I wore my dark glasses and kept well behind him.

Tuesday August 3rd

Eleven days to go and I have already spent all my money on the slot machines.

Wednesday August 4th
Full Moon

The sun came out today!

Also Prince William was christened. The Rio Grande celebrated by giving everyone an extra boiled egg at tea time.

Thursday August 5th

A man called Ray Peabody has joined our table. He is a divorcee from Corby. He spent his *honeymoon* at the Rio Grande. (No wonder he is divorced.) He comes to Skegness to take part in the talent contests. He is a singer and juggler. He showed us a bit of juggling with the cruet until Mr Porke told him to 'stop abusing the facilities'.

Friday August 6th

Sent Pandora a donkey postcard.

Dear Pan,
The sun came out on Wednesday, but it didn't reach into the black despair caused by our separation. It is a cultural desert here.

Thank God I have brought my Nevil Shute books.

Yours unto infinity.

Adrian X

Saturday August 7th

Went to Gibraltar Point in the car to see the wild-life sanctuary. Saw the sanctuary but no wild life. I expect they were all sheltering from the wind.

Read *The Cruel Sea* by a bloke called Nicholas something.

Sunday August 8th
Ninth after Trinity

My father went on a sea fishing trip today with the Society of Redundant Electric Storage Heater Salesmen.

My mother and I spent the day on the beach reading the Sunday papers. She is quite nice when you get her on her own. The sun was dead hot but I've got eighteen spots on my shoulders so I couldn't take my shirt off.

Monday August 9th

We bought day tickets and went to a holiday camp today.

The sight of all the barbed wire and the pale listless people walking aimlessly around inside gave me a weird feeling.

My father started whistling 'The Bridge on the River

Kwai' and it *was* like being in a prisoner of war camp. Nobody was actually tortured or starved, but you got the feeling that the attendants could turn quite nasty. My parents went straight to a bar, so I went on all the pathetic free rides, watched a knobbly knees competition, then a tug of war, then I stood outside the bar waiting for my parents.

They had selfishly chosen a 'No under-eighteens' bar.

At 1.30 my father came out with a bottle of Vimto and a packet of crisps for me.

At 2.30 I put my head round the door and asked how long they would be. My father snarled, 'Stop whining. Go and find something to do.' I watched the Donkey Derby for a bit then got fed up and went and sat in the car.

At 4 p.m. a loudspeaker shouted, 'Would Adrian Mole aged fifteen please go to the lost children's centre where his mummy and daddy are waiting for him.'

The humiliation!

The torment of being given a lollipop by a morose attendant!

My parents thought it was dead funny; they laughed all the way back to the ranch.

Tuesday August 10th

During the evening meal Mr Porke brought my father a message to say that a close friend had been taken into the Royal Hospital and would he please ring ward twelve immediately. It was a mystery to all of us. My father hasn't got any close friends.

My father left the table in a panic. My mother got up to follow him but he said, 'No Pauline, it's got nothing to do with you.'

He was gone for about fifteen minutes, when he came back he said, 'I've got something to tell you both, let's go somewhere private.'

We sat in a wind shelter on the promenade and he informed me and my mother that he was the father of Stick Insect's one-day-old baby boy.

About sixty hours passed, then my mother said, 'What's he called?'

My father said, '*Brett*. Sorry.'

I couldn't think of anything to say so I kept quiet. I still can't think of anything to say so I am going to sleep.

Wednesday August 11th

12.30 p.m. My father has gone to see Brett and Stick Insect. My mother made him go.

I can't think of anything to say to my mother. I always knew I had no small talk, and now I know I've got no big talk either.

8 p.m. She just sits in her attic room with her hands over her lump. She hasn't cried once, I am dead worried.

9 p.m. I phoned Pandora's mother and told her everything. She was very sympathetic. She said she would get Bert settled for the night and then drive to Skegness and pick us up.

I packed all the suitcases and made my mother wash her face and do her hair, then we sat and waited for Mrs Braithwaite.

Thursday August 12th
Moon's Last Quarter

Home.

11 p.m. As soon as she saw Mrs Braithwaite my mother started to cry. Mrs Braithwaite said, 'They're *all* bastards, Pauline,' and gave ME a filthy look! It's just not fair! I intend to stay completely and totally true to Pandora. All else is chaos.

We got home at 4.30 a.m. this morning. Mrs Braithwaite doesn't like driving over 30 mph.

I went straight to bed. I didn't dare to check to see if my father was in his room.

Friday August 13th

The day augured ill.

My father's razor had gone from out of the bathroom so I was forced to use my mother's pink underarm one. It cut my face to ribbons (but there was a very satisfactory amount of bristle around the side of the washbasin).

I had to have a shave because Grandma came round to be told the awful news that her son had fathered an illegitimate child, whilst his wife of fourteen years was expecting a legitimate one.

Grandma took it quite well. She said, 'Which hospital is this woman in?' My mother told her and she straightened her hat and left in a taxi.

Pandora told me that her mother is close to having a nervous breakdown because Bert Baxter has been playing her up all week.

Personally, myself, I think the world has gone mad. Barry Kent won the 'Off the Street' Youth Club poetry competition. His grinning moronic face was in the evening paper. I can't take much more.

Saturday August 14th

Grandma has gone over to the other side!

She has given some of *our* baby's clothes to Brett Slater, Stick Insect's son. I know Grandma doesn't like my mother, but at least my mother is my father's legal wife.

I am just about sick and tired of adults! They have the nerve to tell kids what to do and then they go ahead and break all their own rules.

Pandora's father came round this morning to ask my mother if she wanted any help. My mother said,

'Bugger off home and help your own wife.' At this rate she'll have no men friends left.

Barclays Bank was open this morning. I bet my father was first in the queue. He always forgets to go on Fridays.

Sunday August 15th
Tenth after Trinity

My father came round and asked if he could come home. I wanted my mother to say yes, but she said no. So my father has gone to live with Grandma.

The rat fink has taken the stereo with him. My mother says she doesn't care, she says that after her baby is born she is going to get a highly paid job and buy the best stereo system in the world.

Monday August 16th

Pandora shocked me today by asking if I was curious about my '*brother Brett*'. It's dead strange to think I've got a brother. I hope the poor kid has better luck with his skin than me.

Tuesday August 17th

A cheque for fifty pounds arrived today from my father. My mother ripped it up and posted the pieces back. How stupid can you get?

Even my mother regretted it later on.

Stick Insect, Maxwell House and Brett have moved into Grandma's house.

Wednesday August 18th

Took the dog for a walk and called casually round to Grandma's and casually looked into Brett Slater's cot. The kid's skin is covered in white flaky stuff. He's got loads of wrinkles as well.

I didn't see Stick Insect or my father. Grandma was teaching Maxwell manners at the tea table.

I didn't stay long. I didn't tell my mother I had been, either. It was only a casual visit.

Thursday August 19th
New Moon

Mrs Braithwaite is on Librium because of Bert Baxter, so Mrs Singh has taken over her duties. I haven't seen Bert for ages. I know he will make crude comments about my father's virility, so I am keeping away.

I have gone right off sex. It seems to cause nothing but trouble, especially to women.

Friday August 20th

My mother is too depressed to do any cooking so I am having to do it. So far we have had salad with either corned beef or tuna, but I think I will try something different tomorrow – ham perhaps.

My father keeps ringing up to see how my mother is. Today he asked me if she had mentioned divorce. I said no, she hadn't mentioned it but she certainly looked as if she was thinking about it.

Saturday August 21st

Casually called in at Grandma's again. Brett has got my father's big nose. Grandma was changing his yukky nappy. I was amazed at how big his thing is.

Stick Insect is *breastfeeding* Brett. (The poor kid must be hungry because the last time I had a close look she hadn't got any breasts.)

My father and Stick Insect were out, buying baby equipment between feeds.

Sunday August 22nd
Eleventh after Trinity

Went out and bought the Sunday papers, but didn't bother sneaking a look at the *News of the World* behind the greetings card rack like I usually do. I've got enough sex scandals in my own family without reading about anyone else's.

Mr Cherry, the newsagent, asked if he was to cancel my father's fishing and DIY magazines. I told him to go ahead.

The papers weighed 3 lbs, but there was nothing in them apart from the PLO fleeing from Beirut again.

Monday August 23rd

Barry Kent's mother has had another baby; Pandora passed by the church just as the Kents were emerging from the Christening service. She said the baby looked just like all the other Kents – fierce eyes and massive fists.

They have called the baby Clarke, after Superman. Yuk! Yuk! Yuk!

Tuesday August 24th

Mrs Singh has arranged for Bert to go on holiday with some charity for elderly Hindus. I asked how long Bert had been a Hindu. Mrs Singh said, 'I don't care if he's not a Hindu. I don't care if he's a Moonie or a Divine Light Missionary so long as he is far away from me.'

Sabre is staying at the RSPCA hostel. I hope he is in isolation for the sake of the other dogs.

Wednesday August 25th

Courtney Elliot was sipping Brazilian coffee in the kitchen when I came downstairs. He said, 'I bear an important missive for Master Mole.' It was a letter from the BBC!

I took the letter up to my room and stared at it, willing it to say, 'Yes we are giving you an hour-long poetry programme; it will be called "Adrian Mole, a Youth and his Poetry".'

I wanted it to say that, but of course it didn't. It said:

British Broadcasting Corporation
19th July

Dear Adrian Mole,

Thank you for your very neat letter and for the new poem entitled 'Norway'. It is a considerable development on your previous work and indicates that you are maturing as a poet. If your School Magazine rejected 'Norway' then the Editor of the magazine probably needs his (or her) head seeing to. Unless, of course, you have a lot of very good poets at your school. I agree with you about those boring rhyming poems about flowers and stuff but you must remember that before you can break the rules of rhyme and rhythm you do have to know what those rules are about. It is like a painter who wishes to do abstract paintings – he has to know how to draw precisely from life before he jumbles things up. Picasso is a very good case in point to cite.

I hope you were successful in your test on the Norwegian Leather Industry. The Norwegian colleague (he is a Radio Producer in Bergen, Norway) to whom I showed your poem was very impressed that you were studying his country so diligently. I attach a translation of a letter he sent you which must have been rather difficult to understand since it was in Norwegian. Incidentally, I think 'Fjords' is a better word than 'Inlets'. Don't worry about the spelling, a good editor will always correct details like that. I like your use of the explosive 'But!' in the penultimate line. There isn't anything practical I can do with this particular work but I will put it on the file as an *aide memoire* to your progress as a poet (remember there is not much money in poetry . . .).

I seldom get to see Terry Wogan in the corridors as he works in Radio Two and I work for Radios Three and Four. Also his show goes on the air very early and he has usually left the building by the time I get to my desk.

With my best wishes and again my thanks for having let me see your latest work.

Yours sincerely,

John Tydeman (Radio Four)

Dear Adrian,

John Tydeman showed me your poem 'Norway' and I was very moved by its sentiments. I hope you will be able to visit our country one day. It is very beautiful and you will be able to visit the Fjords and see where Ibsen and Grieg lived. As an intellectual, this should be of interest to you. Perhaps when you visit us and speak with us you will not find our vowels so strange. Remember we only have long nights and short days in winter. In June it is the opposite.

So come in summer and we will make you very welcome.

Good luck with your study of the Norwegian Leather Industry.

Yours sincerely,

Knut Johansen

What a brilliant letter! 'Considerable Development', 'Maturing as a Poet'! The translation was even better; it was an invitation to go to Norway! Well, almost. There was no actual mention of paying my fare, but, 'Come in summer, we will make you very welcome'!

My mother and Courtney Elliot read the letters. Courtney said, 'You have a very singular son, Mrs Mole.'

My mother's reply was brief yet touching. 'I know,' she said.

Thursday August 26th
Moon's First Quarter

I tackled Courtney Elliot about the late delivery of my BBC letter, which was dated July 19th so had taken over a month to travel 104 miles. Courtney said, 'I believe that there was a derailment of the Mail Train at Kettering in July. It is possible that your letter was in one of those unfortunate mail bags that lay at the bottom of the embankment until being discovered by a homeward-bound ploughman.'

The Post Office have always got an excuse!

Friday August 27th

The bank rate has been reduced to 10$\frac{1}{2}$% so my mother has made an appointment to see Mr Niggard, the Bank Manager. She wants to borrow some money because she hasn't got any left.

I hope she gets a loan; I haven't had any pocket money for two weeks.

Saturday August 28th

Pandora is taking canoeing lessons in preparation for her River Wye holiday. She had her first lesson today and she invited me to watch and, if necessary, give her the kiss of life in case she fell out and nearly drowned.

She looked dead erotic in her black wetsuit and crash helmet. And for the first time in yonks I felt my thing moving on its own.

I can't remember anything more about the lesson, so was unable to join in Pandora's enthusiastic conversation on the way home in her dad's car.

Sunday August 29th
Twelfth after Trinity

Stayed in bed all day. My mother went to a picnic with some women at a place called Greenham Common. It was dark when she got back. I was dead worried.

Monday August 30th
Late Summer Holiday (UK except Scotland)

My mother was happy today. She cleaned the house from top to bottom (including the cutlery drawer and understairs cupboard). She sang the same song over and over again.

> You can't kill the spirit
> She is like a mountain
> Old and strong.
> She goes on and on and on!

It looks like her picnic did her good.

Tuesday August 31st

My mother went to see the Bank Manager this morning. I persuaded her to put a loose dress on so that he wouldn't know she was pregnant.

But it turned out that my father had already been whining to the bank for money and while he was there he had blabbed out all our family secrets. Mr Niggard knew that the only income my mother has is Social Security and Family Allowance so he wouldn't lend her any more.

He said she was a bad risk. There is nothing for it, I will have to get a Saturday job. I need money desperately, I've got two months' library fines to pay.

Wednesday September 1st

Got a card from Bert Baxter. It was a picture of Bradford Town Hall. Bert had written,

Dear Laddo,
Having a good laugh with the old 'uns, we are visiting temples and going to weddings nearly every day. The grub is good but I've had to knock off the drink on account of the other old 'uns' religion.

Queenie is coming out next week. So be a good lad and nip round and give the bungalow a bit of a tidy up.

Yours affec'ly,

Bert

Pandora took her One-Star Canoeing test this afternoon. Her instructor, a bloke called Bill Sampson, said that Pandora has got 'great canoeing potential'. He raved on about Pandora's powerful shoulders, limp wrists and gripping thighs. Pandora passed her test easily. Bill Sampson has offered to prepare her for her Two-Star Test.

Pandora has asked me to join her in her new hobby, but I have got a morbid dread of capsizing so I declined. I am quite happy watching from the bank thinking my intellectual thoughts and holding the towels and thermos flask.

Thursday September 2nd

There is now no disguising the fact that my mother is pregnant. She sticks right out at the front and walks in a very peculiar manner. She finds it a bit difficult to bend down, so I spend half my time picking things up for her.

Her dungarees are too tight for her, so I am hoping that she will buy a pretty flowery maternity dress. Princess Diana looked charming during her pregnancy. One of those big white collars would really suit my mother. Also it would distract attention from her wrinkly neck.

Friday September 3rd
Full Moon

Pandora and her parents are leaving for the River Wye tomorrow. I have offered to go in and feed Marley, their big ginger cat. They have accepted my kind offer and have entrusted me with their keys. It is a massive responsibility, their house is chock-a-block with expensive electrical items and ancient antiques.

Saturday September 4th

Waved goodbye to my love today. She blew kisses from the rear windows of the Volvo Estate then vanished round the corner.

I waited half an hour (in case they came back for something they had forgotten) then I let myself into the house, made myself a cup of coffee and sat down to watch their big colour telly. At dinner-time I made myself a tuna sandwich (must remember to replace the tin of tuna before they come back) and ate it at Mr Braithwaite's desk.

I couldn't help noticing a letter on his desk:

Dear Chairperson,

Arthur, it is with the deepest regret that I offer my resignation as vice-chairperson of the Elm Ward Labour Party.

The Committee has moved so far to the right recently that I now find my own moderate views are regarded by them as 'extremist'.

As you know I objected to the Committee sending a telegram of congratulations to Mrs Thatcher during the Falklands Crisis, and, because of my objections, I was called a 'Stalinist' and a 'traitor'. Mrs Benson told me to get back to Russia where I belong.

I know she is a stalwart party member and is indispensable at collecting the tea money, but her constant talk about the Royal Family has no place at a Labour Party meeting, especially with unemployment as high as it is.

And finally and sadly, your own comments about Tony Benn I find absolutely repellent. Calling a member of your own party a 'goggle-eyed goon' is just not on, Arthur. Tony Benn has served this country well in the past, and he may well lead it one day.

I am going on holiday for a week. I will speak to you when I get back.

Yours,
Ivan Braithwaite

There was a stamped, addressed envelope lying next to the letter. Mr Braithwaite had obviously been too busy to post it himself so I posted the letter on my way home.

Sunday September 5th

I have just been to see a brilliant play at our neighbourhood centre. It was called *Woza Albert*. It was all about South Africa and how cruel their government is to the black people who do all the work. I cried a bit at the end. I swear I will never eat another Cape apple as long as I live.

Monday September 6th
Labour Day (USA and Canada)

Spent all day watering the Braithwaites' plants. It can't be healthy living amongst so much vegetation. It's a wonder Pandora and her parents don't die of oxygen starvation. If I was them I would keep a caged canary around the place.

Tuesday September 7th

Went to the ante-natal clinic with my mother. We waited for two hours in a room full of red-faced pregnant women. My mother had forgotten to bring a sample of urine from home, so a nurse gave her a shiny oven tray and told her to, 'Squeeze a few drops out for us, dear.'

My mother had only just been to the loo so she took ages and ended up missing her place in the weighing queue. By the time her blood pressure was taken my mother was in a state of hypertension. She said the doctor warned her about doing too much and told her to relax more.

Wednesday September 8th

Realized with horror that school starts next Monday and I have only done one day's revising for my mock exams. Took my History folder round to the Braith-waites', fed the cat and settled down in the study. I thought perhaps the studious atmosphere might help but I can't say it made much difference. I still can't remember Archduke Ferdinand's middle name, or the date of the Battle of Mons.

Thursday September 9th

Went round to Bert Baxter's bungalow to tidy up. Queenie is coming home from hospital on Saturday. I hope the Hindus bring Bert back in time.

Did revision for mocks until 3 a.m.

Friday September 10th
Moon's Last Quarter

Courtney Elliot said, 'A billet-doux for the Young Master.' It was a letter from Pan.

Adrian Precious,
We started at Builth Wells on Sunday evening and had quite an exciting paddle downstream. Mummy and Daddy were paddling an open Canadian. I was in a single kayak.

We camped overnight at Llanstephan. It was lovely, I left the flap of my tent open and looked up at the stars and thought of you.

Just beyond Llanstephan there is an orgiastic rapid called Hell Hole. The local people fear it and all the canoeing guides describe it as being 'Grade Three, must be portaged', which means you mustn't canoe down it, but instead carry your canoe and equipment *around* it.

Mummy and Daddy managed to get to the side of the river OK but the water carried me ever onwards towards Hell Hole. Honestly Adrian, it was just like *Deliverance*, I half expected a Welsh halfwit to appear on the bridge and start twanging a harp.

Anyway I went rushing into Hell Hole and the canoe turned upside down, but I managed to get out after a while. My boat was smashed in half, but I regained consciousness and swam to the bank.

See you on Sunday.

All my love,

Pandora

P.S. Mummy's nerves are off again.

I felt ill after reading Pandora's letter. I had to take a junior aspirin and lie down.

Saturday September 11th

Had horrible nightmares all night. I kept seeing Pandora's body floating under the remains of Skegness Pier.

Sunday September 12th
Fourteenth after Trinity

Everybody returned home today apart from my father.

Ironed my school uniform: it is much too small for me, but my mother can't afford a new one.

Monday September 13th

I am now a fifth-year and have the privilege of using the side entrance of the school. I can't wait until next year when I will be able to use the *front* entrance (sixth formers and staff only).

Perhaps I have got a perverted streak, but I really enjoyed watching the first-, second-, third- and fourth-years cramming through their low status entrance at the back of the school.

I informed Mrs Claricoates, the school secretary, that once again I am on free school dinners. As usual she was full of empathy for me and said, 'Never mind, pet, it'll all come out in the wash.'

Had mock English exam. I was the first to finish. It was a doddle.

Tuesday September 14th

I have got a new form teacher. His name is Mr Lambert. He is the kind of teacher who likes being friendly. He said, 'Consider me a friend, any problems to do with school or home, I want to hear them.'

He sounded more like a Samaritan than a teacher. I have made an appointment to see him after school tomorrow.

My mother is thirty-eight today. I bought her a card which said 'Happy 18th Birthday', *but*, I cunningly changed the number one into a three by the use of

Tipp-Ex and dried lentils. So it read 'Happy 38th Birthday!' Unfortunately the verse on the inside didn't match my mother's lifestyle much.

> A-tremble on the edge of life,
> One day to be a mum and wife.
> But now it's discos fun and laughter:
> Why should you care what's coming after?

The picture on the front was of a teenage girl going mad to sounds coming out of a record player. On reflection, I think it was a bad choice of card. I wish I wasn't an impulse buyer. Her present was some underarm hair remover. I noticed that the stuff she usually uses had run out.

My father sent a card picturing a sad cat. He had written inside 'Yours as ever, George.' That stinking rat Lucas sent a card from Sheffield. It was in a box and had a cartoon mouse on the front eating a piece of cheese (Edam I think). Inside Lucas had written: 'Pauline, I'll never forget that night in the pinewoods. Yours with undying love, Bimbo.'

She had ten other cards, all from women and all with pictures of flowers on the front. I don't know why women are so mad about flowers. Personally they leave me cold. I prefer trees.

Wednesday September 15th

My father phoned up before I went to school this morning. He wanted to speak to my mother, but she refused to talk to him. Brett was crying. In the background, it sounded as if Grandma and Stick Insect were quarrelling. Somebody (it could only have been Maxwell I suppose) was playing a toy xylophone. My father sounded dead miserable. He said, 'I know I did wrong, Adrian; but the punishment hardly fits the crime.'

Had a long talk with Mr Lambert after school. He took me to a café and bought me a cup of tea and a vanilla slice. As we parted he said, 'Look, Adrian, try to detach yourself from the mess your parents are in. You're a *gifted boy* and you mustn't let them drag you down to their level.'

'*A gifted boy*'! At last someone apart from Pandora has recognized my intellectual prowess.

Had mock biology exam. I was the last to finish.

Thursday September 16th

Barry Kent has made an appointment with Mr Lambert to talk about *his* family problems!

I hope Mr Lambert has got twenty-four hours to spare. Ha! Ha! Ha!

Had mock geography exam. Just my luck – there were no questions about the Norwegian Leather Industry.

Friday September 17th
New Moon

Nearly everyone in our class has made an appointment to see Mr Lambert about their family problems. Even Pandora, whose mother is a Marriage Guidance Counsellor!

Mr Lambert is going about the school biting his nails and looking worried. He has stopped taking people to the café.

Saturday September 18th

A Tydeman letter! Alas, yet another rejection. The gods are not yet smiling on me.

British Broadcasting Corporation
17th September

Dear Adrian Mole,
Thank you for your latest letter (undated – you must, if you are going to be a writer – and even if you are not – DATE your letters. We file them, you know. The BBC has lots of files, some of which are kept in warehouses in Ware, Herts, others of which are at Caversham, nr Reading. Some of the files are very valuable.)

The country seems to have made you gloomy. It often makes poets gloomy, people like Wordsworth & Co. On other occasions it uplifts them – skylarks singing, lambs bounding, daffodils daffing, waterfalls crashing. It provokes odes and things in them. So forget gloom and suicide and write something cheerful.

I'm afraid that the poem is not yet up to broadcast standard but it does show a poetic advance, so keep on trying. We will naturally respect your copyright in your work. (The BBC is usually very good about things like that.) Copyright is dealt with by a special department and we do not bother the Director General directly with such matters. However, you have not got your break (chance) – yet.

Do not kill yourself because of another rejection. If all poets killed themselves because of early rejections there would be no poetry at all.

Yours most sincerely,

John Tydeman

Sunday September 19th
Fifteenth after Trinity

Took a deep breath and went to see Bert and Queenie today. They were hostile to me because I've neglected them for a week.

Bert said, 'He's not bothered about us old 'uns no more, Queenie. He's more interested in gadding about.'

How unfair can you get? I can't remember the last time I gadded about. Queenie didn't say anything because she can't speak properly because of the stroke, but she certainly *looked* antagonistic.

Bert ordered me to come back tomorrow to clean

up. Their home help comes on Tuesdays and Bert likes the place to be tidy for when she comes.

Monday September 20th

Courtney Elliot didn't bring my mother's Social Security giro this morning. I went to school worrying about it and hoping it would come in the second post. I was amazed to learn that I'd only got average marks for my mocks. Surely there has been a serious error.

Tuesday September 21st

My mother and Courtney Elliot had a row over the missing giro this morning. Courtney said, 'Don't shoot the messenger because the news is bad or non-existent, Mrs Mole.'

My mother tried to ring the Social Security office all day, but the line was permanently engaged.

Wednesday September 22nd

I skived off school and went to the Social Security offices with my mother. She couldn't face going on her own. I'm certainly glad I went because it was no place for a pregnant woman.

My mother joined the queue of complaining people

at the reception desk. And I sat down on the screwed-down chairs.

The reception clerk was hiding behind a glass screen, so everyone was forced to shout out their most intimate financial secrets to her. I heard my mother shouting with the rest, then she came back holding a ticket numbered 89, and said that we would have to wait until our number was displayed on an electronic screen.

We waited for yonks amongst what my mother called 'The casualties of Society'. (My father would have described them as 'dregs'.) A group of tramps staggered about singing and arguing with each other. Toddlers ran amok. Teenage mothers shouted and smacked. A Teddy boy on crutches lurched up the stairs helped by an old skinhead in ragged Doc Martens. Everyone ignored the 'No Smoking' notices and stubbed their cigarettes out on the lino. The respectable people stared down at their shoes. About every ten minutes a number flashed up on the screen and somebody got up and went through a door marked 'Private Interviews'.

I didn't see any of the people who'd gone through the door *come out* again. I thought this was a bit sinister. My mother said, 'They've probably got gas chambers out there.'

Our private interview was against the Trades Description Act, because it wasn't private at all. The interviewer was also behind a glass screen, so my mother had to bellow out that she hadn't received her giro and was financially destitute.

The interviewer said, 'Your giro was posted on Friday, Mrs Moulds.'

'MRS MOULDS?' said my mother, 'My name's Mole – MOLE – as in furry mammal.'

'Sorry,' said the interviewer, 'I've got the wrong records.'

We waited another fifteen minutes, then he came back and said, 'Your giro will be put in the post tonight.'

'But I need the money now,' my mother pleaded. 'There's no food in the house and my son needs school trousers.'

'There's nothing I can do,' the bloke said wearily. 'Can't you borrow some money?'

My mother looked the man straight in the eyes and said, 'OK will *you* lend me five pounds, please?'

The man said, 'It's against the rules.'

Now I know why the furniture is screwed down. I felt like flinging a chair about myself.

Thursday September 23rd
Autumnal Equinox

No giro. Courtney Elliot lent my mother £5.

Friday September 24th

8.30 a.m. No giro. But a cheque from my father arrived so we are saved! My mother gave me 15p for a Mars bar, my first in days.

4.30 p.m. My mother took the cheque to the bank this morning, but they wouldn't cash it because it needed four days to clear. Mr Niggard the manager was out officiating at a liquidation, so my mother waited for him to come back then grovelled for a temporary overdraft. Mr Niggard let her have £25.

All this trouble has made my mother's ankles swell up. Somebody is going to pay for this!

Saturday September 25th
Moon's First Quarter

No giro!

Looked Swollen Ankles up in the *Good Housekeeping Family Health Encyclopaedia*. It calls itself the 'Complete Modern Medical Reference Book for the Home', but the index didn't have 'Swollen Ankles'. I used my initiative and looked up 'Pregnancy'. I was interested to see that 'Pregnancy' was adjacent to 'Sex and Reproduction'.

I started reading a section called 'Testes and Sperm' and was astonished to discover that my personal testes make several hundred million sperm *a day*. A DAY! Where do they all go? I know some leak out in the night and some I help to leak occasionally, but what happens to the countless billions that are left swarming around, and what about chaste people like priests? During a lifetime they must collect a trillion trillion. It makes the mind boggle, not to mention the testes.

Sunday September 26th
Sixteenth after Trinity

Read the whole of 'Sex and Reproduction' in bed last night. Woke up to find a few hundred million sperm had leaked out. Still, it will give the remaining sperm room to wag their tails about a bit.

Monday September 27th

No giro!

By a massive stroke of luck we did the storage of semen in human biology today. I was able to give a full and frank account of the life cycle of a sperm.

Mr Southgate the biology teacher was dead impressed. After the lesson he said, 'Mole, I don't know if you've got a natural aptitude for biology or a rather obsessive interest in things sexual. If the former I suggest you change from CSE to 'O' level, if the latter perhaps a chat with the school psychology service may be of use.'

I assured Mr Southgate that my interest was purely scientific.

Tuesday September 28th

No giro!

Pandora and I went for a walk in the woods after

school only to find that a building firm had started to build executive houses in the clearings. Pandora said that the woodlands of England were being sacrificed for saunas, double garages and patio doors.

Some lucky executive is going to have the best conker tree in the Midlands in his back garden. He'll also be as sick as a dog because he'll have Barry Kent's gang chucking sticks at it every autumn. Ha! Ha! Ha!

Went back to Pandora's and watched the Labour Party Conference vote for unilateral disarmament. Mr Braithwaite explained that this means if elected the Labour Party would chuck all their nuclear weapons away. Mrs Braithwaite said, 'Yes and leave us at the mercy of the Soviet threat.' Mr Braithwaite and Mrs Braithwaite started arguing about multilateral versus unilateral disarmament. The argument got a bit nasty and Mr Braithwaite went on to accuse his wife of posting a letter of resignation to the Elm Ward Labour Party. Mrs Braithwaite shouted, 'For the last time, Ivan, I did not post that sodding letter.'

Pandora walked me home and explained that since her mother had joined the SDP her parents had worked in separate studies. She said, 'They are intellectually incompatible.'

I asked Pandora about the letter of resignation. She said that her father had written a letter but decided not to post it. He was therefore hurt when his resignation had been accepted. Pandora said, 'Poor Daddy is in the political wilderness.'

Wednesday September 29th
Michaelmas Day (Quarter Day)

No giro!

My mother had a letter from the bank to tell her that my father's cheque had bounced. I was sent round to Grandma's on my way to school to break the news.

Stick Insect was feeding Brett so I didn't know where to put my eyes. Is it good or bad manners to ignore a suckling baby? I kept my eyes on her neck to be on the safe side.

My grandma was getting Maxwell ready for play school. The poor kid was wrapped in so many layers of clothes that he looked a bit like Scott at the South Pole. Grandma said, 'There's a nip in the air and Maxwell has got a chest.'

My father had gone to the canal bank early, so I left a message with Grandma. She pulled her lips in a straight line and said, 'Another bouncing cheque? Your father ought to take up trampolining.'

I asked Grandma if she ever got fed up with Brett, Maxwell and Stick Insect. Grandma said she thrived on hard work, and it's true, she looks better than when all she had to do was listen to Radio Four all day. She doesn't even listen to 'The World at One' now. Brett doesn't like Robin Day's voice for some reason. It makes him scream and bring his milk up.

Thursday September 30th

No giro!
  Wrote a poem today.

Waiting for the Giro
The pantry door creaks showing empty Fablon shelves.
The freezer echoes with mournful electrical whirrings.
The boy goes ragged trousered to school.
The woman waits at the letterbox.
The bills line up behind the clock.
The dog whimpers empty-bellied in sleep.
The building society writes letters penned in vitriol.
The house waits, waits, waits,
Waits for the giro.

I am reading Philip Larkin's *The Whitsun Weddings*.

Autumn

Friday October 1st

My mother rang up the Citizens' Advice Bureau to find out who her MP is. Then she rang the MP at home, but he wasn't there. His wife said that he had gone on a fact-finding mission to the Canary Isles. She sounded very bitter.

Saturday October 2nd

Courtney brought a letter from the Fens.

King Edward Cottage,
Yosserdyke,
Norfolk.

Dear Pauline,

Your dad and me was sorry to hear about your trouble and we hopes as it is now cleared up. We never did take to George; he had a hasty temper and we think as how you're better off without him. As regards the money, Pauline, well we only got a few good days at the potato picking so we are a bit short ourselves at the moment, but we enclose a postal order for Adrian, as we know he has got a sweet tooth.

If you would put your trust in the Lord, Pauline, you wouldn't keep having such trouble in your life. God only punishes the heathens and the unbelievers. We was shocked last Christmas as to how much smoking and drinking went on under your roof. You wasn't brought up to it, Pauline. Your dad has never touched a drop in his life, nor has he been a slave to nicotine. We are decent God-fearing folk what knows our place and we only wish that you would take after us more before it's too late.

Uncle Dennis, Auntie Marcia and Cousin Maurice have moved out of the caravan and into a council house. They have got all modern facilities, Auntie Marcia jokes that it is just like Buckingham Palace. Perhaps when you have had the unwelcome baby you will come and see it for yourself.

Anyway Pauline

We are praying for you,

Yours affectionately,

Mam and Dad

P.S. Auntie Marcia asks if you ever found Maurice's grey sock that disappeared last Christmas. She's not been able to rest through wondering about it.

Sunday October 3rd
Seventeenth after Trinity. Full Moon

My mother wrote the following reply today:

Dear Mam and Dad,

Sorry about the short delay in replying to your wonderfully comforting letter, but I have only just emerged from a drunken stupor. Adrian was ecstatic to be sent the postal order for 50 pence and rushed straight out to buy me a can of lager. He's such a thoughtful kid.

Nothing would give me greater pleasure than to come down and inspect Auntie Marcia's council house, but I fear that I will be quite unable to drag myself away from the endless round of parties that my life now revolves around. You know what us hedonists are like – living for kicks and not going to church.

I fear that a meticulous search has failed to turn up the missing grey sock. I can appreciate Auntie Marcia's anxiety on this point, so I enclose my last pound note to enable Auntie Marcia to buy a pair and therefore rest in peace.

What you say about George is quite true, but I married him because at that time he laughed a lot. There weren't a lot of laughs in our cottage in the middle of the potato field were there?

Cordial greetings,

Your Daughter Pauline

And Grandson Adrian

I begged her not to send it. She said she would think about it and put it behind the bread bin.

Monday October 4th

NO GIRO!

Tuesday October 5th

No giro!

My mother cracked today. She phoned up the local radio station and told them that she was going to abandon her child at the Social Security office unless she was given her giro.

My digital clock radio woke me up to the sound of my own mother's voice telling the airwaves about our financial difficulties. She was downstairs on the hall phone talking to Mitchell Malone, the halfwit DJ. My mother said she was going to abandon me at the Social Security offices unless the SS Manager contacted her by noon.

Mitchell Malone got dead excited and said, 'Listeners, we're in a High Noon situation here. Will Pauline Mole, pregnant single parent, abandon her only child in the Social Security office? Or will Mr Gudgeon, the Social Security office manager who was on this programme last week, present Pauline with her long overdue cheque? Keep tuned for regular updates on Central, your local Radio Station.'

We sat and waited for the phone to ring. At 12.30 my mother said, 'Put your coat on, Adrian, I'm taking you to be abandoned.'

At 12.35 as we were going out of the door the phone rang. It was my father pleading for his name not to be mentioned on the air.

The presence of radio reporters and journalists caused a mini-riot in the Social Security office. All the claimants wanted to tell their stories. The tramps got over-excited and started brawling amongst themselves. The staff staged a walk-out and the police were called.

Mitchell Malone was doing an outside broadcast, he played a record called 'The Lunatics are taking over the Asylum.'

I was only abandoned for forty-five minutes before Mr Gudgeon gave my mother an 'Emergency Needs Payment' of £25. He said it would see us through the weekend. He asked my mother to come in and see him on Monday morning, but a police sergeant said, 'No, Mr Gudgeon, you will go and see Mrs Mole at home.'

Mr Gudgeon sucked his ragged moustache and said, 'But I've got a meeting on Monday morning.'

The sergeant swung his truncheon about and said, 'Yes, your meeting is with Mrs Mole.' Then he strolled off and started knocking the tramps about.

Wednesday October 6th

A picture of my mother and me was on the front of the paper tonight. (My spots hardly showed up at all.) The headline said: 'A MOTHER'S ANGUISH.' The article underneath said:

Attractive mother-to-be Pauline Vole (58) took the desperate action of abandoning her only child Adrian (5) in the Carey Street Social Security office yesterday.

Mrs Vole claims to have waited three weeks for a giro cheque. She said, 'I was desperate. Adrian means more to me than life itself, but I was driven to take the drastic step of abandoning him to draw attention to our plight.'

Mr Gudgeon (42) the manager of the Carey Street office, said today: 'Mrs Vole has been the unfortunate victim of a staff shortage. The member of staff who deals with the computer broke his toe drinking squash.'

Thursday October 7th

The following corrections appeared in the local paper tonight:

Mrs Pauline Vole would like to correct an inaccurate statement attributed to her in yesterday's edition of the paper.

She did not say, 'Adrian means more to me than life itself.'

In the same article 'drinking squash' should have read 'playing squash'.

We apologize to Mrs Vole and Mr Reginald Gudgeon and thank them for pointing out these unintentional errors.

Friday October 8th

My mother phoned the local paper to demand that they print the following statement:

Mrs Pauline Mole is 38 and not 58, as was reported in Wednesday's edition.

My mother is fed up with the neighbours talking. Last night Mr O'Leary called out, 'Sure you're a fine-looking woman for your age Mrs Mole.'

Saturday October 9th
Moon's Last Quarter

The Guinness Book of Records rang up today. A posh bloke spoke to my mother and asked if she would mind her name being included in the 'Oldest Women to Give Birth' section.

He asked my mother to send her birth certificate. My mother said she hadn't given birth yet and she was only thirty-eight.

The bloke said, 'Sorry for troubling you, Mrs Vole,' and rang off.

Read the paper from cover to cover, but nothing about my mother's age appeared tonight.

Sunday October 10th
Eighteenth after Trinity

My mother spent the day reading the *Observer* with her ankles raised above her head.

I took the dog out. We went to the woods to see the half-built executive houses.

We explored a house called the 'Winchester'. The dog cocked its leg in the master bedroom and started to squat down on the Bar-B-Q patio so I dragged it away.

Monday October 11th
Columbus Day (USA). Thanksgiving Day (Canada)

Courtney brought a dead exciting postcard. It said:

Dear Adrian Mole,
Your work interests me enormously. If you would like to see it published please write to me and I will furnish you with details.
  Sincerely yours,
  L. S. Caton

It was sent from an address in Bolton. I wonder how L. S. Caton heard about me? Perhaps Mr Tydeman mentioned me over the dinner table at a BBC banquet.

I sent Mr Caton a short but dignified reply asking for further details.

Gudgeon turned up and gave my mother the rest of her money. On his way out he asked who the men's size ten shoes under the sofa belonged to. My mother told him that they belonged to her son Adrian. She said, 'I'm not likely to start co-habiting in my condition am I?' Mr Gudgeon blushed and tripped over the dog in his haste to get out.

We had a brillo dinner tonight; chicken curry and my mother put a strand of saffron in the rice. We ate it off our knees (to be strictly accurate my mother ate it off her lump) in front of the television while we watched an old Tudor wreck called the *Mary Rose* get dragged up from the sea bottom.

My mother said, 'From what I can see of it the sea bottom is the best place for it.' I was disappointed not to see any skeletons but the commentator told us that it was an historic occasion, so I tried to feel a bit overawed.

Tuesday October 12th

A first-year called Anne Louise Wirgfield asked me for my autograph today. She said, 'I saw your picture in the paper and told my mummy that you go to our school, but mummy said you didn't because the paper said you're only five. So I want your autograph to prove that I know you.'

I gave the kid my autograph, I will have to get used to being pestered one day, I suppose.

Practised my signature all through Maths. Came

home; watched the Falklands Task Force marching through London. Looked for Clive Kent, but didn't see him.

Wednesday October 13th

My mother has received a clothing voucher for school trousers from the Social Security. It is made out for £10.

To get the trousers though I have to take the voucher to one of three special shops approved by Social Security. All the shops named – Henry Blogetts and Sons, School Outfitters, Swingin' Sixty's and Mick 'n' Dave's – are notorious for selling crap clothes at big prices.

I will not demean myself by taking the voucher in. I have put it in my wallet. When I am rich and famous I will look at it and perhaps show it to my friends to prove that I once knew the sour taste of poverty.

Thursday October 14th

Went to see how Brett is getting on today. He seemed to know I was his brother because when I looked into his cot he gave me a daft gummy smile and held on to my finger dead tight.

His skin has cleared up now so perhaps there is hope for the kid.

Grandma is looking dead haggard, but not as haggard as Stick Insect. The two women are getting on each other's nerves. Grandma doesn't approve of Stick Insect using plain flour for Yorkshire puddings and Stick Insect doesn't like the way Grandma wraps Maxwell's chest up in Vick and brown paper at night. She says the rustling prevents her from sleeping.

When I got home my mother cross-questioned me about Stick Insect and Grandma. She wanted me to recall every expression of face and nuance of voice during my visit.

Friday October 15th

I have put my name down for the school play. We are doing *The Importance of Being Earnest* by Oscar Wilde.

I am having my audition next Monday. I hope to get to play Ernest, although my mother says the handbag is the best part. She thinks she's such a wit.

Monday October 18th

The weekend was far, far, far too boring to write about. Mr Golightly, the Drama teacher, stopped me halfway through my *Henry V* speech. He said, 'Look, Adrian, *The Importance of Being Earnest* is a brittle comedy of manners, not a macho war epic. I want to know if you can time a comic line.' He gave me a speech about

Victoria Station to read, listened, then said: 'Yes, you'll do.'

I have decided to be an actor when I grow up. I will write my novels during breaks in rehearsal.

Tuesday October 19th

Mrs Singh accompanied my mother to the ante-natal clinic today. The gynaecologist has told my mother she must rest more or she will be forced into hospital and made to stay in bed. Her swollen ankles are caused by high blood pressure. She is dead old to be having a baby so the doctors are giving her more attention in case she dies and they get into trouble.

Wednesday October 20th

When I said 'Hello' to Pandora in Geography my voice wobbled out of control. I kept quiet for the rest of the lesson.

Thursday October 21st

My mother asked why I was so quiet. She said, 'You've hardly said a word since *Blue Peter*. Is anything wrong?' I shrilled, 'No,' and left the room.

Friday October 22nd

My voice can't be trusted. One minute it's booming and loud like Ian Paisley, the next it's shrill and shrieking like Margaret Thatcher's used to be before she had voice lessons from an advertising agency.

Saturday October 23rd

Bert Baxter rang up to tell me that my father has got the sack from Manpower Services. I kept silent. Bert said, 'Ain't you got nought to say?'

I wobbled 'No' and put the phone down. I will have to go to the doctor's about my voice. It can't be normal to suffer like this.

Sunday October 24th
Twentieth after Trinity
British Summer Time ends

The dog went beserk and ripped the Sunday papers up today. It had no explanation for its bizarre behaviour.

The hall was covered with pieces of newsprint saying 'Ken Livingstone today defended' ... 'Falklands' upkeep rockets to £700 million' ... 'Israeli soldiers watched helpless as' ... 'trouser zips enquiry' ... 'Firemen will accept 7½% but mood is explosive' ...

I swept the pieces up and put them in the dustbin and put the lid on the outside world.

Monday October 25th
Holiday (Republic of Ireland)
Moon's First Quarter

After a silent day at school I took my unstable voice to Dr Gray's surgery. Dr Gray didn't look up from his horrible scribbling, he just said, 'Yes?' I wobbled and shrilled and boomed all my fears about having a defective voice box.

Dr Gray said, 'For Christ's sake it's only your voice breaking, youth! It's come a bit late but then you're physically immature generally. You should take up a physical sport and get more fresh air.'

I asked how long the uncertainty would last.

He said, 'Who knows? I'm not a bloody prophet, am I?'

I could hardly believe my ears. The first thing I do after leaving school will be to take out a subscription to BUPA.

I have resigned from *The Importance of Being Earnest*. To act you need a reliable voice and I haven't got one.

Tuesday October 26th

Barry Kent has committed educational suicide by wearing his Hell's Angels clothes to school. Mr Lambert pretended not to notice (Barry Kent is four inches taller than him) but Mr Scruton spotted Kent in school dinners and ordered him to take them off, saying that the studs could cause 'somebody to lose an eye'.

Kent went into the fourth-years' cloakroom and took his jacket off. He was wearing a studded death's head shirt underneath so Scruton made him remove that as well, only to reveal a leather-studded vest.

I don't know how Kent manages to carry around so much weight. Mr Scruton has sent Kent home with a note.

Wednesday October 27th

Some of the more impressionable fourth-years came to school with studs on the back of their blazers.

Thursday October 28th

Mr Scruton has added another school rule to the million others. Studs are not allowed to be worn anywhere in school except on the soles of sports boots.

After school Pandora and some of her gang rushed out to buy studs to put on the hem of their underskirts.

Friday October 29th

My mother has the baby in two weeks' time! The hospital did a test on her today. She is getting into a panic because the spare room is still a spare room and not a nursery. We are still dead short of money. The maternity grant only bought half a second-hand pram!

Saturday October 30th

The dog went berserk again and ripped up my priceless collection of old *Beanos*. I have been collecting them since I was seven so I was heartbroken to see them defiled.

I felt like booting the dog around my bedroom but I let it off lightly by chucking it down the stairs.

It's always respected literature in the past. It will have to go to the vet's, just in case it's got a brain malfunction.

Sunday October 31st
Twenty-first after Trinity. Hallowe'en. Daylight Saving Time ends (USA and Canada)

At five o'clock I was asked by my so-called best friend Nigel to go to his Hallowe'en party.

He said, 'Forgot to send you an invite, zit face, but come anyway, dress as a warlock or you won't get in.'

I decided not to go as a warlock; I wanted to break away from stereotypes, so I went as a fiend. My mother helped me to assemble a costume. We used my father's old flippers, one of my mother's long-legged black leotards and an orange fright wig she bought years ago when she went to my father's fishing club dinner and dance.

I looked a bit indecent in the leotard so I put my swimming trunks over the top, but when I got the whole lot on I didn't look a bit fiendish, I just looked dead stupid. My mother had the idea of putting a nylon stocking over my fiendishly made-up face. It looked a bit better but my costume still lacked a certain something.

At seven o'clock I had a crisis of confidence and almost took everything off, but my mother fetched a can of green neon spray paint that we used to perk up last year's Christmas tree. She sprayed me from head to toe with it. The dog whimpered and ran under the draining board. So I knew I must have achieved the right effect.

The short walk to Nigel's house was an ordeal. A gang of little kids in pointed hats ran up to me screaming: 'Trick or Treat.' I kept telling them to bugger off but they followed me to Nigel's, trying to tread on my flippers. Nigel wouldn't let me in at first because I wasn't in warlock costume. (He's so literal! He'll end up working with computers if he's not careful.) But I explained that I was a fiend and he relented. Nigel's mother and father were upstairs watching telly, so we raided their drinks cupboard and drank Tia Maria and Egg Flip Cocktails.

There were no girls at the party, which was a bit strange. Nigel said that girls make him sick. The warlocks and me danced in the pumpkin light to Duran Duran records. It was OK, I suppose, but without girls it lacked a certain *je ne sais quoi* (French for something or other). At ten o'clock Nigel's mother ran in with a running buffet. The food was all gone in ten minutes. Most of it was eaten, but a lot got thrown about. Without the civilizing influence of girls, boys return to the wild.

The school are making me read *Lord of the Flies* by William Golding. I am sharing a book with three dumbos who take half an hour to read one page, so it is turning out to be a frustrating experience.

Monday November 1st
Full Moon

After school I went to the hairdresser's with my massive mother. She didn't want me to go but she can't be allowed out of doors on her own, can she? Women are always having babies in phone boxes, buses, lifts etc. It is a well-known fact.

Franco's is run by an Italian bloke. He shouted at my mother as soon as she got through the bamboo door. He said, 'Hey, Pauline, why you no come to see Franco once a week like before, heh?'

My mother explained that she couldn't afford to have her hair done regularly now.

Franco said, 'What foolish thing you say! Hair first, food second. You want your bambino to open his eyes and see an ugly mama?'

I was astonished to hear the way he bossed my mother about, but for once she didn't seem to mind. He wrapped a sheet around her neck and said, 'Sit down, shut up, and keep still,' then he tipped her backwards and shampooed her hair. He told her off for having a few grey hairs and moaned about split ends and the condition. Then he dried her hair in a towel and made her sit in front of a mirror.

My mother said, 'I'll just have a trim please, Franco.'

But Franco said, 'No way, Pauline. I cut it all off and we start again.' And my mother sat there and let him do it!

She also let him spray her bristle-cut hair purple and she paid him for doing it. *And* gave him a tip!

Tuesday November 2nd

There is a new channel on television. It is called Channel Four and it is for minorities, like intellectuals and people that belong to jigsaw clubs.

At last I have found my spiritual viewing home.

I predict that Channel Four will transform British society. All the morons in the country will start watching it, and get a taste for education and culture! Yes, Britain is in for a new renaissance!

Wednesday November 3rd

My mother has packed her little weekend case and put it in the hall.

Thursday November 4th

My father rang today and asked me how my mother was. I said she was as well as could be expected, for an eight-and-a-half-months pregnant woman.

He asked if the baby's head was engaged yet. I answered coldly that I wasn't conversant with the technicalities of childbirth.

I asked him how his own baby was, he said, 'That's right, Adrian, turn the knife.' Then he put the phone down.

Friday November 5th
Bonfire Night!

Locked the dog in the coal shed, as advised by the media. Then went to the Marriage Guidance Council bonfire party.

It was crowded with couples bickering over the fireworks, so Pandora and I slipped away and shared a packet of sparklers behind the wall of the Co-op bakery. I wrote 'PANDORA' in the air with my sparkler. Pandora wrote 'ADRAIN'. I was very upset: we've been going out for over a year. She ought to know how to spell my name by now.

Went back to the community bonfire and found our dog watching the firework display and chewing a hot-dog.

I lost count of the times nosy adults said, 'That dog should be locked up out of harm's way.'

I tried to explain that our dog is an individualist and can't be treated like other dogs, but what with the exploding of fireworks and the crowds going, 'Oooh!' and, 'Aaaah!' every time a pathetic rocket was launched, it was a bit difficult.

In the end I took the stupid dog home, thus missing the 'Best Dressed Guy' competition.

Saturday November 6th

Wrote a political poem. I am going to send it to the *New Statesman*. Mr Braithwaite told me that they print a seditious poem every week.

Mrs Thatcher by A. Mole
Do you weep, Mrs Thatcher, do you weep?
Do you wake, Mrs Thatcher, in your sleep?
Do you weep like a sad willow?
On your Marks and Spencer's pillow?
Are your tears molten steel?
Do you weep?
Do you wake with '*Three million*' on your brain?
Are you sorry that they'll never work again?

When you're dressing in your blue, do you see the waiting
    queue?
Do you weep, Mrs Thatcher, do you weep?

I think my poem is extremely brilliant. It is the sort
of poem that could bring the government to its knees.

Sunday November 7th

Went to see Bert and Queenie with my mother.

Everyone we met on the way asked my mother when
the baby was due, or made comments like, 'I expect
you'll be glad when the baby's here, won't you?'

My mother was very ungracious in her replies.

Bert opened the door, he said, 'Ain't you dropped
that sprog yet?'

My mother said, 'Shut your mouth, you clapped-
out geriatric.'

Honestly, sometimes I long for the bygone days,
when people spoke politely to each other. You would
never guess that my mother and Bert are fond of each
other.

Everyone was too old, or too ill, or too pregnant to
do any cooking (I developed a sudden ache in both
wrists). So we ate bread and cheese for our Sunday
dinner. Then, in the afternoon we took it in turns to
teach Queenie to speak again.

I got her to say, 'A jar of beetroot please', dead
clearly. I might be a speech therapist when I grow up.
I have got a definite flair for it. We got a taxi back

home because my mother's ankles got a bit swollen. The taxi driver moaned because the distance was only half a mile.

Monday November 8th

I was woken up at 3 a.m. by the sound of my mother crying.

She wouldn't say what was wrong, so after patting her on the shoulder I went back to bed.

I wish she'd let my dad come back. After all he *has* said he's sorry.

Tuesday November 9th

Couldn't concentrate at school for worrying about my mother. Mr Lambert told me off for staring out of the window when I should have been writing about the future of the British Steel Industry.

He said, 'Adrian, you've only got three minutes to finish your essay.' So I wrote: 'In my opinion there *is* no future for the British Steel Industry, while the present government is in power.' I know I'll get into trouble, but I gave it in anyway.

Wednesday November 10th

My mother has gone mad cleaning the house from top to bottom. She has taken all the curtains and nets down. Now anybody passing by in the street can look in and see our most intimate moments.

I was examining my spots in the living-room mirror tonight, when Mr O'Leary shouted from the street: 'There's a fine pimple on the back of your neck, don't miss that one out, boy.'

It's taken me fifteen years to appreciate the part that curtains have played in civilized English life.

Mr Brezhnev, the Russian Prime Minister, died today. World leaders have been sending lying telegrams to the Kremlin saying how sorry they are.

Thursday November 11th
Armistice Day

When I got home from school my mother's little suitcase was missing from the hall. She was nowhere in the house, but I found a note on the biscuit tin. It said:

Waters broke at 3.35. I am in the labour ward of the Royal Infirmary. Call a taxi. £5 note at bottom of spaghetti jar. Don't worry.

　Love, Mum
P.S. Dog at Mrs Singh's.

Her writing looked dead untidy.

The taxi ride was a nightmare. I was struggling to get my hand free of the spaghetti jar all the way. The taxi driver kept saying, 'You should have tipped the jar upside down, you stupid bleeder.'

He parked outside the entrance to the hospital, and watched the jar versus my hand struggle in a bored sort of way. He said, 'I'll have to charge you waiting time.' A hundred years passed: then he said, 'And I can't change a five-pound note either.'

I was almost in tears by the time I managed to pull my hand free. I had a mental image of my mother calling for me. So I gave the taxi driver the fiver, and ran into the hospital. Found the lift and pressed the button which said 'Labour Ward'.

I emerged into another world. It looked like the space control centre at Houston.

A technician asked, 'Who are you?'

I said, 'I'm Adrian Mole.'

'And you've got permission to visit the labour ward?'

'Yes,' I said. (Why did I say yes? Why?)

'Room 13. She's being a bit stubborn.'

'Yes, she's a stubborn kind of person,' I said, and walked down the corridor. Doors opened and shut and I caught glimpses of women hooked up to gruesome-looking equipment. Moans and groans bounced around the shiny floors. I pushed the door of Room 13 open and saw my mother lying on a high bed reading *Memoirs of a Fox-hunting Man* by Siegfried Sassoon.

She looked pleased to see me and then asked why

I'd brought the spaghetti jar into the hospital. I was halfway through telling her, when she screwed her face up and started singing 'Hard Day's Night'.

After a bit she stopped singing and looked normal. She even laughed when I got to the bit about the horrible taxi driver. After a bit a kind black nurse came in and said, 'Are you all right, honey?'

My mother said, 'Yes. This is Adrian.'

The nurse said, 'Put a mask and gown on, Adrian, and sit in a corner; it's going to be action stations soon!'

After about half an hour my mother was singing more and talking less. She kept grabbing my hand and crushing it. The nurse came back in and to my relief told me to go out. But my mother wouldn't let go of my hand. The nurse told me to make myself useful and time the contractions. When she'd gone I asked my mother what contractions were.

'Pains,' she said, between clenched teeth. I asked her why she hadn't had her back frozen to stop the pain. My mother said, 'I can't stand people fiddling around with my back.'

The pains started coming every minute, and my mother went barmy, and a lot of people ran in and started telling her to push. I sat in a far corner at the head end of my mother and tried not to look at the other end where doctors and nurses were clanging about with metal things. My mother was puffing and panting, just like she does at Christmas when she's blowing balloons up. Soon everyone was shouting, 'Push, Mrs Mole, push!' My mother pushed until her eyes nearly popped out. 'Harder,' they shouted. My mother went a bit barmy again, and the doctor said, 'I can see the baby's head!'

I tried to escape then but my mother said, 'Where's Adrian? I want Adrian.'

I didn't like to leave her alone with strangers, so I said I'd stay. I stared at the beauty spot on my mother's cheek for the next three minutes, and I didn't look up, until I heard the black nurse say, 'Pant for the head.'

At 5.19 p.m. my mother had a barmy moment; then the doctor and nurses gave a sort of loud sigh, and I looked up and saw a skinny purple thing hanging upside down. It was covered in white stuff.

'It's a lovely little girl, Mrs Mole,' the doctor said, and he looked dead pleased, as if he were the father himself.

My mother said, 'Is she all right?'

The doctor said, 'Toes and fingers all correct.'

The baby started crying in a crotchety, bad-tempered way, and she was put on my mother's flatter belly. My mother looked at her as if she was a precious piece of jewellery or something. I congratulated my mother and she said, 'Say hello to your sister.'

The doctor stared at me in my mask and gown and said, 'Aren't you Mr Mole, the baby's father?'

I said, 'No, I'm Master Mole, the baby's brother.'

'Then you've broken every rule in this hospital,' he said. 'I must ask you to leave. You could be rife with childish infectious diseases.'

So, while they stood around waiting for something called the placenta to emerge, I went into the corridor.

I found a waiting-room full of worried-looking men, smoking and talking about cars.

(*To be continued after sleep.*)

At 6.15 I rang Pandora and told her the news. She did big squeals down the phone. Next I rang Grandma, who did big sobs.

Then I phoned Bert and Queenie, who threatened to come and see my mother. But I managed to put them off. Then I ran out of five pence pieces, so I called in to see my mum and sister. Then went home. I walked around the empty house, trying to imagine sharing it with a little girl.

I put all my smashable possessions on the top shelf of my unit. Then went to bed. It was only 7.30 but for some reason I was dead tired. The phone woke me up at 8.15. It was my father gibbering about having a girl. He wanted to know every detail about her. I said she took after him. Half bald and angry-looking.

Friday November 12th

The Russians chose their new leader today. He is called Andropov. I am a hero at school. The story has got round that I *delivered* the baby. The dinner lady in charge of chips gave me an extra big portion. Went to the hospital to see my female relations after school.

I am staying at Pandora's house. Over supper I gave them a blow-by-blow account of the birth. Halfway through Mr Braithwaite got up and left the table.

Saturday November 13th

Pandora and I went to see my mother and the baby this afternoon. We had to fight our way through the crowd of visitors round her bed. For such a stubborn person she is certainly popular. The baby was passed around like an exhibit in a court room. Everyone said, 'Isn't she beautiful?'

The women said, 'Ooh it makes me feel broody!'

The men said, 'Small fingernails.'

Then Queenie and Bert arrived, so a space was cleared for Bert's wheelchair, and Queenie sat on the bed and squashed my mother's legs and it was dead chaotic. The nurses started looking efficient and bossy. A staff nurse said, 'You are only allowed two visitors to a bed.' Just then my grandma and father turned up. So everyone else was pleased to go and leave these two particular visitors at the bed.

Sunday November 14th
Remembrance Sunday

My mother phoned me up to tell me that she is coming home at 10.30 tomorrow morning. She told me to make sure the heating is switched on. I asked if she wanted a taxi ordering. She said, 'No, your father has kindly offered to pick us up.'

Us! I am no longer an only child.

Watched the poppies falling on to the heads of the

young kids in Westminster Abbey. My eyes started running: I think I've got a cold coming on.

Monday November 15th

Skived off school. Mrs Singh and Mrs O'Leary came round early to tidy the house. I said I was perfectly capable, but Mrs O'Leary said: 'Sure, you're talking nonsense, child. How would a lump like you know how to make a house nice enough to pass the eagle eyes of a woman?'

At 11.15 I saw the bizarre sight of my father carrying his daughter down the front path. Followed by my thin purple-haired mother. I haven't got enough emotions to cope with all the complexities of my life. After going mad over the baby, Mrs Singh and Mrs O'Leary melted away and left my immediate family staring at each other. To break the tension I made a cup of tea.

My mother took hers to bed and I let mine go cold. My father hung about for a bit then went home to Grandma's.

The midwife came at 2.30. She did mysterious things to my mother in the privacy of the master bedroom. At 3.15 the midwife came downstairs and said my mother was suffering from after-baby blues caused by hormone trouble. She asked me who was looking after my mother. I said I was. She said, 'I see,' in a thin-lipped manner. I said, 'I am perfectly capable of pushing a Hoover around!'

She said, 'Your mother needs more support.'

So I took the pillows off my own bed and gave them to my mother. This act of kindness made my mother cry.

Tuesday November 16th

Phoned the school secretary Mrs Claricoates and enquired about maternity leave. Scruton came on the line. He barked, 'If I don't see you in school tomorrow, Mole, I shall be severely displeased!'

The baby woke up five times in the night. I know, because I sat by her cot, checking her breathing every ten minutes.

My mother has stopped crying and started wearing mascara again.

Wednesday November 17th

Mrs Singh and Mrs O'Leary are taking it in turns to look after my mother and sister. Pandora says I am beginning to be a bore about the baby. She says that my sister's feeding pattern isn't of great interest to her. How callous can you get?

Thursday November 18th

My father was ironing baby clothes when I got home from school. He said, 'If you laugh, I'll kill you.' My mother was feeding the baby, with her feet on the dog's back. It was a charming domestic picture, only spoiled when my father put the ironing board away and went home to his other family.

Friday November 19th

I asked my mother what she was going to call the baby.

She said, 'I can't think beyond the next feed – let alone decide on a name.'

I suggested we both make a list, so after the next feed we did.

My mother's	Mine
Charity	Tracy
Christobel	Claire
Zoe	Toyah
Jade	Diana
Frankie	Pandora
India	Sharon
Rosie	Georgina
Caitlin	
Ruth	

I only liked 'Rosie' and 'Ruth' out of my mother's list. She didn't like any in my list. She said, 'Pandora is a pretentious name!' I think it is the most evocative girl's name in the history of the world. Whenever I say it, or hear it, I get a bursting feeling behind my ribs.

Saturday November 20th

My sister's name is Rosie Germaine Mole.

Everybody likes 'Rosie' but only my mother likes 'Germaine'. The registrar raised his eyebrows, and said, 'Germaine? As in *Female Eunuch*?'

My mother said, 'Yes, have you read it?' 'No, but my wife can't put it down,' he said, smoothing his unironed shirt.

We celebrated Rosie being on the official record sheet of Great Britain by going into a café, and having a meal. Rosie was in a baby sling squashed against my mother's chest. She was dead well-behaved. She only woke up when my mother dropped a warm chip on her head. After the meal, we caught a taxi home. My mother was too tired to walk to the bus stop.

Sunday November 21st

My father came round with £25. He mooned over my mother while she was defrosting a shoulder of lamb under the hot tap. They started having an intense conversation about their future relationship. So I took the dog for a walk into the garden for a session of obedience training, but it was a waste of time. Our dog would have Barbara Woodhouse in tears.

Monday November 22nd

We had to write a description of a person in English. So I wrote about Rosie.

Rosie
Rosie is about eighteen inches long, she has got a big head with fuzzy black hair in a Friar Tuck style. Unlike the rest of our family, her eyes are brown. She has got quite a good skin. Her mouth is extremely small, except when she is screaming. Then it resembles an underground cavern. She has got a wrinkled-up neck like a turkey's. She dresses in unisex clothes, and always wears disposable nappies. She lazes about all day in a carrycot and only gets out when it is time to be fed or changed. She has got a split personality; calm one minute, screaming like a maniac the next.

She is only eleven days old but she rules our house.

Tuesday November 23rd

Rat fink Lucas phoned up tonight. My mother spoke to him for about ten minutes in a mumbling sort of way, as though she didn't want me to hear. But I certainly heard the last thing she said before she threw the phone across the hall. Because it was said at a high rate of decibels.

'ALL RIGHT – HAVE A BLOOD TEST!'

Perhaps Lucas thinks he's got a deadly blood disease. I hope he has.

Wednesday November 24th

Mr O'Leary has gone to Ireland to vote in the Irish election, which is being held tomorrow. I admire his patriotism: but I can't understand why he doesn't live in Ireland all the time. I will ask him when he comes back. Mrs O'Leary is not so patriotic. She stayed at home and threw a party for somebody called 'Ann Summers'. My mother was invited but didn't go. She said Ann Summers was responsible for getting her into her present mess.

I watched the O'Learys' front door all night but all I saw was just a load of middle-aged women giggling and clutching brown paper bags.

Thursday November 25th

Nobody won in the Irish General Election. It was a draw.

Mr O'Leary was detained at East Midlands airport on suspicion of being a terrorist but he was let off with a warning and told not to bring Action Man accessories into the country again.

Friday November 26th

I got a dead horrible shock when I came out of the school gate today. Stick Insect was waiting for me. She stood there rocking an old royal family pram which contained Brett and Maxwell. She looked like a refugee from a Second World War newsreel. Maxwell shouted, 'Hello brudder.' I thought he was talking to Brett, but no, the kid was talking to me! I shoved a bit of Mars bar into his mouth before he could show me up any more, and introduced Pandora to Stick Insect.

I said, 'My girl-friend, Pandora,' to Stick Insect; and, 'Mrs Doreen Slater,' to Pandora. The two women looked each other up and down in a split second, and then smiled in a false way.

'What perfect darlings,' said Pandora, looking in the pram.

'They're both little buggers,' Stick Insect whined. 'I'd never have had them if I'd known.'

'Known what?' said Pandora, pretending to be innocent.

'Known that they take your life over. Don't you have none,' she warned.

Pandora said, 'I hope I shall have six!'

'*And* be editor of *The Times*?' I said sarcastically.

'Yes,' said Pandora, 'and I shall do my own painting and decorating!'

'You wait,' said Stick Insect. 'You just wait.' It was like a gypsy's curse.

I asked S.I. why she'd waited for me, and she told me that my father was awful to live with, and that Grandma was worse.

I said, 'Well what can I do about it?'

Stick Insect said, 'I just wanted to get it off my

chest!' (Flat). Then she wheeled the kids back to Grandma's.

I don't know a single sane adult. They are all barmy. If they are not fighting in the Middle East, they are dressing poodles in plastic macs or having their bodies deep frozen. Or reading the *Sun*, because they think it is a newspaper.

Saturday November 27th

Changed my first nappy tonight.

Tomorrow I am going to try doing it with my eyes open.

Sunday November 28th

How is it that my mother can change Rosie's yukky nappies and at the same time smile and even laugh? I nearly fainted when I tried to do it without a protective device (clothes peg). Perhaps women have got poorly developed nasal passages.

I wonder if research has been done into it? If I pass 'O' level Biology I may even do it myself.

Monday November 29th

My mother's gone right off me since Rosie was born. She was never a particularly attentive mother – I always had to clean my own shoes. But just lately I have been feeling emotionally deprived. If I turn out to be mentally deranged in adult life, it will all be my mother's fault.

I'm spending most of the time reading in my room. I've just finished reading *To Sir with Love*. It's about a black teacher who is badly treated by white yobs. But by persevering, and being kind yet firm, he triumphs over them, and decides not to be an engineer. I give it five out of ten. Which is not bad because I am very discriminating.

Tuesday November 30th
St Andrew's Day

Made my Christmas present list out in order of preference.

Big present list
Word Processor (no chance)
Colour Telly (portable)
Amstrad Hi-Fi unit (for future record collections)
Electronic typewriter (for poems)
3/4-length sheepskin coat (for warmth and status)

Small present list
Pair of trousers (pegs)
Adidas trainers (size ten)
Adidas anorak (36″ chest)
Anglepoise lamp (for late-night poetry)

Gigantic tin of Quality Street
Solid gold pen set (inscribed A. Mole)
Pair slippers
Electric razor
Habitat bath robe (like Pandora's dad's)

Things I always get whether I want them or not
Beano Annual
Chocolate smoking set
Pkt felt-tip pens
False nose/glasses/moustache

I gave my mother the list, but she wasn't in the mood for talking about Christmas. In fact just mentioning Christmas put her in a bad mood.

Wednesday December 1st

An emotion-packed phone call from Grandma: Stick Insect has taken Brett and Maxwell to stay with Maxwell's father, who has just come back from the Middle East, loaded with tax-free money and stuffed toy camels!

Apparently my father doesn't mind being deprived of his paternal rights and Maxwell's dad doesn't care that Stick Insect has had a baby in his absence. I am shocked. Am I to be the sole guardian of the little morality left in our society?

Thursday December 2nd

Maxwell's dad, Trevor Roper, doesn't mind about Brett because he thinks Brett is the result of having faulty coitus interruptus!

Stick Insect is getting married to Mr Roper as soon as his divorce is through. It's no wonder the country is on its knees. I am seriously thinking about returning to the church. (Not to go to Stick Insect's wedding either.) I have made an appointment to see a vicar, Reverend Silver. I got him out of the Yellow Pages.

Friday December 3rd

The vicar was mending his bike when I first saw him. He looked quite normal except that he was wearing a black dress.

He got up and gave me a bone-crushing handshake. Then he took me to his study and asked me what I wanted to see him about. I said I was worried about the disintegration of morals in modern life. He lit a cigarette with trembly hands, and enquired if I had asked God for guidance. I said I had stopped believing in God. He said, 'Oh God, not another one!' He talked for ages. It all boiled down to having faith. I said I hadn't got faith and asked him how to get it.

He said, 'You must have faith!' It was like listening to a stuck record. I said, 'If God exists how come He allows wars and famines and motorway crashes to happen?'

Rev. Silver said: 'I don't know, I lie awake wondering that myself.'

Mrs Silver came in with two mugs of Nescafé, and a box of Mr Kipling's iced fancies.

She said, 'Derek, your Open University thing is starting in ten minutes.'

I asked the Rev. Silver what he was studying. He said, 'Microbiology. You know where you are with microbes.'

I said goodbye and wished him luck in his change of career. He told me not to despair, and showed me out into the mad, bad, world. It was cold and dark and some yobs were throwing chips about in the street. I went home feeling worse than ever.

Saturday December 4th

I am having a nervous breakdown. Nobody has noticed yet.

Sunday December 5th

Went to see Bert; he is my last hope. (Pandora failed me. She blamed my mental state on my being a meat eater.) I said, 'Bert, I am having a breakdown!' Bert said that he had had a breakdown in the First World War. He said his was caused by seeing thousands of dead men and being constantly afraid for his life. He asked what mine was caused by.

I said, 'The lack of morals in society.'

Bert said, 'You daft bugger, what you need is a good stint of hard work. You can start on the washing up.'

When I'd finished Queenie made me a cup of tea, and a pile of crab paste sandwiches. While I ate I watched *Songs of Praise* on the television. The church was full of happy-looking people all singing their hearts out.

How come they've got faith and I've not? Just my luck!

Monday December 6th

I was woken up at 1 a.m., 2.30 a.m. and 4 a.m. by Rosie screaming.

I got up at 6 a.m. and listened to a farming programme on Radio Four. Some old rustic gasbag was drivelling on about geese farming in Essex. At 8.30 I went into my mother's room, to ask for my dinner money, and found Rosie fast asleep in my mother's bed. This is strictly forbidden by the baby books.

I checked that Rosie could breathe properly, then, after taking three pounds out of my mother's purse, I went to school and tried to behave normally.

Tuesday December 7th

Queenie died at 3 o'clock this morning. She had a
stroke in her sleep. Bert said that it was a good way to
go, and I am inclined to agree with him. It was strange
to go into Bert's house and see Queenie's things all
over the place. I still can't believe she is dead and that
her body is in the Co-op Funeral Parlour.

I didn't cry when my mother told me the news, in
fact I felt like laughing. It wasn't until I saw Queenie's
pot of rouge standing on the dressing table that tears
leaked out. I didn't let Bert see me crying, and he
didn't let me see him crying. But I know he has been.
There are no clean hankies left in his drawer.

Bert doesn't know what to do about death certificates, and funeral arrangements etc. So Pandora's
father came round to do all the death paperwork.

Wednesday December 8th

Bert has asked me to write a poem to put in the Deaths
column of the local paper.

10 p.m. I am terrified. In fact I have got writer's block.

11.30 p.m. Unblocked. Finished poem.

Thursday December 9th

The following announcements appeared in the paper tonight:

BAXTER, Maud Lilian (Queenie). Passed away peacefully at home on 7th December 1982. To the best girl that ever was. Bert, Sabre and Adrian.

White face, red cheeks.
Eyes like crocus buds.
Hands deft and sure, yet worked to gnarled roots.
A practical comfortable body, dressed in young colours.
Feet twisted, but planted firmly on the ground.
A sure soft voice, with a crackly sudden laugh.
Her body is lifeless and cold,
But the memory of her is joyful and as warm as a rockpool in August.

Funeral service and cremation, Monday 13th December at 1.30 p.m. at Gilmore's crematorium. Floral tributes to Co-operative funeral service.
Written with love, from Adrian, on the instructions of Mr Bertram Baxter.

BAXTER, Queenie: Sadly missed, Pauline and Rosie Mole.

BAXTER, Maud Lilian:
The parting was so sudden.
We sit and wonder why.

> The saddest thing of all,
> Is that we never said goodbye.

From your grieving son, Nathan, and your daughter-in-law, Maria, and Jodie and Jason, grandchildren.

BAXTER, Queenie: Adieu Queenie, Mr and Mrs Braithwaite and Pandora.

BAXTER, Queenie:
> Always a smile and a kindly word.
> She'd never pass on the things she heard.
> She bore her troubles with never a moan.
> To every stray dog she would give a bone.

God Bless Queenie. From your friends at the 'Evergreens'.

BAXTER, Queenie: Life is a struggle in search of a vision. You have found your vision we hope. From your friends, the Singh Family.

BAXTER, Queenie: Words can't express how much I will miss my old pal. Your neighbour, Doris.

BAXTER, Queenie: Deepest sympathy, from John the milkman.

BAXTER, Queenie: We have lost a dear old friend. Julian and Sandy, at the 'Jolie Madame' Hair Salon.

BAXTER, Queenie: A sad loss. May and George Mole.

BAXTER, Queenie: I'll miss you, Queenie. Betty in the sweet shop and her husband, Cyril, and children Carol and Pat.

My tribute to Queenie has caused a stir. People have said it's in bad taste, and have complained that it doesn't rhyme. Must I live amongst uneducated peasants – for the rest of my life? I long for the day when I buy my first studio flat in Hampstead. I will have a notice on my door: 'NO HAWKERS TRADERS OR PHILISTINES.'

Friday December 10th

Mr Braithwaite is very worried about Queenie's funeral. The cheapest he can arrange will cost £350. (Plain coffin, one hearse, one mourners' car.) But Queenie's funeral insurance is only worth £30. She took it out in 1931 when £30 would buy you: a fancy coffin, two teams of black horses with plumes, a funeral tea, and a gang of top-hatted attendants. The death grant the government gives you is no help. It doesn't buy a brass coffin nail.

The only solution is for Bert to take out hire-purchase and have Queenie's funeral on the never-never.

Saturday December 11th

The finance company have turned down Bert's request for a loan. They say he is too old at nearly ninety, so it looks like Queenie will have to be buried by Social Security (grey van, plywood coffin, ashes put in a jam jar).

Bert is dead upset. He said, 'I wanted my girl to go out properly!' I spent all night phoning around to everyone who knew Queenie, getting them to donate money. I was called a saint several times.

Sunday December 12th

My mother has gone out with Mrs Singh, Mrs O'Leary and her women's group to have a picnic on Greenham Common. She has taken Rosie, so the house is dead peaceful.

I played my 'Toyah' records at full volume and had a bath with the door open.

10.02 p.m. I have just seen the Greenham women on the telly! They were tying babies' bootees on to the wire surrounding the missile base. Then they held hands with each other. The newscaster said that 30,000 women were there. The dog was sulking because my mother had gone out for the day. It didn't understand that she was miles away safeguarding its future.

They got back safely. The women's group came back to our house. They talked about female solidarity, while I served them coffee and tuna sandwiches. I felt excluded from the conversation so I went to bed.

2.00 a.m. Just woken up by Mr Singh and Mr O'Leary banging on our door demanding entrance. I got up and explained to them that there were about twenty women in our living room. Mr O'Leary said, 'Tell Caitlin to hurry up; I can't find my pyjamas.' Mr Singh said, 'Ask Sita to tell me how to work our electric kettle.'

I advised them to go home for their own safety.

Monday December 13th

Queenie's funeral.
We dropped Rosie off at Mrs Singh's and walked round to Bert's bungalow. All the curtains in the street were shut out of respect for Queenie. The neighbours were out looking at the floral tributes, which were lined up alongside the little path to the front door. Bert was sitting in his wheelchair wearing his wedding suit. Sabre was sitting by his side. My mother gave Bert a kiss.

Bert said, 'I don't like to think about her lying in an unheated coffin, she never did like the cold.'

My mother acted as hostess because none of Queenie's relations came. (Queenie quarrelled with them because they disapproved when she married Bert.)

The mourners' cars arrived so me and the Co-op men carried Bert out to the leading car, then me and my mother and Doris from next door, and Mr and Mrs Braithwaite and Pandora sat in the leading car. The second car filled up with less important mourners and we set off very slowly to Gilmore's Crematorium. As we passed the cemetery gates, an old man took his hat off and bowed his head. Bert said that the old man was a stranger. I was very touched by this gesture of respect.

My mother and father sat together in the chapel, briefly united. Me and Pandora sat either side of Bert. He said he wanted to have 'young 'uns' around him.

The service was short; we sang Queenie's favourite carol, 'Away in a Manger', and her favourite song, 'If I ruled the World'.

Then, while the organ played sad music, the coffin started sliding towards purple curtains around the altar. When the coffin reached the curtains Pandora whispered, 'God, how perfectly barbaric.'

I watched with horror as the coffin disappeared. Bert said, 'Tara old girl' and then Queenie was burnt in the oven.

I was so shocked, I could hardly walk up the aisle. Pandora and I both looked up when we got outside. Smoke was pouring out of the chimney, and was carried away by the wind. Queenie always said she wanted to fly.

I suppose there is a sort of logic to life and death. Rosie was born and so Queenie had to make way for her. The funeral tea was held at Pandora's house; it was a very jolly affair. Bert held up well, and even cracked a few jokes. But I noticed that whenever I mentioned Queenie's name, people looked away, and pretended not to hear. So Bert is on his own again, and will need more looking after than ever!

How will I cope? I've got my 'O' levels in June.

Tuesday December 14th

It was on Radio Four that the government is spending a billion pounds on buying war equipment. Yet one of our science laboratories at school is closing down after Christmas, because our school can't afford to pay a new teacher. Poor old Mr Hill is retiring after thirty years of sweating over the Bunsen burners. He will be sadly missed. He was dead strict but dead fair with it. He was never sarcastic and seemed to listen to what you were saying. Also he gave out mini Mars bars for good work.

Wednesday December 15th

We put the Christmas tree up tonight. It had gone a bit rusty, but I tied tinsel round the worst bits. My mother insisted on hanging up the decorations I made when I was a little kid. She said they had sentimental value for her. It looked OK when all the flashy balls and bad-taste angels were bunged on it.

I picked Rosie up and showed her the finished tree, but I can't say she was overjoyed. In fact she just yawned. The dog, on the other hand, had one of its mad fits, and had to be restrained with a rolled-up *Guardian*.

Thursday December 16th

Bought a pack of cheap Christmas cards from Cherry's, but didn't write in them. I will wait and see who sends me one first.

Friday December 17th

The school's internal Christmas post service is as bad as the GPO's. I posted Pandora a card before assembly but she still hadn't had it by the end of the last lesson.

I will find out which first-years were on Elf duty today, and severely rebuke them.

Saturday December 18th

Courtney has made £150 in tips from his post round. He is spending it on a weekend in Venice. He says that Christmas in Venice is an experience that everyone should have at least once in their lives. I wish I could have that experience. Courtney said that English canals are not a patch on Venetian ones.

Sunday December 19th

Today Rosie Germaine Mole smiled for the first time. The recipient of the smile was the dog.

My father rang to ask what we are doing for Christmas. My mother said, 'The usual seasonal things, George: eating turkey, getting drunk, buying replacement bulbs for the fairy lights.'

My father said, 'Mother and me will be having *a quiet time, on our own, alone. Just the two of us. Away from our nearest and dearest.*'

My mother said, 'It sounds divine. Well I must dash. A crowd of pre-Christmas revellers have just turned up with the champagne.'

This was a complete and utter lie. It was only me coming into the room with a cup of cocoa.

Monday December 20th

We break up tomorrow. So the school has gone a bit wild. The girls are doing no work at all, they just sit around the classrooms counting how many Christmas cards they've received from each other, and writing out hundreds more. The Elf postal service is being swamped.

I haven't sent any cards at all yet. I'm still waiting to see if anybody sends me one.

Tomorrow is the day of the school concert. It will be the first year I have had nothing to do. My mother is glad because it means she won't have to go.

Tuesday December 21st

Last day of school
Thank God! I got seven Christmas cards. Three tasteful. Four in putrid taste and printed on flimsy rubbish paper that won't stand up. On receipt I quickly wrote out seven cards and gave them to a passing elf. Mr Golightly, director of the Christmas play, *The Importance of Being Earnest Christmas Show*, was very irritable today when I wished him good luck for tonight. He said, 'Thanks to your abdication, Adrian, I have got a midget playing Ernest.' (Peter Brown, whose mother smoked throughout her pregnancy!)

I'm glad I did abdicate from my role, because the play was a complete fiasco. Lady Bracknell forgot to say, 'A handbag?' And Peter Brown stood behind a chair so that the audience only saw the top of his head. Simone Bates, as Gwendoline, was quite good but what a shame her costume didn't hide her tattoos! The other parts are just not worth writing about.

The best thing in the show was the scenery. I congratulated Mr Animba, the woodwork teacher, on his dedication. He said, 'Do you think anybody noticed that it was adapted from the *Peter Pan* scenery of three years ago?' I assured him that nobody had complained that the view from the french windows was of a palm-fringed island.

Mr Golightly was nowhere to be seen at the end of the play. Somebody told me that he had run from the wings shortly before the end, saying he had to visit his mother in hospital.

The best thing about the evening was the interval when Pandora played her viola in the refreshment room.

Wednesday December 22nd

Drew £15 out of my Building Society today.

I know it's a lot but I've got an extra person to buy for: Rosie.

9.30 p.m. Forgot that Queenie isn't here any more. I needn't have been so extravagant. My memory!

Thursday December 23rd

Made a list and went to Woolworth's, as they have got a good selection of festive gifts.

Dog	False bone	(£1.25)
Pandora	Solid gold chain	(£2.00)
Mother	Egg Timer	(About £1.59)

Rosie	Chocolate Santa	(79p)
Bert	20 Woodbines	(£1.09)
Nigel	He gets nothing this year	His best friend is now Clive Barnes
Father	Festive tin of anti-freeze	(£1.39)
Grandma	Gift pack of dusters	(£1.29)
Auntie Susan	Hankie Set	(99p)
Sabre	Dog Comb	(£1.29)

Woolworth's was swarming with last-minute shoppers, so I had to queue for half an hour at the checkout till. Why do people wait to do their shopping until there are only two days left before Christmas?

I couldn't get on a bus home because of the stupid lemmings. Went to the 'Off the Streets' Youth Club party with Pandora. Nigel caused a scandal by dancing with Clive Barnes who was wearing lipstick and mascara!

Everyone was saying that Nigel is gay, so I made sure that everyone knew that he is no longer my best friend. Barry Kent smuggled two cans of 'Tartan' bitter through the fire doors. His gang of six shared them, and got leglessly drunk. At the end of the party Rick Lemon put 'White Christmas' by some old crumblie on the record deck and all the couples danced romantically together. I told Pandora how much I adored her and she said, 'Aidy, my pet, how long will our happiness last?'

Trust Pandora to put a damp cloth on everything.

Saw her home. Kissed her twice. Went home. Fed dog. Checked Rosie's pulse. Went to bed.

Friday December 24th
Christmas Eve

My mother is being kept a prisoner by Rosie; so I have had to do all the Christmas preparations. I was up at 7.30 queuing in the butcher's for a fresh turkey, pork joint, and sausage meat.

By 9 a.m. I was in the queue at the greengrocer's: 3lbs sprouts, 24 tangerines, 2lbs mixed nuts, 2 bunches of holly (make sure they have berries), salad (don't forget green pepper), 2 boxes of dates (get those with camel on lid), 3lbs of apples (if no Cox's get G. Smith), 6lbs potatoes (check each one for signs of sprouting).

By 11.15 I was in the launderette washing and drying the loose covers off the three-piece suite.

2 p.m. saw me at the grocer's with a long list, and Rosie's pram outside to cart everything home. £2.50's worth of Stilton (make sure good blue colour, firm texture), 2 boxes sponge fingers, red and yellow jelly . . . tin of fruit salad. . . . It went on for ever.

At 4.10 p.m. I was struggling into Woolworth's front doors, and trying to fight my way to the fairy-light counter. At 4.20 I got to the counter only to find empty shelves and other desperate people swapping rumours: 'Curry's have got some lantern style', 'Rumbelow's have got two packets of the "star type"', 'Habitat have got the High Tech styles but they're pricey!'

I went to all the above shops and more, but at 5 p.m. I admitted defeat and joined the long queue at the bus stop.

Drunken youths covered in 'crazy foam' and factory girls wearing tinsel garlands paraded around the town singing carols. Jesus would have turned in his tomb.

At 5.25 I had a panic attack and left the queue and rushed into Marks and Spencer's to buy something.

I was temporarily deranged. A voice inside my head kept saying: 'Only five minutes before the shops shut. Buy! Buy! Buy!'

The shop was full of sweating men buying women's underwear. At 5.29 I came to my senses, and went back to bus stop. Just in time to see the bus leaving. I got home at 6.15 after buying a packet of fairy lights from Cherry's shop which is just around the corner from our house.

My mother has made the lounge look especially nice (she'd even dusted the skirting board) and when the new fairy lights were switched on, and the fruit arranged, and the holly stuck up etc, it looked like a room on a Christmas card. Me and my mother had a quick drink before Bert arrived in an Age Concern car, driven by a kind volunteer.

We settled him in front of the telly with a beetroot sandwich and a bottle of brown ale, and we went into the kitchen to start the mincepies and trifles.

*

1 a.m. Just got back from the Midnight Service. It was very moving (even for an atheist), though I think it was a mistake to have a live donkey in the church.

2 a.m. Just remembered, forgot to buy nutcrackers.

Saturday December 25th
Christmas Day

Got up at 7.30.

Had a wash and a shave, cleaned teeth, squeezed spots then went downstairs and put kettle on. I don't know what's happened to Christmas Day lately, but something has. It's just not the same as it used to be when I was a kid. My mother fed and cleaned Rosie, and I did the same to Bert. Then we went into the lounge and opened our presents. I was dead disappointed when I saw the shape of my present. I could tell at a glance that it didn't contain a single microchip. OK a sheepskin coat is warm but there's nothing you can *do* with it, except wear it.

In fact after only two hours of wearing it, I got bored and took it off. However, my mother was ecstatic about her egg timer; she said, 'Wow, another one for my collection.' Rosie ignored the chocolate Santa I bought her. That's 79 pence wasted! *This is what I got:*

³/₄ length sheepskin coat (out of Littlewoods catalogue)

Beano Annual (a sad disappointment, this year's is very
   childish)

Slippers (like Michael Caine wears, although not many
   people know that)

Swiss army knife (my father is hoping I'll go out into the
   fresh air and use it)

Tin of humbugs (supposedly from the dog)

Knitted Balaclava helmet (from Grandma Mole. Yuk!
   Yuk!)

Boys' Book of Sport (from Grandma Sugden: Stanley
   Matthews on cover)

I was glad when Auntie Susan and her friend Gloria
turned up; at 11 o'clock. Their talk is very metropolitan
and daring; and Gloria is dead glamorous and sexy.
She wears frilly dresses, and lacy tights, and high
heels. And she's got an itsy-bitsy voice that makes my
stomach go soft. Why she's friends with Auntie Susan,
who is a prison warder, smokes Panama cigars and
has got hairy fingers, I'll never know.

   The turkey was OK. But would have been better if
the giblets and the plastic bag had been removed
before cooking. Bert made chauvinist remarks during
the carving. He leered at Gloria's cleavage and said,
'Give me a nice piece of breast.' Gloria wasn't a bit
shocked, but I went dead red, and pretended that I'd
dropped my cracker under the table.

   When my mother asked me which part of the turkey
I wanted, I said, 'A wing please!' I really wanted breast,
leg, or thigh. But wing was the only part of the bird
without sexual connotations. Rosie had a few spoons

of mashed potato and gravy. Her table manners are disgusting, even worse than Bert's.

I was given a glass of Bull's Blood wine and felt dead sensual. I talked brilliantly and with consummate wit for an hour, but then my mother told me to leave the table, saying, 'One sniff of the barmaid's apron and his mouth runs away with him.'

The Queen didn't look very happy when she was giving her speech. Perhaps she got lousy Christmas presents this year, like me. Bert and Auntie Susan had a disagreement about the Royal Family. Bert said he would 'move the whole lot of 'em into council houses in Liverpool.'

Gloria said, 'Oh Bert that's a bit drastic. Milton Keynes would be more suitable. They're not used to roughing it you know.'

In the evening I went round to see Grandma and my father. Grandma forced me to eat four mincepies, and asked me why I wasn't wearing my new Balaclava helmet. My father didn't say anything; he was dead drunk in an armchair.

Sunday December 26th
First after Christmas

Pandora and I exchanged presents in a candlelit ceremony in my bedroom. I put the solid gold chain round her neck, and she put a 70% wool, 10% cashmere, 20% acrylic scarf round my neck.

A cashmere scarf at fifteen!

I'll make sure the label can be seen by the public at all times.

Pandora went barmy about the solid gold chain. She kept looking at herself in the mirror, she said, 'Thank you, darling, but how on earth can you afford solid gold? It must have cost you at least a hundred pounds!'

I didn't tell her that Woolworth's were selling them cheap at two pounds a go.

Monday December 27th
Boxing Day, Holiday (UK except Scotland).
Holiday (Canada). Bank Holiday (Scotland).
Holiday (Rep of Ireland)

Just had a note handed to me from a kid riding a new BMX.

Dear heart,
I'm awfully sorry but I will have to cancel our trip to the cinema to see *ET*.

I woke up this morning with an ugly disfiguring rash around my neck.

Yours sincerely,
Pandora
P.S. I am allergic to non-precious metal.

Tuesday December 28th

Walked up and down the High Street in my sheepskin coat and cashmere scarf. Saw Nigel in his new leather trousers posing at the traffic lights. He suggested we go to his house to 'talk'. I agreed. On the way he told me that he was trying to decide which sort of sexuality to opt for: homo, bi or hetero. I asked him which he felt more comfortable with. He said, 'All three, Moley.' Nigel could never make up his mind.

He showed me his presents. He had: a multi gym, Adidas football boots, a Mary Quant make-up hamper, and a unisex jogging suit.

Wednesday December 29th

Danny Thompson has turned into a Rasta. I met him when I was walking up and down the High Street this morning. He asked me if I could play a musical instrument. I said, 'No.'

He said, 'Too bad, man, I needs a bass player real quick.'

I said I was surprised that a reggae band should need a double bass.

He did fancy hand-clapping and laughed and said, 'Bass *guitar*, what give out de rhythm.'

I said that my only contribution to the band could be as a lyricist.

He suggested I try writing a few songs and submit-

ting them to the brothers. Then he gave me a complicated handshake and went off down the street with a
springy step and with his blond plaits bobbing up and
down.

Thursday December 30th
Full Moon

Me, Mum, Rosie, Auntie Susan and Gloria went to
Bridgegate Park today. Bert doesn't like fresh air so he
stayed at home with the dogs and leftover Christmas
food. We walked four boring miles. I walked behind
Gloria so that I could watch her bum and legs properly.
Auntie Susan and Gloria are going back to Holloway
prison tonight. They will be sadly missed, they are so
gay and vital. Bert is going back to his council bungalow. He will *not* be missed. He watches ITV all day
and won't let anybody else hold Rosie.

Friday December 31st

Bert has asked if he can stay on until New Year's Day.
He said he can't face seeing the New Year in with only
a Voluntary Social Worker's company. My mother
agreed but she took me into the kitchen and whispered,
'Look, Bert's not living here for ever, Adrian. I can't
look after a small baby and a geriatric at the same
time!'
    At eleven o'clock my father rang up to wish us all a

Happy New Year. My mother's face went a bit blotchy and soft, and she invited him round for a drink.

At 11.15 rat fink Lucas rang from Sheffield, whining on about the fact that he was alone with a bottle of 'Johnnie Walker'. My mother said, 'How appalling! You should have bought a decent brand – after all it is New Year's Eve.'

She looks dead nice again now that her figure is nearly back to normal. In fact after the phone calls she looked her old cocky self. My father crossed our doorstep at one minute to twelve, with a packet of 'Zip' firelighters (the nearest he could get to coal). Then, when the Scottish people on the telly went berserk at midnight, we all stood around Bert's wheel-chair, holding hands and singing 'Auld Lang Syne'. Then we talked about Queenie and Stick Insect and said things like, 'Well I wonder what 1983 will bring us?'

Personally, nothing would surprise me any more. If my father announced that he was really a Russian agent or my mother ran away with a circus knife thrower, I wouldn't raise an eyebrow.

Pandora rang at 1 a.m. to say 'Happy New Year'. The Braithwaites' party sounded good. I wished I'd gone instead of being kind and staying at home. Went to bed rigid with fear. 1983 is my 'O' level year.

Winter

Saturday January 1st 1983
New Year's Day

These are my New Year resolutions:

1. I will revise for my 'O' levels at least two hours a night.
2. I will stop using my mother's Buff-Puff to clean the bath.
3. I will buy a suede brush for my coat.
4. I will stop thinking erotic thoughts during school hours.
5. I will oil my bike once a week.
6. I will try to like Bert Baxter again.
7. I will pay my library fines (88 pence) and rejoin the library.
8. I will get my mother and father together again.
9. I will cancel the *Beano*.

Sunday January 2nd

Took stock of my appearance today. I have only grown a couple of inches in the last year, so I must reconcile myself to the fact that I will be one of those people who never get a good view in the cinema.

My skin is completely disfigured, my ears stick out and my hair has got three partings and won't look fashionable whichever way I comb it.

Monday January 3rd

Negotiations are going on between my parents for a return to their married state. My mother said, 'But how can it ever work, Adrian? There is so much to forget.' I suggested hypnosis.

Tuesday January 4th

More negotiations behind closed doors. As he left, I asked my father for a report on the meeting. He said, 'No comment!' and got in his car.

Wednesday January 5th

Negotiations have broken down.

I heard the sugar bowl crashing to the kitchen floor then raised voices. Then the door slamming.

Thursday January 6th

A message was passed to an intermediary (me) that fresh negotiations would be welcomed. The message was passed on and the response was favourable, so it was left to me to arrange time, venue and baby-sitting details.

Friday January 7th

The meeting took place in a Chinese restaurant at 8 p.m. Negotiations went on throughout the evening and were only adjourned when one party returned home to feed the baby.

Saturday January 8th

Both parties have issued the following bulletin:

It is agreed that Pauline Monica Mole and George Alfred Mole will attempt to live in mutual harmony for a trial period of one month. If during that time Pauline Monica Mole, hereafter known as P.M.M., and George Alfred Mole, hereafter known as G.A.M., break the following agreement, then the agreement shall be declared null and void, and divorce proceedings will automatically follow.

The Agreement
1. G.A.M. SHALL CHEERFULLY AND WITHOUT NAGGING OR REMINDING DO HIS RIGHTFUL SHARE OF HOUSEHOLD TASKS.
2. P.M.M. SHALL KEEP HER SIDE OF THE BEDROOM IN A HYGIENIC AND PRESENTABLE CONDITION.

3. BOTH PARTIES TO GO TO THE PUB AT SUNDAY LUNCHTIMES.

4. THE CHILDREN OF THE MARRIAGE, ADRIAN AND ROSIE MOLE, TO BE GIVEN FAIR AND EQUAL ATTENTION FROM BOTH PARENTS.

5. FINANCIAL MATTERS TO BE DISCUSSED EACH FRIDAY NIGHT AT 7 P.M.

6. A SEPARATE BANK ACCOUNT TO BE OPENED FOR P.M.M.

7. NEITHER PARTY TO INDULGE IN FLIRTATION, SEDUCTION OR ADULTERY WITH THE OPPOSITE SEX WITHOUT THE FULL KNOWLEDGE, OR CONSENT, OF THE OTHER PARTY.

8. P.M.M. TO REPLACE CAP ON TOOTHPASTE AFTER USE.

9. G.A.M. TO WASH OWN HANDKERCHIEFS.

10. BOTH PARTIES TO HAVE UNLIMITED FREEDOM FOR THE PURSUIT OF HOBBIES, POLITICAL INTERESTS, DEMONSTRATIONS, AND SOCIAL INTERCOURSE OUTSIDE THE HOME.

11. G.A.M. TO THROW BOTH PAIRS OF CAVALRY TWILL TROUSERS AWAY.

12. P.M.M. WILL NOT CONSTANTLY HARP ON DOREEN SLATER EPISODE. G.A.M. WILL NOT DO THE SAME RE: LUCAS EPISODE.

Signed on this day the 8TH JANUARY 1983
Pauline Mole
George Mole
A. Mole, 1st Witness
Rosie Mole, 2nd Witness. Her mark. X

Sunday January 9th

My father burnt his cavalry twills in the back garden
today. As he poked the gobs of burning cloth he said,
'Well, it's the straight and narrow for me from now
on.' I don't know whether he meant his life or his
trousers.

Monday January 10th

Lousy stinking school started today. Everybody was
flashing their new calculators around. My sheepskin
caused a bit of a stir wherever it went – and it went
everywhere. It is far too valuable to leave in the cloakroom. Pandora and I held hands in assembly. But were
spotted by Mr Scruton. He said, 'Keep your silly
adolescent courtship rituals to outside school hours.'
Pandora was still upset at break, but I comforted
her in the Boys' toilets, by explaining that Mr Scruton
was probably impotent, and it enraged him to see
young lovers who were brimming with Eastern
promise.

Tuesday January 11th

Saw Roy Hattersley on the television tonight. He is
putting weight on. He ought to go on a diet in case
there's a General Election. The viewers don't like fat

politicians. Look what happened to Churchill after the war. He was slung out because he got too fat. I know all this because we had a film of the Second World War in History today. I might be a historian if my memory improves.

Wednesday January 12th

Nigel has formed a Gay Club at school. He is the only member so far, but it will be interesting to see who else joins. I noticed Brain Box Henderson hovering around the poster looking worried.

Thursday January 13th

Mr Scruton has ordered the closure of the Gay Club, saying that he and the school governors couldn't sanction the use of the school gym for 'immoral purposes'. Nigel pretended to be innocent. He said, 'But sir, the Gay Club is for pupils who want to be frisky, frolicsome, lively, playful, sportive, vivacious or gamesome during the dinner break. What is immoral about gaiety?'

Mr Scruton said, 'Nigel, the word "Gay" has changed its meaning over the past years. It now means something quite different.'

Nigel said, 'What does it mean, sir?'

Scruton started sweating and messing about with his pipe, and not answering, so Nigel let him off the hook by saying: 'Sorry, sir, I can see that I will have to get an up-to-date dictionary!'

Friday January 14th

Must go and see how Bert is getting on. God! I wish I'd never got involved with him; he is like an Ancient Mariner around my neck.

Saturday January 15th

There is a new joke craze sweeping the school. In my opinion these so-called jokes are puerile. I watch in amazement as my fellow pupils roll helplessly in the corridors with tears of laughter coursing down their cheeks after relating them to each other.

1. Q. What do you call a man with a seagull on his head?
   A. Cliff.
2. Q. What do you call a man with a shovel in his head?
   A. Doug.
3. Q. What do you call a man without a shovel in his head?
   A. Douglas.
4. Q. What do you call an Irishman who's been buried for fifty years?
   A. Pete.
5. Q. What do you call a man with fifty rabbits up his bum?
   A. Warren.

Come back, Oscar Wilde. Your country needs you.

Sunday January 16th

6 p.m. My father put on his new straight-legged jeans today. He looks dead stupid in them. Talk about mutton dressed as lamb. He looks like stewing steak dressed as 'Flash Fry'.

I had to look after Rosie while my parents swanned down to the pub. I was also in charge of the pork and roast potatoes, and switching on the greens. I fed Rosie OK but it took ages to get her wind up. I patted her back for ages but it wasn't until I turned her upside down that she burped. I pretended not to notice that her nappy needed changing and acted surprised when my mother pointed out that there was a yukky smell in the room.

10 p.m. Now I come to a difficult entry. How exactly do I feel about my father's return home? It's been a week now and I've had plenty of time to think about it, but they've had these reconciliations before and they've ended in tragedy. So, I think I'll reserve my judgement until the slopping has stopped and they are back to normal.

12.15 a.m. Why didn't I go and see Bert? Why are you such a rat fink, Mole?

Monday January 17th

Breakfast telly started today. I got up at 5.45 a.m. so I wouldn't miss history in the making. I made breakfast for me and the dog, and took it into the lounge. Normally cornflakes are banned from the lounge, on account of the odd one falling out of the bowl and sticking to the carpet, but I felt sure my mother wouldn't mind on this special occasion.

The dog fouled things up a bit by trampling into its bowl and scattering Pedigree Chum and Winalot into the shag pile. But I scraped the worst of the mess up with an empty fag packet, and we settled down to wait for 6.30. At 6.25 I woke my parents up by shouting loudly up the stairs that Breakfast Television was starting. My father shouted loudly down the stairs that he didn't want to see bloody Frank Bough at 6.30 a.m. in the morning, and that he'd break my neck if I didn't turn the volume down.

Rosie woke up and started crying. I got the blame for that, and what with all the rowing and screaming I missed the very beginning. This is just my luck!

I enjoyed the Horoscopes, the News, the Celebrities and Frank Bough. He looks a steady sort of bloke. I wouldn't mind having a father like him. But best of all was Selina Scott, with her ravishing looks and quicksilver brain.

Courtney Elliot joined me in front of the screen at 7.45 a.m. He pronounced it 'lacking in intellectual fibre' and said he would stick to listening to Radio

Four on his headset. I was late for school because Frank wasn't allowed to open the champagne until nearly nine o'clock!

I have written to the Director General to complain.

Dear Sir,
I wish to convey to you my congratulations on your new programme *Breakfast Time*. I saw the first episode and I thought it was a remarkable achievement considering. However, me and my fellow pupils were late for school, due to the late opening of the champagne.

Either this shows a flagrant disregard for your teenage audience, or a woeful ignorance on your part, of the time I and my cohorts have to arrive at school in the morning.

I suggest, Sir, that you do your research rather more thoroughly. Finally can I make a plea that in future episodes, any special items ie Ernest Hemingway chatting about his latest book, or Princess Diana having her horoscope read, will take place *before* 8.30 a.m. (except on Fridays when we don't have assembly).

Thanking you in anticipation of a reply,

Your most obedient servant,

A. Mole (aged 15 and 9 months)

Tuesday January 18th

Lord Franks has published his report on the Falklands War, but I will make no further comment until I have studied today's *Guardian* editorial on the matter.

10.30 p.m. Can't find *Guardian*: it's not in its usual place in the dog's basket.

Wednesday January 19th

Found *Guardian* in dust-bin wrapped round yesterday's supply of disposable nappies. I made strong objections to my mother. Her feeble excuse was that she'd run out of plastic pedal bin liners.

Thursday January 20th

Selina Scott is haunting my dreams: last night she was walking down our street selling cucumbers door to door. I bought half a dozen with a £50 note I had in my wallet. She smiled shyly and said, 'Prithee, how old are you, sire?' I answered, 'I be fifteen years, pretty maid.' Then the dog jumped on my face and woke me up.

I tried to tell my mother about my dream, but she refused to listen. She said, 'There is only one thing more deadly boring than listening to other people's dreams, and that is listening to other people's problems.'

Friday January 21st

Last night Selina Scott and I were rowing the Atlantic single handed. Selina fell overboard and was swallowed by a dolphin. I swam into the dolphin's belly, and joined Selina: it was quite cosy. We had a glass of champagne then swam out and got back into the boat where we found Frank Bough teaching Pandora how to read out football results.

I told my father every detail of my dream (what Selina was wearing, etc) but I could tell he wasn't really interested. Now I know why people pay to go to psychiatrists. (They are the only people who will listen.)

Saturday January 22nd

No Selina this morning, so I had to make do with going into town with Pandora, who wanted to buy a pair of neon pink legwarmers. After trekking round fifty shops while Pandora sneered at inferior pinks and rejected them all, I suggested we went for a cup of coffee. While I scraped the froth off, I confessed to Pandora how I felt about Selina. Pandora took it very calmly. She said, 'Yes, Selina Scott is to be congratulated, not many women could have borne the pain of so much plastic surgery!'

According to Pandora, Selina has had her nose, mouth, breasts, ears, and eyes remodelled by the surgeon's knife. Poor Selina has to spend three hours in the make-up chair in order to disguise the operation scars. Pandora went on to say, 'Of course she booked into the clinic under her real name, which is Edna Grubbe!'

I asked Pandora how she got her insight into the lives of the famous. Pandora stubbed her cigarette out and said, 'My family used to be on intimate terms with a high-up in the BBC.'

I asked who, a window-cleaner? But I said it quietly because Pandora had got into one of her moods. We resumed our search but none of the legwarmer shops had neon pink so Pandora is getting an 'Awayday' and going to London to buy some. She said, 'God how I hate the wretched provinces.'

Sunday January 23rd

Rat fink Lucas rang up today. I told him that my mother was at the pub with my father. He asked me which pub, so I told him but instead of ringing off he asked me loads of questions about Rosie, and even asked me to bring her to the phone so that he could hear her gurgling. I told him that she was a late developer and was still at the screaming stage. Then Lucas said a weird thing: he said, 'That's my girl!'

My mother came home in a bad mood and my father came home in an even worse mood. It seems that my mother had left the pub's darts match at a crucial point in order to answer a telephone call.

Monday January 24th

The water workers have gone on strike, so my father made us all have a bath tonight. The dog included. Then he went around collecting containers and filling them up. While he was doing it he was whistling and looking cheerful. My father loves a crisis.

Tuesday January 25th

Fabulous! Amazing! Brilliant! Magic!

Showers have been banned at school!

The twice-weekly torture of displaying my inferior muscle development is over. I hope the water workers prolong the strike until I've left full-time education. They should stick out for £500 a week, in fact.

Wednesday January 26th

Courtney Elliot has offered to give me private tuition for my 'O' levels. It seems he is a Doctor of Philosophy who left academic life after a quarrel in a university common room about the allocation of new chairs. Apparently he was promised a chair and didn't get it.

It seems a trivial thing to leave a good job for. After all, one chair is very much like another. But then I am an existentialist to whom nothing really matters.

I don't care which chair I sit in.

I am reading *On the Road* by Jack Kerouac.

Thursday January 27th

Ken Livingstone was on the telly tonight, talking about his triumph in getting the High Court to cut bus fares in London. This led to me asking my parents for the bus fare to get to school. I am tired out by the time I have walked a whole mile in the morning. My father said that he used to walk four miles to school and four miles back, through wind, rain, snow, hail, and broiling sun and fog.

I said sarcastically (though wittily), 'What strange climatic conditions prevailed in the Midlands in the nineteen-fifties!'

My father said, 'Weather was weather in those days. You wouldn't know proper weather if it came up and smashed you in the face.'

Friday January 28th

I reminded my father that the law about seat belts comes into force on Monday. He said, 'Nobody makes George Mole wear a baby harness.'

My mother said, 'A policeman will, so belt up!'

Saturday January 29th

Bert Baxter rang to ask why I hadn't been round. I said I'd been too busy.

Bert said, 'Yes, too busy to visit an old lonely widower.'

I promised to go round tomorrow after dinner. Bert said, 'Dinner? What's that?'

I said, 'You remember, Bert, it's meat and three veg and gravy and stuff.'

Bert said that it was so long since he'd eaten properly that his vocabulary was suffering.

I asked him round for dinner tomorrow and told him that my father would give him a lift. But when I told my parents they went mad, and said that they'd arranged to visit some *properties* tomorrow and were planning to get a Chinese take-away.

Properties! Why didn't they consult me? After all, it is my 'O' level year and it is most important that I suffer no violent change, trauma or neurosis.

Sunday January 30th

Spent Sunday afternoon reading the *News of the World* out loud to Bert. I was amazed at how many vicars are leaving their flocks and running away with attractive divorcees.

I also read him a few bits from *The Sunday Times* colour supplement, but Bert stopped me, saying, 'Do you think I'm interested in bleedin' Italian furniture, or "A day in the life" of a soddin' piano player?'

I said, 'I think you ought to keep up with modern cultural patterns!'

Bert said that whenever he heard the word 'culture' he reached for his bottle opener.

At 7 p.m. Bert's Age Concern volunteer turned up to take Bert to the pub. He is a thin, nervous-looking man called Wesley. Sabre growled and bared his horrible fangs when he came into the room. Bert said, 'Don't make any sudden moves, Wesley, Sabre's bite is worse than his bark.'

I couldn't resist showing off by throwing Sabre about and tickling his belly. I even did my party trick of putting my head in Sabre's mouth. I didn't leave it in long though; Sabre's breath stank of cheap dog meat.

After Wesley and Bert left I tidied up a bit. I found Bert and Queenie's wedding photo under Bert's pillow. Funny to think that old, smelly, unattractive people can be sentimental.

Monday January 31st

On the way to school me and Nigel had a dead good time signalling to car drivers who had forgotten to put their seat belts on. Hardly any of them thanked us.

Tuesday February 1st

The first cracks in the new marital alliance appeared today: an argument about money.

We are kept by the state in the style that the state wants to keep us, ie in poverty. My parents just can't cope with being poor. It's all right for me because I'm used to it. I've never had more than three quid a week to call my own.

Wednesday February 2nd

Lucas turned up on our doorstep halfway through *Coronation Street* demanding to see Rosie. My father said that Rosie was busy and couldn't be disturbed, but Lucas started shouting in his loud sing-song voice, so my father let him in to stop the neighbours talking.

My mother went dead pale under her Max Factor. Lucas said, 'Pauline, I want access to my child!'

My father's knees buckled a bit and he sat down on the arm of the settee to recover. He said weakly, 'Pauline, tell me that Rosie is mine!'

My mother said, 'Of course she's yours, George!'

Lucas took out a black 1982 diary and said, 'Pauline and I resumed our affair of the heart on February 16th 1982. However we did not consummate our new relationship until Sunday March 13th 1982, when Pauline came to a protest rally in Sheffield.'

My mother shouted, 'But I was wearing my new cap, I couldn't have got pregnant.'

My father said, 'Adulteress!'

'I'm not an adulteress,' my mother sobbed.

My father yelled, 'If the cap fits, wear it!'

'But I *did* wear it,' said my mother in anguish.

Lucas tried to put his arms around her but she karate-chopped him on the back of the neck.

Everybody had forgotten I was there until I ran from the room, saying, 'I can't stand this eternal insecurity!'

As I ran to my room I passed Rosie in her cot. She was playing with her toes, unaware that her paternity was being settled downstairs.

Thursday February 3rd

During the month of March 1982 it would seem that both my parents were carrying on clandestine relationships, which resulted in the birth of two children. Yet my diary for that period records my childish fourteen-year-old thoughts and preoccupations.

I wonder, did Jack the Ripper's wife innocently write:

10.30 p.m. Jack late home. Perhaps he is kept late at the office.

12.10 a.m. Jack home covered in blood; an offal cart knocked him down.

Pandora is standing by me at this time of crisis. She is a true pillar of salt.

Friday February 4th

I had to spend the day in matron's office due to feeling weak in the first lesson (PE).

She asked me if there was anything wrong at home. I started to cry and said that everything was.

She said, 'Adults have complicated lives, Adrian. It's not all staying up late and having your own door key!'

I said that *parents* ought to be moral and consistent and have principles.

She said, 'It's a lot to ask.'

I made her promise not to tell anyone that she'd seen me crying. She promised and kindly let me stay until my eyes had got back to normal.

Saturday February 5th

Lucas continues to persecute us.

A solicitor's letter arrived today. He is taking us to court unless he is allowed access to Rosie.

Courtney Elliot suggested we find a good solicitor and get him to write a letter back saying that, unless Lucas stops his campaign, we will get an injunction out.

I don't know what it means, but it sounds dead threatening.

Sunday February 6th

I broke the silence of months and went to make my peace with Grandma. She was a bit frosty at first, but then she offered to make me some treacle toffee, so I knew I was forgiven.

She has bought a budgie called Russell. (Named after Russell Harty, her favourite person in the world after me.) She said, 'This little bird has given me more pleasure than my whole family put together, and what's more he listens and doesn't answer back.'

I didn't tell her about the Lucas affair. A further shock could kill her. She said that after the Stick Insect/ Trevor Roper scandal, her hair fell out and has not grown back.

This explains why she was wearing her hat in the house.

Monday February 7th

Michael Heseltine has chickened out of a public debate on cruise missiles with CND. I expect he is scared of being shown up.

A similar thing is happening in our house; my father is refusing to talk to Pandora's mother, who is a marriage guidance counsellor.

Rosie is teething. She is getting through six bibs a day. Dribble hangs permanently from her mouth. She looks like a rabid dog.

Tuesday February 8th

Don't ask me how I am getting through the long school day. Just don't ask. I am walking around like a smiling robot. But my soul is weeping, weeping, weeping. If only the teachers knew that an unkind word from them brings tears to my eyes.

I am getting away with it by saying I've got conjunctivitis but it's a near thing sometimes.

The trial period is up today.

1 a.m. The two parties have agreed on an extension.

Wednesday February 9th

The racehorse Shergar has been kidnapped by the IRA. Pandora seems more concerned about the horse's troubles than mine. I said, 'Haven't you got things out of perspective Pandora?'

She said, 'No, Shergar is highly bred and extremely sensitive. He must be suffering terribly.'

I don't know who to turn to for help. I might run away to London.

Thursday February 10th

I've changed my mind about going to London.

According to the *Guardian* lead pollution is sending the cockneys who live there mad.

Friday February 11th

We have got a solicitor called Cyril Hill. He has written a stern letter to rat fink Lucas, warning him to lay off our family.

The letter cost us £20.

Saturday February 12th

The atmosphere at home is as thick as treacle, so I went to see Bert. I could hardly get in the door for Voluntary Social Workers, queuing up to be given their orders. None of them wanted to attend to Sabre's needs, however, so I mucked his kennel out and brushed his coat and then took him for his daily prowl round the recreation ground.

Barry Kent and his gang were there – tying the swings in knots, but with Sabre by my side I felt confident enough to have a go on the slide.

On the way back I passed several Alsatians and their male owners; perhaps it was a coincidence but *every* owner was practically a midget. Their Alsatians came up to their waists. I don't know what it means. But it must mean something.

Sunday February 13th

It's Valentine's Day tomorrow. I think I'll have the day off school. I can't stand being the only kid in my class who doesn't come into the classroom with a fistful of garish cards, and a self-congratulatory smile. I know I'll get one from Pandora, but she doesn't count; I've been going out with her for over a year.

Monday February 14th
St Valentine's Day

Got four cards: one from Pandora, one from Grandma, one from my mother and one from Rosie.

Big, big deal!

I got Pandora a Cupid card and a mini pack of 'After Eights'. Lucas sent one to Rosie. My parents didn't bother this year, they are saving their money to pay for the solicitor's letter.

Tuesday February 15th
Shrove Tuesday

Pandora is not speaking to me because I absent-mindedly wrote 'Best Wishes' in her Valentine's card.

She said, 'It's symptomatic of our decaying relationship, Adrian.'

I think she could be right. I'm going off her. She is too clever by half. My mother was too busy with Rosie to make pancakes, so I had a go. I don't know why my father went so mad, the kitchen ceiling needed decorating anyway.

Wednesday February 16th
Ash Wednesday

Today is my parents' special day.

They are getting through thirty fags a day each. If Social Security hear about it they will get done and quite rightly!

Thursday February 17th

I wrote a poem on the toilet wall at school today.

I thought it was a good way of getting a bit of political consciousness over to my moronic fellow pupils.

> *The Future*
> What future is there for the young?
> What songs are waiting to be sung?
> There are no mountains left to climb,
> No poetry without a rhyme.
> No jobs to go to after school.

We divide and still they rule.
They give us Job Creation Schemes.
When what we want are hopes and dreams.
A. MOLE

Friday February 18th

I was sent to see the headmaster today. He has found out about my toilet poem. I asked him how he knew I'd written it. He said, 'You signed it, idiot boy.' I have been suspended for a week.

Saturday February 19th

Barry Kent and his gang called for me today. Kent said, 'We're going down town, you can come if you like!'

I was feeling a bit nihilistic so I went.

Sunday February 20th

Hung around the deserted shopping centre with Barry Kent and the lads. I feel a curious affinity with the criminal classes. I am beginning to understand why Lord Longford (another noted intellectual) spends his time hanging around prisons.

Barry graciously gave me permission to call him 'Baz'.

Monday February 21st
Washington's Birthday Observance

Baz took me home and introduced me to his family today.

Mrs Kent said, 'Ain't you the lad what's 'ad all the scandal?'

I said, 'Yeah that's me, but so what?'

Mrs Kent said, 'That's no way to talk, young man.'

Mr Kent said, 'You keep a civil tongue in your head. That's my wife you're talking to.' I immediately apologized and remembered my manners. In fact I got up and offered Mrs Kent the unbroken chair.

The Kent children were swarming about in the living room, watching a television programme about the population explosion. A lurid coloured photo of Clive Kent in his army uniform stood on top of the radiogram. I asked how he was. Mrs Kent said, 'He's in an army hospital: his nerves is shot to pieces after the Falklands.'

I had a nice tea with the family; chip sandwiches with tomato sauce, and once I'd got used to the funny smell in the house I was able to relax for the first time in weeks.

Tuesday February 22nd

A note from Pandora:

Adrian,
As you seem to prefer the company of louts and anti-social drop-outs, I think it best if we finish. You have chosen to tread a different path from the one I intend to make my way on in the world.

Thank you for the good times.

Pandora Braithwaite

Wednesday February 23rd

Today I drew some money out of my Building Society account, and bought my first pair of Doc Marten's. They are bully-boy brown and have got ten rows of lace holes.

They add an inch to my height.

Thursday February 24th

Spent the early part of the evening standing outside the off-licence with the gang. I made witty remarks about passing girls and made the gang laugh. They have started calling me 'Brains'. Baz has hinted that I have got leadership qualities.

Friday February 25th

Mrs Kent has decided to have some new furniture, so the gang went to the rubbish tip to see what we could find. We came back with two almost unbroken kitchen chairs, a wicker linen basket, and a fireside rug. We are going back tomorrow with Rosie's pram to fetch a washing machine with mangle attachment.

Mrs Kent was very pleased with our haul: she said, 'It's a crying shame what folks chuck away!' Mr Kent lost his job two months ago, when the dairy closed down. He looked a bit ashamed when we brought the new furniture in. I heard him say to his wife, 'For better or worse, eh, Ida?'

Saturday February 26th

I borrowed the pram OK but unfortunately Rosie was in it. She had to be taken out and carried for our journey back from the rubbish tip.

But she was a good kid and didn't cry once. Mrs Kent was overjoyed with her new washing machine. It looked OK when it had been wiped down. Mr Kent unscrewed the faulty motor, and started cleaning it down on the hearth rug, and Mrs Kent didn't murmur! My mother would have gone beserk. She won't let my father fill his lighter in the lounge.

Sunday February 27th

Good news. The washing machine is working. There was a line of grey nappies on Mrs Kent's washing line today. I told her about 'Ariel' washing powder and she said, 'I'll buy some tomorrow when I get my family allowance.'

Monday February 28th

Rosie has got her first tooth. My index finger is still bleeding.

Tuesday March 1st

Spent the evening outside the Chinese chip shop chucking prawn crackers about with the gang. I haven't read a book for ages. Instead of reading about life I am living it.

Wednesday March 2nd
St David's Day

We are being persecuted by the police!

Tonight, as we were messing about in the shopping precinct, a police patrol car went by dead slowly, and the driver *looked* at us.

Talk about a police state!

Thursday March 3rd

The community policeman, PC Gordon, has been to see my parents, to warn them that I am running wild with a notorious gang. He is calling round tomorrow to give me a lecture on responsible citizenship.

Friday March 4th

PC Gordon is the sort of bloke you can't help liking. He is thin and jolly and he calls everybody 'Bucko'. But he said things like: 'You're obviously a clever lad, Adrian'; and: 'You're from a good family' (Ha!); and 'Kent and his gang are no-hopers, they'll do you no favours.'

He asked me why I had suddenly gone off the rails. I said that I was an existentialist nihilist.

He said, 'Lads usually say they get into trouble because they're bored.'

I smiled cynically and said, 'Yes existential nihilism is just one step further.' I could tell he was impressed by my vocabulary.

Later on my parents came in and used clichés like: 'He's a good lad at home' (my father); and: 'Barry Kent has led him astray' (my mother).

When he'd gone I polished my boots and went to bed with the dog.

Saturday March 5th

Grandma rang and said that it was all round the Evergreens that I was 'keeping bad company'. She made me go round for tea. I didn't want to go, but there is something about Grandma's voice that makes you obey orders so I went.

While Grandma toasted crumpets on the electric coal fire she told me that my father had been in trouble with the police in 1953. She said, 'He got caught scrumping apples. The shame nearly killed me and your poor dead Grandad.'

I asked if my father had continued his criminal career.

She said, 'Yes, in fact he went from bad to worse, he went on to scrump pears and plums.'

I was curious to know how my father had been persuaded from taking up a life of crime. Grandma said, 'Your Grandad gave him a good thrashing with the buckle end of his belt.' Poor Dad! It explains why he is full of inner rage.

Sunday March 6th

Being in a gang is not as exciting as I thought it would be. All we do is hang around shopping precincts and windy recreation grounds. Sometimes I long to be in my bedroom, reading, with the dog at my side.

Monday March 7th

Just got back after a cold boring night of shouting in quiet streets. Barry Kent tipped a rubbish bin over for a laugh, but in fact it wasn't very funny and I had to force myself to guffaw with the others in the gang. Barry Kent said, 'If it wasn't for me, my Uncle Pedro would lose his job!' His Uncle Pedro is a street cleaner.

After Barry went home I picked the broken glass up and replaced it in the bin. I wouldn't like a little kid to fall on it.

Tuesday March 8th

There was a very unpleasant incident tonight.

Barry Kent shouted horrible names at two of the Singh kids. I said, 'Oh lay off em eh, Baz, they're all right!'

Barry sneered and said, 'I 'ate anyone who ain't English.'

I reminded him about his Uncle Pedro and he said, 'Except Spaniels.'

I can't go on leading this double life for much longer.

Wednesday March 9th

I have decided not to take my 'O' levels. I am bound to fail them anyway so why waste all that neurosis in worrying? I'll need all the neurosis I can get when I start writing for a living.

Thursday March 10th

The first page of my new novel:

Precinct by A. Mole, aged 15 years 11 months
Jake Butcher closed his eyes against the cruel wind that whistled over the paving slabs of the deserted shopping precinct. His cigarette dropped with a curse from his lips. 'Damn,' he expectorated.

It was his last cigarette. He ground the forlorn fag under the sole of his trusty Doc Marten's boot. He dug both fists into the womb-like pockets of his anorak, and with his remaining hand he adjusted the fastening on his Adidas sports bag.

Just then a sudden shaft of bright sunlight illuminated the windows of Tesco's. 'Christ,' said Jake to himself, 'those windows are the same yellow as in Van Gogh's sunflower painting!' Thus, ruminating on art and culture, did Jake pass the time.

Quite soon a sudden clap of thunder announced itself. 'Christ,' said Jake, 'that thunder sounds like the cannons of the 1812 Symphony!'

He bitterly drew his anorak hood over his head, as raindrops like giant's tears fell on to the concrete wasteland. 'What am I doing here?' questioned Jake to himself. 'Why did I come?' he anguished. 'Where am I going?' he agonized. Just then a sudden rainbow appeared.

'Christ,' said Jake, 'that rainbow looks like . . .'

I had to stop there; I don't know where Jake came from, or where he's going either.

Friday March 11th

Pandora Braithwaite is going out with Brain Box Henderson. I hope they'll both be very happy. Nigel says they spend all their time together talking about higher mathematics.

Did a bit of shouting outside the Youth Club doors tonight.

Rick Lemon pretended not to hear us, but I noticed that the vein in his temple was throbbing. Why don't my parents notice that I am turning into a yob?

Saturday March 12th

Saw Danny Thompson, the white Rasta, outside the Chinese chip shop tonight. He asked me if I'd written any lyrics for the group yet. I said I'd go home straight away and write some. I was glad of an excuse to leave.

I was tired of Barry Kent shoving his prawn balls down my trousers.

Sunday March 13th
Mothering Sunday

Rat fink Lucas sent my mother a mother's day card signed 'Rosie'.

Grandma sent Stick Insect a card signed 'Brett'.

My mother sent Grandma Mole a card signed 'George'.

My father sent my Grandma Sugden a card signed 'Pauline'.

I didn't send the woman who gave birth to me a card this year. Interpersonal relationships in our family have gone completely to pot. This is what living with the shadow of the bomb does to you.

Monday March 14th
Commonwealth Day

Barry Kent has been arrested for vandalizing hyacinths in the town hall square yesterday morning at 7 a.m.

He is pleading extenuating circumstances; they were to be a gift for his mother.

Tuesday March 15th

Reasons for living	*Reasons for not living*
Things might get better	You die anyway
	Life is nothing but anguish
	There is too much cruelty in the world
	'O' levels in June
	My parents hate me
	I've lost Pandora
	Nobody leaves Barry Kent's gang alive.

Wednesday March 16th

Elizabeth Sally Broadway keeps snatching my school scarf from round my neck and running away with it. forcing me to chase her. This is a sure sign that she is romantically interested in me. I can feel my hormones stirring for the first time in months.

Thursday March 17th
St Patrick's Day

Elizabeth grabbed my executive brief case and sprinted across the sports field during the afternoon break.

I caught up with her in the shrubbery where we had a very enjoyable tussle which lasted five minutes and climaxed in me removing her glasses and hair pins.

She looked different unspectacled and with her hair down her back.

I said, 'But Elizabeth, you're beautiful.'

God knows what would have happened if the bell hadn't rung for the next lesson.

2 a.m. Can't sleep for the noise of Irish bagpipes leaking out of the O'Learys' house.

4 a.m. Just woken up by the sound of breaking glass.

6 a.m. A police car has just left the O'Learys' house taking Sean O'Leary with it. Sean looked quite cheerful, in fact he was singing a song about Forty Shades of Green.

Friday March 18th

At last! My parents have noticed that I am out of control, and have banned me from going out after school.

Spent the evening re-reading *Black Beauty* for the fifth time.

Saturday March 19th

I have written a letter to Barry Kent, resigning from the gang.

Dear Baz,
The crumblies have said I've got to stay in for a week. So I'll have to give hanging about with you and the lads a miss. Also Baz, they are forcing me to take my stinking exams in June, so I'd better resign from my place in the gang and leave it open for somebody who needs it. I hope your court case goes well. No hard feelings eh?
    Yours Fraternally,
    Brains

Sunday March 20th
British Summer Time begins

8 p.m. Rained solidly all day.

10.30 p.m. How can it rain 'solidly'? What a strange mistress is the English language.

Monday March 21st

My parents have hardly spoken to me since Friday night. They are too busy watching Rosie's manual dexterity develop.

Every time the kid grabs a plastic brick or shoves a rusk in her mouth, she gets a round of applause.

Tuesday March 22nd

I have decided to leave home.

Nobody will care. In fact my parents probably won't notice that I've gone. I have given the Building Society one week's notice of my intention to withdraw £50. There is no point in losing interest unnecessarily.

Wednesday March 23rd

I am making preparations to leave. I have already written my goodbye letters.

Pandora,
I may be gone for some time.
  Adrian

Dear Mum and Dad,
By the time you read this I will be far away. I know I am breaking the law in running away before my 16th birthday, but, quite honestly, a life as a fugitive is preferable to my present miserable existence.
  From your son,
  A. Mole

Dear Bert,
I've taken your advice and gone off to see the world.
You don't need me now that you've got all those wimpy
volunteers hanging around you. But watch out, Bert, you
are only popular because they think you are a character.
Any day now they will find out that you are bad-tempered
and foul-mouthed. I will send you a postcard from one of
the corners of the world.

   Adios Amigo,
P.S. Give my love to Sabre, and don't forget to give him his
Bob Martins.

Dear Grandma,
Sorry to worry you but I have gone away for a bit. Please
stop feuding with Mum and Dad. 'They know not what
they do.' Rosie is lovely now, she would really like to see you.

   Lots of love,
   Adrian

Dear Mr Scruton,
By the time you read this I will be miles away from your
scabby school. So don't bother sending the truant officer
round. I intend to educate myself in the great school of life,
and will never return.

   A. Mole
P.S. Did you know that your nickname is 'Pop-Eye'? So-
called because of your horrible manic sticking-out eyes.
Everybody laughs at you behind your back, especially Mr
Jones the PE teacher.
P.P.S. I think you should be ashamed of the fact that Barry
Kent *still can't read* after spending five years in your school.

Dearest Elizabeth,

I'm sorry that I have to leave just as our love was bursting into bud. But a boy has to do what a boy has to do.

Don't wait for me, Elizabeth. I may be gone for some time.

Yours with regrets and fondest memories,

Aidy Mole

Baz,

I've blown town. The pigs will be looking for me. Try and put 'em off the scent will you?

Brains

Nige,

Good luck with being gay. I, too, am different from the herd; so I understand what it is like to be always out of step.

It's the ordinary people who will have to learn to accept us.

Any road up as we say in these parts.

Rock on Tommy!

Your old mate,

Aidy

Thursday March 24th

Five days to go. I am growing a beard.

I have borrowed my dead grandad's suitcase. Luckily he had the same initials as me. His name was Arnold.

Grandma thinks I am using it for a camping trip with the Youth Club. The truth would kill her.

Friday March 25th

I have started packing my case. A certain amount of rationalization has had to take place regarding clean socks and underwear.

I will have to lower my standards and only change them every other day. No sign of the beard yet.

Saturday March 26th

Courtney Elliot has been instructed by my father not to deliver any letters with a Sheffield postmark. But he brought one into the kitchen this morning saying, 'The Royal Mail has to get through, Mr Mole. We're like the Pony Express in that respect!'

My father ripped the letter into tiny pieces and foot-pedalled them into the bin.

Later on I retrieved the bits and stuck them together.

. . . ole.

. . . structed . . . client . . . ucas, civil action unless . . . Ros . . . ole . . . is his daughter. He wishes the aforesaid child to . . . Rosie Lucas.

My client . . . blood test . . . under oath that . . . inter-course took . . . Pauline Mole . . . to hear from you . . .

Yours Faithfully,

Coveney, Tinker, Shulman, Solicitors.

Sunday March 27th

The crumblies spent three hours forcing Rosie to sit up on her own. But she kept sliding down the cushions and laughing. If she could talk I know what she would say, 'Stop interfering in my development, I'll do it when I'm ready!'

I pointed out that her back muscles are not strong enough yet, but the crumblies wouldn't listen. They said things like, 'Rosie is exceptionally forward,' and 'You were nowhere near as advanced as she is at five months!'

They will be sorry for these cutting words on Tuesday.

Monday March 28th

An old American bloke called Ian MacGregor has been put in charge of the National Coal Board. It is a disgrace!

England has got loads of ruthless, out-of-work executives who would be delighted to be given the chance to close their own country's coalmines down. Mr Scargill is quite right to protest, he has my full support on this issue.

Packed my pyjamas and dressing gown.

It is RA day tomorrow. I have made out a list of vital equipment, clothing etc.

Roller skates
Shaving kit
3 jumpers
2 shirts
3 pairs trousers
5 pairs socks
Wellingtons
Doc Marten's
Plimsolls
Orange waterproof
    trousers
4 pairs underpants
4 vests
Diary
Survival handbook
Robinson Crusoe
Down and Out in Paris and
    London

Penguin Medical
    Dictionary
Junior aspirins
First aid box
Sleeping bag
Camping stove
Matches
6 tins beans
Spoon
Knife
Fork
Cruet
Serviettes
Transistor radio
The dog

Tuesday March 29th

6 a.m.	Packed everything on list apart from the dog.
6.05	Took everything out.
6.10	Repacked.
6.15	Took everything out.
6.30	Repacked, but no good. Still can't get suitcase lid to shut. Decide not to take roller skates.
6.33	Ditto wellingtons.

6.35	Ditto camping stove.
6.37	Suitcase lid shuts.
6.39	Try to pick up suitcase. Can't.
6.40	Take out tins of beans.
6.44	Repack.
6.45	Get in a rage.
6.48	Take cruet and serviettes out.
6.55	Take Doc Marten's out of suitcase. Decide to wear them instead. Spend fifteen precious minutes in doing the sodding laces up.
7.10	Examine spots in bathroom.
7.13	Check farewell letters have got stamps on.
7.14	Pick suitcase up. Not bad. Not good.
7.15	Repack suitcase with half previous clothes.
7.19	Pick suitcase up. Better.
7.20	Remember sleeping bag. Try to pack it in suitcase.
7.21	Get in another rage.
7.22	Kick suitcase across bedroom floor.
7.22.30 secs.	Crumblies shout from their bedroom. Demanding to know what all the noise is about.
7.24	Make tea. Crumblies ask why I have got a tin opener in the breast pocket of my blazer. I lie and say that I've got Domestic Science for my first lesson.
7.31	Feed dog, make baby's breakfast slops.
7.36	Check Building Society account book.

7.37	Groom dog. Pack its personal possessions in suitcase: dog bowl, brush, vaccination certificate, worm tablets, lead, choke chain, 5 tins Chum, bag of Winalot.
7.42	Try to pick up suitcase, can't.
7.47	Decide to leave dog behind. Break the news to it.
7.49	Dog cries. Crumblies shout at it to be quiet.
7.50	Decide to take the dog after all.
8.00	Pack minimum amount of stuff in Adidas bag.
8.10	Hide Grandad's suitcase in wardrobe.
8.15	Say goodbye to Rosie.
8.20	Put dog on lead.
8.21	Wait until crumblies are distracted.
8.25	Leave house with dog.
8.30	Post farewell letters.
9.00	Draw £50 out of Building Society, and head North.

Wednesday March 30th

3 p.m. Watford Gap Service Station. MI Motorway.

My first mistake was waiting for a lift on the southern bound side of the motorway approach road.

My second mistake was bringing the dog.

7.31 Sheffield.
Got a lift in a pig delivery lorry. This is just my luck!

I had a very long conversation with the driver, which is a miracle really, because I couldn't hear a word he was saying over the noise of the engine. I am having to keep a low profile. Sheffield is rat fink Lucas's stamping ground.

Why doesn't my beard hurry up and grow?

9.30 p.m. Leeds.
Tuned into the Radio Four nine o'clock news. But no mention was made of my mysterious disappearance. I am writing this at the side of the canal. A man has just come up and asked me if I want to sell the dog. I was tempted but said no.

11.00 p.m. Rang home but the phone wasn't snatched up immediately like it is in the films about runaway children.

Another sign of their indifference.

Thursday March 31st

1 a.m. The man who asked about the dog has just approached me and asked me if I want to sell *myself.* I said, 'No,' and told him my father was the Chief Constable of Wales.

He said, 'Why are you sleeping rough in Leeds?'

I told another lie, I said, 'My father has sent me on

an initiative test. If I survive this he'll put me down for Hendon Police College.'

Why did I tell him such an elaborate lie? Why? I had to listen while he told me his many grievances against the police. I promised to pass them on to my father and copied his name and address into my diary:

Stanley Gibbons,
c/o Room 2,
The Laurels Community Care Hostel,
Paradise Cuttings,
Leeds

He invited me to spend the night on his put-u-up, but I demurred, saying that my father was checking up on me via a long-distance telescope. He went then.

Spring

Friday April 1st
Good Friday. All Fools' Day

10 a.m. Leeds. (A launderette.)
Thank God for launderettes, if they hadn't been invented I'd be dead of hydrophobia by now. Nowhere else is open.

It cost a *pound* to dry my sleeping bag. But I was so wet and cold that I didn't care at the time.

I am waiting for the dog to wake up. It was on guard duty last night protecting our respective bodies from Stanley Gibbons. I am sixteen tomorrow. But still no sign of a beard. Good Friday!

Saturday April 2nd
Manchester Railway Station.

Got here by fish lorry. Pretended to be asleep in order to avoid driver's conversation.

10.31 a.m. I wonder what my mum and dad have bought me for my birthday. I hope they are not too worried. Perhaps I ought to ring them and convince them that I am well and happy.

12.15 p.m. We have been ordered out of the railway station café by a bad-tempered waitress. It's the stupid dog's fault. It kept going behind the counter and begging for bits of bacon.

Yet I bought it a bacon roll all to itself this morning.

3 p.m. Nobody has said 'Happy Birthday' to me.

3.05 p.m. I'm not well (I've got a cold) and I'm not happy. In fact I'm extremely unhappy.

5.30 p.m. Bought myself a birthday card. Inside I wrote:

To our darling first-born child on his sixteenth birthday.
With all the love it is possible to give,
From your admiring and loving parents.
PS. Come home son. Without you the house is devoid of life and laughter.

6.15 p.m. There was nothing about me on the six o'clock news.

7.30 p.m. Can't face another night in the open.

9 p.m. Park bench.
I have asked three policemen the time, but none of them have spotted me as a runaway. It's obvious that my description hasn't been circulated.

9.30 p.m. Just rang the police station, using a disguised voice. I said, 'Adrian Mole, a sixteen-year-old runaway, is in the vicinity of the Blood Transfusion Headquarters. His description is as follows: small for his age, slight build, mousey hair, disfigured skin. He is wearing a green school blazer. Orange waterproof trousers. A blue shirt. Balaclava helmet. Brown Doc Martens. With him is a mongrel dog, of the following description: medium height, hairy face, squint in left eye. Wearing a tartan collar and matching lead.'

The desk sergeant said, 'April Fool's Day was yesterday, sonny.'

10.00 p.m. Waited outside the Blood Transfusion place but there wasn't a policeman in sight. There is never one around when you need one.

11.39 p.m. I have walked past the police station twenty-four times, but none of the cretins in blue have given me a second glance.

11.45 p.m. I have just been turned away from an Indian Restaurant on the grounds that I wasn't wearing a tie, and was accompanied by a scruffy dog.

Sunday April 3rd
Easter Sunday

Still in Manchester. (St Ignatius's church porch.)

*

1 a.m. It is traditional for the homeless to sleep in church porches so why don't vicars make sure that their porches are more comfortable? It wouldn't kill them to provide a mattress, would it?

7.30 a.m. Got up at six. Had a wash in a bird bath. Read the inscriptions on the gravestones. Then went in search of a shop. Found one; bought two Cadbury's creme eggs. Ate one myself, gave the other to the dog. The poor thing was so hungry it ate the silver paper as well. I hope it won't be ill; I can't afford to pay for veterinary attention. I've only got £15.00 left.

Monday April 4th
St Ignatius's church porch, Manchester.

6 a.m. For two days I have had the legal right to buy cigarettes, have sex, ride a moped, and live away from home. Yet, strangely, I don't want to do any of them now I'm able to.

Must stop. A woman with a kind face is coming through the gravestones.

9 a.m. I am in the vicar's wife's bed. She is a true Christian. She doesn't mind that I am an existentialist nihilist. She says I'll grow out of it. The dog is downstairs lying on top of the Aga.

10 a.m. Mrs Merryfield, the vicar's wife, has phoned my parents and asked them to come and fetch me. I asked Mrs Merryfield for my parents' reactions. She crumpled her kind face up in thought then said, 'Angry relief is the nearest I can get to it, dear!'

I haven't seen the vicar yet. He is having a lie-in because of being so busy yesterday. I hope he doesn't mind that a stranger is occupying his wife's bed.

12.30 p.m. The vicar has just gone. Thank God! What a bore! No wonder poor Mrs Merryfield sleeps apart from him. I expect that she is scared he'll talk about comparative religions in his sleep. I have just spent a week living rough. The last thing I want is a lecture on 'Monophysitism'.

2.30 p.m. The Reverend Merryfield brought my dinner in at 1.30, then gabbled on about 'Lamaism', the Tibetan religion, while my dinner got cold, and eventually congealed.

6 p.m. I notice my parents are not breaking their necks to get here. I wish they would hurry up. I've had 'Mithraism', 'Orphism' and 'Pentecostalism' up to here.

I'm all for a man having outside interests, but this is ridiculous.

Tuesday April 5th

Bedroom. Home.
Well, there were no banners in the street, or crowds

of people jostling to get a view as I got out of my father's car. Just my mother's haggard face at the lounge window, and Grandma's even haggarder one behind her.

My father doesn't talk when he's driving on motorways, so we had hardly said a word to each other, since leaving St Ignatius's vicarage. (And Reverend Merryfield saw to it that we didn't talk *at* the vicarage, what with his rabbiting on about Calvinism and Shakers. Mrs Merryfield tried to stop him: she said, 'Please be quiet, darling,' but it just set him off on Quietism.)

But my mother and Grandma said a great many things. Eventually I pleaded for mercy and went to bed and pulled the crispy white sheets over my head.

Wednesday April 6th

Dr Grey has just left my bedside. He has diagnosed that I am suffering from a depressive illness brought on by worry. The treatment is bedrest, and no quarrelling in the family.

My parents are bowed down by guilt.

I can't rest for worrying about the letter I wrote to 'Pop-Eye' Scruton.

Thursday April 7th

The dog is at the vet's, having the blisters on its paws treated. I got up for five minutes and looked out of my bedroom window today. But there was nothing in the urban landscape to interest me, so I got back into bed.

I haven't opened my birthday presents yet.

Friday April 8th

Ate a Mars bar.

I can feel my physical strength returning, but my mental strength is still at rock bottom.

Saturday April 9th

10 a.m. I suffered a relapse so Dr Grey called round.

I lay back listlessly on the pillows and let him feel my pulse etc.

He muttered, 'Bloody Camille,' as he left the room.

Perhaps Camille is a drug that he's thinking of using on me.

12 noon. I asked my mother to draw the curtains against the sun.

Sunday April 10th

Lay all day with my head turned to the wall. Rosie was brought in to cheer me up, but her childish gibbering merely served to irritate so she was taken away.

Monday April 11th

Bert Baxter was carried up to my bedside, but his coarse exhortation, 'Get out of your pit, you idle bugger!' failed to stir me from my nihilistic thoughts.

Tuesday April 12th

Nigel has just left, after trying to arouse me by playing my favourite 'Toyah' tapes at a discreet volume.

I signalled that I would prefer both his and Toyah's absence.

Wednesday April 13th

A sign that my parents are now frantic with worry about me; Barry Kent was allowed into the house.

His inarticulate ramblings about the gang's activities failed to interest or stimulate me, so he was led out of the darkened room.

Thursday April 14th

A consultant psychologist has been ordered.

Dr Grey has admitted his failure.

Friday April 15th

Dr Donaldson has just left my bedside after listening to my worries with grave attention.

When I'd sunk back on to my pillows he said, 'We'll take them one by one.'

1. Nuclear war *is* a worry, but do something positive about your fear – join CND.
2. If you fail your 'O' levels you can retake them next year, or never take them – like the Queen.
3. Of course your parents love you. They didn't sleep during the time you were away.
4. You are *not* hideously ugly. You are a pleasant, average-looking boy.
5. Your sister's paternity problems are nothing to do with you, and there is nothing you can do to help.
6. I've never heard of a sixteen-year-old having their own poetry programme on Radio Four. You must set yourself realistic targets.
7. I will write to Mr Scruton ('Pop-Eye') and inform him that you were under great stress at the time you wrote the letter.

8. Pandora comes under the heading of insoluble problems.

Saturday April 16th

Grandma came to my room at 8 a.m. this morning and ordered me out of bed!

She said, 'You've been pampered enough. Now pull yourself together, and go and shave that bum-fluff off your face!'

I weakly protested that I needed more time to find myself.

Grandma said, 'I need to wash those sheets so get out of bed!'

I said, 'But I'm angst-ridden.'

'Who wouldn't be after lying in a bed like a dying swan for a week!' was her callous reply.

My Grandma is a good honest woman, but her grasp of the intellectual niceties is minimal.

Spent the day on the settee sipping Lucozade.

Sunday April 17th

Settee.

My parents are speaking to me in tones of forced gaiety. They are making pathetic attempts to bring me back into normal life by drawing my attention to items of interest on the television. 'Watch the news!' they brightly exclaimed. I did.

It was full of stories about murder, bombing, uncovered spies and disasters of rail, road and air. The only remotely cheerful item was about a man with no legs who'd walked from John O'Groats to Land's End. This proof of the cruelty of fate versus the magnificence of the human spirit reduced me to silent sobs into the Dralon cushions.

Monday April 18th

The school holidays started today.

It is just my luck to be too ill to appreciate the break.

Tuesday April 19th

> *Daffodils by A. Mole*
> While on my settee I lie
> From out of the corner of my eye
> I spot a clump of Yellow Daffodils,
> Bowing and shaking as a lorry goes by.
> Brave green stalks supporting yellow bonnets.
> Like the wife of a man who writes Love Sonnets.

Wednesday April 20th

Ate four Shredded Wheat today.

I can feel my strength slowly returning.

Thursday April 21st

Pandora came to see me for ten minutes this afternoon.

Brain Box Henderson stood at our gate, fiddling with his calculator. Perhaps he was trying to work out how much he loves Pandora.

Well it won't be as much as me, Henderson. I can assure you of that fact!

Pandora was wearing Monochromatic rags. She told me it was the latest fashion. She is coming back tomorrow.

Friday April 22nd

I asked my mother if she would go to town and buy me three tee-shirts. One black, one white and one grey.

When she came back I set about the tee-shirts with a pair of scissors. Grandma took this to be a symptom of my escalating madness. I tried to explain that it was how we in the teenage sub-culture are dressing now. But she couldn't take it in.

When my father saw me wearing rags he went pale and almost said something. But my mother whispered, 'Not now, George, don't send him off again!'

Pandora came round at 5 p.m. By the end of *John Craven's News Round* we were in each other's arms. Our rags entangled, our lips on fire.

Saturday April 23rd

Pandora went round to Brain Box Henderson's house to break the news, but he was out buying floppy discs, so she left a message on his word processor. Getting Pandora back from him is a triumph of Art over Technology.

Sunday April 24th

I am reading *Kingsley, The Life, Letters and Diaries of Kingsley Martin*, by C. H. Rolf. Strangely, it doesn't mention that he wrote *Lucky Jim*.

Monday April 25th

Went for a walk with Pandora and Rosie.

(That is to say Pandora and I walked, but lucky Rosie was pushed in her pram.) We called in to see Bert. He was dead pleased to see us. He has been deserted by his voluntary helpers, and hadn't got any Woodbines in the house. He smelt rotten so we stripped him off and put him in the bath. (Bert insisted that Pandora put a flannel over her eyes for this part of the operation.) Then I washed his bit of remaining hair and gave him a good scrub down, while Pandora took Rosie and Sabre and went to Mr Patel's for Woodbines.

When Pandora came back we lifted Bert out of the bath (Pandora promised to keep her eyes shut) and I dried him and put him into clean pyjamas. He looked lovely with his white hair all fluffy and sticking out at the back of his head. If I'd been a householder I would have invited him to stay there and then. Bert needs twenty-four-hour round-the-clock care, by people who love him.

The problem is that very few people, apart from Mother Teresa and a few nuns, could put up with Bert for more than a couple of days.

I asked him if there was any chance of him turning Catholic, he said, 'About as much chance as there is of Mrs Thatcher turning into a woman!'

On the way home we played a good game. We pretended we were married and that Rosie was our baby. Pandora tired of the game before I did but not before several people had been fooled.

Tuesday April 26th

The dog had an unfortunate accident on the kitchen floor this morning. Unfortunate for me, that is, because I had to clear it up. Knowing its use for such emergencies, I grabbed this week's copy of the *Sunday Times*, and made the thrilling discovery that HITLER'S DIARIES HAVE BEEN FOUND! I quote, 'After being hidden in a German hayloft for nearly forty years, the *Sunday Times* today tells the full story of this historic discovery!' I read on avidly. And to think I nearly used such a revelatory article to wipe up a piece of dog crap!

Wednesday April 27th

Is there no trust left in the world?

The Hitler Diaries are being subjected to meticulous tests by scientists. Why can't they take the *Sunday Times*'s word for it that the diaries are genuine? Even a sceptic like me knows that the *Sunday Times* wouldn't risk its reputation if there was the faintest chance that the diaries were a forgery.

Thursday April 28th

Herr Wolf-Rudiger Hess, son of Rudolph Hess (Hitler's Deputy Maniac), has said that the Hitler Diaries are genuine. So there, Pandora! Incidentally, Rudolph Hess is eighty-nine. The same age as Bert Baxter.

Friday April 29th

My father took me and Rosie to the bank. To help him get a bank loan. Mr Niggard, the Bank Manager, looked at my rags in a pitying way. Then said, 'Why do you require this loan, Mr Mole? A car, a house extension or clothes for the children perhaps?'

My father said, 'No. I can't afford to *buy* anything. I just want to feel some money in my hand again.'

But, after hearing that my parents were both out of work and on the Social, Mr Niggard refused the loan, saying: 'I am saving you from yourself. You will thank me one day.'

My father said, 'No I won't, I'm taking my overdraft elsewhere.'

Saturday April 30th

My mother has decided that sugar is the cause of all the evil in the world, and has banned it from the house.

She smoked two cigarettes while she informed me of her decision.

Sunday May 1st

I overheard my father say, 'Well it looks like the North Sea for me, Pauline.'

I ran into the kitchen and said, 'Don't do it, Dad. The economy is bound to pick up!'

My father looked puzzled. Perhaps he was surprised to hear such an emotional outburst from me.

I was surprised myself.

Monday May 2nd
Bank Holiday

Lord Dacre has vouched for the Hitler Diaries' authenticity.

So Pandora owes me £1.50 in a lost bet. Ha! Ha! Ha!

Tuesday May 3rd
Back to School

Quite a few changes have taken place since I was last at school. Mr Jones the PE teacher has got the sack, and Mr Lambert has married Ms Fossington-Gore; he is now called Mr Lambert-Fossington-Gore. She is called Ms Fossington-Gore-Lambert.

Mr Scruton is on sick leave, suffering from a breakdown due to compiling the timetable, so Podgy Pickles the Deputy Head has taken over his functions. The new regime is a bit more relaxed, though not yet liberal enough to enable me to wear my rags to school.

We spent the first day back being taught how to revise for the dreaded 'O' levels.

6 p.m. Started revising English, Biology and Geography.

7 p.m. Decided to concentrate on one subject at a time. Chose English.

8 p.m. Finished revising when Bert Baxter phoned and requested my help. His toilet is blocked again.

Wednesday May 4th

Got a letter from L. S. Caton – the man who recognizes my writing talent. The postmark said '*New York*'.

Dear Adrian Mole,
Thank you for sending me the first page of your novel, *Longing for Wolverhampton*. I am sure that any publishing house worth its salt would jump at the chance to publish such a promising piece of work.

For a small consideration (shall we say, $100), I would be pleased to promote your book.

Make your cheque out to: L. S. Caton Ltd and send it to me, c/o The Dixon Motel,
1,599 Block 19,
NY State
USA

My father refused to give me the money after reading the first page of *Longing for Wolverhampton*! He said, 'I've read some rubbish in my life, but this . . .'

Thursday May 5th

My father has gone for an interview to be a roustabout on an oil rig in the North Sea.

My father a roustabout!

It is nearly as good as having a cowboy for a father. I hope he gets the job. He will be away one fortnight in two.

Friday May 6th

Yet another disenchantment.

The Hitler Diaries are a hoax. I have paid Pandora £1.50.

I am dead disappointed, I was looking forward to reading about what maniacs eat for breakfast, and how they behave in private.

Saturday May 7th

Spent all day revising with Pandora in her mother's study.

Our house is intolerable because my father is beside himself with grief at being turned down by the oil rig firm.

I *told him* it was a bit premature to buy the check shirts and jeans, before he'd been notified that he'd got the job, but he wouldn't listen.

Now he owes Grandma £38.39.

Sunday May 8th

The *Sunday Times* has printed a grovelling apology to its readers, and ex-readers.

I will save today's edition and use it to clean up any future dog crap. Adrian Mole does not like being made to look a fool.

Especially in front of the future Mrs Adrian Mole, *née* Pandora Braithwaite.

Monday May 9th

Mrs Thatcher has called a General Election for June 9th!

How selfish can you get?

Doesn't she know that the May and early June period is supposed to be kept quiet, while teenagers revise for their exams? How can we study when loudspeakers are blaring out lying promises, day and night and canvassers are continually knocking on the door, reminding floating voters that it's 'make your mind up' time? It's all right for her to announce she is going to the country, but some of us can't afford that luxury.

Tuesday May 10th

I keep getting anxiety attacks every time I think about the exams.

I know I'm going to fail.

My overriding problem is that I'm *too* intellectual: I am constantly thinking about things, like: was God married? and: if Hell is other people, is Heaven empty?

These thoughts overload my brain, causing me to forget *facts*. Such as: the average rainfall in the average Equatorial Forest and other boring stuff.

Wednesday May 11th

Grandma has given me some brain pills as a revision aid.

They are concocted from a disgusting part of a bull. She said, 'Your dead Grandad swore by them.' I swallowed two this morning but by the afternoon I still couldn't remember the capital of British Honduras.

I swore by them as well.

Thursday May 12th

I thought my parents had given up the idea of moving house, but no! My mother struck terror into my heart and bowels at breakfast time by announcing that after the exams, we are going to sell our house and move to a desolate area of Wales! She said, 'I want to give us a chance of surviving a nuclear attack.'

I have written to the Council asking to be put on the waiting list.

I requested a two-bedroom flat facing south, with balcony and a working lift.

Friday May 13th

My mother and father are having to negotiate a new Marriage Contract. I'm not surprised; my father hates Wales. He even complains when it is shown on television.

My mother has borrowed ominous books from the library: *The Treatment of Radiation Burns; Bee-Keeping, an Introduction*; and *Living without Men – A Practical Guide*.

Saturday May 14th

10 a.m. A bloke in a blue-and-white pin-striped suit, blue shirt, blue tie, blue rosette, has just knocked at the door. Thrust his hand out, said, 'Julian Pryce-Pinfold: your Conservative candidate, I trust I have your vote!'

I was quite pleased to be taken for eighteen. But I said, 'No, you are planning to exterminate the working class!'

Pryce-Pinfold laughed like a horse and said, 'I say, don't go over the top old chap, we're just trying to trim 'em down a bit!'

He left his poster so I drew devil's horns on his head

and wrote '666' on his forehead, and put it up in the lounge window.

Sunday May 15th

A bloke in a grey suit, white shirt, and red tie, has just disturbed my Biology revision by knocking on the door and announcing that he is the Labour candidate. He said, 'I'm Dave Blakely and I'm going to get Britain back to work!'

My father asked him if there were any jobs going in the Labour Party headquarters. (A sign of his desperation.)

Dave Blakely said that he had never been to the headquarters so he didn't know.

He said, 'I disagree with official Labour policy.'

My mother harangued him about nuclear disarmament and criticized the Labour Party's record on housing, education and trade union co-operation.

Dave Blakely said, 'I suppose you're a Tory are you madam?'

My mother snapped: 'Certainly not, I have voted Labour all my life!'

Monday May 16th

A blond man in a blazer, with a regimental badge, stood outside the school gates handing out election leaflets this afternoon. I read mine on the way home. The man is called Duncan McIntosh and his party is called 'The Send 'Em Back Where They Come From Party'. Its policy is the compulsory repatriation of: black people, brown people, yellow people, tinged people, Jewish, Irish, Welsh, Scottish, Celtic and all those who have Norman blood.

In fact only those who can prove to be pure-bred flaxen-haired Saxons are to be allowed to live in this country.

My mother has worked out that if he came to power the population of Great Britain would be reduced to one.

Tuesday May 17th

Barry Kent has threatened Duncan McIntosh with grievous bodily harm unless he keeps away from our school.

He has joined 'Rock against Racism' (Barry Kent not Duncan McIntosh).

Wednesday May 18th

The SDP candidate (green suit, orange shirt, neutral tie, nervous smile) has just left our house on the verge of tears, after my mother refused to let her kiss Rosie.

Thursday May 19th

I was shown a blurred picture of a broken-down cottage this morning, and asked if I would like to live there.

I replied in the negative.

My mother said, 'It sounds perfect. It's two miles from the nearest shop and fifty-five miles from the nearest American Air Base! Wouldn't you like to get up in the morning and feed the chickens, Adrian?'

I replied, 'I hate chickens. Their nasty beaks and cruel eyes absolutely repel me.'

Friday May 20th

Scruton has retired on the grounds of ill health (gone barmy) and Podgy Pickles has got his name screwed on to the Headmaster's door.

I have never been taught by Podgy, but by all accounts he is a nice bloke who talks about his family, and informs his class when he is thinking of buying a new car.

He took assembly this morning. He had dried egg yolk running down the length of his tie. I know because I was standing next to him. He had called me up to the stage to address the school on 'Why I think school uniform should be abolished!' I spoke from the heart, citing my parents' poverty, and bringing tears to the eyes of Ms Fossington-Gore-Lambert.

Saturday May 21st

My father ordered three politicians out of the front garden this morning. He said, 'My son is upstairs studying for a better future, and your constant clamouring for attention is distracting him!'

Actually I was measuring my thing at the time, but their noise *was* distracting. I kept losing my place on the tape-measure.

Sunday May 22nd

Rosie started crawling at 5 p.m.

My parents gave her a standing ovation.

Monday May 23rd

My English essay 'Despair' was read out to the class.

Everyone looked dead miserable at the end. It is a story about a hamster with an incurable disease. I asked Mr Lambert-Fossington-Gore if it was of sufficient quality to send to the BBC.

He laughed and said, 'Only the Natural History Unit at Bristol.'

I have taken his advice and sent it.

Tuesday May 24th

I have hung a notice on my door. It says: 'ATTEN-TION! NO ONE ALLOWED PAST THIS POINT!'

I am sick of having my privacy invaded.

Wednesday May 25th

No one came into my room to wake me up. So I was late for school and when I got home my dirty washing was still on the floor and my curtains were drawn.

Thursday May 26th

My racing bike has been stolen from out of the back garden.

The prime suspects are the dustmen. They have never forgiven us for having maggots in our dustbin last summer.

Friday May 27th

Followed the dustbin men up our road and tried to overhear any suspicious conversation, but they were only talking about Len Fairclough.

One of them warned me to keep away from the

mangling machinery at the back. Was this a hint of the violence to come, if I voice my suspicions to the police?

Saturday May 28th

Nigel brought my bike back today.

He intended to run away on it to avoid his 'O' levels, but decided not to after his father bought him a set of video cassette study aids. We are the only family in our street who haven't got a video, so there's no point in asking my parents for similar technological help. I will just have to rely on my brain.

Sunday May 29th

Stayed in bed all day revising.

Bert Baxter phoned three times but each time I told my parents to tell him that I was out of town.

The third time he rang, my mother said, 'Was it anything important, Bert?' Bert said, 'Not really, I just wanted to tell him that I think I'm ninety today.'

Felt such a rat fink that I pretended to return from out of town. I went to see him and gave him ninety gentle bumps (although I'm sure he's due at least one more).

It seemed to do him good.

Monday May 30th

Wrote some lyrics for Danny Thompson's reggae band.

Hear what he saying by A. Mole
Sisters and Brothers listen to Jah,
Hear his words from near and far,
Haile Selassie he sit on the throne.
Hear what he saying. Hear what he saying. (*Repeated 10 times.*)
JAH! JAH! JAH!

Rise up and follow Selassie, the king.
A new tomorrow to you he will bring. (*Repeat.*)
E-thi-o-pi-a,
He'll bring new hope to ya.
Hear what he saying. Hear what he saying. (*Repeated 20 times.*)

I gave it to Danny Thompson in Geography.
He read it, and said, 'Not bad, for a honky!'
What a cheek, he's twice as white as I am!
Pandora's mother has decided that the dynamics in our family are beyond her. She has recommended that we go to see a family therapist.

Tuesday May 31st

Got a letter from Johnny Tydeman.

I can't remember any of the references it contains. Did I really write a poem called 'Autumn Renewal'?

I must have written it while the balance of my mind was disturbed in April.

British Broadcasting Corporation

30th May

Dear Adrian Mole,

I do not think I will call you 'Aidy' and I think that it is a little premature in our correspondence for you to call me 'Johnny'. In fact I am never known as 'Johnny', only as 'John'. I do not wish to sound like a stuffy old grown-up, but when you are writing to people officially it is polite for one of your years to address them formally – though I do not mind, at this stage in our correspondence, your addressing me as 'Dear John Tydeman'. But 'Johnny', no! I do have several nicknames by which my friends know me but I am not going to reveal them to you. They relate largely to my surname rather than my Christian name.

Your last letter was altogether rather peculiar. Had you been at your parents' cocktail cabinet by any chance? Or had you drained the dregs of the previous night's vino? I do hope you had not tried glue-sniffing again. At least I am very pleased to hear that you have decided not to kill yourself this year. It would be a shocking waste. A poet can only die young when he has written a number of successful poems – *vide*: Keats, Shelley, Chatterton and co. Most poets write drivel in their old age – *vide*: Wordsworth and quite a lot of Tennyson. I am sure your mother would miss you very much, so it is best that you remain alive.

Perhaps under the influence of something or other, your grammar seems to have gone to pot, eg: 'I have wrote some.' But your poem 'Autumn Renewal' certainly has its moments. I like the pun about chaps. A bit rude though. 'Dandeline' (sic – not 'sick'!) is actually spelt 'dandelion' so you can't make it rhyme with 'decline' nor 'Vaseline' – try as you will.

Do not worry about our files. They will be shredded before the KGB can get to them. Your secrets are safe in Ware and Caversham.

With my best wishes and continued good luck with your writing efforts.

Yours,

John Tydeman

Wednesday June 1st

This will be my last entry; until the exams are over.

Courtney Elliot is coming round to give me last-minute coaching; must stop, his taxi has just drawn up outside.

Thursday June 2nd

My parents went to see a family therapist last night. During their absence Pandora and I indulged in extremely heavy petting; so heavy that I felt a weight fall from me.

If I don't pass my exams it won't matter.

I have known what it is to have the love of a good woman.

ADRIAN MOLE:
THE WILDERNESS
YEARS

'What's gone and what's past help
Should be past grief.'

William Shakespeare
The Winter's Tale

Winter

Tuesday January 1st 1991

I start the year with a throbbing head and shaking limbs, owing to the excessive amounts of alcohol I was forced to drink at my mother's party last night.

I was quite happy sitting on a dining chair, watching the dancing and sipping on a low-calorie soft drink, but my mother kept shouting at me: 'Join in, fishface,' and wouldn't rest until I'd consumed a glass and a half of Lambrusco.

As she slopped the wine into a plastic glass for me, I had a close look at her. Her lips were surrounded by short lines, like numerous river beds running into a scarlet lake; her hair was red and glossy almost until it reached her scalp and then a grey layer revealed the truth: her neck was saggy, her cleavage wrinkled and her belly protruded from the little black dress (*very* little) she wore. The poor woman is forty-seven, twenty-three years older than her second husband. I know for a fact that he, Martin Muffet, has *never* seen her without make-up. Her pillow slips are a disgrace; they are covered in pan-stick and mascara.

It wasn't long before I found myself on the impro-vised dance floor in my mother's lounge, dancing to

'The Birdie Song', in a line with Pandora, the love of my life; Pandora's new lover, Professor Jack Cavendish; Martin Muffet, my boyish stepfather; Ivan and Tania, Pandora's bohemian parents; and other inebriated friends and relations of my mother's. As the song reared to its climax, I caught sight of myself in the mirror above the fireplace. I was flapping my arms and grinning like a lunatic. I stopped immediately and went back to the dining chair. Bert Baxter, who was a hundred last year, was doing some clumsy wheelchair dancing, which caused a few casualties; my left ankle is still bruised and swollen, thanks to his carelessness. Also I have a large beetroot stain on the front of my new white shirt, caused by him flinging one of his beetroot sandwiches across the room under the misapprehension that it was a party popper. But the poor old git is almost certain to die this year – he's had his telegram from the Queen – so I won't charge him for the specialist dry cleaning that my shirt is almost certain to require.

I have been looking after Bert Baxter for over ten years now, going back from Oxford to visit him, buying his vile cigarettes, cutting his horrible toenails, etc. When will it end?

My father gate-crashed the party at 11.30. His excuse was that he wanted to speak urgently to my grandma. She is very deaf now, so he was forced to shout above the music. 'Mum, I can't find the spirit level.'

What a pathetic excuse! Who would be using a spirit level on New Year's Eve, apart from an emergency plumber? It was a pitiful request from a lonely, forty-nine-year-old divorcee, whose navy blue mid-eighties suit needed cleaning and whose brown moccasins needed throwing away. He'd done the best he could with his remaining hair, but it wasn't enough.

'Any idea where the spirit level is?' insisted my father, looking towards the drinks table. Then he added, 'I'm laying some paving slabs.'

I laughed out loud at this obvious lie.

My grandma looked bewildered and went back into the kitchen to microwave the sausage rolls and my mother graciously invited her ex-husband to join the party. In no time at all, he had whipped his jacket off and was frugging on the dance floor with my eight-year-old sister Rosie. I found my father's style of dancing acutely embarrassing to watch (his role model is still Mick Jagger); so I went upstairs to change my shirt. On the way, I passed Pandora and Bluebeard Cavendish in a passionate embrace half inside the airing cupboard. He's old enough to be her father.

Pandora has been mine since I was thirteen years old and I fell in love with her treacle-coloured hair. She is simply playing hard to get. She only married Julian Twyselton-Fife to make me jealous. There can be no other possible reason. Julian is a bisexual semi-aristocrat who occasionally wears a monocle. He strains after eccentricity but it continues to elude him. He is a deeply ordinary man with an upper-class accent. He's not even good-looking. He looks like a horse on two legs. And as for her affair with Cavendish, a man who dresses like a tramp, the mind boggles.

Pandora was looking particularly beautiful in a red off-the-shoulder dress, from which her breasts kept threatening to escape. Nobody would have guessed from looking at her that she was now Dr Pandora Braithwaite, fluent in Russian, Serbo-Croat and various other little-used languages. She looked more like one of those supermodels that prowl the catwalks than a Doctor of Philosophy. She certainly added glamour to the party: unlike her parents, who were dressed as usual in their fifties beatnik style – polo necks and corduroy. No wonder they were both sweating heavily as they danced to Chuck Berry.

Pandora smiled at me as she tucked her left breast back inside her dress, and I was pierced to the heart. I truly love her. I am prepared to wait until she comes to her senses and realizes that there is only one man in the world for her, and that is *me*. That is the reason I followed her to Oxford and took up temporary residence in her box room. I have now been there for a year and a half. The more she is exposed to my presence, the sooner she will appreciate my qualities. I have suffered daily humiliations, watching her with her husband and her lovers, but I will reap the benefits later when she is the proud mother of our six children and I am a famous author.

As the clock struck twelve, everyone joined hands and sang 'Auld Lang Syne'. I looked around, at Pandora; at Cavendish; at my mother; at my father; at my stepfather; at my grandma; at Pandora's parents,

Ivan and Tania Braithwaite; and at the dog. Tears filled my eyes. I am nearly twenty-four years of age, I thought, and what have I done with my life? And, as the singing died away, I answered myself – nothing, Mole, nothing.

Pandora wanted to spend the first night of the New Year in Leicester at her parents' house with Cavendish, but at 12.30 a.m. I reminded her that she and her aged lover had promised to give me a lift back to Oxford. I said, 'I am on duty in eight hours' time at the Department of the Environment. At 8.30 sharp.'

She said, 'For Christ's sake, can't you have one poxy day off without permission? Do you have to kow-tow to that little commissar Brown?'

I replied, with dignity, I hope, 'Pandora, some of us keep our word, unlike you, who on Thursday the second of June 1983 promised that you would marry me as soon as you had finished your "A" levels.'

Pandora laughed, spilling the neat whisky in her glass. 'I was sixteen years old,' she said. 'You're living in a bloody time warp.'

I ignored the insult. 'Will you drive me to Oxford as you promised?' I snapped, dabbing at the whisky droplets on her dress with a paper serviette covered in reindeer.

Pandora shouted across the room to Cavendish, who was engaged in conversation with Grandma about the dog's lack of appetite: 'Jack! Adrian's insisting on that lift back to Oxford!'

Bluebeard rolled his eyes and looked at his watch.

'Have I got time for one more drink, Adrian?' he asked.

'Yes, but only mineral water. You're driving, aren't you?' I said.

He rolled his eyes again and picked up a bottle of Perrier. My father came across and he and Cavendish reminisced about the Good Old Days, when they could drink ten pints in the pub and get in the car and drive off 'without having the law on your back'.

It was 2 a.m. when we finally left my mother's house. Then we had to call at the Braithwaites' house to collect Pandora's overnight bag. I sat in the back of Cavendish's Volvo and listened to their banal conversation. Pandora calls him 'Hunky' and Cavendish calls her 'Monkey'.

I woke up on the outskirts of Oxford to hear her whisper: 'So, what did you think of the festivities at Maison Mole, Hunky?'

And to hear him reply: 'As you promised, Monkey, delightfully vulgar. I enjoyed myself enormously.' They both turned to look at me, so I feigned sleep.

I began to think about my sister Rosie, who is, in my view, totally spoilt. The *Girls' World* model hairdressing head she had demanded for Christmas had stood neglected on the lounge window sill since Boxing Day, looking out onto the equally neglected garden. Its retractable blonde hair was hopelessly tangled and its face was smeared with garish cosmetics. Rosie was dancing earlier with Ivan Braithwaite in a manner totally unsuited to an eight-year-old. They looked like Lolita and Humbert Humbert.

Nabokov, fellow author, you should have been alive on that day. It would have shocked even you to see Rosie Mole pouting in her black miniskirt, pink tights and purple cropped top!

I have decided to keep a full journal, in the hope that my life will perhaps seem more interesting when it is written down. It is certainly not interesting to actually live my life. It is tedious beyond belief.

Wednesday January 2nd

I was ten minutes late for work this morning. The exhaust pipe fell off the bus. Mr Brown was entirely unsympathetic. He said, 'You should get yourself a bicycle, Mole.' I pointed out that I have had three bicycles stolen in eighteen months. I can no longer afford to supply the criminals of Oxford with ecologically sound transport.

Brown snapped, 'Then *walk*, Mole. Get up earlier and *walk*.'

I went into my cubicle and shut the door. There was a message on my desk informing me that a colony of newts had been discovered in Newport Pagnell. Their habitat is in the middle of the projected new ring road. I rang the Environmental Office at the Department of Transport and warned a certain Peter Peterson that work on the ring road could be subject to delay.

'But that's bloody ludicrous,' said Peterson. 'It would cost us hundreds of thousands of pounds to re-route that road, and all to save a few slimy reptiles.'

That is also my own private point of view of newts. I'm sick of them. But I am paid to champion their right to survive (in public at least), so I gave Peterson my standard newt conservation lecture (and pointed out that newts are amphibians, not reptiles). I spent the rest of the morning writing up the Newport Pagnell case.

At lunchtime I left the Department of the Environment and went to collect my blazer from the dry cleaner's. I had forgotten to take my ticket. (It was at home, being used as a bookmark inside Colin Wilson's *The Outsider*. Mr Wilson is Leicester-born, like me.)

The woman at the cleaner's refused to hand over my blazer, even though I pointed to it hanging on the rack! She said, 'That blazer has got a British Legion badge on it. You're too young to be in the British Legion.'

An undergraduate behind me sniggered.

Enraged, I said to the woman, 'You are obviously proud of your powers of detection. Perhaps you should write an *Inspector Morse* episode for the television.' But my wit was lost on the pedant.

The undergraduate pushed forward and handed her a stinking duvet, requesting the four-hour service.

I had no choice but to go home and collect the ticket, go back to the cleaner's, and then run with the blazer, encased in plastic, slung over my shoulder, all the way back to the office. I have got a blind date tonight and the blazer is all I've got to wear.

My last blind date ended prematurely when Ms Sandra Snape (non-smoking, twenty-five-year-old, vegetarian: dark hair, brown eyes, five foot six, not unattractive) left Burger King in a hurry, claiming she'd left the kettle on the stove. I am now convinced, however, that the kettle was an excuse. When I returned home that night, I discovered that the hem was down at the back on my army greatcoat. Women don't like a scruff.

I was twenty-five minutes late getting back to work. Brown was waiting for me in my cubicle. He was brandishing my Newport Pagnell newt figures. Apparently I had made a mistake in my projection of live newt births for 1992. Instead of 1,200, I had put down 120,000. An easy mistake to make.

'A hundred and twenty thousand newts in 1992, eh, Mole?' sneered Brown. 'The good citizens of Newport Pagnell will be positively inundated with amphibia.'

He gave me an official warning about my time-keeping and ordered me to water my cactus. He then went to his own office, taking my paperwork with him. If I lose my job, I am done for.

11.30 p.m. My blind date did not turn up. I waited two hours, ten minutes in the Burger King in the town centre. Thank you, Ms Tracy Winkler (quiet blonde, twenty-seven, non-smoker, cats and country walks)!

That is the last time I write to a box number in the *Oxford Mail*. From now on, I will only use the personal column of the *London Review of Books*.

Thursday January 3rd

I have the most terrible problems with my sex life. It all boils down to the fact that I *have* no sex life. At least not with another person.

I lay awake last night, asking myself why? Why? Why? Am I grotesque, dirty, repellent? No, I am none of these things. Am I normal-looking, clean, pleasant? Yes, I am all of these things. So what am I doing wrong? Why can't I get an average-looking young woman into my bed?

Do I exude an obnoxious odour smelled by everyone else but me? If so, I hope to God somebody will tell me and I can seek medical help from a gland specialist.

At 3 a.m. this morning my sleep was disturbed by the sound of a violent altercation. This in itself is not unusual, because this house provides a home for many people, most of them noisy, drunken undergraduates, who sit up all night debating the qualities of various brands of beer. I went downstairs in my pyjamas and was just in time to see Tariq, the Iraqi student who lives in the basement, being led away by a gang of criminal-looking men.

Tariq shouted, 'Adrian, save me!' I said to one of the men, 'Let him go or I will call the police.'

A man with a broken nose said, 'We *are* the police, sir. Your friend is being expelled from the country, orders of the Home Office.'

Pandora came to the top of the basement stairs. She was wearing very little, having just left her bed. She said in her most imperious manner: 'Why is Mr Aziz being expelled?'

'Because,' said the thuggish one, 'Mr Aziz's presence is not conducive to the public good, for reasons of national security. Ain't you 'eard there's a war on?' he added, ogling Pandora's satin nightshirt, through which the outline of her nipples was clearly visible.

Tariq shouted, 'I am a student at Brasenose College and a member of the Young Conservatives: I am not interested in politics!'

There was nothing we could do to help him, so Pandora and I went back to bed. Not the same bed though, worse luck.

At nine o'clock the next morning, I rang the landlord, Eric Hardwell, on his car phone and asked if I could move into the now vacant basement flat. I am sick of living in Pandora's box room. Hardwell was in a bad mood because he was stuck in traffic, but he agreed, providing I can give him a £1,000 deposit, three months' rent in advance (£1,200), a banker's reference and a solicitor's letter stating that I will not burn candles, use a chip pan, or breed bull terrier dogs in the basement.

I shall have to stay here in the box room. I need to use my chip pan on a daily basis.

Lenin was right: all landlords *are* bastards.

Somebody who looked like Tariq was on *Newts At Ten*; he was waving from the steps of an aeroplane which was bound for the Gulf. I waved back in case it was him.

Correction: I meant, of course, to write *News At Ten*.

Friday January 4th

Woke up at 5 a.m. and was unable to get back to sleep. My brain insisted on recalling all my past humiliations. One by one they passed in front of me: the bullying I endured from Barry Kent until my grandma put a stop to it; the day at Skegness when my father broke the news to me and my mother that his illegitimate son, Brett, had been born to his lover, Stick Insect; the black day when my mother ran away to Sheffield for a short-lived affair with Mr Lucas, our smarmy neighbour; the day I learned that I had failed 'A' level Biology for the third time; the day Pandora married a bisexual man.

Then, after the humiliations came the *faux pas*, a relentless march: the time I sniffed glue and got a model aeroplane stuck to my nose; the day my sister, Rosie, was born and I couldn't remove my hand from the spaghetti jar where the five pound note for the taxi fare to the maternity hospital was kept; the time I wrote to Mr John Tydeman at the BBC and addressed him as 'Johnny'.

The procession of *faux pas* was followed by a parade of bouts of moral cowardice: the time I crossed the road to avoid my father because he was wearing a red pom-pom hat; my craven behaviour when my mother was stricken with a menopausal temper tantrum in the Leicester market place – I should not have walked away and hidden behind that flower stall; the day I had a jealous fit, destroyed the complimentary tickets for Barry Kent's first professional gig on the poetry circuit and blamed the dog; my desertion of Sharon Bott when she announced she was pregnant.

I despise myself. I deserve my unhappiness. I am truly a loathsome person.

I was relieved when my travelling alarm clock roused me from my gloomy reverie and told me that it was 6.30 a.m. and time to get up.

> *Nipples by A. Mole*
> Like raspberries
> taken from the freezer
> Inviting tongue and lips
> but warning not to bite
> Not yet
> soon
> But not yet

I am on flexitime and had agreed to start work at 7.30 a.m., but somehow, although I left my box room at 7 a.m., I didn't arrive at work until 8 a.m. A journey of half a mile took me an hour. Where did I go? What did I do? Did I have a blackout on the way? Was I mugged and left unconscious? Am I, even as I write, suffering from memory loss?

Pandora is constantly telling me that I am in urgent need of psychiatric help. Perhaps she is right. I feel as though I am going mad; that my life is a film and that I am a mere spectator.

Saturday January 5th

Julian, Pandora's upper-crust husband, has returned from his Christmas sojourn in the country with his parents. He shuddered when he walked through the front door of the flat.

'God!' he said. 'The pantry of Twyselton Manor is bigger than this bloody hole.'

'Then why come back, sweetie?' said Pandora, his so-called wife.

'Because, *ma femme*, my parents, poor, deluded creatures, are paying mucho spondulicks to keep me here at Oxford, studying Chinese.' He laughed his neighing horse's laugh. (And he's certainly got the teeth for it.)

'But you haven't been to a lecture for over a year,'

said Dr Braithwaite (12 'O's, 5 'A's, BA Hons. and D. Phil.).

'But my lecturers are all such boring little men.'

'It's such a waste, husband,' said Pandora. 'You're the cleverest man in Oxford *and* the laziest. If you're not careful, you'll end up in Parliament.'

After Julian had thrown his battered pigskin luggage into his room, he returned to the kitchen, where Pandora was chopping leeks and I was exercising my new sink plunger. 'So, darlings, what's new?' he said, lighting one of his vile Russian cigarettes.

Pandora said, 'I'm in love with Jack Cavendish, and he's in love with me. Isn't it absolutely marvellous?' She grinned ecstatically and chopped at the leeks with renewed fervour.

'Cavendish?' puzzled Julian. 'Isn't he that grey-haired old linguistics fart who can't keep his plonker in his pants?'

Pandora's eyes flashed dangerously. 'He's sworn to me that from now on his lifestyle will be strictly non-polygynous,' she said.

She stretched up to replace the knife on its magnetic rack and her cropped T-shirt rode up, revealing her delicate midriff. I thrust the plunger viciously into the greasy contents of the sink, imagining that Cavendish's head was on the end of the wooden stick, instead of the black rubber suction pad.

Julian neighed knowingly. 'Cavendish doesn't know

the meaning of the word "non-polygynous". He's a notorious womanizer.'

'*Was*,' insisted Pandora, adding, 'and *of course* he knows the meaning of the word "non-polygynous": he is a professor of Linguistics.'

I left the plunger floating in the sink and went to my box room, took my *Condensed Oxford Dictionary* from its shelf and, with the aid of the magnifying glass, looked up the word 'non-polygynous'. I then uttered a loud, cynical laugh. Loud enough, I hoped, to be heard in the kitchen.

Sunday January 6th

Woke at 3 a.m. and lay awake remembering the time when Pandora and I nearly went All the Way. I love her still. I intend to be her second husband. And what's more, she will take my name. She will be known as 'Mrs Adrian Albert Mole' in private.

> *On Seeing Pandora's Midriff*
> The glorious shoreline from ribcage
> To pelvis
> Like an inlet
> A bay
> A safe haven
> I want to navigate
> To explore
> To take readings from the stars

To carefully trace my fingers
Along the shoreline
And eventually to guide my ship, my destroyer,
    my pleasure craft
Into and beyond your harbour

6.00 p.m. Sink still blocked. Worked for three hours in the kitchen, adding vowels to the first half of my experimental novel *Lo! The Flat Hills of My Homeland*, which was originally written with consonants only. It is eighteen months since I sent it to Sir Gordon Giles, Prince Charles's agent, and he sent it back, suggesting I put in the vowels.

Lo! The Flat Hills of My Homeland explores late twentieth-century man and his dilemma, focusing on a 'New Man' living in a provincial city in England.

The treatment is broadly Lawrentian, with a touch of Dostoevskian darkness and a tinge of Hardyesque lyricism.

I predict that one day it will be a GCSE set book.

I was driven out of the kitchen by the arrival of that wrinkled-up ashtray on legs, Cavendish, who had been invited to Sunday lunch. He hadn't been in the flat two minutes before he was pulling a cork out of a bottle and helping himself to glasses out of the cupboard. He then sat on *my* recently vacated chair at the kitchen table and began to talk absolute gibberish about the Gulf War, predicting that it would be over within months. I predict that it will be America's second Vietnam.

Julian came into the kitchen, wearing his silk pyjamas and carrying a copy of *Hello!*

'Julian,' said Pandora, 'meet my lover, Jack Cavendish.' She turned to Cavendish and said, 'Jack, this is Julian Twyselton-Fife, my husband.' Pandora's husband and Pandora's lover shook hands.

I turned away in disgust. I'm as liberal and civilized as the next person. In fact, in some circles I'm regarded as quite an advanced thinker, but even I shuddered at the utter depravity that this introduction signified.

I left the flat to get some air. When I returned from my walk around the Outer Ring Road two hours later, Cavendish was still there, telling tedious anecdotes about his numerous children and his three ex-wives. I microwaved my Sunday lunch and took it into my box room. I spent the rest of the evening listening to laughter in the next room. Woke at 2 a.m. and was unable to get back to sleep. Filled two pages of A4 devising tortures for Cavendish. Not the actions of a rational man.

Tortures for Cavendish
1) Chain him to the wall with a glass of water *just* beyond his grasp.
2) Chain him naked to a wall while a bevy of beautiful girls walk by, cruelly mocking his flaccid *and* aroused penis.
3) Force him to sit in a room with Ivan Braithwaite, while Ivan talks about the finer details of the Labour Party's

Constitution, with particular reference to Clause Four.
(This is true torture, as I can bear witness.)
4) Show him a video of Pandora getting married to me.
   She radiant in white, me in top hat and tails, putting
   two gloved fingers up at Cavendish.

Let the punishment fit the crime.

Monday January 7th

Started my beard today.

Some of the Newport Pagnell newts have crossed
the road. I telephoned Peterson at the Department of
Transport, to inform him. There has obviously been
a split in the community. I expect a female newt is at
the bottom of it: *cherchez la femme.*

Wednesday January 9th

For the first time in my entire life I haven't got a single
spot, pustule or pimple. I pointed out to Pandora over
breakfast that my complexion was flawless, but she
paused in applying her mascara, looked at me coldly,
and said, 'You need a shave.'

Spent ten minutes at the sink with the plunger
before going to work, but to no avail. Pandora said,
'We'll have to get a proper man in.'

Does Pandora realize the impact the above words,

so apparently casually uttered, have had on me? She has disenfranchised me from my gender! She has cut my poor, useless balls off!

Thursday January 10th

Brown has advised me to shave. I refused. I may have to seek the advice of the Civil and Public Service Union.

Friday January 11th

Applied to join the CPSU.

Pandora found Cavendish's A4 torture list. She has made an appointment for me to see her friend Leonora De Witt, who is a psychotherapist. I agreed reluctantly. On the one hand, I am terrified of my unconscious and what it will reveal about me. On the other, I am looking forward to talking about myself non-stop for an hour without interruption, hesitation or repetition.

Saturday January 12th

Pandora's most recent ex-lover, Rocky (Big Boy) Livingstone, came round to the flat today, asking for the return of his mini sound-system. At six foot three and fifteen stone of finely honed muscle, Rocky is a 'proper' man, if ever I saw one. Pandora was out, meeting some of Cavendish's children at the Randolph Hotel. So, in her absence, I gave the sound-system to him. Since he and Pandora split up, Rocky has opened new gyms in Kettering, Newmarket and Ashby de la Zouch. He and his new girlfriend, Carly Pick, are still happy.

Rocky said, 'Carly's a real star, Aidy. I respect the lady, y'know.' I told Rocky about Professor Cavendish. He was disgusted.

He said, 'That Pandora is a *user*. Just 'cos she's clever, she finks she's . . .' He flailed about for the right word and finished, 'clever'.

Before he went he unblocked the sink. I was very grateful. I was getting sick of washing the pots in the bathroom hand basin. None of the saucepans would fit under the taps.

I went to the window and watched him drive away. Carly Pick had both her arms around his neck.

Sunday January 13th

The Gulf War deadline expires on the 15th, at midnight. What will I do if I am called up to fight for my country? Will I cover myself with honour, or will I wet myself with fear on hearing the sound of enemy gunfire?

Monday January 14th

Went to Sainsbury's and stocked up with tins of beans, candles, Jaffa cakes, household matches, torch batteries, paracetamol, multivitamins, Ry-King and tins of corned beef and put them in the cupboard in my box room. Should the war spread over here, I will be well prepared. The others in the flat will just have to take their chance. I predict panic buying on a scale never seen before in this country. There will be fighting in the aisles of the supermarkets.

Appointment with Leonora De Witt on Friday 25th of this month at 6 p.m.

Tuesday January 15th

Midnight. We are at war with Iraq. I phoned my mother in Leicester and told her to keep the dog in. It is twelve years old and reacts badly to unexpected noises. She laughed and said, 'Are you going mad?' I said, 'Probably,' and put the phone down.

Wednesday January 16th

Bought sixteen bottles of Highland Spring water, in case water supply is cut off owing to bombardment by Iraqi airforce. It took me four trips from the Spar shop on the corner to the flat, but I feel more secure knowing I will not go thirsty during the coming *Blitzkrieg*.

Brown has not mentioned my beard for some days now. He is preoccupied with the effect that 'Operation Desert Storm' will have on the desert wildlife. I said, 'I'm afraid I regard Iraqi wildlife as being on the side of the enemy. I'm more worried about my dog, at home in Leicester.'

'Ever the parochial, Mole,' said Brown, in a lip-curling manner. I was quite insulted. Brown reads nothing, apart from journals on wildlife, whereas I have read most of the Russian Greats and am about to embark on *War and Peace*. Hardly parochial, Brown!

Thursday January 17th

I have hired a portable colour television, so I can watch the Gulf War in bed.

Friday January 18th

The spokesperson for the USA military is a man who calls himself 'Colon Powell'. Every time I see him, I think of intestines and the lower bowel. It detracts from the gravity of the War.

Saturday January 19th

Bert Baxter rang me up at the office today. (I will kill whoever gave him the number.) He wanted to know 'when you and my favourite gal are comin' to see me?' His 'favourite gal' is Pandora. Why doesn't Bert just *die* like other pensioners? His quality of life can't be up to much. He is nothing but a burden to others (me).

He was entirely ungrateful when I dug a grave for his dog, Sabre, last year, though I challenge anyone to dig a neater hole in compacted soil with a rusty garden trowel. If I'd had a decent spade at my disposal, then, *naturellement*, the grave would have been neater. The truth is that I hated and feared Sabre. The day the wretched Alsatian died was a day of rejoicing for me. No more smelling its noxious breath. No more forcing Bob Martin's conditioning tablets between its horrible vicious teeth.

Bert burbled on about the war for a while, and then asked me if I had heard my old enemy Barry Kent on *Stop the Week* this morning. Apparently, Kent was publicizing his first novel, *Dork's Diary*. I am now utterly convinced there cannot be a God. It was me that encouraged Kent to write poetry, and now I find out that the ex-skinhead, frozen peabrain has written a novel, *and got it published!!!*

Pandora told me this evening that Kent made Ned Sherrin, A. S. Byatt, Jonathan Miller and Victoria

Mather laugh almost continuously. Apparently the phone lines at the BBC were jammed with listeners asking when *Dork's Diary* will be published (Monday). This is absolutely and totally the last straw. My sanity hangs by a fragile thread.

Sunday January 20th

I was passing Waterstone's bookshop when I saw what appeared to be Barry Kent standing in the window. I lifted my hand in greeting and said, 'Hello, Baz,' then realized that the smirking skinhead was only a cardboard cut-out. Copies of *Dork's Diary* filled the window. I'm not ashamed to say that curses sprang from my lips.

As I flicked through the pages of the slim volume, my eye was caught not only by the many obscenities with which the book is littered, but by the name – 'Aiden Vole' – given to one of the characters. This 'Aiden Vole' is obsessed with matters anal. He is jingoistic, deeply conservative and a failure with women. 'Aiden Vole' is an outrageous caricature of me, without a doubt. I have been slandered. I shall see my solicitor in the morning. I shall instruct him or her (I haven't actually got a solicitor yet) to demand hundreds of thousands of pounds in damages. I couldn't bring myself actually to buy a copy of the book. Why should I add to Kent's royalties? But I noticed as I left the shop that Kent is giving a reading from *Dork's Diary* on Tuesday evening at 7 p.m. I will be in the audience. Kent will leave Waterstone's a broken man when I have finished with him.

Monday January 21st

The Cubicle, DOE
Just listened to Kent on *Start the Week* on my portable radio. He has certainly extended his vocabulary. Melvyn Bragg said that the Aiden Vole character was 'wonderfully funny' and asked if he was based on anybody real. Kent laughed and said, 'You're a writer, Melv; you know what it's like. Vole is an amalgam of fact and fantasy. Vole stands for everything I hate most in this country, after the new five-pence piece, that is.' The other guests – Ken Follett, Roy Hattersley, Brenda Maddox and Edward Pearce – laughed like drains.

Spent the rest of the morning looking through the Yellow Pages for a solicitor with a name I can trust. Chose and rang 'Churchman, Churchman, Churchman and Luther'. I am seeing a Mr Luther at 11.30 a.m. on Thursday. I am supposed to be visiting the Newport Pagnell newts on Thursday morning with Brown, but he will just have to face them alone. My reputation and my future as a serious novelist are at stake.

Alfred Wainwright, who wrote guides to the fells of the Lake District, died today. I once used Mr Wainwright's maps when I attempted to do the 'coast to coast' walk with the 'Off the Streets' Youth Club. Unfortunately, I developed hypothermia within half an hour of leaving the Youth Hostel at Grimsby and my record-breaking attempt had to be abandoned.

Tuesday January 22nd

Review of *Dork's Diary* in the *Guardian*:

'A coruscating account of *fin de siècle* provincial life. Brilliant. Dark. Hilarious. Buy it!' Robert Elms

Box Room 10 p.m.
Couldn't get in to see Kent; all the tickets were sold. Tried to speak to him as he entered the shop, but couldn't get near to him. He was surrounded by press and publicity people. He was wearing sunglasses. In January.

Wednesday January 23rd

Beard coming along nicely. Two spots on left shoulder blade. A slight pain in anus, but otherwise I am in superb physical condition.

Read long interview in the *Independent* with Barry Kent. He told lies from start to finish. He even lied about the reason for his being sent to prison, claiming he was sentenced to eighteen months for various acts of violence, when I know very well that he got four months for criminal damage to a privet hedge. I have faxed the *Independent*, putting the record straight. It gave me no pleasure to do this, but without the Truth we are no better than dogs. Truth is the most important thing in my life. Without Truth we are lost.

Thursday January 24th

Lied on the phone to Brown this morning and told him that I could not visit the Newport Pagnell newt habitat on account of a severe migraine. Brown ranted on about how he had 'never taken a day off work in twenty-two years'. He went on to brag that he had 'even passed several massive kidney stones into the lavatory at work'. Perhaps that explains why the lavatory basin is cracked.

I was late for my appointment with Mr Luther, the solicitor, though I left the flat in plenty of time – another time warp or memory-loss – a mystery, anyway. As I told Luther (in great detail) about Kent's slander of me, I noticed him yawning several times. I expect he was up late; he looks the dissolute type. He was wearing braces covered in pictures of Marilyn Monroe.

Eventually he raised his hand and said, 'Enough, I've heard enough,' in an irritable sort of way. Then he leaned across his desk and said, 'Are you vastly rich?'

'No,' I replied, 'not vastly.'

He then asked, 'Are you desperately poor?'

'Not desperately. That's why I . . .'

Luther interrupted before I could finish my sentence, 'Because unless you are vastly rich, or desperately poor, you can't possibly afford to go to court. You don't qualify for Legal Aid and you can't afford to pay a barrister a thousand pounds a day, can you?'

'*A thousand pounds a day?*' I said, absolutely aghast.

Luther smiled, revealing a gold back molar.

I remembered my grandma's advice, 'Never trust a man with a gold tooth.' I thanked Mr Luther politely but coldly and left his office. So much for English justice. It is the worst in the world. As I passed the waiting room, I noticed a copy of *Dork's Diary* on the coffee table, next to copies of *Amnesty* and *The Republican*.

Got home to find a note from Leonora De Witt informing me that she is unable to keep our appointment tomorrow. Why? Is she having her hair done? Is double-glazing being installed in her consulting room? Have her parents been found dead in bed? Am I so unimportant that my time is a mere plaything to Ms De Witt? She suggested a new appointment: Thursday 31st January at 5 p.m. I left a message on her Ansafone, agreeing to the new arrangement, but announcing my displeasure.

Saturday January 26th

I was awake all last night, watching 'Operation Desert Storm'. I feel it's the least I can do – after all, it is costing HM Government thirty million pounds a day to keep Kuwait a democracy.

Sunday January 27th

According to the *Observer* today, Kuwait is not and has never been a democracy. It is ruled by the Kuwaiti Royal Family.

Bluebeard laughed when I told him. 'It's all to do with *oil*, Adrian,' he said. 'Do you think the Yanks would be in there if Kuwait's main product was *turnips*?'

Pandora bent down and kissed the back of his withered neck. How she could allow her young, vibrant flesh to come into contact with his ancient, wrinkled skin, I'll never know. I had to go into the bathroom and take deep breaths and control the urge to vomit. Why slobber over *him* when she could have *me*?

My mother rang at 4 p.m. I could hear my young stepfather, Martin Muffet, hammering in the background. 'Martin's putting some shelves up for my knick-knacks,' she shouted over the row. Then she asked me if I had read the extracts from *Dork's Diary* in the *Observer*. I was able to answer truthfully. 'No,' I said. 'You should,' said my mother. 'It's totally brilliant. When you next see Baz, will you ask him for a free copy, signed to Pauline and Martin?'

I said, 'It is highly unlikely that I will see Kent. I do not move in the same illustrious circles as him.'

'Which illustrious circles *do* you move in, then?' asked my mother.

'None,' I answered truthfully. Then I put the phone down and went to bed and pulled the duvet over my head.

Monday January 28th

Britain's Jo Durie and Jeremy Bates won the mixed doubles in Melbourne. This surely points to a renaissance in British tennis.

> *Pandora's Little Pussy*
> I love her little Pussy
> Her coat is so warm
> But if I should stroke her
> She'll call the police and identify me in
> A line-up
> And do me some harm

Wednesday January 30th

Shocked to hear on Radio Four that King Olav the Fifth of Norway was buried today. His contribution to the continuing success of the Norwegian leather industry is something that is little appreciated by the vast majority of the Great British Public. Prince Charles was England's graveside representative.

Borrowed *Scenes from Provincial Life* by William Cooper from the library. I only had time to choose one book, because a 'suspicious package' was found in the Romantic Fiction section and the library was evacuated.

Sink blocked again. Plunged for the duration of *The Archers*, but to no avail.

Thursday January 31st

I didn't arrive at the consulting room on Thames Street until 5.15 p.m. Leonora De Witt was not pleased.

'I'll have to charge you for the full hour, Mr Mole,' she said, seating herself in an armchair which was covered in old bits of carpet. 'Where would you like to sit?' she asked. There were many chairs in the room. I chose a dining chair which was standing against a wall.

When I was seated, I said, 'I was under the impression that our sessions were to be under the auspices of the National Health Service.'

'Then you were gravely mistaken,' said Ms De Witt. 'I charge thirty pounds an hour – under the auspices of the private enterprise system.'

'*Thirty pounds an hour!* How many sessions will I need?' I asked.

She explained that she couldn't possibly predict, that she knew nothing about me. That it depended on the cause of my unhappiness.

'How do you feel at the moment?' she asked.

'Apart from a slight headache, I feel fine,' I replied.

'What are you doing with your hands?' she said quietly.

'Wringing them,' I replied.

'What is that on your brow?' she asked.

'Sweat,' I answered, taking out my handkerchief.

'Are your buttocks clenched, Mr Mole?' she pressed.

'I suppose they are,' I said.

'Now answer my first question again, please. How do you feel at this moment?'

Her large brown eyes locked into mine. I couldn't avert my gaze.

'I feel totally miserable,' I said. 'And I lied about the headache.'

She talked at length about the *Gestalt* technique. She explained that it was possible to teach me 'coping mechanisms'. Apart from Pandora, she is probably the loveliest woman I have ever spoken to. I found it hard to take my eyes off her black-stockinged feet, which were slipped into black suede shoes with high heels. Was she wearing tights or stockings?

'So, Mr Mole, do you think we can work together?' she said.

She looked at her watch and stood up. Her hair looked like a midnight river pouring down her back. I eagerly affirmed that I would like to see her once a week. Then I gave her thirty pounds and left.

Friday February 1st

Just returned from Newport Pagnell. My nerves are shot to pieces. Brown drove like a man possessed. At no time did he exceed the speed limit, but he drove onto the kerb, scraped against hedgerows and on the motorway section of our journey he left only a six-inch gap between our fragile Ford Escort and the monolithic juggernaut in front of us.

'It saves precious fuel if you can stay in the lorry's slipstream,' he said by way of explanation. The man is an environmental fanatic. He spent last Christmas Day classifying seaweed at Dungeness. I rest my case. Thank God for the weekend. Or *le weekend*, as our fellow Europeans say.

Saturday February 2nd

Viscount Althorp, Princess Diana's brother, has confessed to his thin wife and the rest of the world that he had an affair in Paris. Prince Charles and Princess Diana must have been horrified to find out that there was an adulterer in the family. He should be stripped of his title immediately. The Royal Family and their close connections should be above such brutish instincts. The country looks to them to set the moral standard.

Had bath, shampooed beard, cut fingernails and toenails. Put hot oil on hair to nourish it and give it shine and the outward illusion of health.

11.45 p.m. Bert Baxter has just telephoned. He sounded pathetic. Pandora was out and in a moment of weakness I agreed to go and visit him in Leicester tomorrow. Wrote a note to Pandora, left it on her pillow.

Pandora,

Baxter rang in considerable distress, something about killing himself – I intend to visit him tomorrow. He intimated to me that he wished to see you too. I plan to rise at 8.30 to catch the train, or, should you wish to accompany me, my alternative *modus operandi* will be to rise at nine and be driven by you in your motor car, thus arriving in Leicester at approximately 11 a.m. Would you please inform me of your decision by the method of slipping a note under my door? Please do not disturb me tonight with the sounds of your wild love-making. The walls of my box room are very thin and I am sick of sleeping with my Sony Walkman on.

Adrian

Sunday February 3rd

At 2.10 a.m., Pandora burst into my box room and hurled abuse at me. She flung my note to her into my face and screamed, 'You pompous *nerd*, you pathetic *dork*! "*Modus operandi*"! 'Be driven by you in your motor car"! I want you out of this box room and out of my life, *tomorrow*!'

Bluebeard came in and led her away and I lay in bed and listened to them murmuring together in the kitchen. What brought on such an unprovoked outburst?

At 3.30 a.m. they went into Pandora's bedroom. At 3.45 a.m. I put Dire Straits into my Sony and turned the volume up to full.

Didn't wake until midday. Phoned Bert and said I was unable to visit him owing to being awake all night with intestinal pains. I could tell Bert didn't believe me. He said, 'You're a bleedin' liar. I've just spoken to my gal Pandora. She rang me on her car phone. She looked in your room before she set out for Leicester and she said you were sleepin' like a newborn.'

'Why didn't she wake me then?' I asked.

''Cos she 'ates the bleedin' sight of you,' said the diplomatic one.

Monday February 4th

Inexplicably late for work by twenty-three minutes. Brown was practically frothing at the mouth. Also accused me of stealing postage stamps. He said, 'Every penny is needed by the DOE if our wildlife is to be preserved.' As if! Are the badgers and foxes and tadpoles and lousy, stinking newts going to pop their clogs because I, Adrian Mole, made use of two second-class postage stamps paid for out of my taxes in the first place? No, Brown. I don't think so.

Tuesday February 5th

Pandora still in Leicester. Trimmed beard around mouth. Swallowed clippings. One lodged at back of throat; annoying.

Wednesday February 6th

Brown came into my cubicle today and demanded to see my 'A' level certificates! He had heard on the office grapevine that I had failed 'A' level Biology three times.

The only person in Oxford – apart from Pandora – who knows about my triple failure is Megan Harris, Brown's secretary. I confessed to her whilst in a drunken and emotional state at the DOE Christmas Party last year. She alone knows that my job as a Scientific Officer Grade One was granted to me under false pretences. Has Megan blabbed? I must know.

I told Leonora De Witt my family history tonight. It's a tragic story of rejection and alienation, but Leonora simply sat and picked balls of fluff from her sweater, which drew my attention to the shape of her comely breasts. It was obvious that she was not wearing a bra. I wanted to leave my chair and sink my head into her bosom. I went into some detail about my parents' deviant behaviour, but the only time she showed obvious interest was when I mentioned my dead grandfather, Albert Mole, whom I have to thank for my middle name.

'Did you see his dead body?' she asked.

'No,' I replied. 'The Co-op undertaker had screwed the coffin lid down and nobody could find the screw-driver at Grandma's house, so . . .'

'Continue,' ordered Leonora. So I did. Through fat, hot tears. I told about my feeling of exclusion from 'normal' life; of how I long to join my fellow human beings, to share their sorrows, their joys, their sing-songs in pubs.

Leonora said, 'People sing awful songs in pubs. Why do you feel a need to join in singing those mawkish lyrics and banal tunes?'

'I stood outside such pubs as a child,' I said. 'Everybody sounded so happy.'

Then the alarm went off on her watch and it was time to cough up thirty quid and leave.

On my way home I went into a pub and had a drink. I also initiated a conversation about the weather with an old man. There was no singing, so I went home.

Thursday February 7th

I asked Megan outright this morning. I approached her in the corridor as she was being scalded by the Autovent tea/coffee/oxtail soup machine. She admitted that she had let it 'slip out' that I was totally unqualified for my position. Then she swore me to secrecy and informed me that she and Brown have been having an affair since 1977! Brown and the lovely Megan! Why do women throw themselves at worn-out old gits like Brown and Cavendish, and ignore young, virile, bearded men like me? It defies logic.

Megan was eager to talk about her affair with Brown. Apparently he had sworn to leave Mrs Brown in 1980, but has not yet done so. I feel sorry for Mrs Brown every time she comes into the office. It is not her fault that she looks like she does. Some women have got good dress sense and some women haven't. Mrs Brown obviously does not know that pop socks should only be worn under trousers or long skirts. Also, somebody should tell her that warts can be cured nowadays.

Friday February 8th

Pandora is back in Oxford, but not speaking to me much, apart from the bare facts that Bert is no longer suicidal. She bought him a kitten and also installed a cat flap in his back door. Brown asked me again for my Biology 'A' level certificate. I looked at him enigmatically and said, 'I think you'll find that Megan has the information you require.' God, blackmail is an ugly word. I hope Brown doesn't force me to use it.

I have thrown my condom away. It had exceeded its 'best before' date.

Monday February 11th

Megan came into my cubicle today, sobbing. Apparently Brown forgot her birthday, which was yesterday. Alack, alas! It looks as if I am cast into the role of Megan's only confidant. I put my arms around her and kissed her. She felt lovely and soft and squashy. She pulled away quite soon, however, and said, 'Your beard is scratchy and horrible.'

But was my beard the *real* reason?

Does my breath stink? Does my body stink?

Who can I trust to tell me the truth?

I can certainly see what Brown sees in Megan, but I will never in a billion years see what she sees in him. He is forty-two, thin, and wears atrocious clothes from 'Man at C&A'. Megan says he is good in bed. Who is she trying to kid? Good at what in bed? Doing jigsaws? Sleeping? Perhaps she means that he is unselfish with the duvet? If Brown is good in bed, then I am a tractor wheel.

Tuesday February 12th

Tried to visit newt habitat in Northamptonshire, but 'wrong kind of snow' caused Class 317 engine to fail. Was forced to sit in freezing carriage whilst buffet bar attendant gave out continuous announcements in annoying adenoidal voice. Was pleased when buffet car ran out of all supplies and closed. Got back to Oxford at 10.30 p.m., to find message from Megan. Rang her to find out that she and Brown had had a row; their affair is over. I was distraught. This means I no longer have a hold over Brown. It could signal the end of my career with the DOE.

Wednesday February 13th

Brown/Megan affair is on again. Apparently Brown cycled round to Megan's flat in the early hours, after telling Mrs Brown he was going bat-watching. Their reconciliation was very passionate.

I cannot imagine anything in the world more distasteful than seeing Brown in a state of orgasmic pleasure. Apart from *being* with Brown in a state of orgasmic pleasure.

Bought new condom – spearmint flavoured.

Also bought bunch of bananas. Megan says they are very good for those, like me, who suffer from an irritable bowel.

Thursday February 14th

Valentine's Day card from my mother as usual. Megan in tears again. Brown forgot. Bought economy box of tissues at lunchtime for Megan's sole use. I can't afford to keep wasting Kleenex on her. Bluebeard has sent Pandora a disgracefully extravagant bouquet (it is disgusting when people are starving), and at seven o'clock this evening he called with champagne, an Art Nouveau brooch and a pair of satin pyjamas. Then, as if that wasn't enough, he took her out for dinner in a hired car with uniformed driver! Most unacademic behaviour.

Cavendish behaves more like a pools winner than a professor of Linguistics at an ancient seat of learning.

Left to myself, I ate a simple meal of bread, tuna and cucumber and went to bed early. I am reading *English Love Poems*, edited by John Betjeman. Valentine's Day is a ridiculous charade, the ignorant masses are manipulated by the greetings card companies into forking out millions – and for what? For the illusion of being loved.

Friday February 15th

A Valentine's Day card! Signed 'A Secret Admirer'! I sang in my bath. I walked to work without touching the pavement! Who is she? The signature told me that she is educated and uses a felt-tip pen, like me.

Leonora had her hair pinned up today; she was wearing silver earrings so long that they brushed her slim shoulders. She was wearing a scooped-neck black top. A bra strap was visible. Black lace. She occasionally pushed it back inside her top. Every time she did so her sparkling bracelet fell down her arm towards her elbow. I am not in love with Leonora De Witt. But I am obsessed with her. She invades my dreams. She made me talk to an empty chair and pretend that it was my mother. I told the chair that it drank too much and wore its skirts too short.

Saturday February 16th

I finally took my library books back today: *A Single Man* by Christopher Isherwood, *English Love Poems* by John Betjeman, *Scenes from Provincial Life* by William

Cooper and *Notes from the Underground* by Dostoevsky. I owed seven pounds, eighty pence in fines. My least favourite librarian was on duty at the desk. I don't know her name, but she is the Welsh one with the extroverted spectacles.

After I'd written out my cheque and handed it to her, she said, 'Do you have a cheque card?'

'Yes,' I replied. 'But it's at home.'

'Then I'm afraid I cannot accept this cheque,' she said.

'But you know me,' I said. 'I've been coming here once a week for eighteen months.'

'I'm afraid that I don't recognize you at all,' she said and handed me my cheque back.

'This beard is quite recent,' I said coldly. 'Perhaps you could try to visualize my face without it.'

'I don't have time for visualization,' she said. 'Not since the cuts.'

I showed her a small photograph of myself that I carry in my wallet. It was taken pre-beard.

'No,' she said, after giving it a cursory glance. 'I don't recognize that man.'

'But that man is *me*!' I shouted. A queue of people had built up behind me and they were listening avidly to the exchange. The librarian's spectacles flashed in anger.

'I have been doing the job of three people since the cuts began,' she said. 'And you are making my job even more difficult. Please go home and find your cheque card.'

'It is now 5.25 p.m. and the library closes in five minutes,' I said. 'Even Superman couldn't fly back in time to pay the fines, choose four books and leave before the doors close.'

Somebody behind me in the queue muttered, 'Get a bleedin' move on, Superman.'

So I said to the spectacled one, 'I'll be back tomorrow.'

'Oh no you won't,' she said, with a tiny smile. 'Due to the cuts this library doesn't open again until Wednesday.'

On my way home I railed internally against a government that is depriving me of new reading matter. Pandora has forbidden me to touch her books ever since I left a Jaffa cake inside her Folio Society edition of *Nicholas Nickleby*; Julian's books are in Chinese and I'm finding the last hundred pages of *War and Peace* heavy going. There is no way I can afford to buy a new book. Even a paperback costs at least a fiver.

I have to cough up thirty pounds a week for Leonora. I have even had to cut down on my consumption of bananas. I am down to one a day.

I have been forced to read my old diaries. Some of the entries are incredibly perceptive. And the poems have stood the test of time.

Sunday February 17th

Pandora spoke to me today. She said, 'I want you to leave. You stultify me. We had a childhood romance, but we are both adults now: we have grown in different directions and the time has come to part.' Then she added, cruelly, I thought, 'And that bloody beard makes you look absolutely ridiculous. For God's sake, shave it off.' I went to bed shattered. Read page 977 of *War and Peace*, then lay awake staring into the darkness.

Monday February 18th

I looked into the newsagent's on my way to work. I saw the following advertisement, written in a reasonably educated hand, on a Conqueror postcard:

Large sunny room to let – in family house.
Fire sign preferred. Use of W machine/dryer.
£75pw inclusive to N/S male professional. Ring Mrs Hedge.

I rang Mrs Hedge as soon as I got to my cubicle. She asked for my date of birth. I told her it was April 2nd, which excited the response, 'Aries, good. I'm Sagittarius.'

I went to see her at 7 p.m. and inspected the room. 'It's not very sunny,' I said.

She said, 'No, but would you expect it to be on an evening in February?'

I like the cut of her jib. She is oldish (thirty-five to thirty-seven, I would guess), but has not got a bad figure, although it's hard to tell with the clothes women wear nowadays. Her hair is lovely; treacle-coloured, like Pandora's used to be before she started mucking about with Colour-Glo. She was wearing quite a bit of make-up and her mascara had smudged. I hope this is not a sign of sluttishness. She was recently divorced and needs to let the room in order to continue paying the mortgage. Apparently the Building Society (my own, coincidentally) has turned nasty.

She invited me to test the bed. I did so and had a sudden vision of myself and Mrs Hedge engaging in vigorous sexual intercourse. I said aloud, 'I'm sorry.'

Naturally Mrs Hedge was completely in the dark as to the reason for my apology and said, '"Sorry"? Does that mean you don't like the bed?'

'No, no,' I gibbered. 'I love you; I mean, I love the bed.'

I was concerned that I hadn't made a good impression, so I rang Mrs Hedge when I got home (in an effort to impress her) and informed her that I was a writer; would the scratching of my pen in the small hours bother her?

'Not at all,' she replied. 'I am visited by the Muse myself in the night occasionally.'

You can't walk on the pavement in Oxford without bumping into a published or unpublished writer. It's no wonder that the owner of the stationery shop where I buy my supplies goes to the Canary Islands twice a year and drives a Mercedes. (He drives a Mercedes in *Oxford*, not the Canary Islands, though of course it is perfectly feasible that he has the use of a Mercedes *in* the Canary Islands as well. But I doubt, given the comparative infrequency of his visits, if he actually *owns* a Mercedes in the Canary Islands though I suppose it could be leased.) I don't know why I felt the need to explain the Canary Islands/Mercedes confusion. I suppose it may be another example of what Leonora calls my 'childish pedantry'.

Tuesday February 19th

My mother rang in a panic at 11.00 p.m., to ask if Martin Muffet, my young stepfather, had turned up at the flat. Quite frankly, I laughed out loud. Why would Muffet want to visit *me*? He knows I disapprove of my mother's foolhardy second marriage. Apart from the age difference (which is as wide as the mouth of the Amazon), they are physically and mentally incompatible.

Muffet is a six foot six bag of bones, who thinks the Queen works hard and that Paddy Ashdown is incapable of telling a lie. My mother is five foot five and squeezes herself into clothes two sizes too small for her and thinks that Britain should be a republic and that our first president should be Ken Livingstone, the well-known newt lover. On my last visit, I noticed that young Mr Muffet was far less attentive to my mother than of late. I expect he is regretting his mad rush into matrimony.

My mother said, 'He went to London this morning, to visit the Lloyd's building for his Engineering course.'

My mother's grasp of the geographical layout of the British Isles has always been minimal. I informed her of the distance from the Lloyd's building in the City of London to that of my box room in Oxford.

She said in a pathetic voice, 'I thought he might have popped in on his way back to Leicester.'

She phoned back at 2 a.m. Muffet was trapped in an underground train in a tunnel for six hours, or so he said.

Thursday February 21st

This time Leonora invited me to imagine that the chair was my father. She gave me an African stick and I beat the chair until I lay limp and exhausted and physically unable to lift the stick again.

'He's not a bad bloke, my dad,' I said. 'I don't know why I went so berserk.'

Leonora said, 'Don't talk to me, talk to him. Talk to the chair. The chair is your father.'

I felt stupid addressing the empty chair again, but I wanted to please Leonora, so I forced myself to look the upholstery in the eye and said, 'Why didn't you buy me an anglepoise lamp when I was revising for my GCSEs?'

Leonora said, 'Good, good, take it further, Adrian.'

'I hate your Country and Western cassettes,' I said.

'No,' Leonora whispered. 'Deeper, darker, an earlier memory.'

'I remember when I was three,' I said. 'You came into the bedroom, yanked my dummy out of my mouth and said, "*Real* boys don't need a dummy."'

I then grabbed the stick from where it was lying on the floor and once again began to beat the chair. Dust flew.

Leonora said, 'Good, good. How do you *feel*?'

I said, 'I feel terrible. I've wrenched my shoulder beating that chair.'

'No, no,' she said, irritably. 'How do you feel *inside*?'

I cottoned on.

'Oh, at peace with myself,' I lied. I got up, gave my therapeutic dominatrix the thirty quid and left. I needed to buy some Nurofen before the late-night chemist closed. I was in agony with my shoulder.

Friday February 22nd

Another split in the Newport Pagnell newts. There are now three separate habitats. Something fishy is happening in the newt world. Brown is phoning newt experts worldwide, droning on about this phenomenon.

Mrs Hedge has interviewed other potential tenants, but has chosen me! I was racked all night by erotic dreams, concerning me, Brown, Megan and Mrs Hedge. I am ashamed, but what can I do? I can't control my subconscious, can I? I was forced to go to the launderette, though it is not my usual day.

Saturday February 23rd

Norman Schwarzkopf was on television tonight, pointing a stick at an incomprehensible map. Why he was dressed in army camouflage is a mystery to me:

a) there are no trees in the desert
b) there were no trees in the briefing room
c) he is obviously too important to go anywhere near the enemy; he could go around dressed like Coco the Clown and still not be shot at

Tuesday February 26th

Visited Mrs Hedge today, to finalize arrangements for renting the room and to discuss our tenancy agreement. She had a picture of the charred head of an Iraqi soldier who was found dead in a vehicle held against her fridge by a Mickey Mouse magnet. I averted my eyes and asked her for a drink of water.

Wednesday February 27th

Yesterday evening I informed Pandora that I am moving out of the flat at the weekend. I had hoped that she would fall on my neck and beg me to stay, but she didn't. At 1 a.m. I was woken by the sound of a champagne cork popping, glasses clinking and wild, unrestrained laughter from Pandora, Cavendish and Julian. The Infernal Triangle.

Thursday February 28th

Leonora did most of the talking tonight. She told me that I expect too much of myself, that I have impossibly high standards. She told me to be kind to myself and made me draw up a list of ten things I enjoy doing. Every time I banish a negative thought about myself, I am allowed to treat myself.

She asked if I can afford the occasional self-indulgence. I confessed that I have savings in the Market Harborough Building Society. She gave me a piece of paper and a child's crayon and told me to write down ten treats.

Treats
1) Reading novels
2) Writing novels
3) Sexual intercourse

4) Looking at women
5) Buying stationery
6) Eating bananas
7) Crab paste sandwiches
8) Watching boxing on television
9) Listening to Tchaikovsky
10) Walking in the countryside

I asked Leonora what her treats were.

She said in a husky low voice, 'We're not here to talk about me.' Then she smiled and showed her beautifully white teeth and said, 'We have a few things in common, Adrian.'

I felt a throb of sexual desire surge through me.

'I too like to watch the boxing on television,' she said. 'I'm a Bruno fan.'

Friday March 1st

At breakfast this morning, I asked Cavendish if he would help me to move my things to Mrs Hedge's. He has got a big Volvo estate. He said, 'Can't think of anything I'd rather do, Aidy.' He offered to move me immediately, but I said, 'Tomorrow morning will do. Some of us have to *work*.'

He laughed and said, 'So you think teaching Linguistics is a soft option, do you, Aidy?'

I said, 'Yes, as a matter of fact, I do. I doubt if *work* is a four-letter word to you.'

'Speaking as a professor of Linguistics,' he snarled, 'I can assure you that work is indeed a four-letter word.' As he reached for the ashtray, his dressing gown fell open, revealing withered nipples and grey matted chest hair. I was almost physically sick. I could hardly swallow my Bran Flakes.

Took the portable TV back to the shop. On my return, I wrote a poem to Pandora and slipped it under her door. It was my last-ditch attempt to seduce her away from Cavendish.

> *Pandora! Let Me! by A. Mole*
> Let me stroke your inner thighs
> Let me hear your breathy sighs
> Let me feel your silky skin
> Let me make your senses spin
> Let me touch your soft white breast
> Let us stop and have a rest.
> Let me join our beating hearts
> Let me forge our private parts
> Let me delve and make you mine
> Let me give you food and wine
> Let me lick you with my tongue
> Let me do whatever's wrong
> Let me watch you take your pleasure
> Let me dress you in black leather
> Let me fit you like a glove
> Let me consummate our love.

At 1 a.m. Pandora pushed a note under my door.

Adrian,

   If you continue to send such filth to me, I will, in future, pass it on to the police.

   Pandora

Saturday March 2nd

As I packed my belongings, I reflected that I have not acquired much in my life. A basic wardrobe of clothes. A few hundred books. A Sony Walkman. A dozen or so cassettes. My own mug, cup, bowl and plate. A poster by Munch, a cactus, a magnifying mirror on a stand, a bowl for bananas, and a lamp. It is not much to show for a year and a half of toil at the DOE. True, I have got £2,579 saved in the Market Harborough Building Society, and £197.39 in Nat West, but even so.

   I found the blue plastic comb I have been searching for since last year. It was on top of the wardrobe. Why? How did it get there? I have never climbed on the wardrobe to comb my hair. I suspect Julian. He is a big fan of Jeremy Beadle's.

11 p.m. Too tired to write much, just to put it on the record that I am lying in Mrs Hedge's bed. It is very comfortable. My new address is now:

8 Sitwell Villas
Summertown
Oxford.

Sunday March 3rd

I didn't know where I was when I woke up, then I
remembered. I smelt bacon cooking, but I didn't go
downstairs. I felt like an intruder. I got up, tiptoed to
the bathroom, got dressed, made my bed, then sat
on the bed listening to sounds from below. Eventually,
driven by hunger, I went downstairs. Mrs Hedge was
not there. The breakfast plates were still on the kitchen
table. The kitchen pedal bin was overflowing. There
were eggshells on the floor. The cupboard under the
sink was full of filthy yellow dusters. The fridge was
full of little saucers containing mouldy leftovers. The
grill pan was unwashed. The *Observer* was speckled
with tinned tomato juice.

It is as I feared: Mrs Hedge is a slut. The phone rang
non-stop. Took messages: 'Ted phoned.' 'Ian rang.'
'Martin called.' 'Call Kingsley back.' 'Julian rang: Are
you going to the launch on Tuesday?'

I was mopping the kitchen floor when Mrs Hedge
returned. She was carrying a large shrub and four tins
of Carlsberg.

'Christ,' she said. 'It looks like I've struck lucky. Do
you like housework, Mr Mole?'

'I find it difficult to tolerate disorder,' I said.

She went out into the garden to plant the shrub, then sat on the patio on an iron chair, swigging Carlsberg out of the tin. She didn't seem to notice the cold. When it started to rain, she came into the house, got a golfing umbrella from the jar in the hall, and went back out again. I went up to my room to work on my novel, *Lo! The Flat Hills of My Homeland*.

When I next went downstairs, there was no sign of Mrs Hedge. I was pleased to see three tins of Carlsberg still left in the fridge. She may be a slut and an eccentric, but, thank God, she is not yet an alcoholic.

Monday March 4th

Mrs Hedge was still in bed when I got back from work. The kitchen was a disgrace. The Carlsberg was gone from the fridge. She must have drunk them in bed! It is the only conclusion.

Wednesday March 6th

Went to Pandora's to pick up my post. Nothing exciting. Letters from the Market Harborough Building Society, *Reader's Digest* and Plumbs, a firm promoting stretch covers. How did Plumbs get hold of my name and address? I have never shown the slightest interest in soft furnishings. Pandora has turned my box room into a study. I opened a file on her desk marked, 'Lecture Notes'. Didn't understand a word. They were written in what was probably Serbo-Croat.

Thursday March 7th

I walked into the bathroom tonight without knocking. Mrs Hedge was in the bath, shaving her legs. I will buy a bolt for the door tomorrow. I'd guess she is at least 38C.

Friday March 8th

Mrs Hedge said, 'Feel free to invite your friends round, Mr Mole.' I told her that I hadn't got any friends. I walk alone.

When I told Leonora the same thing, she said, 'Before our next session, please try to speak to a stranger; smile and initiate a conversation; and make a new female friend.'

Saturday March 9th

There was a stranger in the kitchen when I came down. He was eating Marmite on toast. He said, 'Hi. I'm Gerry.'

I smiled and said, 'Good morning. I'm Adrian Mole.'

That was the extent of our social intercourse. I found it difficult to initiate a conversation with a man wearing a woman's negligee and nothing else.

I made myself a cup of tea and left.

I wish I was back in my box room.

Monday March 11th

Mr Major on the news. He said, 'I want us to be where we belong, at the very heart of Europe, working with our partners in building the future.'

A peculiar thing: Mr Major cannot say the word 'want' to rhyme with 'font', which is the correct English pronunciation. For some reason, he says '*went*'. I suspect that this disability stems from childhood. When little John lisped, 'I want some sweeties,' etc., etc. Did his father leap down from his trapeze and shout, 'I'll give you *want*!'? Or shout, 'Say *want* again and I'll beat you black and blue,' thus leaving little John sobbing into the sawdust of the Big Top and unable to pronounce that little English word?

My heart goes out to him. He is obviously in urgent need of therapy. It seems to me that we have both suffered for having embarrassing fathers. I will bring the subject up when I next see Leonora.

Tuesday March 12th

Brown slipped down a grassy bank and bruised his coccyx at the weekend. He was collecting owl droppings. He has been incapacitated and is lying on a plank on his bedroom floor. Ha! Ha! Ha! Ho! Ho! Ho! Three cheers!

Wednesday March 13th

Brown's deputy, Gordon Goffe, is throwing his weight (twenty stone) about. He is conducting an enquiry into 'postage stamp pilfering'. This is just my luck. I was about to send the opening chapters of my novel *Lo! The Flat Hills of My Homeland* off to Faber and Faber today. I shall have to fork out for the stamps myself. Once they have read these chapters, they will be panting for the rest.

Thursday March 14th

The Birmingham Six have been released from prison.

Gordon Goffe is lumbering around the offices, carrying out spot checks on our drawers. Megan was found to have an illicit box of DOE ballpoints. She has received an oral warning. No session with Leonora this week. She is attending a conference in Sacramento.

Friday March 15th

Barry Kent was on *Kaleidoscope* reading from *Dork's Diary*. The little I heard was nihilistic rubbish. Goffe barged into my cubicle and said that I was not allowed to listen to Radio Four during office hours. I pointed out that Mr Brown had never objected.

Goffe said, 'I am not Mr Brown,' a statement so stupid that I was lost for an answer. I've got an answer now, at three minutes past midnight, but it is obviously too late.

Saturday March 16th

Called round to Pandora's flat for my letters. Nothing of interest: circular for thermal underwear; *Reader's Digest* competition entry form – prize: a gold bar; Plumbs catalogue, offering discount on mock velvet curtains. I am twenty-four next month and I must confess, dear journal, that I had expected by now to be in correspondence with interesting and fascinating people. Instead, the world seems to think of me as a person who gets up in the morning, puts on his thermal underwear, draws his mock velvet curtains and settles down to read his new copy of *Reader's Digest*.

The cat looked thin, but was pleased to see me. I gave it a whole tin of cat food. Pandora was out, so

I had a good look around the flat. Her underwear drawer is full of disgusting sex aids. Bluebeard is obviously not up to it.

Sunday March 17th

Had an interesting talk about the Russian elections with the girl in the local newsagent's this morning. Then, as she handed me my *Sunday Times*, she remarked (joking, I presume), 'It's very heavy. Would you like me to help you carry it home?'

'No,' I jocularly replied. 'I think I can just about manage.' Though, as I took it, I pretended to buckle under its weight. How we laughed.

She is quite pleasant-looking in a sort of un-assuming sort of way.

6.00 p.m. On rereading the above, I think I have been unfair to the girl in the newsagent's. A gingham nylon overall is not the most flattering of garments. And I didn't see her legs, as they were behind the counter at all times.

I have just read the *Sunday Times* books section and was appalled, astonished and disgusted to see that *Dork's Diary* is at number ten in the hardback bestseller list today!

Monday March 18th

Called in at the newsagent's for a packet of Polos on the way to work. The girl joked that I was paying for fresh air, i.e. the hole! This hadn't occurred to me before, so I handed the Polos back to her and said, 'Okay, I'll have Trebor Mints instead.' Again, we laughed uproariously. She has certainly got a good sense of humour. Legs still behind the counter. Brown still malingering at home. Goffe still rampaging in the office. Leonora will be pleased to hear about the girl in the newsagent's.

Tuesday March 19th

A letter from Pandora, my first at Sitwell Villas:

Sunday, March 17th

Adrian,

I have asked you many times to return the front door key to this flat. You have not yet done so. I'm afraid I must give you an ultimatum. Either the key is in my possession by 7 p.m. on Tuesday night, or I call out a locksmith, have the lock changed and send the bill to you. The choice is yours. I will no longer tolerate you:

a) interfering in the cat's feeding pattern;

b) snooping in my underwear drawer; or

   c) helping yourself to food from the refrigerator when I
      am not there.

As I have said, I will continue to redirect your post (such
as it is) and relay any messages that I consider to be urgent.

At 6.59 p.m., I pushed an envelope containing the key,
a ten-pence piece and a terse note under the door of
Pandora's flat. The note said:

Pandora,
a) In my opinion, the cat is too thin and appears to be
   lacking in energy;
b) I vividly remember you saying that 'Suspenders, etc.
   are symbols of women's enslavement to men's lust.'
   Ditto vibrators;
c) The pot of crab paste in the refrigerator was *mine*. I
   purchased it on February 20th this year. I have the
   receipt to prove it. I admit that I did help myself to a
   slice of bread. I enclose, as you cannot fail to see,
   a ten-pence coin, as remuneration for the slice of
   granary.

Wednesday March 20th

How do I get the legs out from behind the counter?

Thursday March 21st

Her name is Bianca. A strange name for somebody
working in a newsagent's. They are usually called Joyce.
I saw her carrying boxes of crisps from a delivery lorry
into the shop. Legs okay, but ankles a bit bony, so, on
a scale of one to ten, only five.

9.00 p.m. Leonora was in a strange mood tonight. She
was annoyed because I was fifteen minutes late. I
pointed out to her that she would be paid for the full
hour.

She said, 'That's not the point, Adrian. Our sessions
together are carefully structured. I insist that you are
punctual in future.'

I replied, 'My chronic unpunctuality is one of my
many problems. Shouldn't you be addressing it?'

She crossed her shapely legs under her black silk
skirt and I saw a flash of white. From that point on I
was helpless and could only nod or shake my head in
answer to her questions. Speech was beyond me. I
felt that if I opened my mouth I would utter crude
inarticulate protestations of lust, which would frighten
her and signal the end of our time together.

Ten minutes before the end of our session she said,
'You are displaying typically regressive behaviour at
the moment, shall we take advantage of it?'

I nodded and she encouraged me to talk about my
earliest memories. I remembered being bitten by a

dog and my grandma applying iodine to the wound. I also remember my (now dead) grandad kicking the dog round the kitchen.

Then it was time to fork out £30 and leave.

Saturday March 23rd

Mrs Hedge asked me if she should marry Gerry, sell up and move to Cardiff. I advised against it. I have only just settled in, found out how to work the grill pan, etc. I can't face looking for alternative accommodation. Anyway, why ask me? I've only spoken to the ugly brute a few times.

Sunday March 24th

The lavatory seat was up, so I guessed that Gerry was *in situ*. I went to buy my newspaper from Bianca and, on my return, sure enough, Gerry and Mrs Hedge were in the kitchen eating eggs and bacon. Mrs Hedge didn't look pleased to see me. I threw a few Rice Krispies into a bowl and took them up to my room. But, by the time I'd got upstairs, they had stopped snapping and crackling and popping, which annoyed me considerably. I loathe soggy cereals.

Monday March 25th

Gerry is now a fixture. I am like a cuckoo in the nest.
A gooseberry in the strawberry patch. A piranha in
the goldfish bowl. Conversation stops when I enter the
kitchen or sitting room and they are there. I wanted
to watch the Oscar ceremony on television tonight,
but Gerry snatched the remote control and kept it on
his lap, thus denying me the pleasure of *seeing* that
gifted and modest actor Jeremy Irons win an Oscar
for Britain. I had to hear this wonderful news on Radio
Four and visualize Mr Irons's delight myself. Whoever
said that the 'pictures are better on the radio' was
completely wrong.

Tuesday March 26th

I have asked Bianca to give me prior warning, should a
suitable-sounding postcard arrive at the shop offering
accommodation. She agreed. I think she finds me
personable. Haste has changed the meaning of the
above sentence: postcards cannot walk into a newsagent's and talk suitably. Leonora cancelled tonight's
appointment. 'An emergency,' she said.

Am I not an emergency? My sanity hangs by a
gossamer thread. Leonora is the only barrier between
me and the public ward in a lunatic asylum. How will

she live with herself if I am admitted foaming at the mouth and struggling inside a straitjacket?

Wednesday March 27th

Mr David Icke, who is a famous Leicester person, has revealed that he is a 'channel for the Christ spirit'. He went on television and told the goggling press that his wife and daughter were 'incarnations of the archangel Michael'. He blamed the planet Sirus for bringing earthquakes and pestilence to the world. Gerry and Mrs Hedge mocked him and said he is barmy, but I'm not so sure. We Leicester people are known for our level heads. Perhaps Mr Icke knows something that we ordinary mortals cannot even guess at.

Thursday March 28th

Bianca studied Astronomy in the sixth form. She said this morning, 'There is no such planet as Sirus.' But, as I pointed out to her, 'David Icke did say that Sirus was *undiscovered*, so naturally no reference *would* be found to it in the books, would it?'

A queue formed, so we were forced to break off our discussion. I called in on my way home from work, but Bianca was busy – some old git was complaining about his newspaper bill.

Friday March 29th

The more I think about David Icke's predictions, i.e.
that the world will end unless it 'purges itself of evil',
the more it makes sense. He is a successful man, who
was employed by the BBC, no less! He was also a
professional goalkeeper for Hereford City. We should
not be too quick to scoff. Columbus was once mocked
for remarking that the world was round. Something
that was verified by the first US astronauts.

My mother rang tonight to ask me what I want for
my birthday next week. I told her to get me the usual,
a book token. She went on to say that Leicester was
agog about David Icke, and that 'there has been a run
on turquoise track suits' (worn by Mr Icke's followers).
She said she felt sorry for his mother. Apparently, Mr
Icke claimed he was born on the planet Sirus, whereas
his mother said in the *Leicester Mercury* that she distinctly remembers giving birth to him in the Leicester
General Maternity Hospital.

I ran out of bananas tonight. I had to walk to
the outer suburbs before finding an off-licence that
stocked them.

Saturday March 30th

Posted two birthday cards to myself. I put second-class stamps on, so they should get here by Tuesday morning.

Spring

Spring

Monday April 1st

A man with a Glaswegian accent rang me in my cubicle this morning and said, 'I have just finished reading the opening chapters of your novel *Lo! The Flat Hills of My Homeland* and I want to publish it next year. Would an advance of £50,000 be acceptable?'

I stammered out, 'Yes,' and asked to whom I was speaking.

'A. *Fool!*' laughed the imposter, and slammed the phone down.

How cruel can you get? For fifteen seconds, I had achieved my ambition. I was a professional writer living in my own house. I'd learned to drive. I had a car in the garage. I had a Rolex watch and a Mont Blanc pen. There was an air ticket to the USA in the pocket of my cashmere coat. Fan letters bristled inside my leather briefcase. Invitations to literary events were stacked on the mantelpiece. Then my dream was shattered by the hoaxer and I went back to being simple Adrian Mole, who was halfway through writing a report on newt movements, in a cubicle in a DOE building in Oxford. I suspect Goffe.

Tuesday April 2nd

Birthday cards from Mother, Rosie, Father, Grandma, Mrs Hedge and Megan. Six cards in all. Not bad, I needn't have posted two to myself.

Presents
1) Ten pound book token from mother.
2) W. H. Smith voucher from father (fiver).
3) 2 pairs of socks from Mrs Hedge (white).
4) Cactus plant from Megan (obscene).

No surprise party. No candles to blow out. No singing. No Leonora until Thursday.

Wednesday April 3rd

I am twenty-four and one day old. *Question*: What have I done with my life? *Answer*: Nothing.

Graham Greene died today. I wrote to him four years ago, pointing out a grammatical error in his book *The Human Factor*. He didn't reply.

Thursday April 4th

I trimmed my beard this morning. Mrs Hedge screamed when I came out of the bathroom. When she recovered, she said, 'Christ, you look like the Yorkshire Ripper.'

I had a terrible session with Leonora. I went into her room with the self-esteem of an anorexic aphid and came out feeling worse.

My low self-esteem on entering Leonora's room was due to an acrimonious phone conversation I'd had with my mother earlier. She had rung the office to ask me if I would like to go to a party given by Barry Kent to celebrate the success of *Dork's Diary*. The venue is the North East Leicester Working Men's Club, and half of Leicester has been invited.

I said to my mother, 'I would sooner wash a corpse.'

My mother accused me of petty jealousy, and then had a tantrum and recited my faults: arrogance, over-weening pride, snobbery, pretension, phoney intellectualism, wimpishness, etc., etc.

I recited this to Leonora who said, 'I suggest that you take on board what your mother is saying. I also suggest that you *go to the party*.' She said that she had bought five copies of *Dork's Diary*: for her husband, Fergus; for her best friend, Susan Strachan; for her therapist, Simon; for her supervisor, Alison; and for herself. I was totally gobsmacked. When Leonora said that it was time to go, I refused to leave my chair.

I said, 'I can't bear the thought of you enjoying Barry Kent's work.'

Leonora said, 'Tough, give me thirty pounds and leave.'

I said, 'No, I am totally sexually obsessed by you.

I think about you constantly. I have revealed my innermost feelings to you.'

Leonora said, 'Yours is a standard reaction. You'll get over it.'

I said, 'Leonora, I feel betrayed. I refuse to be treated like an example from a text book.'

Leonora stood up and tossed her magnificent head and said, 'Ours is a professional relationship, Mr Mole. It could never be anything else. Come and see me next Thursday.'

'Okay,' I said. 'Take your thirty pieces of silver.'

I flung a Market Harborough Building Society cheque made out for thirty pounds onto the desk and left, slamming the door.

If my father had allowed me to abandon that dummy in my own time, I'm convinced I would now be enjoying perfect mental health.

Saturday April 6th

Am I the only person in Britain who has an open mind re the David Icke sensation? Bianca described him as a 'barmpot' this morning – but as I pointed out to her, Jesus himself was reviled in his day. The press were against him and the money-lenders slagged him off to all and sundry. Also, Jesus was a bit of an eccentric as regards clothes. He would not have won a 'Best Dressed Palestinian of the Year Award'. But, had track suits been around in Christ's day, he would almost certainly have opted for the comfort and wash-ability of such garments.

Sunday April 7th

Dork's Diary is now at number eight. Glanced through my *Illustrated Bible Stories* tonight and was startled to find on page 33 (Raising Lazarus) that Jesus is wearing turquoise robes!!!

Monday April 8th

Brown is back, but he is wearing a noisy surgical corset, which is quite useful (the noise, not the corset), because Megan is seeing Bill Blane (Badger Dept) on the side. I like Bill. He and I discussed David Icke at the Autovent today. Bill agrees with me that Sirus could have been overlooked by the astronomers. It could well have been hidden behind another, bigger planet.

The emir of Kuwait has promised to hold parliamentary elections next year. He has announced that women will be allowed to vote. Good for you, Sir!

Tuesday April 9th

John Major has been cross-examined by the press about his 'O' levels. I hope this won't remind Brown about my own, non-existent, Biology 'A' level. Why, oh why, couldn't I have been born an American? College students there are given multiple choice type exams. All the dumbos have to do is put a tick against what they think is the right answer.

    Example: Question: Who discovered America?
                Was it: a) Columbus?
                          b) Mickey Mouse?
                          c) Rambo?

Wednesday April 10th

Bill Blane has asked me to go for a drink after work tomorrow. This could be the start of a new friendship.

Thursday April 11th

Bill wanted to talk about Megan. In fact, he talked about her all night. I couldn't get a word in edgeways, apart from saying, 'Same again?' when it was my turn to buy a round. I drank far too much (three pints) and in my muddled state started walking back to

Pandora's flat before realizing my mistake and turning my steps towards the Hedge household.

Friday April 12th

Worked on *Lo! The Flat Hills of My Homeland* tonight. Started Chapter Eleven:

As he skirted the top of the hill, he looked east and saw the city of Leicester glowing in the dying embers of the setting sun. The tower blocks reflected the scarlet rays and bounced them against the factory chimneys and the Royal Infirmary multi-storey car park. He sighed with the glorious anticipation of knowing that he would soon be tramping the reconstituted concrete streets of his home town. He could have entered the city by a more discreet route – turned off the motorway at Junction 23 – but he preferred this, the route of the sheep drovers, and anyway, he hadn't got a car.

He had been away too long, he thought. He had grown tired of the world and its attractions. Leicester was where his heart was. He strode down the hill, his eyes were wet. The wind, perhaps? Or the pain of absence? He would never know. The sun slipped away behind the grand edifice of the Alliance and Leicester Building Society headquarters and he felt the stealthy black fingers of night collect around him. Soon it was dark. Still he descended. Down. Down.

Not many people know that Leicester lies in a basin, he ruminated. No wonder it is the bronchitis centre of the world, he thought. Before long, he had descended the hill and he was on flat ground.

I think this is probably the best writing I have ever done. It is magnificent. I hope I can maintain this standard throughout the novel.

Saturday April 13th

Notes on *Lo!*:

a) Should I give my hero a name? Or should I continue to call him '*he*', '*him*', etc.?
b) Should the narrative be stronger? At the moment, not much happens. *He* leaves Leicester, then comes back to Leicester. Should the reader know what *he* does in between?
c) Should *he* have sex, or go shopping? Most modern novels are full of references to one or the other – the reading public obviously relishes such activities.

Descriptions (to be slotted in somewhere):

The tree bent in the wind, like a pensioner at Land's End.

The fried egg spluttered in the frying pan like an old man having a tubercular coughing fit in a 1930s National Health Service hospital.

Her breasts were as full as hot air balloons. Her face was infused with anger, her eyes flashed like a manic lighthouse whose wick needed cleaning.

The tea was welcome. *He* sipped it gratefully, like an African elephant which has previously found its waterhole to be dry, but then remembered, and walked to, another.

From now on, I shall write down these thoughts and ideas as they come to me. They are far too good to waste. Publication looks to be within my grasp.

Sunday April 14th

Woke at 8.30, had breakfast: cornflakes, toast, brown sauce, two cups of tea. Collected *Sunday Times* and *Observer*. Bianca not there. *Dork's Diary* has gone to number seven. Changed into blazer. Walked round Outer Ring Road, came back. Brushed and hung up blazer. Lay on bed. Slept. Woke up, put on blazer, went out, had pizza in Pizza Hut. Came back, lay on bed, slept. Woke, had bath, changed into pyjamas and dressing gown. Cut toenails, trimmed beard, inspected skin. Tidied tapes into alphabetical order, Abba to Warsaw Concerto. Went downstairs. Mrs Hedge in kitchen, in tears at kitchen table. 'I've got nobody to confide in,' she cried. Made crab paste sandwiches. Went to bed. Wrote up journal.

I can't go on like this; I'd have more of a social life in prison.

Monday April 15th

Went to see DOE doctor, Dr Abrahams. I told him I was depressed. He told me he was depressed. I told him that my life was meaningless, that my ambitions remained unrealized. He told me that his dream was to become the Queen's gynaecologist by the age of 44. I asked him how old he was. He told me that he was 45. Poor old git. He gave me a prescription for my depression. I asked the chemist if there were any side effects.

She said, 'Well, there's lack of concentration. Your physical movement may be reduced. You'll notice an increase in heart rate. There'll possibly be sweating and tremors, constipation and perhaps difficulty in urinating. Bit depressing, really, isn't it?'

I agreed with her and tore the prescription into pieces.

Wednesday April 17th

Rocky gave me a lift to work this morning in his limo. We discussed Pandora, how arrogant she is, etc. Rocky said, 'But, y'know, Aid, I'll always love the girl, she's, y'know, kinda like *unique.*'

I congratulated Rocky on his use of the word 'unique'.

Rocky told me that Carly Pick, his girl friend, is teaching him new words.

I said, 'So, she's extending your vocabulary, is she?' But he looked at me blankly, from which I inferred that she hadn't been at it for long.

When the car drew up outside the DOE, I was pleased to see that Brown was looking out of his office window. He ducked out of sight, but he couldn't have failed to see me exiting from the limousine. It won't hurt Brown to know that I mingle with the rich and powerful.

Robert Maxwell has saved the *Mirror*. He is a saint!

Thursday April 18th

The Newport Pagnell newts seem to have settled down, thank God. The road plans are finalized and construction is due to start next month.

Mrs Brown came to the office today. She had lost her handbag in the Ashmolean Museum. Brown was entirely unsympathetic. Before he closed his office door, I heard him say, 'That's the second time this year, you stupid cow.' He would not have spoken to Megan like that. Mrs Brown is very pretty. It's just that her clothes are horrible. It's as though there is a lunatic living in her wardrobe who orders her what to wear every morning. She can get away with looking ridiculous in Oxford. People probably assume that she is just another barmy professor, but she would be a laughing stock in Leicester.

Saturday April 20th

Mrs Hedge crying again this morning. I must away from this Vale of Tears. I need cheerful people around me.

Bianca handed me a card this morning. It said, in mad handwriting:

ROOM TO LET
Academic household willing to let room free to tolerant person of either gender, in return for light household duties/babysitting/cat-sitting. Would suit working person with most evenings free. Please ring Dr Palmer.

I rang immediately from the phone box outside the newsagent's. A bloke answered.

DR PALMER: Christian Palmer speaking.
ME: Dr Palmer, my name is Adrian Mole. I've just seen your postcard in the newsagent's.
DR P: When can you start?
ME: Start what?
DR P: Looking after the bloody kids.
ME: But you don't know me.
DR P: You sound okay and you've already proved you can

use a telephone. So you can't be a total simpleton.

Have you got all your faculties: four limbs, eyesight?

ME: Yes.

DR P: Ever been done for molesting kiddie-winkies?

ME: No.

DR P: Got any particularly nasty personal habits?

ME: No.

DR P: Good. So when can you start? I'm on my own here.
My wife's in the States.

The telephone receiver was dropped. Suddenly I heard Palmer shout, 'Tamsin, put the top back on that bottle of bleach! Now!'

He came back on the phone and gave me his address in Banbury Road.

I went into the newsagent's and asked Bianca what newspapers and magazines Palmer read. This is a sure sign of character. It was a baffling list:

Newspapers: the *Observer*, the *Daily Telegraph*, the *Sun*, the *Washington Post*, the *Oxford Mail*, the *Independent*, the *Sunday Times*, *Today*.

Magazines: *Time Out*, *Private Eye*, *Just Seventeen*, *Vogue*, *Brides*, *Forum*, *Computer Weekly*, *Woman's Own*, *Paris Match*, *Gardening Today*, *Hello!*, the *Spectator*, the *Literary Review*, *Socialist Outpost*, the *Beano*, *Angler's Weekly*, *Canoeist*, *Viz*, *Interiors*, *Goal!*

I stopped her and said, 'Palmer's newspaper bill must be enormous. How does he pay it?'

'Infrequently,' she replied.

Sunday April 21st

Dr Palmer is tall and thin and wears his hair like Elvis Presley did during his silver-cloaks-in-Los-Angeles phase. His first words to me were, 'On your way to a fancy dress party?' He laughed and fingered the lapels of my blazer.

I mumbled something neutral and he asked, 'Is that beard *real*?'

I assured him that I had grown it myself and he said, 'How old are you?'

I answered, 'Twenty-four,' and he laughed a strange laugh, like a dog's bark, and said, '*Twenty-four*: so why the hell do you want to walk round looking like bloody Jack Hawkins?'

'Who's Jack Hawkins?' I asked.

'He's a film star,' he replied. 'Everybody's heard of Jack Hawkins.' He looked annoyed for some reason. Then he said, 'Well, unless you're twenty-four, that is.'

We were still standing on the doorstep of his decrepit house. A line of dirty, unrinsed milk bottles stood on the step. A little kid of unknown sex ran up the hall and tugged at Palmer's trousers. 'I've done a great big one! Come and look, Daddy!' it said.

We all three went into a gigantic room which seemed to be a kitchen, living-room and study combined. In the middle of the floor stood a potty in the shape of an elephant. Dr Palmer looked in the potty and exclaimed, 'Tamsin, that is a truly wonderful piece of shit.'

I averted my eyes as he carried the potty out of the room. Then I heard him shouting, 'Alpha! Griffith! Come and see what Tamsin's done!' There was a thundering on the stairs. I looked into the hall and saw two other androgynous children looking into the potty, saying, 'Wow!' and 'Mega shit!'

I adjusted my blazer in the mirror over the large fireplace and thought that the Dr Palmer household was unsuited to one of my temperament. I do not like to hear little children swear and I prefer them to be dressed in proper clothes and to have hairstyles which give a clue to their sexual orientation. However, when Dr Palmer came back from emptying the potty, I was pleased to see that he was drying his hands, which indicated to me that he knew the fundamentals of hygiene. I agreed to inspect the free room. We climbed the stairs, followed by Tamsin, Griffith and Alpha, who spoke to each other in a language I was not familiar with.

'Is it Welsh they're speaking?' I asked.

'No,' Palmer laughed. 'It's Oombagoomba. It's their own language. They're wearing their Oombagoomba clothes.'

I looked at the rags and bits of cloth and shawls, etc. with which the kids were festooned and was relieved to find out that it was not their usual mode of dress. I too used to have my own made-up language (Ikbak), until my father beat it out of me during a long car journey to Skegness.

The 'free room' turned out to be the whole of the attic floor. It had a kitchen at one end, and a private bathroom at the other. There was a proper desk. I could imagine reading the proofs of *Lo!* at that desk.

'You can do what you like up here,' said Palmer, 'apart from serial killing.'

'Are you a teacher?' I ventured.

'No,' he said. 'I'm leading a research project on popular culture. We are trying to establish why people go out to pubs, discos, bingo sessions, to the cinema, that sort of thing.'

'It's to enjoy themselves, isn't it?' I said.

Palmer laughed again. 'Yeah, but I've got to stretch that very simplistic answer into a three-year study and a seven-hundred page book.'

As we went down the stairs, I mentioned to Dr Palmer that as well as being an excellent tenant, I am also a novelist and a poet.

He groaned and said, 'So long as you *never* ask me to look at your manuscripts, we'll stay the best of friends.'

He made me a cup of coffee after grinding up some beans and he told me a bit about his wife, Cassandra, who is in Los Angeles directing a film about mutilation. She sounds horrific, although he claims to miss her. I am too tired and confused to write more. Dr Palmer has told me he must know by Wednesday if I want the room. He's got to go out on Friday to a darts competition.

Monday April 22nd

Should I go, or should I stay?

Can I stand babysitting for three children, four nights a week?

I could save £75 a week. In a year, that is . . .? As usual, when faced with mental, or even physical, arithmetic, my brain has just left my body and walked out of the room.

Thank God for calculators. Nine hundred pounds! It's not as if I would be sacrificing my social life. I haven't got one and, with a bit of luck, Mrs Palmer will stay in America, or fall over Niagara Falls, or something.

Thursday April 25th

Rang Palmer from the office and told him that I would be moving in tonight. Rang Pandora; asked if Cavendish would help me to move.

'Moving?' she said. 'Again?' Then, 'You make more moves than a tiddlywink.'

Rang Mrs Hedge, asked her to take my Y-fronts out of the washer and hang them on my bedroom radiator to dry. Mentioned that I would be moving on.

She said, 'Everybody does, eventually.'

*

Rang my mother and gave her my new address in case of a family tragedy. She yakked on for half an hour about President Gorbachev's threat to resign and predicted that the USSR was in danger of collapse. I cut in eventually and said, 'I no longer take an interest in world events. There is nothing I can do to influence them, so why bother?'

Rang Grandma, in Leicester. Had a long chat about Princess Diana. Grandma doesn't think she's been looking happy lately. I voiced my own concern. Diana is too thin.

Rang Market Harborough Building Society to notify change of address.

Rang Waterstone's. Pretended to be irate reader; threatened to sue them for selling pornography, i.e. *Dork's Diary*.

Rang Megan. Pretended to be Brown. Said, 'God, I love you, Megan,' in his horrible squeaky voice.

Eventually, Brown burst in and demanded that I get off the phone. I sincerely hope he hasn't been listening outside the door.

I had a compulsion to visit Leonora again. She agreed to see me immediately. She was wearing a white dress. She looked like a sacrificial virgin. I wanted to deflower her, but I found myself talking about Bianca.

Leonora leant forward in her chair, displaying her dark cleavage. I found myself saying that I was quite interested in Bianca, although I found her lack of cleavage disappointing.

Leonora said, 'But could you love Bianca?'

I said, 'The idea is ridiculous. The thought of *her* doesn't keep me awake at night, but the thought of *you* does.'

Leonora sighed and said, 'I suggest you cultivate this friendship with Bianca. I am a married woman, Adrian. Your obsession with me is typical of a therapist/client relationship. It is called transference. You must face the truth about your feelings.'

I said, 'The truth about my feelings is that I don't love you. I just want to go to bed with you.'

Leonora said, 'Thirty pounds please.'

I felt like a client paying a whore.

Friday April 26th
Moving Day

Cavendish and Palmer are old friends. When they saw each other, they did that arms-clasped-on-each-other's-shoulders, then grin-and-shake, which so many men in Oxford seem to go in for these days. As I removed my possessions from the back of the Volvo and tried to stop Tamsin, Griffith and Alpha from interfering, I heard Cavendish and Palmer laughing like madmen in the living-room. I'm not sure, but I think I heard the word 'blazer' mentioned. The children spoke Oombagoomba all night until their father returned at 11.30 p.m. They flatly refused to go to bed, or to converse with me in English. Instead, they lay under the massive pine table on a pile of cushions and jabbered away in that made-up lingo. It was like being abroad; if you closed your eyes.

Saturday April 27th

Bought *The White Hotel* by D. M. Thomas this morning. If it is even half as good as *The Great Babylon Hotel* by Arnold Bennett I will be more than satisfied. When Christian saw me take it out of the carrier bag, he raised his eyebrows and said, 'Don't leave it lying around. Alpha's got a reading age of thirteen.'

I said, 'You should encourage your child to read.'

Christian snapped, '*The White Hotel* is a bit heavy for a kid who still believes that fairies live at the bottom of the garden.'

I must say this surprised me. I went down to the bottom of the garden yesterday. It is covered in rusting toys and stinking garden rubbish. It is hardly Fairyland.

At 11.30 p.m., I opened *The White Hotel*, read for ten minutes, then got out of bed and bolted the door. It must never fall into Alpha's hands.

Monday April 29th

Babysat. Christian is at the semi-final of a darts competition with his dictaphone and clipboard. Do the big-bellied darts players realize that they are taking part in a research project? I doubt it. They all seem to have tunnel vision, which I suppose is an advantage if you play darts for a living.

Christian told me today that Bianca was enquiring about me, asking if I'd settled in. He told her that the kids like me. I wish he'd told me. Christian asked me why I don't ask Bianca for a date. I answered nonchalantly that I was too busy. But, dear journal, the truth is that I'm afraid *she might refuse.* My ego is but a frail and fragile thing and furthermore am I sure I want to commit myself to a person who works in a newsagent's shop?

Notes on Bianca:

Negative

1. She is pleasant-looking but certainly not a head-turner, unlike Leonora, who is capable of stopping the traffic.
2. When I mentioned that my walk to work was 'pleasantly Chekhovian', largely due to the blossoming cherry trees, she looked at me blankly and asked me what 'Chekhovian' meant.
3. Her hips do not look capable of bearing a child.
4. She wears Doc Marten boots.

5. She is a Guns 'n' Roses fan.

Positive
1. She is kind, especially to the children who linger over the sweets section in the newsagent's.
2. I seem to be able to make her laugh.
3. Her skin looks like white silk. I have a strange desire to stroke her face whenever I am close to her.

Tuesday April 30th

I'm glad April is over. It is a bitter-sweet month. The blossom is out, but the wind still swells around and flaps the bottoms of your trousers unless you tuck them into your socks.

Beard bushy now. Food gets caught in it. Brown pointed out a piece of egg white at 9.30 a.m. I ate my boiled egg at 7.39 this morning. Since that time, I have spoken to, or been seen by, at least thirty people. Why did no one else point out that I had egg white in my beard? It is not as if it was a *small* piece. As egg white goes, it was quite a large piece, and as such, impossible to overlook. I will have to buy a small hand mirror and check my beard regularly after meals. I cannot risk such social embarrassment happening again.

Wednesday May 1st

Babysat. Griffith asked me to help him with his model of a Scud missile, which he is making out of a toilet roll tube and cut-up bits of washing-up liquid bottle. I pointed out to him that I am a pacifist.

Griffith (six) said, 'If your sister was being threatened by a gang of vicious thugs, would you stand by and do nothing?'

I said, 'Yes.' Griffith doesn't know my sister Rosie. She is quite capable of seeing off a gang of vicious thugs.

Christian was back from his karaoke evening by 11 p.m. Apparently, he'd been forced to sing 'Love is a Many Splendoured Thing' in order to keep his cover. So his research project *is* an undercover operation. That explains why Christian changes out of his ragged denims and into his Sta-Pressed polyesters before joining his unsuspecting fellow low-culture vultures.

Thursday May 2nd

Read through the whole of *Lo! The Flat Hills of My Homeland* manuscript so far. It is crap from start to finish.

Friday May 3rd

Perhaps I was too harsh last night. *Lo!* has passages of sheer brilliance. About five.

Saturday May 4th

Left *Lo!* on kitchen table overnight. No comment from Christian this morning, though Alpha said, 'You've spelt "success" wrong on page four. It's got two c's and two s's.' Christian didn't even look up from his *Sun*.

If there's one thing I can't bear, it's a precocious child. It's completely unnatural. I was tempted to tell Alpha that any fairy living in the Hell Hole at the bottom of her garden should have a tetanus jab, but I didn't.

I received the new Plumbs catalogue this morning, offering me four tapestry-look cushions with frilled edges at the bargain price of £27.99. How did they track me down? The envelope came direct from Plumbs to the Banbury Road. Are they watching me?

Sunday May 5th

Put blazer on and went for my customary Sunday walk around the Outer Ring Road at 2 p.m. Some old git

in a Morris Minor stopped and asked me for directions
to the Oxford Bowling Club. As if *I*'d know! Returned to find house full of Christian's friends having
what he described as a 'fondue party'. They were
dipping raw vegetables into a stinking pot of what
looked like yellow emulsion paint. I declined to join
them.

Monday May 6th

Bianca was passing as I left for work this morning, so
we walked part of the way together. As we crossed at
the lights, her hand brushed mine. An electric shock
passed through me. I apologized and put my hand in
my raincoat pocket to prevent another such occur-
rence. She took off her Sony headset and invited me
to listen to her Guns 'n' Roses tape. After five minutes
I handed it back to her. I couldn't stand the din.

Tuesday May 7th

Bianca was there again outside the house this morning.
I don't know why she keeps coming down this road.
It's not on her route to work.

Babysat. The kids went to bed at 9.30 p.m., after I'd
read them the first three chapters of *Lo!* For once, they
seemed quite tired, yawning, etc.

Wednesday May 8th

Bianca there yet again, tying the laces on her Docs. She told me that she gets bored in the evenings – she hasn't got that many friends in Oxford. She misses the cinema especially, but she is fed up with going on her own. She went on and on about Al Pacino. She has seen *Sea of Love* eleven times. I haven't seen it once. Personally, I can't stand the man. I told her that I too haven't seen a film in ages. When she left me and went into the newsagent's, she looked irritable. Premenstrual, probably.

Thursday May 9th

Babysat. At 7.30 p.m. I offered to read more of *Lo!* to the kids, but they said, as one, that they were very tired and wanted to go to bed! I had a peaceful night washing my working wardrobe and shampooing my beard. Christian got back at 1 a.m. after observing a fight in an Indian restaurant. I advised him to put his trousers in cold water to soak overnight. Turmeric is one of the most stubborn stains known to man. It is a pig to shift once it has gained a hold.

Monday May 13th

A terrible scandal at lunchtime today! Megan Harris and Bill Blane were caught in the act of photocopying their private parts! They would have got away with it, had the machine not jammed. They have both been suspended on full pay, pending an internal enquiry. I am quite pleased. It has saved me from having to photocopy two hundred pages of Newport Pagnell newt drivel.

Tuesday May 14th

It is totally unfair. Because of Bill's suspension, I have been given responsibility for the entire Badger Department. Brown threw the badger case histories on my desk and said, 'You're a friend of Bill's. Sort this out.'

Just because Brown was the one to force the photocopy room door open yesterday, there's no need to take it out on me. He may have lost a mistress and a secretary, but he must remember what he learned on his managerial training course and keep his head.

Wednesday May 15th

Up at dawn to catch taxi to badger set. I must learn to drive. On the return journey, the taxi driver kept complaining about the smell. I had the fresh badger droppings in a sealed DOE jar, so how the aroma came in contact with the taxi driver's nose is a mystery to me. Personally, I found the fresh air 'pine tree' hanging from the roof of his taxi to be much more olfactorily offensive.

Friday May 17th

I am already up to my ears in newts and badgers, and now Brown is hinting that I may also be given responsibility for *natterjack toads*! He is obviously trying to force me into resigning or having a nervous breakdown due to overwork.

Photocopies of Megan's and Bill's private parts are being passed around the office. I think this is absolutely disgusting – a total invasion of their private lives, not to mention their private parts. Anyway the copies are so blurred that it is impossible to tell which is Bill's and which is Megan's. That photocopier never did work properly.

Bianca came round with Palmer's newspaper bill tonight. I answered the door and would have invited her in, but I didn't want her to think that sexual intercourse was on my mind – though, of course, it was. It's never off my mind. She had obviously gone to some trouble with her clothes, for a change. She was wearing tight denim jeans, high-heeled ankle boots and a white shirt which was tucked into a brown leather belt. She had recently washed her hair. I could smell Wash 'n' Go – the shampoo I use myself. It was on the tip of my tongue to ask her if she would come in for coffee, but something held me back.

She didn't seem to want to move off the doorstep – she kept talking about how fed up she was with having nothing to do in the evening. I was forced to stand in a cold wind, wearing only a shirt and trousers. This could result in a severe chill. I must check my tempera-ture over the next few days.

Sunday May 19th

As predicted, I woke up yesterday feeling feverish, so I had three tablespoons of Night Nurse (though it was only 8.30 in the morning) and went back to sleep. Today, Christian knocked on my door at 12.30 p.m. and asked if I could watch the kids for three hours while he attended a 'Stag Strip' at a Working Men's Club. I reluctantly agreed and dragged myself out of bed.

I myself, personally, have never watched a strip show. I wouldn't know how to arrange my facial features. Would I watch with studied indifference like

TV detectives when they are forced to interview scumbag low-life in strip joints? Would I smile and laugh as though *amused* by the sight of a young woman taking her clothes off? Or would I swallow frequently, pant and goggle my eyes and reveal to onlookers that I am sexually excited? I fear the latter.

When Christian returned, he went upstairs. The shower was running for at least three quarters of an hour. I suspect he was symbolically cleansing himself.

Today was an Oombagoomba day, so I didn't – indeed, *couldn't* – talk to the kids.

The Chancellor, Norman Lamont, is going to sue a sex therapist for damages. But *how* did she damage you, Lamont? The British people should be told.

A letter from *Reader's Digest* arrived on Saturday, informing me that my name has been shortlisted out of many hundreds of thousands to receive a huge cash prize! All I have to do is agree to subscribe to the *Reader's Digest* magazine! It is easy to sneer at *Reader's Digest*, but it has to be said that they are an extremely handy way for busy bibliophiles to keep abreast of matters literary.

Plumbs have also written to me, offering to supply a lace circular tablecloth, plus a plywood circular table, should I not already have one. I must say I was quite tempted by both.

Thursday May 23rd

Christian held a drinks party last night and Cavendish and Pandora came round. I tried to engage Pan in conversation, but every time I did, I could see her eyes looking past me over my shoulder. Am I such boring company?

At 8 o'clock, Bianca turned up in a shiny, tight black dress. I introduced her to Pandora. Pandora said to her, 'That's a great dress, Bianca. God, don't you love lycra? What did we do without it?' They then yakked on about lycra for half an hour. In my opinion, Pandora's expensive education has been entirely wasted.

There must have been at least fifty people in the living-room/kitchen/study at one point. The majority of them were graduates, but you would never have known it from their conversation. The main topics were, in order:

1) *The Archers*
2) Football (Gazza)
3) Lycra
4) University cuts
5) Princess Diana
6) Alcoholism
7) The Oxford murder
8) Oats
9) Rajiv Gandhi being burnt
10) The Gossard Wonderbra

Call themselves intellectuals! My efforts to talk about my book, *Lo! The Flat Hills of My Homeland*, were met with cool indifference. Yes! The so-called 'best brains' in the land listened to me for a few minutes, then made feeble excuses to leave my company. At one point, just as I was telling him about my hero's apprenticeship to a cobbler in Chapter Eleven, a man called Professor Goodchild moved away, saying: 'Please spare me the sodding details.'

Yet only minutes later, I overheard him talking about his fish tank and how best to clean it.

Bianca left at 11.30 in the company of a dubious-looking type in a black leather jacket. He is something big in astrophysics, apparently, though in my opinion he looked like the type of moron who wouldn't know which end of a telescope to put his eye to.

As we were cleaning up after the party, Christian said, 'Adrian, take a tip from me, throw that bloody blazer away. Buy yourself some fashionable, young man's clothes!'

I replied (quite wittily, I thought), 'Lycra doesn't suit me.' He looked puzzled for a moment, then continued to wash the glasses.

Pandora also commented unfavourably, saying, 'That fucking awful blazer: give it to Oxfam, for Christ's sake.'

Perhaps I will.

I lay awake for hours imagining Bianca and the astrophysicist gazing at the stars together. Would he trust her with his telescope?

Friday May 24th

A household on my route to work has acquired an American pit bull terrier. On the surface, it seems to be a friendly beast. All it does is stand and grin through the fence. But in future I will take a different route to work. This is a considerable inconvenience to me, but I cannot risk facial disfigurement. I would like the photograph on the back of the jacket of my book to show my face as it is today, not hideously scarred. I know that plastic surgeons can work miracles, but from now on I am taking no chances.

Brown was in a foul mood today. He has had a letter from Megan's solicitor. She is threatening to sue him for defamation of character, unless she is reinstated immediately. I hope Brown caves in. Megan's replacement, Ms Julia Stone, is one of those superior types who never lose their money in chocolate machines in railway stations.

Saturday May 25th

Oxford is full of sightseers riding on the top deck of the tourist buses and walking along the streets gazing upwards. It is extremely annoying to us residents to be asked the way by foreigners every five minutes. Perhaps it is petty of me, but I quite enjoy sending them in the wrong direction.

I have just remembered! When I gave my blazer to the Oxfam shop yesterday, my condom was in the top pocket. This means that, should a sexual opportunity arise today, I will be unprepared. It also means that I can no longer go into the Oxfam shop – at least, not until Mrs Whitlow, the volunteer helper I gave it to, dies or retires. Mrs Whitlow has often congratulated me on being a 'decent, clean-living young man', though I have given her absolutely no grounds for thinking so.

Monday May 27th

Why do the banks have to close just because it is a Bank Holiday? It is a day when people want to *spend* money, isn't it? Borrowed £5 from Christian for Durex and bananas.

Tuesday May 28th

I have just finished Chapter Twelve of *Lo! The Flat Hills of My Homeland*, 'The Dog It Had To Die':

He closed the front door of his mother's house with a sigh. He had left her slumped on the kitchen table surrounded by brimming ashtrays and empty Pilsner cans. Upstairs, his father was injecting heroin into his collapsed veins. The family pet, an American pit bull terrier, looked out from the front window of the squalid terraced house and growled, showing its fearsome jaws. He walked down the street and tossed off greetings to the stunted neighbours. A couple fornicated in an alley, their eyes dead, their motions automatic. He wept internally. Anguish gripped his soul. He rued the day he had been born. Then, suddenly, a shaft of sunlight fell across his path. He stood, mesmerized. Was it a sign, a portent, that his life would improve from now?

He turned and went back to the house. He opened the front door. The dog, Butcher, growled at him, so he strangled it until the dog lay dead at his feet. He felt Evil, but at the same time strangely Good. The dog had been nothing but a nuisance and nobody ever took it for a walk. His conscience was clear.

Wow! Powerful writing, or what? I believe Dostoevsky would be proud of me. Canine murder is surely a first in English fiction. I expect I'll get a few letters from English dog lovers when *Lo! The Flat Hills of My Homeland* is published, but I shall write back and point out that I am an artist and must go where my pen takes me.

Wednesday May 29th

Julia Stone and I had a brief conversation at the Autovent machine today, while my oxtail soup was pouring into my plastic cup. She asked me not to use the ladies' lavatory again. I pointed out to her that the men's lavatory had run out of toilet paper, but she said if I continued to 'invade female space', she would report me for sexual harassment. She also said that she had checked the post book and that I used more postage stamps than any other member of staff.

I told her in cold tones – though not as cold as my oxtail soup – that I wrote more letters, therefore I needed more stamps. But I fear I have made an enemy.

Ms Julia Stone is a daunting woman. My throat constricts whenever I have to talk to her. Lipstick might help. Her, not me.

Christian returned from the Golden Gate nightclub with a black eye. His crime was to look at a yob. Yes, the yob accused Christian of 'looking' at him. This is a frightening example of the disintegration of British society. Yobs used to *enjoy* people looking at them. From now on, I shall avert my eyes whenever I see a yobbish person approaching me.

After Christian had stopped fussing with his eye and gone to bed, I sat at the kitchen table and tried to get some sex into *Lo! The Flat Hills of My Homeland*.

Chapter Thirteen: Deflowering

He lay in bed in his Parisian bedroom. Fifi began to remove her lycra dress. His breathing rate increased. She stood revealed before him, her chest strained beneath her Gossard Wonderbra, her knickers were clean and nicely ironed. He reached out for her, but she said to him in her French accent, 'No, no, *mon amour*, I am thinking you must wait.'

His ardour increased as he noticed that her bottom was smooth and had no pimples. He groaned and . . .

It's no good. I can't write about sex. Not even French sex in Paris.

Saturday June 1st

Two letters, one from Plumbs, offering me a set of matching towels with my personal monogram embroidered on the hems; the other from Sharon Bott.

Dear Adrian,

I hope you are well long time no see I saw your mum in town and we had a talk she said how much Glenn looked like you I said yes and she said is he our Adrians Sharon I must know she just came out with it like that I din't know what to say I have got to confess I was seeing someone else at the time as I was seeing you I din't want to double time you Adrian but you was sometimes moody and I wanted some laffs I was only young. Glenn is going to school now and is a big boy. My mum says you should pay some money but I said no mum it would not be fair cause I dont no if Glenn is Adrians or not Your mum gave me this address to write to you I hope they're is not to many spelling mistakes and that but I never write anything now since I left school their is no need I saw Baz on the telly did you   He has done alright for himself I have not got a bloke now sinse Daryl run off with the video and

£35 I had saved for the gas   I have put a bit of wait on but I am going to go to Waitwatchers and get it off   You mum said she would babysit   she is so good to me.

  Cheers,

    Sharon

Sunday June 2nd

I spoke to my mother this morning and ordered her to keep her nose out of my affairs. She said, 'Glenn is the *result* of one of your affairs,' and put the phone down. From then on, I got the engaged signal.

I was enraged by my mother's interference. How dare *she* pontificate about *anybody*'s morals? I know for a fact that she was not a virgin on her wedding night. Grandma told me.

And anyway, my mother should not have spoken in the plural. I have not had *affairs*. I have had *an* affair. In the singular. With Sharon Bott, a simpleton who cannot differentiate between 'they're', 'there' and 'their' and is a virtual stranger to the comma and full stop. She probably thinks that a semi-colon is a partial removal of the intestines.

Memo to self: Is the kid mine? Blood test? Letter of denial?

2 a.m. Wrote to Sharon.

3 a.m. Destroyed the letter. (My reply to her must be carefully crafted. I need time to read up on the law relating to paternity.)

Tuesday June 4th

Thank God, Prince William has made a full recovery after being bashed on the head by a golf club. When I think how close we came to losing our future King, my heart stands still. Well, not literally *still*, it doesn't *stop*, but I'm glad the kid is better. I phoned Grandma in Leicester. She wanted to know why Prince Charles didn't pick his son up from the hospital. She said, 'Doesn't he know that it is traditional in our English culture?' She thinks that the monarchy is losing touch with the common herd and she complained bitterly that the Royal Yacht *Britannia* costs thirty-five thousand pounds a week to run.

5.00 p.m. The *Oxford Mail* has just informed me that the emir of Kuwait has yet to announce the date for democratic elections to be held in his country. Puzzling, considering all the trouble and expense the allies went to only recently. Get a move on, emir! I'm also informed by the *Oxford Mail* that the Royal Yacht *Britannia* costs thirty-five thousand pounds *a day*! *A day*! I phoned Grandma immediately and put her right. She was disgusted.

Query: Why does the emir of Kuwait spell his name with a small 'e'?

Friday June 7th

I spent the morning writing a report on a projection of newt births and the early afternoon on a report on the distribution of badgers. But I fear some of the paperwork has got mixed up. As I was photocopying the reports, I noticed that I had muddled a few facts. However, Brown was shouting down the corridor for the reports, so what could I do? His management meeting was due to start at 4 p.m., so I had no choice but to hand him the papers.

Saturday June 8th

Wrote to Sharon:

Dear Sharon,

How very nice to hear from you after all this time.

I'm afraid that there is no chance at all that I can be the father of your child, Glenn.

I have recently had my sperm counted and I was informed by the Consultant Spermatologist that my sperms are too weak to transform themselves into a child. This is a personal tragedy to me, as I had planned on having at least six children.

You mention in your letter that you were double-timing me. I was most upset to read this – our relationship was not ideal, I know; we came from different backgrounds: me: upper working/lower middle; you: lower working/underclass. And, of course, our educational attainments are worlds apart, not to mention our cultural interests. But despite these differences, I had thought that we rubbed along quite well sexually. I see absolutely no reason why you should have betrayed me and sought out another sexual partner. I confess that I am devastated by your revelation. I feel cheap and used. I would be most obliged to you if you would stop seeing my mother. She is addicted to human dramas of any kind. She thinks of herself as a character in a soap opera. I suggest that you should go to Weight-watchers (not *Wait*watchers, by the way), and hire yourself a competent child-minder. My mother is not to be trusted with young children: she dropped me on my head at the age of six months, whilst taking a boiled egg out of a saucepan.

Anyway, Sharon, it was very nice to hear from you.

Regards,

Adrian

PS. Who were you double-timing me with? Not that it matters, of course. I have had a constant stream of lovers since our relationship ended. It is simple curiosity on my part. But I would like to know the youth's name, though it is not in the least important. Don't feel obliged to let me know. I just think it may help you to get it off your chest. Guilt can eat away at you, can't it? So would you please write to me and let me know the youth's name? I think you would feel better about yourself.

Sunday June 9th

I spent the day quietly, working on Chapter Fourteen of my novel.

He looked at the young boy, who was poking a stick at a natterjack toad. 'Stop!' he cried. 'It is one of an endangered species. You must be kind to it.' The young child stopped poking at the toad and came to hold his hand.

'Who are you?' lisped the child. He longed to shout, 'I am your *father*, boy!' but it was impossible. He looked at Sharon Slagg, the boy's mother, who weighed twenty-one stone and had numerous split ends. How could he have once enjoyed sexual congress with her?

He let go of the boy's hand and said, 'I am nobody, boy. I am a stranger to you. I am simply a person who loves the planet we live on – including the dumb creatures that we share our planet with.'

With that, he walked away from his son. The boy exclaimed, 'Please, stranger, don't go.' But he knew he must, before Sharon Slagg looked up from *Damage*, the book she was reading on the park bench. The boy said, 'I wish you were my father, stranger, then I too would have a daddy to come to parents' evenings.'

He thought his heart would break. Sobbingly, he walked

away across the grass until the boy was the size of an ant in the distance.

I don't mind admitting that this piece of writing had me wiping my eyes. God, I'm clever. I can tug at the heart strings like no other writer I know. I do feel that my book is now vastly improved by these additions. It still lacks narrative thrust (or does it?), but nobody can say that it doesn't engage the reader's emotions.

Thursday June 20th

Bianca came round tonight to borrow a cup of Basmati rice. She has stopped going out with the Stargazer: she said his breath smelled constantly of kiwi fruit.

She is a nicely spoken girl, with quite an extensive vocabulary. I asked her why she was serving in a newsagent's. She said, 'There are no jobs for qualified engineers.'

I was totally gobsmacked to learn that Bianca has an upper second degree in Hydraulic Engineering – from Edinburgh University. Before she left with the rice, I asked her to mend the leaking shower in my room. She said she would be pleased to come round tomorrow night and see to it for me. She asked if she should bring a bottle of wine with her. I said there was no need. She looked disappointed. I sincerely hope she is not an alcoholic or a heavy drinker who needs a 'nip' before she can do a job of work.

I am making good progress on the novel. I took out my epic poem *The Restless Tadpole* tonight. It is amazingly good, but I can't spare the time to finish it. The novel has to come first. There is no money in poetry. Our Poet Laureate, Ted Hughes, has been wearing the same jacket in his photograph for the past twenty years.

Friday June 21st

Bianca came round *avec* tool box, but *sans* wine. She hung about after she'd fixed the shower and talked about how lonely she is and how she longs to have a regular boy friend. She asked me if I have a regular girl friend. I replied in the negative. I sat in the armchair under the window and she lay on my bed in what an old-fashioned kind of man could have interpreted as a provocative pose.

I wanted to join her on the bed, but I wasn't sure how she would react. Would she welcome me with open arms and legs? Or would she run downstairs screaming and ask Christian to call the police? Women are a complete mystery to me. One minute they are flapping their eyelashes, the next they are calling you a sexist pig.

While I tried to work it out, a silence fell between us, so I started to talk about the revisions I am making to my book. After about twenty minutes, she fell into a deep sleep. It was a most awkward situation to be in.

Eventually, I went downstairs and asked Christian to come and wake her up. He sneered and said, 'You're unbelievably stupid at times.' What did he mean? Was he referring to my inability to fix my own shower head, or to my timidity regarding sex?

When Bianca woke up she looked like a sad child. I wanted to put my arms round her but before I could she had grabbed her tool box and run down the stairs without saying goodnight.

Saturday June 22nd

Had a most satisfactory shower this morning. The force of the water has improved considerably.

2.00 p.m. Worked on Chapter Fifteen. I have sent *him* to China.

11.30 p.m. I have brought *him* back from China. Can't be bothered to do all that tedious research. I just got him walking along the Great Wall, then flying back to East Midlands Airport. I went down to the kitchen to make myself a cup of hot chocolate and told Christian about my hero's trip to China. Christian said, 'But you told me that he is a pauper. Where would he get the money for his air ticket?' God, how I hate pedants!

1.00 a.m. Insert for Chapter Fifteen:

What was this on the mat? He bent down and picked up a letter from the *Reader's Digest*. On the front of the expensively papered envelope was written 'OPEN AT ONCE'. He obeyed. Inside was a letter and a cheque for one million pounds! He was fabulously rich! 'How shall I spend it all?' he asked the cat. The female cat looked back at him inscrutably. 'China?' he said. 'I'll have a day trip to China!'

I hope this satisfies my pedantic landlord and my most critical of readers.

Sunday June 23rd

At breakfast, I told Christian how my hero got the money to go to China. He now wants to know what my hero does with the *remaining* money. There is no pleasing him.

12 noon

Chapter Sixteen: A Gratuitous Act
The beggar outside Leicester bus station stared in disbelief as £999,000 showered down onto his head. *He* walked away, a pauper once again.

5.00 p.m. Saw Bianca walking towards me as I was returning from my perambulations around the Outer

Ring Road this afternoon. She was wearing shorts and a T-shirt: her legs, apart from the ankles, looked superb, long and slim. I hurried towards her. To my astonishment, she crossed over the road and ignored me. So much for Christian telling me that she fancies me! It's certainly a good job I didn't join her on the bed the other night. I could be in prison now, on a sexual assault charge.

The next time I go to the library I will try to find a book that explains to the intelligent layman how women's brains work.

Summer

Wednesday July 3rd

Brown reminded me today that I have two weeks'
holiday entitlement which I will lose unless I take it
within the next two months.

Rang my travel agent. Told her I want two weeks in
Europe in a four star hotel with half board, but for no
more than £300. She promised to ring back if anything
turned up in Albania. I said, 'Not Albania, I hear the
food is inaudible.' After I'd put the phone down, I
remembered that the word for bad food is, of course,
'inedible'. I hope I'm not suffering from an early onset
of senile dementia. Word-loss is an early signal.

Friday July 5th

The travel agent rang today. Unfortunately, the call
was put through to Brown's office, where I was being
reprimanded because of a mix-up over the newt and
badger reports. The Department of Transport had
received the erroneous intelligence that a family of
badgers had appeared on the route of the projected
Newport Pagnell bypass. Naturally, I was constrained

by Brown's presence, so I was unable to concentrate on what the travel agent was saying.

I said that I would ring her back, but she said, 'You must book it *now* if you want it.'

I said, 'Book what?'

She said, 'Your holiday. A week on the Russian lakes and rivers, and a week in Moscow. A fortnight for £299.99, full board.'

'Go ahead,' I said.

Saturday July 6th

Rang 'Easy-pass' Driving School and booked a free lesson as advertised in the *Oxford Mail*. I take to the road on Thursday, July 18th.

I have taken driving lessons before, but have been badly let down by my previous instructors. They were all incompetent.

Sunday July 7th

Babysat while Christian went to bingo. He won £7.50 and was near to winning the area prize of £14,000. He only needed two fat ladies.

Monday July 8th

Worked on *Lo*! Shall I give *him* a name? If so, what shall it be? It needs to express his sensitivity, his courage, his individualism, his intellectual vigour, his success with women, his affinity with nature, his proletarian roots.

Tuesday July 9th

How about Jake Westmorland?

Wednesday July 10th

Maurice Pritchard?

Thursday July 11th

Oscar Brimmington?

Friday July 12th

Jake Pritchard?

Saturday July 13th

Maurice Brimmington?

Sunday July 14th

A decision will have to be made soon. I can't move on with my book until it has. Christian prefers 'Jake Westmorland'. However, the man in the greengrocer's likes the sound of 'Oscar Brimmington'. Whereas a bus conductor, whose opinion I sought, was very keen on 'Maurice Westmorland'.

Monday July 15th

Spent the day babysitting. I got the kids to test me on the Highway Code. Somebody kept ringing the house tonight. A woman. All she said was, 'Hello.' But when I asked who was calling she put the phone down. It sounded like Bianca, but why should she behave in such a childish manner?

Tuesday July 16th

Brown had to have his surgical corset adjusted at the Radcliffe Hospital this morning, so I took the opportunity to go into his office and look at my file: 'MOLE – ADRIAN.'

FORESIGHT – NONE

PUNCTUALITY – POOR

INITIATIVE – NONE

RELIABILITY – QUITE GOOD

HONESTY – SUSPECTED OF PILFERING POSTAGE
    STAMPS

ACCEPTANCE OF RESPONSIBILITY – POOR

RELATIONS WITH OTHERS – QUITE GOOD

I believe his 'A' level Biology qualification to be
    bogus.

Wednesday July 17th

Dear Mr Brown,

It is with great regret that I write to inform you of my intention to resign from the Department of the Environment. I will of course serve out my statutory two months' notice. I have been unhappy for some time now with how the department is run. I feel that my talents have been wasted. Collecting badger faeces was not in my original job description.

Also, in my opinion, the protection of animals has reached ludicrous levels. The beasts have more rights than I do. Take bats. If I were to hang upside down and defecate in a church, I would be taken away to an institution. Yet bats are *encouraged* by conservationists such as yourself,

Mr Brown. It's no wonder that our churches are empty of parishioners.

I remain, sir,
    Adrian Mole

At 10.00 a.m. I wrote the above letter, put it into an envelope and wrote 'FOR THE ATTENTION OF MR BROWN'.

At 11.00 a.m., after staring down at the envelope for a full hour, I put it under my blotting pad. Thinking perhaps that I could brazen it out regarding the bogus 'A' level.

At midday, while I was at the Autovent, the envelope disappeared. I searched my cubicle but found nothing, apart from my little blue comb.

At 1.00 p.m., I was summoned to Brown's office and told to clear my desk and leave the premises immediately. He gave me an envelope which contained a cheque for £676.31 = two months' pay plus holiday money less tax and National Insurance.

Who delivered my resignation letter? I suspect the Sexually Harassed One.

So, like three and a half million of my fellow citizens, I am without work.

1 a.m. Christian got me drunk tonight. I had two and a half glasses of Vouvray and a pint of draught Guinness in a can.

Thursday July 18th
Driving Lesson

Stayed in bed until 2 p.m. My driving instructor is a woman called Fiona. She is old (47) and has got lots of loose skin around her neck, which she pulls at in times of crisis. I did *tell* her that it is over a year since I was behind the wheel. I did *ask* if I could practise first on Tesco's Megastore out-of-town car park, but Fiona refused and forced me to drive on real roads with real traffic. So what happened at the roundabout was not my fault. Fiona should have been quicker with the dual controls.

Friday July 19th

A letter from Faber and Faber:

Dear Mr Mole,

   I am afraid that I am returning your manuscript, *Lo! The Flat Hills of My Homeland.*

   It is a most amusing parody of the English *naïf* school of fiction.

   However, we do not have a place for such a book on our list at the moment.

   Yours sincerely,
      Matthew Evans

After reading the letter six times, I tore it in pieces. Mr Evans will be sorry one day. When my work is being auctioned in hotel rooms, I will instruct my agent to disqualify Mr Evans from the bidding.

There was no reason to get up, so I stayed in bed all day, wondering if there was any point in going on. Pandora despises me, I am out of work and I am incapable of driving a car in a straight line. At 7 p.m. I got out of my bed and rang Leonora. A man answered the phone: 'De Witt.'

'It's Adrian Mole,' I said. 'Could I speak to Leonora?'

'My wife's dressing,' he said; which threw me for a while. Images of Leonora in various lingerie outfits flashed into my mind.

'It's an emergency,' I managed to croak out. I heard him put the receiver down with a crack and shout, 'Darling, it's for you. Something about moles.'

There was a muttered oath, and then Leonora came on the phone.

'Yes?'

'Leonora, I'm in despair. Can I come round and see you?'

'When?'

'Now.'

'No, I'm giving a dinner party at eight and the first course is an asparagus soufflé.'

I wondered why she would think I was remotely interested in her menu.

'I need to talk to you,' I said. 'I've lost my job, my

novel's been rejected and I crashed the driving school car yesterday.'

'They are all life experiences,' she said. 'You will come out of this a stronger man.'

I heard her husband shouting something in the background. Then she said, 'I have to go. Why don't you talk to that girl, Bianca? Goodbye.'

I did as I was told. I went and stood outside Bianca's house and looked up at her flat. Nobody went in or came out.

After watching for an hour I went home and got back into bed. I hope the De Witts and their guests all choked on their asparagus soufflé.

Saturday July 20th

Cassandra Palmer turned up on the doorstep this afternoon. Christian's face turned white when he saw his wife. The children greeted her politely, but without much enthusiasm, I noticed. She looks as though she wrestles in mud for a living. I loathed her on sight. I cannot stand big women who shave their heads. I prefer them with hair.

Her first words to me were, 'Oh, so *you*'re the cuckoo in the nest.'

Sunday July 21st

The dictatorship of Cassandra started this morning. Our household is not allowed to drink tap water, coffee, tea or alcohol, nor to eat eggs, cheese, chocolate, fruit yoghurt, Marks & Spencer's lemon slices . . . etc., etc. The list goes on forever. There are also things we mustn't say. I happened to mention that Bianca's boss, the newsagent, is a fat man. Cassandra snapped, 'He's not fat, he's dimensionally challenged.'

I laughed, thinking this was a good joke, but Cassandra's mouth turned into a grim slit and with horror I realized she was serious.

Christian remarked to his wife over lunch that he was losing his hair, 'going bald' were his words. Once again, Cassandra snapped into action.

'You're a little follicularly disadvantaged, that's all,' she said, as she inspected the top of her husband's head.

I cannot share this house with that woman, or *her* language. It is not as though she is pleasant to look at. She is as ugly as sin, or, as she might put it, she is facially impaired.

Monday July 22nd

I asked Bianca if she would keep a lookout for suitable accommodation. She agreed, though there is nothing to keep me here in Oxford any more, apart from my unrequited love for Dr Pandora Braithwaite.

Tuesday July 23rd

> *Dr Braithwaite*
> Since you gained your Ph.D.
> You have had no time for me.
> You loved me once, you could again.
> Pandora, give up other men!
> You swore to love me for all time.
> As long as Moon and June would rhyme.
> Please marry me and be my wife.
> For you I'll sacrifice my life.
> I'll stay at home, I'll cook and clean
> In the background, never seen.
> When you return from brainy toil,
> I'll have the kettle on the boil.
> While you translate from Serbo-Croat,
> I will shake our coco doormat.
> I'll gladly wash your duvet cover,
> If only I can be your lover.

I put the poem through Pandora's door at 4 a.m. This is my last-ditch attempt to sound out Pandora's true feelings for me. Leonora has said that I must move on emotionally. What will Pandora's reaction be?

Wednesday July 24th

I found this letter on the doormat.

Dear Adrian,

You woke me at 4 a.m. with your clumsy manipulation of my letter box. Your poem caused my lover and me much merriment. I hope, for your sake, that it was *meant* to be funny. If it was *not*, then I urge you to seek further psychiatric advice from Leonora. She told me that you have stopped seeing her regularly. Is it the cost?

I *know* you can afford £30 a week. You don't drink, or smoke, or wear decent clothes. You cut your own hair, you don't run a car. You don't gamble or take drugs. You live rent-free. Withdraw some money from your precious Building Society and *get help*.

Regards,
  Pandora

PS. Incidentally, I am *not* a Ph.D., as you state in your poem. I am a D. Phil. A subtle but important difference here in Oxford.

So that's it. If Pandora came to me tomorrow, begging to be Mrs A. A. Mole, I would have to turn her down. I have moved on. It's Leonora I must see. Must.

Thursday July 25th

5.15 p.m. I have just phoned Leonora and insisted that she gives me an emergency appointment. I said I had something momentous to tell her. She agreed reluctantly.

5.30 p.m. I burst into Leonora's room this evening and found her with another client, a middle-aged man who was sobbing into a Kleenex (woman trouble, I suppose). I was ten minutes early and Leonora was furious and ordered me to wait outside. At 6.30 p.m. precisely, I knocked on her door and she shouted, 'Come.' She was still in a bad mood and so I tried to make conversation and asked her what had upset the sobbing middle-aged man. This angered her even more. 'What is said to me in this room remains confidential,' she said. 'How would *you* feel if I talked about *your* problems to my other clients?'

'I don't like to think about you having other clients,' I confessed.

She sighed deeply and curled a hank of black hair around her finger. 'So what's the momentous happening?' she said eventually.

'I've moved on from Pandora Braithwaite,' I said, and I told her about the poem and Pandora's reaction to it and my reaction to Pandora's reaction. At that moment, a tall, dark man wearing a suede shirt came in. He looked surprised to see me.

'Sorry, darling. I can't find the small grater, for the parmesan.'

'Second drawer down, darling, next to the Aga,' she said, looking up at him in rapt adoration.

'Terribly sorry,' he said.

When he'd gone out, I stood up and said, 'How dare your husband interrupt my consultation with his petty domestic enquiries?'

Leonora said, 'My husband didn't know you were here. I squeezed you in, if you remember.' Her tone was carefully measured, but I noticed that a vein was pulsating on the side of her temple and that she was wringing her hands.

'You should learn to express your anger, Leonora. It's no good for you to bottle it up,' I said.

She then said, 'Mr Mole, you are not making progress with me. I suggest you try another analyst.'

'No,' I said. 'It's you I want to see. You're my reason for living.'

'So,' she said. 'Think what you're saying. Are you saying that without me you would commit suicide?'

I hesitated. Noises of pans banging and glasses tinkling came up from the basement, as did a delicious smell that made my mouth water. For some reason I blurted out, 'Could I stay to dinner?'

'No. I never socialize with my clients,' she said, looking at her slim, gold watch.

I sat down and asked, 'How mad am I, on a scale of one to ten?'

'You're not mad at all,' she said. 'As Freud said, "It

is impossible for a therapist to treat either the mad or those in love."'

'But I *am* in love. With you,' I added.

Leonora sighed very deeply. Her breasts rose and fell under her embroidered sweater.

'That is why I think that seeing another therapist would be a good idea. I have a friend, Reinhard Kowolski, who has a superb reputation . . .'

I didn't wait to hear any more about Herr Kowolski. I left her room and put three ten pound notes on the hall table, next to the laughing Buddha and walked out into the street.

I felt angry, so I decided to express my anger and I kicked an empty Diet Coke can all the way home.

When I got to the attic, I laid out all my job-searching clothes ready for the morning. Then I lay on my bed with the *Oxford Mail* and ringed all the likely looking jobs in the situations vacant columns.

There was nothing that required one 'A' level in English.

Friday July 26th

Went to the Job Centre, but the queue was too long, so returned to find Cassandra in the kitchen, examining the children's books, pen in hand. She picked one up and changed *Winnie the Pooh* to *Winnie the Shit*. 'I hate ambiguity,' she explained, as she snapped the cap back on her Magic Marker.

Saturday July 27th

Saw Brown in W. H. Smith's, buying the current wild-life magazines. He smiled and said, 'Enjoying your life of leisure, Mole?'

I forced a smile to my lips and said, 'On the contrary, Brown, I am working as hard as ever. I am a middle manager at the Book Trust in Cambridge, at £25,000 a year, plus car. I got the position thanks to my having English Literature at "A" level.' Brown stormed off, forgetting to pay for his magazines. He was stopped on the pavement by a security guard. I didn't hang around to watch Brown's humiliation.

Sunday July 28th

Stayed in room all day, out of Cassandra's way. She is insisting that everyone in the house meditates for half an hour each morning. Christian has stopped doing his research into popular culture. Cassandra objected to the smell of cigarette smoke on his clothes when he returned from his low-class haunts. If she is not careful, she will wreck his academic career.

I am living on my savings, but I cannot continue to do so. The State will have to keep me – after all, I didn't ask to be born, did I? And one day the State will be glad it supported me. When I am a high-rate taxpayer.

However, before I throw myself on its mercy, I am going to tramp the streets of Oxford tomorrow and look for a job, any job that doesn't involve driving or working with animals.

Next year, I will have lived for a quarter of a century and as yet I have made no mark on the world – apart from winning a *Leicester Mercury* literary prize when I was seventeen.

If I died tomorrow, what would be written on my tombstone?

> Adrian Albert Mole
> Unpublished novelist
> and pedestrian
>
> Mourned by few
> Scorned by many
> Winner of the *Leicester Mercury*
> 'Clean Up Leicester' Essay Prize

Tuesday July 30th

Why do beggars *always* want money for a cup of tea? Don't any of them drink coffee?

Wednesday July 31st

Why didn't palace flunkies arrange for Princess Diana to be kept dry at the open-air Pavarotti concert last night? If she develops pneumonia and dies, the country will be plunged into crisis and Charles will be devastated with grief. He obviously adores her. Somebody's head should roll.

Thursday August 1st

Dear Adrian,

I was sorry to read about your poor cwallity seed   the person I was seeing on the side was barry kent   I feel better now it is off my chest.

Yours sinserely,
Sharon

Barry Kent! I should have known! He is an amoral, talentless turd! He is lower than a cesspit. He has the prose style of a *Daily Sport* leader writer. He wouldn't know what a semi-colon was if it fell into his beer. The little I have read of *Dork's Diary* forced me to the conclusion that Kent should be arrested and charged with criminal assault on the English language. He deserves to burn in everlasting hell with a catherine wheel tied to his cheating penis.

Friday August 2nd

Dear Sharon,

Many thanks for your commiserations regarding my 'seed', as you put it. May I suggest that you get in touch with Barry Kent (who, as you know, is now both *rich* and famous) and ask him to contribute to Glenn's upbringing? The least Kent can do is to send Glenn to a private school, thus giving his child an excellent start in life.

I remain,

Yours,

Adrian

PS. I am absolutely sure that Barry will be thrilled to hear that he has a child.

PPS. Eton is quite a good private public school.

Sunday August 4th

Cassandra announced at breakfast that she has taken the locks off the bathroom and lavatory doors. 'Inhibitions about nakedness and bodily functions are the reason why the English are no good at sex,' she said. She looked pointedly at her husband, who blushed and rubbed the side of his nose.

The Queen Mother is 91 today. I suppose she doesn't think it is worth getting her teeth seen to now. I can see her point.

Monday August 5th

Contacted Foreign Parts, the travel agents, about my Russian cruise and explained that I have been made redundant and would like to cancel and have my money back. The travel agent told me that it was impossible and told me to refer to the small print on my documents. I peered in vain and eventually went to Boots and bought a pair of 'off the peg' reading spectacles for £7.99. The travel agent was right; I will have to go.

Tuesday August 6th

Christian told me (shamefaced) that Cassandra requires my attic room. She is opening a reincarnation centre where people can get in touch with their former selves. She wants me out of the attic by mid-September. I couldn't help myself. I burst out, 'Your wife is a cow!' Christian said, 'I know, but she used to be a kitten.'

So, no job and, when I get back from the Russian cruise, nowhere to live.

Thursday August 8th

Dear John Tydeman,

The last time I wrote to you, it was to apologize for clogging up the BBC's fax machines with my 700-page novel, *Lo! The Flat Hills of My Homeland*. You sent it back to me (eventually) and said, and I quote: 'Your manuscript is awash with consonants, but vowels are very thin on the ground, thin to the point of non-existence.'

You will, I am sure, be delighted to hear that I have now reinstated the vowels and have spent this year rewriting the first sixteen chapters, and I would value your comments on them. They are enclosed with this letter. I know you are busy, but it wouldn't take you long. You can read them in the BBC's coffee lounge during your coffee breaks, etc.

I remain, Sir,

Yours,

Adrian Mole

10.30 p.m. I have seen Leonora for the last time. She has dismissed me from my post as her client. I over-played my hand and declared my love for her. In fact, it wasn't so much a declaration, it was more of a proclamation. It was probably heard all over Oxford. Her husband heard it because he came into the room with a tea towel and a little blue jug in his hand and asked Leonora if she was all right.

'Thank you, Fergus, darling,' she said. 'Mr Mole will be leaving soon.'

'I'll be outside if you need me,' he said, and left, leaving the door slightly open.

Leonora said, 'Mr Mole, I am calling a halt to our professional relationship, but before you leave I would like to reassure you that your problems are capable of being solved.

'You expect too much of yourself,' she said, leaning forward sympathetically. 'Let yourself off the hook. Be *kind* to yourself. You've expressed your worries about world famine, the ozone layer, homelessness, the Aids epidemic, many times. These are not only your problems. They are shared by sensitive people all over the world. You can have no control over these sad situations – apart from donating money. However, over your personal worries, lack of success with your novel, problems with women, you do have a certain amount of control.' Here she stopped and she looked as though she wanted to take my hand, but she didn't.

'You are an attractive, healthy young man,' she said. 'I have not read your manuscript, so I can't comment on your literary talent or otherwise, but what I do know is that there is somebody out there who is going to make you happy.'

I turned on my dining chair and looked out of the window. 'Not literally out there, of course,' she snapped, following my glance. She stood up, shook my hand and said, 'There will be no charge for this session.'

I said, 'It isn't transference: it's true love.'

'I've heard that at least twenty times,' she said, softly. She rose to her feet. Her rings sparkled under the light and she shook my hand. As I left, I passed her husband, who was still drying the little blue jug twenty minutes later. A suitable case for treatment if ever I saw one.

'I intend to marry your wife one day,' I said, before closing the front door.

'Yes, that's what they all say. Cheerio.' He smiled and went towards Leonora and I closed the door on a painful – and expensive – period of my life.

Friday August 9th

Adrian,

What the fuck are you playing at, getting Sharon Bott to write to me and ask for money to send her sprog to fucking Eton? I'm down here at Jeanette Winterson's place, trying to finish my second novel and I can do without all this fucking rubbish.

Baz

Saturday August 10th

I looked in the Job Centre window today. There were three vacancies in the window. One for a 'mobile cleansing operative' (road sweeper?), one for a 'peripatetic catering assistant' (pizza delivery?) and one for a 'part-time clowns enabler' (!). I didn't exactly reach excitedly for the Basildon Bond on my return to Stalag Cassandra.

Sunday August 11th

Went to the newsagent's. Bianca is back from Greece. She has got a fantastic tan. She was wearing a low-cut white tee shirt, which displayed her breasts. They looked like small, ripe, russet apples. I asked her facetiously if she had had a holiday romance. She laughed and admitted that she had – with a fisherman who had never heard of Chekhov. I asked if she was going to continue the romance. She gave me a strange look and said: 'How would you *feel* about it if I did, Adrian?'

I was about to reply when a member of the underclass thrust a *Sunday Sport* into her hands, so the moment was lost.

10.00 p.m. How do I feel about Bianca's holiday romance? I'm always pleased to see her, but I can't stop comparing her to the lovely Leonora: Bianca is a Malteser: Leonora is an Elizabeth Shaw gold-wrapped after dinner mint.

Tuesday August 13th

I leave for Russia on Thursday. I bought myself a new toiletry bag – it's time I treated myself. I hope there are some decent women of childbearing age aboard.

I spent the evening packing. I decided not to take any books. I expect there will be a library on the ship, well stocked with the classics of Russian literature in good translations. I hope my fellow passengers are cultured people. It would be intolerable to have to share the dining room and decks with English lager louts. I decided to include a huge bunch of semi-ripe bananas amongst my luggage. I am used to eating a banana a day and I have heard they are in short supply in Russia.

Saturday August 17th

River camp – Russia
It is 7.30 p.m. There is no cruise ship. There are no passengers. Each member of our party is paddling their own canoe. I am crouched inside a two-man tent. Outside are swarms of huge, black mosquitoes. They are waiting for me to emerge. I can hear the river throwing itself over the rapids. With a bit of luck, I will die in my sleep.

The man I have been sharing my tent with, Leonard Clifton, is out chopping trees down with a machete, borrowed from Boris, one of our river guides. I sincerely hope that one of Clifton's trees falls on his horrible bald head. I cannot stand another night listening to his interminable anecdotes about the Church Army.

I told Boris earlier today that I would give him all my roubles if he would arrange for me to be airlifted to Moscow. He paused from repairing the hole in my canoe and said, 'But you must paddle now to the river's end, Mister Mole; there is no inhabitations, peoples or telephonings here.'

On my return to civilization, I will sue Foreign Parts for every penny they've got. At no time did they mention that I would be paddling a canoe, sleeping in a tent, or drinking water from the river. The worst privation of all is that *I have got nothing to read*. Clifton lent me his Bible, but it fell overboard at the last rapids. As I watched it sink, I shouted 'My God, my God, why hast thou forsaken me?' To the bewilderment of the rest of the group and of myself, I must admit.

Monica and Stella Brightways, the twins from Barnstaple, are outside leading the singing of 'Ten Green Bottles'. Leonard and the rest of the gang are joining in lustily.

10.00 p.m. Tent. I have just returned from the forest, where I was forced to urinate into the darkness. I stood with the others round the fire for a moment, drinking black tea.

Monica Brightways had a serious argument with

the scoutmaster from Hull. She claimed she saw him take two slices of black bread from the sack at lunchtime. He denied it vehemently and accused her of hogging the camp fire. Everyone took sides, apart from me, who loathes them both equally.

Capsized eleven times earlier today. The rest of the hearties were furious with me for holding them up. It is all right for them. They are all members of the British Canoe Union. I am a complete novice and crossing a lake in a force-nine gale is something out of my worst nightmare. The Waves! The Wind! The Water! The lowering black Russian sky! The Danger! The Fear!

I pray to God we may soon come to our journey's end. I long for Moscow. Though I will have to stay in my hotel room; the mosquitoes have attacked my face unmercifully. I look like the Elephant Man on acid.

Midnight The drinking of vodka is now taking place. From my tent I can hear every word. The Russians are maudlin. Every time they talk about 'our souls', the English snigger. I crave sleep. I also crave hot water and a flushing lavatory.

Moscow! Moscow! Moscow!

Wednesday August 21st

Moscow train
The lavatory on the train defies description. However, I'll try. After all, I am a novelist.

Imagine that twenty buffalo with loose bowels have been trapped inside the lavatory for two weeks. Then try to imagine that an open sewer runs across the floor. Add an IRA prisoner on dirty protest. Then concoct a smell by digging up a few decomposed corpses, add a couple of healthy young skunks and you come quite near to what the lavatory looks and smells like.

Leonard Clifton is writing to President Gorbachev to complain.

I said, 'I think Gorbachev has other things on his mind at the moment, such as preventing civil war and feeding his fellow citizens.'

A harmless remark, you might think, but Clifton went mad. He screamed, 'You have ruined my holiday, Mole, with your pathetic whingeing and nasty, cynical comments.'

I was totally gobsmacked. Nobody in the group came to my defence – apart from the Brightways twins, who had already informed the group at frequent intervals that they 'loved all living things'. So anything they had to say was irrelevant. They no doubt equate my life with that of a lugworm.

Thursday August 22nd

Hotel room – Moscow
I am staying in the 'Ukraina', near the Moskva River. It looks like a hypodermic syringe from outside. Inside,

it is full of bewildered guests of all nationalities. Their bewilderment stems from the hotel staff's reluctance to pass on any information.

For instance, hardly anybody knows *where* meals are being served, or even *if* meals are being served.

For breakfast this morning I had a piece of black bread, four slices of beetroot, a sprig of fresh coriander and a cup of cold, black tea.

An American woman in the queue behind me wailed to her husband, 'Norm, I gotta have juice.'

Norm left the queue and went up to a group of loitering waiters.

I watched him mime an orange, first on the tree and then off the tree. The waiters watched him impassively, then turned their backs on him and huddled around a portable radio. Norm returned to the queue. His wife shot him a contemptuous look.

She said, 'I just gotta have some fruit in the morning. You *know* that, Norm. You know how my system seizes up.'

Norm pulled a face indicating that he remembered *exactly* what happened to his wife's system when it seized up. I thought fondly about the bunch of bananas upstairs in my room.

They were worth their weight in gold.

At nine-thirty, most of our group gathered in the foyer of the hotel ready to start our visit to Red Square. I lurked behind a pillar, dabbing TCP onto the fourteen mosquito bites which disfigured my face.

The Barnstaple twins, Monica and Stella Brightways,

kept us waiting for ten minutes, claiming that they had to wait for the lift to ascend to where their room was on the nineteenth floor. Eventually we set off in a bus which seemed to have an interior exhaust pipe next to my seat at the back. I coughed and choked on the diesel fumes and made a futile attempt to open the window. The coach driver was wearing a Gorbachev badge and seemed to be in a bad mood. Our coach parked on the edge of Red Square and we got out and gathered around our Intourist guide, Natasha. She held up a red and white umbrella, and we followed behind like moronic sheep. When we got to the Square, it became obvious that something was happening, a protest march or a demonstration of some kind was taking place. I lost sight of the red and white umbrella and became lost in the crowd. I heard an ominous rumbling behind me, but was unable to move.

An old lady in a headscarf shook her fist towards the noise. She screamed something in Russian. Spittle flew out of her mouth and landed on my clean sweater. Then the crowd parted and the rumbling grew nearer and the tracks of a Russian army tank clanked past an inch away from my right shoe. The tank stopped and a young man clambered aboard and began to wave a flag. It was the hammer and sickle flag I'd been used to seeing everywhere. The crowd roared its approval. What was happening? Had Moscow Dynamo won at football? No, something more important was taking place.

A young woman who wore too much blue eye-shadow said to me, 'Englishman, today you have witnessed the end of Communism.'

'I nearly got run over by a tank,' I said.

'A proud death,' she said. I reached into my pocket for a banana to boost my blood-sugar level. I started to peel it. The young woman's eyes filled with tears. I offered her a bite, but she misinterpreted my gesture and shouted something in Russian. The crowd roared and cheered. She then turned and told me she was shouting 'Bananas for all under Yeltsin!' The crowd began to chant. Then the young woman ate my banana.

'A symbolic gesture, of course,' she said.

When I returned to my room, I found a hefty young Russian woman sitting on a chair outside the door. She was wearing a low-cut brown lamé minidress.

She said, 'Ah, Mr Mole, I am Lara. I come to your room, to sleep, of course.'

I said, 'Is this part of the Intourist programme?'

Lara said, 'No. I am, of course, in love with you.'

She followed me into my room and went to the bunch of bananas on the bedside table. She looked down at them with lust in her eyes and I understood. It wasn't me she wanted: it was the bananas. I gave her two. She went away. Intercourse with her might have done me some harm. She had thighs like Californian redwoods.

Friday August 23rd

I lay awake most of the night, scratching at my mosquito bites and regretting my hasty decision and wondering how news about my bananas had spread. The next day the streets were full of rioting Muscovites and we were confined to the hotel.

After lunch (black bread, beetroot soup, a wizened piece of meat, one cold potato), I returned to my room to find that my bananas had gone. I was outraged.

I complained to Natasha, but she only said, 'You had *ten* bananas?' She looked misty-eyed and then snapped, 'You should, of course, have put them in the hotel safe. They will be changing hands on the black market by now.'

I found Leonard Clifton in the gloomy basement bar. There had been a coup against Gorbachev and then a counter-coup by Boris Yeltsin.

'This is bad news for Soviet Communism,' he said, 'but good news for Jesus.'

England! England! England!

I long for my attic room.

Monday September 2nd

Oxford

I am in bed, exhausted and hideously deformed. Why do mosquitoes exist? Why? Cassandra said they are 'a vital component of the food chain'. Well, I Adrian Mole, would gladly *pull* the chain on them. And, if the food chain collapses and the world starves, so be it.

I have written to Foreign Parts, threatening to report them to ABTA unless I receive *all* my money back, plus compensation for the double trauma suffered from the mosquitoes and the revolution.

Tuesday September 3rd

Christian passed by Foreign Parts today. He said it looked deserted. There was a pile of unopened letters on the doormat inside the shop.

Thursday September 5th

A reply from John Tydeman, Head of Drama, BBC Radio.

Dear Adrian,

To be perfectly honest, Adrian, my heart sank when I returned from holiday and saw that your manuscript, *Lo! The Flat Hills of My Homeland* had landed on my desk yet again. You say in your letter, 'I expect you are busy'. Yes, I damned well *am* busy, incredibly so.

What exactly is a 'coffee break'? I've never had a 'coffee break' during the whole of my long career with the BBC.

I drink coffee at my desk. I do not go to a 'coffee break' lounge where I loll about on a sofa and read handwritten manuscripts, 473 pages long. My advice to you (without reading your wretched MS) is to:

1) Learn to type
2) Cut it by at least half
3) Supply a SAE and postage. The BBC is suffering from a cash crisis. It certainly cannot afford to subsidize your literary outpourings.
4) Find yourself a *publisher*. I am *not* a publisher. I am the Head of Radio Drama. Though sometimes I wonder if I am Marjorie Proops.

I am sorry to have to write to you in such terms, but in my experience it is best to be frank with young writers.

Yours, with best wishes,

John Tydeman

Poor old Tydeman! He has obviously gone mad. 'Sometimes I wonder if I am Marjorie Proops' (!) – perhaps the Director General should be told that his Head of Radio Drama is suffering from the delusion that he is an agony aunt.

And he admitted that he hadn't even read the re-edited *Lo! What do we licence-payers pay for*?

Dear Mr Tydeman,

I would appreciate it if you could send my MS back, ASAP. I do not want it circulating around the corridors of the BBC and being purloined by a disaffected freelance producer, anxious to make his or her mark on the world of broadcasting.

    Adrian Mole

PS. Allow me to inform you, sir, that you are *not* Marjorie Proops.

Saturday September 7th

Spent most of the day in a futile search for a reasonably priced room. As I made my weary way back home, I passed Foreign Parts. There was a note on the door:

This business is closed. All enquiries to Churchman, Churchman, Churchman and Luther, Solicitors.

I didn't take down the telephone number. It was already in my filofax, under 'S'. A middle-aged couple *were* taking the number down, though. They were due to depart tomorrow on a cycling holiday in 'Peter Mayle Country', Provence. They were facing the awful realization that they were not going to see the famous table on the infamous terrace, and possibly take tea with Pierre Mayle plus *femme*.

    As the couple walked away, I heard her say to him: 'Cheer up, Derek, there's always the caravan at Ingoldmells.' A fine woman, indomitable in the face of disaster. Mr Mayle has been cheated of meeting a true Brit.

Sunday September 8th

I have decided to go with Jake Westmorland.

Chapter Seventeen: Jake – A Hero of Our Time
Jake stood on top of the tank in Red Square. What a good job I took Russian at school, instead of French, he thought. Then, quieting the multitudes by a small gesture of his hand, he spoke.

'I am Jake Westmorland,' he shouted. The revolutionary hordes bellowed their grateful recognition. A sea of banners waved joyously. The sultry Russian sunlight glinted on the dome of St Basil's Cathedral as Jake tried to quieten the crowds and begin his speech. The speech that he hoped would prevent the disintegration of the Soviet Union . . .

Monday September 9th

I have written eleven speeches for Jake and thrown them all in the bin. None of them was capable of changing the course of world history.

. . . But before Jake could make the speech that would almost certainly have saved the Soviet Union, a shot rang out and Jake fell off the tank and into the arms of Natasha, his Russian mistress. She threw Jake over her shoulder and the silent crowd parted to let them through.

Thursday September 12th

Cassandra has ordered me to be out of the house by noon on Saturday! The lousy, stinking undergraduates have hogged all the private rented accommodation. I had no choice but to throw myself on the mercy of Oxford Council. But the Council official I spoke to today maintained that I am 'intentionally homeless' and refused to help me. I have started collecting cardboard boxes. Either to pack my belongings in, or to sleep in – who knows?

Friday September 13th

Christian has taken the children to see his mother in Wigan. He is a spineless coward. The hideous Cassandra is walking around the house in her absurd clothes, singing her ludicrous rapping songs. I asked her tonight if I could store my books in the attic until I've found a place of my own. She replied, 'Books?' as though she'd never heard the word before.

I said, 'Yes, *books*. You know, those things with cardboard covers stuffed with paper. People read them, for pleasure.'

Cassandra snorted contemptuously. 'Books belong in the past, together with stiletto heels and Gerry and the Pacemakers. This is the nineties, Adrian. It's the age of technology.'

She went to her word processor and pressed a button. A series of little green men wearing Viking helmets filled the screen and began to fight with little red men wearing baseball caps, who came out of a cave. Cassandra leaned eagerly towards the screen. I sensed that our conversation was over and left the room.

Query: Is the world going mad, or is it me?

Saturday September 14th

8.30 a.m.

Options
1) Pandora (no chance)
2) Bianca (possible)
3) Mother (last resort)
4) Bed and breakfast (expensive)
5) Hostel (fleas, violence)
6) Streets

11.30 a.m.

1) Pandora turned me down flat. She is a true *Belle Dame sans Merci*.
2) Bianca is away attending a Guns 'n' Roses convention in Wolverhampton. Left note at newsagent's.
3) My mother is out gawping at a new crop circle just outside Kettering.

4) The cheapest B&B is £15.99 a *night*!

5) There is nothing under 'Hostel' in the phone book.

6) I hit the road at high noon.

11.35 p.m. Leicester. Bert Baxter's house

So, it has come to this. I am reduced to sleeping on a Put-U-Up in a pensioner's living-room, which stinks of cats. Baxter is charging me £5 for tonight, plus £2.50 for bacon and eggs. My mother's house is locked and dark, and the key is not in its usual place under the drain cover. In normal circumstances I would have broken the small pantry window and climbed in, but my mother has had a security system installed. Delusions of grandeur, or what?

My father, supposedly penniless, is on holiday in Florida with a rich divorcee called Belinda Bellingham. I know I could go to my grandma's but I can't bear her to find out that I am unemployed and homeless. The shock could kill her. She has my GCSE certificates framed on the hall wall. My 'A' level English certificate is in a silver frame on the mantelpiece in her front room. Why give such anguish to an elderly diabetic?

Monday September 16th

1.35 a.m. I am now trying to sleep on the sofa-bed in my mother's living-room. As I write, the television in my mother's bedroom is blaring. The washing machine is on its spin cycle. The dishwasher is shrieking and somebody is taking a shower. Subsequently, the water pipes are banging all over the house. My stepfather, Martin Muffet, has just gone upstairs with his DIY toolbox. Does nobody sleep in this house?

Tuesday September 17th

My grandma knows all. My mother has told her everything. She is disgusted. I hope she never finds out that Bert Baxter gave me a bed for the night.

Wednesday September 18th

G knows about B&B at BB's. She saw BB in C&A.

Friday September 20th

A postcard of Clifton Suspension Bridge came this morning.

Dear Adrian,

I've only just got your message! Sorry I didn't see you before you left. That Cassandra is a sad woman all right!

I've never been to Leicester. Is it nice? Hope so for your sake!

There's a floor here for you if you fancy coming back to Oxford! I know where I can borrow a double mattress.

Let me know soon, please!
Love,
B.

The exclamation marks gave me some pain. Could I share a floor with a woman who was so profligate with them? And what would the sleeping arrangements be? This 'double mattress' she mentioned. Was it for me only? If so, why a double? I presume she has an adequate bed of her own. I decided to write an ambiguous reply, keeping my options open, but committing myself to nothing. My mother, who had brought the postcard to me in bed, wanted to know *everything* about 'B'. Height, weight, build, colouring, education, class, accent, clothes, shoes. 'Is she nice?' Have I 'slept with her'? 'Why not?' The Spanish Inquisition would be nothing compared to my mother. Nothing.

Dear Bianca,

It was most kind of you to write to me and offer the use of a double mattress and your floor.

I confess to you that when I asked you for your help in solving my temporary difficulty regarding my lack of accommodation, I was in somewhat of a panic.

I am surprised that you responded as you did. Ours has not been a long acquaintanceship. For all you know, I could have severe character faults or a psychotic personality.

I would urge caution in the future. I would not like to see you taken advantage of. I am not sure about my future plans. Leicester has a certain *je ne sais quoi*: it is quite pleasant in the autumn, when the fallen leaves give the pavements a little colour.

Yours,
Best wishes,
Adrian

Sunday September 22nd

I was looking forward to a traditional Sunday dinner with Yorkshire pudding and gravy, etc. But my mother informed me at 1.00 p.m. that she doesn't *do* Sunday dinner any more. Instead, we were driven four miles in Muffet's car to a 'Carvery' where we paid £4.99 a head to be served with slices of cardboard and dried up vegetables by a moronic youth in a chef's that. My sister Rosie spilt Muffet's half pint of Ruddles all over our table. I tried to come to the rescue with half a dozen beer mats – but the beer mats refused to soak up any beer. They repelled all liquid. In the end, the moronic one threw us a stinking dishcloth.

Query: What is the purpose of modern beer mats? Are they now merely symbolic, like the crucifix?

6.00 p.m. My mother has informed me that I have got to pay her board of 'a minimum of thirty-five pounds a week, or you're out on your ear'. Does blood count for nothing in 1991?

Tuesday September 24th

My grandma has said I can move in with her, rent free, providing I cut the grass, wind the clocks and fetch the shopping. I agreed immediately.

Wednesday September 25th

I read the first three chapters of *Lo!* aloud to Grandma tonight. She thinks it is the best thing she has ever heard. She thinks that the publishers who rejected it are barmy. And she has got nothing but contempt for Mr. John Tydeman. She recently wrote to him to complain about the sex in *The Archers*. She claims that he didn't reply personally. Apparently he got a machine to do it for him.

Sunday September 29th

Archers omnibus. Egg, bacon, fried bread, the *People*. Roast beef, roast potatoes, mashed potatoes, cabbage, carrots, peas, Yorkshire pudding, gravy. Apple crumble, custard, cup of tea, extra strong mints, *News of the World*. Tinned salmon sandwiches, mandarin oranges and jelly, sultana cake, cup of tea.

Monday September 30th

Chapter Eighteen: Back to the Wolds
Jake settled back in the rocking chair and watched his grandmother making the corn dolly. Her apple cheeks glowed in the flames from the black leaded range. The copper kettle sang. The canary in the cage by the window trilled along with it. Jake sighed a deep, contented sigh. It was good to be back from Russia and all that unpleasantness with Natasha. Here, he could truly relax, in his grandma's cottage on the Wolds.

Autumn

Autumn

Tuesday October 1st

My father brought Mrs Belinda Bellingham round to
meet me at Grandma's house tonight. I was totally
gobsmacked; she is a posh person! My father has
started to pronounce his aitches religiously and to say
'barth' instead of 'bath'. And he has also discovered
manners: every time my grandma came into the room,
he leapt out of his chair.

Eventually she snapped, 'Sit *down*, George. You're
up and down like a window cleaner's ladder.'

Mrs Bellingham is blonde and pretty, with those
cheekbones that denote centuries of wise breeding. I
thought she was very pale, considering she had just
spent two weeks in the sun. Later in the evening, I
found out that she lives in fear of skin cancer. Apparently she spent her holiday running from one patch
of shade to another. Mrs Bellingham is the managing
director of 'Bell Safe' – a burglar alarm company. My
father starts work next Monday as Mrs Bellingham's
sales director. They tried to persuade my grandma to
allow them to install a burglar alarm at cost price, but
she refused, saying, 'No, thank you. If I have to go

out, I turn the volume up on Radio Four and leave my front door open.'

Mrs Bellingham and my father exchanged scandalized glances. Grandma continued, 'And I've never been burgled in sixty years, and anyroad up, if I had an alarm on the front of the house, folks'd know I've got something valuable, wouldn't they?'

There was an awkward pause, then my father said, 'Well, Belinda, I'll see you home, shall I?'

He fetched her coat and held it out while she put it on. He has obviously been having lessons in social etiquette. When they'd gone, my grandma shocked me by saying, 'Your dad's turned into a right brown-nosing bugger, hasn't he?'

Perhaps she is suffering from the early symptoms of senile dementia. I have never heard her swear before.

Sir Alan Green, the Director of Public Prosecutions, has been caught talking to a prostitute and has resigned. Under the 1985 Sexual Offences Act, a man seen approaching a woman more than once can be stopped by the police. This is news to me. I shall certainly be more careful whom I approach in the street from now on.

Friday October 4th

Grandma and I have scoured the house from top to bottom today. Grandma has a fixation about germs. She is convinced that they are lying in wait for her, ready to pounce and bring her down. I blame the television advertisement for a lavatory cleaner which depicts 'germs' the size of gremlins, who lurk about in the 'S' bend, chuckling malevolently. Although I've seen this advertisement hundreds of times, I simply can't remember what the product is called.

Query: Is television advertising effective?

Later, Grandma sat down and watched the Labour Party singing 'We Are the Champions' as the finale to their conference in Brighton. Not many of the shadow cabinet knew the words. I hope Freddie Mercury wasn't watching – it would have stuck in his teeth, not to mention his craw.

Sunday October 6th

Turning the pages of my *Observer* today, I saw Barry Kent's ugly face staring out at me. Apparently he is a new member of a place called the Groucho Club. I read the accompanying article avidly. It is exactly the sort of place I would like to be a member of. Should I ever reach that goal, I shall tell the manager (Liam) the truth about Kent's past and have him blackballed.

Elizabeth Taylor has married a bricklayer with a bad perm. He is called Larry Fortensky. Michael Jackson's ape, Bubbles, was the best man.

Chapter Nineteen: Time to Move On
Jake slipped out of the cottage as the village church struck

midnight. He ran stealthily down the lane and towards the minicab which was waiting, as instructed, by the post office. As he threw his rucksack into the back of the car and climbed in after it, he sighed with relief. He never again wanted to see the apple cheeks of his grandmother and he vowed to burn the next corn dolly he came across.

'Put your foot down!' Jake barked to the minicab driver. 'Take me to the nearest urban conurbation.'

The minicab driver's brow was furrowed. 'What's an urban conurbation when it's at 'ome?' he said.

Jake snapped, 'Okay, dolt! You want specifics, take me to the Groucho Club.'

At the mention of the magic words, the cab driver's shoulders straightened. The dandruff stayed on his scalp. He had waited years to hear the words, 'Take me to the Groucho Club'. He looked at Jake with a new respect and he did as he was told. He put his foot down on the clutch and the minicab sped away from the Wolds and towards the great metropolis where, in the Groucho, the Great were no doubt quaffing the house wine and exchanging witticisms. Jake hoped Belinda would be there, at the bar, showing her legs and laughing hysterically at one of Jeffrey Bernard's jokes.

Monday October 7th

Barry Kent is making a film for BBC2 about his 'roots'. The television cameras were in the Co-op, blocking the aisles. I couldn't get to the cat food, so I complained to the manager (who, incidentally, didn't look a day older than seventeen). He replied, 'Barry Kent's comin' here in person this afternoon.' It was as though he were talking about royalty.

I said, 'I don't give a toss. I want three tins of Whiskas, *now*!' The boy manager went off and, in crawling tones, asked the cameraman to pass him three tins of cat food. With what I thought was ill grace, the cameraman obliged and, after paying the starstruck child, I left the shop.

Tuesday October 8th

My mother has been persuaded to give a talk to camera about 'the Barry Kent she once knew'. I urged her to tell the truth, about the bullying, lying, scruffy, thick youth we knew and despised.

But my mother said, 'I always found Barry to be a sensitive child.' The director made her stand by her overflowing wheelie bin in the side yard.

My mother said, 'Shouldn't I be made-up, by a proper make-up artist?' Nick, the director, said, 'No, Mrs Mole, we're going for actuality.' My mother touched the cold sore on her lip and said, 'I'd counted on a bit of camouflage to hide this.' A strong light was turned on her, which showed every line, wrinkle and bag on my mother's face.

Then the director shouted, 'Go!' and my mother went. To pieces. After seventeen attempts, BBC2 gave up, packed their gear and went off. My mother ran upstairs and threw herself on the bed. There is nothing so pitiful as a failed interviewee.

Saturday October 12th

Kent is still poncing around the neighbourhood. I saw him being filmed walking up our street. He was wearing a floor-length overcoat, cowboy boots and dark glasses. I ducked out of sight. I have no wish to be publicly identified as the dork in *Dork's Diary*.

I took the dog for a walk to the field where Pandora used to ride Blossom, her pony. It tired very quickly. I had to carry it back.

I saw Mrs Kent, Barry's mother, on the way home. She was walking her pit bull terrier. I asked her if she had registered the beast yet (as required by law).

She said, 'Butcher wouldn't hurt a fly.'

I said, 'It's not flies I'm worried about. It's the tender flesh of small children.'

She changed the subject and told me that Barry had bought her the council house she now lives in. This made me laugh quite a lot. The Kents' house is a byword for squalor in our neighbourhood. They chop the internal doors up for firewood every winter.

Sunday October 13th

Finished Chapter Nineteen tonight.

Jake was sick of being interviewed. He ordered the journalists to leave the Groucho Club and leave him alone. He turned to Lenny Henry and said, 'Let's have a drink, Len.' Lenny smiled his thanks and Jake snapped his fingers. A waiter came running immediately and bent deferentially towards Jake. 'A bottle of champagne – a big one – and make that three glasses,' for Jake had just seen one of his best friends, Richard Ingrams, of *News Quiz* fame, come through the hallowed swing doors. 'Hey, Rich, over here!' shouted Jake. There was a sound of scuffling coming from the reception area. Jake turned his head round to see Liam, the manager, throwing Kent Barry, the failed writer, out of the club and into the gutter.

Monday October 14th

Dear Bianca,

After further reflection, can I take you up on your offer? It would be most convenient for me to spend a few days sleeping on your floor in Oxford. Quite honestly, I cannot tolerate another moment living with my family. It isn't just the noise level and the constant bickering; it's the small things – the encrusted neck of the HP Sauce bottle; the slimy soap dish; the dog hairs in the butter.

You can telephone me on the above number, any time, night or day. Nobody sleeps in this house.

All my very best wishes,

Adrian Mole

Tuesday October 15th

My sister Rosie told me that she hated me this morning. Her outburst came after I suggested that she comb her hair before going to school. My mother got out of bed and came downstairs. She lit her second cigarette of the day (she smokes the first in bed) and immediately took Rosie's side. She said, 'Leave the kid alone.'

I said, 'Somebody has to maintain standards in this house.'

My mother said, 'You can talk. That beard looks like a ferret's nest. I don't know how you can bear to have it so near to your mouth. A public health inspector would close it down.'

During the ensuing row, nasty things were said on both sides, which I now regret. I accused her of being a neglectful mother, with loose morals. She counter-attacked by describing me as 'a fungus-faced dork'. She said she had secretly read my *Lo!* manuscript and thought it was 'crap from start to finish'. She said, 'in the unlikely event of it being published, I hope you will use a pseudonym, because, to be honest, Adrian, I couldn't stand the public shame.'

I put my head on the kitchen table and wept.

My mother then put her arm around me and said, 'There, there, Adrian. Don't cry. I didn't mean it, I think *Lo! The Flat Hills of My Homeland* is a very interesting first attempt.'

But it was no good. I wept until dehydration set in.

10.00 p.m. Why hasn't Bianca phoned? I used a first class stamp.

Thursday October 17th

Drew more money out of the Market Harborough Building Society. My dream of being an owner-occupier has receded even further into the realms of fantasy.

I have received a postcard of the Forth Bridge, with no address but posted in London.

Dear Adrian,

I'm going to London to try for a proper job. I've got an interview with British Rail. In a rush. Please reply c/o my friend Lucy:

Lucy Clay
Flat 10
Dexter House
Coghill Street
Oxford

She has promised to pass on any messages.

I hope you are well and happy. I miss you!
  Love,
    B.
PS. How about a London floor when I find one?

Friday October 18th

Chapter Twenty: The Reckoning
Jake pushed the earth wire out of the lawnmower plug, then screwed the plug together again. He could hear his mother on the telephone to her new lover (a schoolboy called Craig).

He waited for her to finish cooing her endearments down the phone and re-emerge on the terrace. 'I've cut half the lawn, mother,' he shouted, 'but I've got to go to the barber's now.'

His mother frowned and dropped ash all down her cashmere dress. 'But Jake, darling,' she remonstrated. 'You know I hate to see a job half done.' She went towards the lawnmower.

Jake chuckled inwardly. He had banked on this trait of his mother's. As he passed through the french windows, he heard the hover-mower whir into life, to be followed immediately by the high-pitched scream.

Jake immediately felt guilty, then comforted himself by thinking that he had advised his mother time after time to install a circuit breaker; advice she had foolishly chosen to ignore.

Sunday October 20th

It was my father's access day today. He came to take Rosie out to McDonald's as usual. While she looked for her shoes, my father and I talked man to man about my mother. We agreed that she was an impossible person to live with. We had a good laugh about Martin Muffet, who was in the back garden building a lean-to conservatory with the assistance of his Black and Decker work bench. We agreed that, since marrying my mother, Muffet has aged ten years.

I congratulated my father on capturing Mrs Belinda Bellingham, and confessed that I didn't have much luck with women. My father said, 'Tell them what they want to hear, son, and buy them a bunch of flowers once a fortnight. That's all there is to it.'

I asked him if he intended to marry Mrs Bellingham, but before he could answer, my mother staggered into the room carrying a large cardboard box which contained the swag she'd bought from a car boot sale. She'd bought a painting of Christ on the cross; an ashtray with two scottie dogs painted on it; an aluminium toast rack; twenty-seven bent candles; a chenille tablecloth; a Tom Jones LP; six cooking apples; and a steering wheel. As she excitedly unpacked the junk onto the kitchen table, I saw my father looking at her with what I can only describe as lovelight in his eyes.

Monday October 21st

Bianca rang, but I was out cutting Bert Baxter's disgusting toenails. My mother wrote down a telephone number where I could contact Bianca, but then lost it almost immediately. We searched the house, but failed to find the scrap of paper. I expect the dog ate it. It has recently taken to scoffing whole pages of the *Leicester Mercury*, a sign of its increasing neurosis or a vitamin deficiency – who knows? Nobody can afford to take it to the vet to find out.

Tuesday October 22nd

I sent a postcard of Leicester Bus Station to Bianca c/o Lucy Clay:

Dear Bianca,

Thank you for your postcard of the Forth Bridge.

I was most surprised to hear that you were leaving Oxford and going to the 'Smoke', as the cockneys say.

I wish you luck in your search for a 'proper' job. Keep me posted. I have had no luck yet, but I keep trying.

It is very difficult living here with my family. There is a total clash of lifestyles. I strive to be tolerant of the noise and disorder, but it is hard, very hard.

Yours,

With very best wishes,

Adrian

Mrs Bellingham has offered me a job selling security devices. It is evening work. I have to call on nervous householders after dark and put the fear of God into them until they sign up for a burglar alarm or security lights. I said I would think about it.

Mrs Bellingham said in her careful voice, 'There are three million unemployed. Why do you need to think about it?'

I said I hoped that beggars could still be choosers.

She is offering me £3.14 an hour. No commission, no insurance stamp, no contract of employment – cash in hand. I asked her if she objected to my belonging to a union. Her face went whiter than ever and she said, 'Yes, I'm afraid I do. Mrs Thatcher's greatest achievement was to tame the unions.' My father is a Thatcherite's lackey!

Thursday October 24th

I despise myself. I have only been working for two nights, but I have already sold a whole house security system, six car alarms, four peepholes and half a dozen bike locks. My method is simple. I get into the house and show the householders the portfolio that Mrs Bellingham has assembled. It consists of lurid stories cut out of the tabloid newspapers and police press releases. After leafing through this alarming document, it would take great insouciance for the householder to deny that more security in the home is a desirable thing.

Mrs Bellingham has instructed me to ask the question, 'Don't you think your family deserves more protection from the dark forces of evil that are at large in our community?'

So far only one person has said, 'No,' and he was the defeated-looking father of six teenage boys.

Monday October 28th

Shaved beard off. Mrs Bellingham said it made me look untrustworthy. I am completely in her power. If she ordered me to go to work wearing a Batman outfit, I would have to obey her. I have no legal rights of employment.

Thursday October 31st

At last! The economic recovery is on its way! The Confederation of British Industry has reported that they expect outputs and exports to increase in the years ahead. According to the CBI, manufacturers are expecting huge new orders. I broke this good news to my mother. She said, 'Yes, and the dog is getting married on Saturday and I'm its Matron of Honour.' Then she and Martin Muffet went off into one of their mad laughing fits.

Ken Barlow of *Coronation Street* fame has been on

trial for being boring. He was found 'Not Guilty' and awarded £50,000.

My mother has got a job as a security guard in the new shopping centre that has just opened in Leicester city centre. She looks like a New York City police-woman in her uniform. She told the security firm, 'Group Five', that she was *thirty-five years old*! She is now living in fear that her true age, forty-seven, will be revealed. Is everybody partially sighted at Group Five? Did her interview take place in a candlelit office? I asked her these questions.

She said, 'I bunged on rather a lot of Max Factor's pan-stick and sat with my back to the window.'

Friday November 1st

In view of my continuing success in flogging her security paraphernalia, Mrs Bellingham has raised my hourly rate from £3.14 to the heady sum of £3.25! Gee whiz! Fire a cannon! Release the balloons! Open the Bollinger! Issue a press release! Inform the Red Arrows!

Saturday November 2nd

Jake used his Swiss Army knife to dismantle the burglar alarm and in a matter of moments he had circumnavigated the padlocks, bolts and chains on the front door and was standing in the front hall of Bellingham Towers.

Upstairs, sleeping after an hour of arduous lovemaking, were the owners of the historic country house, Sir George and Lady Belinda, and their daughter, the Honourable Rosemary. Jake chuckled as he stuffed silver and *objets d'art* into a black plastic bag. He felt no guilt. He was robbing the filthy rich to feed the filthy poor. He was the Robin Hood of Leicestershire.

My mother claims that I look exactly like John Major, especially when I am wearing my reading glasses. This is total rubbish: unlike Mr Major, I have got lips. They may be on the thin side, but they are distinctly there. If I were Major, I'd have a lip transplant. Mick Jagger could be the donor.

Tuesday November 5th

Robert Maxwell, the mogul, has fallen overboard from his yacht, the *Lady Ghislaine*.

Went to Age Concern Community Bonfire Party. Pushed Bert Baxter there in his wheelchair. Baxter was asked to leave after half an hour because he was seen (and certainly heard) to throw an Indian firecracker into the bonfire. The organizer, Mrs Plumbstead, said apologetically, 'Safety has to be paramount.'

Baxter said scornfully, 'There were no such thing as *safety* when I were a lad.'

I pushed him home in silence. I was furious. Because of him, I missed the baked potatoes, sausages and soup. I had to wait for an hour for the district nurse to come and put him to bed.

Thursday November 7th

Kevin Maxwell has denied that his deceased father's businesses have financial problems.

Query: Would our banks lend £2.5 billion to a man with money problems?

Answer: Of course not! Our banks are respected financial institutions.

Sunday November 10th

To Grandma's for the Remembrance Day poppy-laying ceremony. I am proud of my dead grandfather, Albert Mole. He fought valiantly in the First World War so that I would not have to live under the tyranny of a foreign oppressor.

I cannot let the above sentence lie. The truth is that my poor, dead grandfather fought in the Great War because he was ordered to. He always did what he was told. I take after him in that respect.

Monday November 11th

A gang of Leicester yobs shouted out, 'Hey, John Major, how's Norma?' tonight, as I came out of the cinema. I looked around, thinking that perhaps the Prime Minister was visiting the Leicester Chamber of Commerce, or something, but there was no sign of him. I then realized, to my horror, that they were addressing their yobbish remarks to me.

Wednesday November 13th

A letter from Bianca.

Dear Adrian,

Thank you for your letter, which Lucy forwarded to me. As you can see from my address, I am living in London. I am renting a small room in Soho at the moment, but it is costing £110 per week, so I won't be here long!

I've got a job as a waitress in a restaurant called 'Savages'. The owner is a bit strange, but the staff are very nice. It would be lovely to see you when you're next in London. My day off is Monday. How is the novel going? Have you finished your revisions? I can't wait to read it in full!

Love,

Bianca (Dartington)

Thursday November 14th

Dear Bianca,

Many thanks for your letter of the 11th. I must confess that I was rather surprised to hear from you. I am hardly ever in London, but I may drop in and see you on my next visit. Isn't Soho a dangerous place in which to live? Please take care as you walk the streets. Personally, I am ossifying in this provincial hell.

Lo! is going very well. I have called my hero Jake Westmorland. What do you think?

Please write back.

Yours as ever,

Adrian

Friday November 15th

The New York Stock Exchange collapsed today. I hope this won't affect the interest rates of the Market Harborough Building Society.

Saturday November 16th

No reply from B.

Sunday November 17th

Why isn't there a Sunday delivery in this country? I expect it is because of objections from the established Church. Do the clergy imagine that God gives a toss if humans receive letters or not on a Sunday?

Monday November 18th

By second post. A postcard of Holborn Viaduct.

Dear Adrian,
   No. Soho is not dangerous. I *love* Jake Westmorland. When are you coming to London?
   Lots of love,
      Bianca

Tuesday November 19th

I sent Bianca a postcard of the Clock Tower, Leicester.

Dear Bianca,
   As it happens, I shall be in London next Monday. Would you like to have lunch? Please write or ring to confirm.
   Very warm wishes,
      Adrian

PS. I have shaved my beard off. It was the television pictures of Terry Waite that decided me.

Wednesday November 20th

Grandma's Christmas card arrived. The shops are full of Santa Clauses ringing bells and getting in the way of legitimate shoppers. My mother said that whilst on duty she saw an old lady shoplifting a Cadbury's Selection Box. I asked her what action she'd taken. She said, 'I turned and walked the other way.'

There is a rush on for burglar alarms. Everybody wants them fitted before Christmas when they fill their homes with consumer durables and Nintendo games.

Saturday November 23rd

A postcard from Bianca, of the original Crystal Palace.

Dear Adrian,

I have got to work on Monday. The office party season has started, but come down anyway. I will get off early. I look forward to seeing you. Come to 'Savages', Dean Street, at 2.30 p.m.

Love,
Bianca

Sunday November 24th

Freddie Mercury has died of Aids. There was no time for me to mourn, but I put 'Bohemian Rhapsody', which is one of my favourite records, on the record player.

I laid my wardrobe on my bed (or rather, the *contents* of my wardrobe) and tried to decide what to wear for my trip to London. I do not wish to be marked out as a provincial day-tripper by sneering metropolitans. Decided on the black shirt, black trousers and Oxfam tweed jacket. My grey slip-on shoes will have to do. Set my alarm for 8.30 a.m. I catch the 12.30 p.m. train.

Monday November 25th

Soho
I am in love with Bianca Dartington. Hopelessly, help-lessly, mindlessly, gloriously, magnificently.

Tuesday November 26th

I am still here, in Soho, in Bianca's room above Brenda's Patisserie in Old Compton Street. I have hardly seen daylight since 3.30 p.m. on Monday.

Wednesday November 27th

Poem to Bianca Dartington:

> Gentle face,
> Night black hair,
> Natural grace,
> Love I swear.
> Marry me, be my wife,
> Make me happy, share my life.

Thursday November 28th

Phoned my mother and asked her to send my books to Old Compton Street. Informed her that I am now living in London, with Bianca. She asked for the address, but I wasn't falling for that. I hung up.

Friday November 29th

God, I love her! I love her! I love her! Every minute she is away, working at 'Savages', is torture for me.

Query: Why didn't I *know* that the human body is capable of such exquisite pleasure?

Answer: Because, Mole, you had not made love to Bianca Dartington – somebody who loves you body and soul – before.

Saturday November 30th

What did I ever see in Pandora Braithwaite? She is an
opinionated, arrogant ball-breaker. An all-round nasty
piece of work. Compared to Bianca, she is nothing,
nothing. And as for Leonora De Witt, I can hardly
remember her face.

I never want to leave this room. I want to live
the whole of my life within these four walls (with
occasional trips to the bathroom, which we have to
share with a fire-eater called Norman).

The walls are painted lavender blue and Bianca has
stuck stars and moons on the ceiling which glow in
the dark. There is a poster of Sydney Harbour Bridge
on the wall between the windows. There is a double
bed with an Indian bedspread covered in cushions; a
chest of drawers that Bianca has painted white; an old
armchair covered in a large tablecloth. A wonky table,
half painted in gold, and two pine chairs. Instead of a
bedhead, we have got a blown-up photograph on the
wall of Isambard Kingdom Brunel, Bianca's hero.

Every morning when I wake up, I can't believe that
the slim girl with the long legs who is lying next to
me is mine! I always get out of bed first and put the
kettle on the Baby Belling cooker. I then put two slices
of toast under the grill and serve my love with her
breakfast in bed. I won't allow her to get out of bed
until the gas fire has warmed the room. She catches
cold easily.

I want to please her more than I want to please myself.

This morning, 'Stand By Me', sung by Ben E. King, was playing on Capital Radio.

I said, 'I love this song. My father used to play it.'

Bianca said, 'So do I.'

We danced to it, me in my boxer shorts and Bianca in her pink knickers with the flowers on.

'Stand By Me' is now our song.

Sunday December 1st

Went to the National Gallery today. We walked around the Sainsbury Wing like Siamese twins, fused together. We cannot bear to be apart for even a moment. The renaissance pictures glowed like jewels and inflamed our passion. Our mutual genitalia are a bit sore and bruised, but it didn't stop us making love as soon as we got back to the room. Norman next door banged on the wall and nearly put us off, but we managed to ignore him.

Monday December 2nd

I was putting my socks and shoes on this morning, when I noticed a strange expression on Bianca's face.

I said, 'What is it, darling?'

After a lot of cajoling, Bianca confessed that she

adored everything about me except my grey slip-on shoes and white towelling socks. As a mark of my love for her, I opened the window and hurled my only pair of socks and shoes into Old Compton Street. I was unable to go out all day as a consequence. I was a barefoot prisoner of love.

Late that afternoon, Bianca bought me three pairs of socks from Sock Shop, and one pair of dark brogues from Bally. They all fitted perfectly. The shoes are *serious*. I felt like a grown-up in them as I walked around the room. I then walked to the Nat West Bank in Wardour Street and removed £100 from the Rapid Cash machine. This is the most I have ever withdrawn in one go. I paid Bianca for the shoes (£59.99), which is also the most I have ever paid for a pair of shoes. Incidentally, it is now late evening and the grey slip-ons are still in the gutter. I *did* see a tramp try them on, but he scowled and took them off immediately, though they looked a good fit.

Wednesday December 4th

I telephoned my mother today and asked her why she hadn't sent my books on as I had asked.

She screamed, 'Mainly because you refused to give me your address, you stupid sod.' She then went on to say that she had asked our postman, Courtney Elliot, for an estimate of the cost of sending the books by Parcel Post. Apparently, he 'guestimated' (her word, not mine) that it would cost about a hundred quid! She said that my father is driving to London on Friday to attend a conference on Home Security. She said she would ask him to drop the books, and the rest of my worldly goods, off. I agreed reluctantly and gave her the address.

When Bianca had gone to work, I walked to Oxford Street and bought a dustpan and brush, a packet of yellow dusters, Mr Sheen, a floor cloth, some liquid Flash, a bottle of Windolene and a pair of white satin knickers from Knickerbox.

Bianca was thrilled when she returned at 3.00 p.m. to find our room cleaned and sparkling. Almost as thrilled as I was at 1.00 a.m. when she put the satin knickers on.

Friday December 6th

My father was in a foul temper when he got here tonight. The conference was in Watford, so he had to go considerably out of his way (backwards) in order to deliver my stuff. When he eventually found Old Compton Street, it was 9.30 p.m.

He parked outside on double yellow lines, with his hazard lights flashing. Together, we lugged the boxes of books and plastic bags of clothes four floors up to the room. When we'd finished, my father collapsed on the bed. His bald patch was glistening with sweat. I was glad that Bianca was at work. When he'd recovered, I went down to see him off. Mrs Bellingham had ordered him to be home at a reasonable time. He is obviously afraid of her. As we walked to the car, my father stopped, pointed to the gutter and shouted, 'What the bleeding hell is that?'

His Montego had been wheel-clamped. I thought he was going to break down and cry in the street, but instead he went berserk and kicked at the yellow clamp and shouted obscenities. It was highly amusing to the posing idiots who were drinking cappuccino in the cold wind on the opposite pavement.

I offered to go with him to the outer reaches of London, to start the long, bureaucratic process of declamping the car, but my father snarled, 'Oh, bugger off back upstairs to your cowing love nest.' He hailed a black cab and jumped in. As it turned into Wardour Street, I could tell that it wouldn't be long before my father was whining to the cab driver about his bad luck, his ungrateful son, his fearsome mistress and his feckless ex-wife.

Saturday December 7th

Spent a pleasant day cataloguing and then arranging my books on the bookshelves I constructed from three planks and nine old bricks I found in a skip in Greek Street. Cost? Nil. In the same skip, I found *Moral Thinking* by John Wilson. It was printed in 1970, before sex came into *The Archers*, however, so I suppose the morality may be out of date.

Bianca came home at lunchtime and asked if I wanted a job as a part-time washer-up in 'Savages'. It is cash in hand, off the books. I said, 'Yes.'

We went to see the Thames Barrier and talked about our future. We pledged that we would not let riches and fame divide us.

I start washing up on Monday.

Monday December 9th

Peter Savage, the owner of 'Savages', is certainly aptly named. I have never known a man with such a bad temper. He is rude to everybody, staff and customers. The customers think he is amusingly eccentric. The staff hate him and spend their meal breaks fantasizing about killing him. He is a tall, fat man with a face like a beef tomato. He dresses like Bertie Wooster and talks like Bob Hoskins of *Roger Rabbit* fame. He wears a CND tiepin on his Garrick Club tie.

Culturally, he is all over the place.

Tuesday December 10th

Savage was drunk at 10 a.m. At 12 noon he vomited into the yukka plant in the corner of the restaurant.

At 1 p.m. his wife came, abused him verbally and then carried him out to her car, helped by Luigi, the head waiter.

I am reading *The Complete Plain Words* by Sir Ernest Gowers. I am on page 143: *Clichés*. Far be it from me to say so, but I'm sure my writing style will improve by leaps and bounds.

Bianca startled me this evening by suddenly shouting, 'Please, Adrian, can't you stop that perpetual sniffing. Use a handkerchief!'

Wednesday December 11th

I toil over greasy pots and pans for £3.90 an hour, and the customers fork out £17 for a monkfish and £18 for a bottle of wine! Savage is obviously not as stupid as he looks.

Fogle, Fogle, Brimmington and Hayes, the advertising firm, held their Christmas party in 'Savages' at lunchtime. The restaurant was closed to ordinary customers. Bianca said that the managing director, Piers Fogle, told her that they were in a celebratory mood because they had just won a contract worth £500,000 on the strength of a slogan for an advertising campaign for condoms.

'What the well-dressed man is wearing' is to appear on billboards all over the country.

Their bill came to over £700. They gave Bianca and the other waitresses £5 each. I, the serf in the kitchen, got nothing, of course. Luigi put two fingers up to Fogle's back as he staggered out of the restaurant.

Saturday December 14th

We haven't made love for over twenty-four hours. Bianca has got cystitis.

Sunday December 15th

Bought *The Joy of Sex* in the Charing Cross Road. Cystitis is called 'The Honeymooners' Illness'. It can be caused by vigorous, frequent sex. Poor Bianca is in the toilet every ten minutes. Why is there *always* a price to pay for pleasure?

Monday December 16th

Savage was in court this morning, charged with assaulting a customer last April. He was fined £500 and ordered to pay costs and damages totalling my wages for five years. He came back to the restaurant with Mrs Savage and his lawyer to celebrate the fact that he hadn't been sent to prison, but after the champagne had been drunk and the tagliatelle consumed, Savage spotted a group of Channel Four executives on table eight and began to abuse them because they didn't show enough tobogganing on their sports programmes.

According to Bianca, Mrs Savage said, 'Darling, do be quiet, you're starting to get a little tedious.'

Savage shouted, 'Shut your mouth, you fat cow!'

She shouted, 'I'm a size *ten*, you callous bastard!'

The lawyer tried to conciliate, but Savage tipped the table up and Luigi ended up throwing his boss out of his own restaurant.

Personally, I would be happy to see Savage chained up in prison, on bread and water, with rats gnawing at his feet – and I'm a supporter of prison reform.

Tuesday December 17th

Experimented with making very gentle love. I was the passive partner.

Later, we had our first argument. Where are we spending Christmas Day and Boxing Day? In our room? At her parents'? At my parents'? Or with Luigi, who has invited us to his house in Harrow? We didn't shout at each other, but there was (and still is) a distinct lack of seasonal goodwill. Bianca turned her back on me in bed tonight.

Thursday December 19th

We woke up tangled together, as usual. Christmas wasn't mentioned, but love, passion and marriage were. We are going to spend Christmas with her parents in Richmond. Her father is going to pick us up on Christmas Eve. It will save me having to buy presents for my family.

Saturday December 21st

Tonight, Savage promenaded around the restaurant with a miniature Christmas tree on his head, complete with twinkling lights. He kissed all the women and blew cigar smoke at all the men. Luigi led him into the kitchen and propped him up against the sink. Savage then proceeded to tell me that his mother had never loved him and that his father had run away with an alcoholic nurse when he was eight. (When Savage *junior* was eight.) He broke down and wept, but I was too busy to comfort him. The cook was screaming for side plates.

Sunday December 22nd

Bianca stayed in bed today, tired out, poor kid, which gave me a chance to work on chapter twenty-one of *Lo! The Flat Hills of My Homeland.*

Jake ran his fingers down the length of her back. Her skin felt like the finest silk, even to his fingers, roughened by years of immersion in washing-up water. She sighed and squirmed into the flannelette sheet. 'Don't stop,' she said, her voice cracking like a whip. 'Don't ever stop, Jake . . .'

Tuesday December 24th
Christmas Eve

I braved the maddening crowds today and went out to buy Bianca's Christmas present. After tramping the streets for two hours, I ended up in Knickerbox and bought her a purple suspender belt, scarlet knickers, and a black lace bra. When the saleswoman asked me about size, I confessed I didn't know. I said, 'She's not Rubenesque, but she's not Naomi Campbell.'

The woman rolled her eyes and said, 'Okay, she's medium, yeah?'

I said, 'She looks a bit like Paula Yates, but with black hair.'

The woman sighed and said, 'Paula Yates breast-feeding or not breastfeeding?'

I said, 'Not breastfeeding,' and she snatched some stuff off the racks and gift-wrapped it for me.

I agonized in Burger King over whether or not to buy her parents presents. At four-thirty, I decided that, yes, I would ingratiate myself with them and bought her mother some peach-based pot-pourri. I phoned Bianca at 'Savages' and asked what I should get for her father. She said her father was fond of poetry, so I went and bought him a book of poems by John Hegley, called *Can I Come Down Now Dad?* which has a picture of Jesus on the cross on its cover. I also managed to track down a copy of *The Railway Heritage of Britain* by Gordon Biddle and O. S. Nock for Bianca.

Thursday December 26th
Boxing Day

Richmond
Bianca's mother is allergic to peaches; and her father, the Reverend Dartington, thought that the John Hegley book was in extremely bad taste. Also, I hate Bianca's brother and sister. How my sweet, darling Bianca could have come from such a vile family is a mystery to me. We slept in separate beds in separate rooms. We had to go to a wooden hut of a church on Christmas Day and listen to her father rant on about the commercialization of Christmas. Bianca and I were the only people to buy presents. Everyone else had given money to the Sudanese Drought Fund. Bianca bought me a Swatch watch and the *Chronicle of the Twentieth Century*, which will be an invaluable work of reference to me. I was very pleased. She was pleased with the Biddle and Nock.

Her brother, Derek, and her sister, Mary, obviously disapprove of our love affair. They are both unmarried and still live at home. Derek is thirty-five and Mary is twenty-seven. Mrs Dartington was forty-eight when Bianca was born.

There was no turkey, no drink and no celebration. It made me long for my own family's vulgarity.

This afternoon, we had to go for a walk alongside the river. Little kids were out in force, wobbling on new bikes and pushing prams with new-looking dolls inside. Derek has now taken a shine to me. He thought I was a fellow trainspotter; I quickly put him right. Bianca and I managed a quick embrace in the kitchen tonight before being interrupted by Mary, who came in looking for her constipation chocolate.

Mrs Dartington had a convenient 'turn' just before dinner and took to her bed. Bianca and I cooked the meal. We had salad, corned beef and baked potatoes. I cannot wait to get back to our room. I need Bianca. I need onions. I need garlic. I need Soho. I need Savage. I need air. I need freedom from the Dartingtons.

There are four beige car coats hanging up in the downstairs cloakroom.

Friday December 27th

The Reverend Dartington drove us back to Soho in martyred silence. Every time he stopped at a red light or pedestrian crossing, he drummed his fingers on the steering wheel impatiently.

Two days with her family have had a deleterious

effect on Bianca: she seems to have shrunk physically and regressed mentally. As soon as she got back into the room she burst into tears and shouted, 'Why didn't they *tell* me they were giving their Christmas presents to the Sudanese?'

I said, 'Because they wanted to claim the moral high ground and make you feel foolish. It's obviously a punishment because you are living in sin, in Soho, with a lowly washer-upper.'

An hour later, Bianca had sprung back in size and mental capacity. We made love for one hour, ten minutes. Our longest yet. It is quite useful having a stopwatch facility on my new Swatch.

Sunday December 29th

We went to Camden Lock today to buy Bianca a pair of boots. The whole area was thronging with young people who were both buying and selling. I said to Bianca, 'Isn't it nice to see the young out and about and enjoying themselves?'

She looked at me in a funny way and said, 'But *you* are young. You're only twenty-four, though sometimes I find it hard to believe.'

She was right, of course. I am young, officially, but I have never felt young. My mother said I was thirty-five on the day I fought my way out of her womb.

The cystitis is back. Bianca has reluctantly put the

satin knickers back in her underwear drawer and gone back to the cotton gussets.

I am reading a play, *A Streetcar Named Desire* by Tennessee Williams. Poor Blanche Dubois!

Winter

Wednesday January 1st 1992

'Savages' was closed last night, so we went to Trafalgar Square at 11.30 p.m. to see the New Year in. The crowd was like a drunken field of corn rippling and swaying in a storm. For over two hours I lost myself and went with the flow. It was frightening, but also exhilarating to find myself in a line doing the conga up St Martin's Lane. Unfortunately, the person in front of me had extremely fat buttocks. It was not an attractive sight.

When Big Ben struck twelve, I found myself kissing and being kissed by strangers, including foreigners. I tried to get to Bianca, but she was surrounded by a party of extrovert Australian persons who were all over seven foot tall. But finally, at 12.03 a.m. on the 1st of January, we kissed and pledged our troth. I can't believe I've got such a wonderful woman. Why does she love me? I live in fear that one day she will wake up and ask herself the same question.

We went to Tower Bridge today. It left me cold, but Bianca was enraptured by the structural design of the thing. I practically had to drag her away.

Thursday January 2nd

Got up at 3.30 a.m. and joined the queue outside Next in Oxford Street. The sale started at 9.00 a.m. I got into conversation with a man who had his eye on a double-breasted navy suit, marked down from £225 to £90. He is getting married to a parachute packer, called Melanie, next Saturday.

In my new black leather jacket, white T-shirt and blue jeans, I look like every other young man in London, New York and Tokyo. Or Leicester, come to think of it. For Leicester is at the very epicentre of the Next empire.

Bianca wanted to visit Battersea Power Station today and asked me to go with her, but I pointed out to her that *Lo!* was about to develop in a revolutionary direction and that I needed to work on Chapter Twenty-two.

She left the flat without saying a word, but her back looked very angry.

Jake pulled the collar of his Next black leather jacket up against the cruel wind that blew across the Thames. He stared down into the ebbing water. It was time he did something with his life other than help with famine relief in Sudan. He knew what it was. It was something he had fought against – God knows how he had fought! But the compulsion was overwhelming now. He had to do it. He had to write a novel . . .

Wednesday January 8th

President Bush vomited into the lap of the Japanese Ambassador at an official banquet in Tokyo tonight. We watched it on the portable television in the kitchen at 'Savages'. Mrs Bush shoved her husband under the table, then left the room. She didn't look too pleased. The television news showed the whole incident in slow motion. It was sickening. The Japanese people looked horrified. They are sticklers for protocol.

Savage has fired little Carlos for smoking a joint in the yard at the back of the restaurant. Savage then drank half a bottle of brandy, three bottles of Sol, stole various drinks from customers' tables and ended up fighting with the palm tree at the bar after accusing it of having an affair with his wife. Alcohol is certainly a dangerous drug in the wrong hands.

Wednesday January 15th

Jake sat in front of his state of the art Amstrad and pressed the glittery knobs. The title of his novel appeared on the screen.

SPARG FROM KRONK
Chapter One: Sparg Returns
Sparg stood on the hilltop and looked down on Kronk, the settlement of his birth. He grunted to his woman,

Barf, and she grunted back wordlessly, for the words had not yet been found.

They ran down the hill. Sparg's mother, Krun, watched her son and his woman come towards the fire. She grunted to Sparg's father, Lunt, and he came to the door of the hut. His eyes narrowed. He hated Sparg.

Krun threw more roots into the fire: she had not expected guests for dinner. It was typical of her son, she thought, to arrive unexpectedly and with a woman with a swollen belly. She hoped there would be enough roots to go round.

She was glad the words had not been found. She hated making small talk.

Sparg was here, in front of her. She sniffed his armpit, as was the custom when a Kronkite returned from a long journey. Barf hung back and watched the greeting ceremony. Her mouth salivated. The smell of the burning roots inflamed her hunger.

Because the words had not been found no news could be exchanged between mother and son.

Jake fell back from his computer terminal with a contented sigh. It was good, he thought, damned good. The time was right for another prehistoric novel without dialogue.

Tuesday January 21st

A letter from Bert Baxter. Almost illegible.

Dear Lad,

It seems a long time since I saw you. When are you coming to Leicester? I've got a few jobs that need doing. Sorry about the writing. I've got the shakes.

Yours,

Bertram Baxter

PS. Bring your toenail scissors.

Had a serious row with Bianca tonight. She accused me of:

a) Never wanting to go out
b) Excessive reading
c) Excessive writing
d) Contempt for Britain's industrial heritage
e) Farting in bed

Monday January 27th

At last reconciled, we went to the National Film Theatre tonight and saw a film about a Japanese woman who cuts her lover's penis off. During the rest of the film, I sat with my legs tightly crossed and at intervals looked nervously across at Bianca, who was staring up at the screen and smiling.

My hair is almost long enough for a pony tail. *The Face* tells me that pony tails are becoming passé. But it may be my last chance to try one. So I am going for it. Savage has been boasting that he has had his for five years.

Bianca has bought a secondhand electric typewriter and is typing *Lo!* She has already presented me with seventy-eight beautifully laid-out pages. It is amazing how much a novel is improved by being typed. I should have taken Mr John Tydeman's advice years ago.

Wednesday January 29th

UK heterosexual Aids cases rose by fifty per cent last year. I gave this information to Bianca as we walked to 'Savages' early this evening. She went very quiet.

I had to wait ages outside the bathroom tonight to clean my teeth. Eventually Norman came out and apologized for the new scorch marks on the frame of the mirror. He has been *told* not to practise in there.

When I got back to our room, I found Bianca reading a pamphlet written by the Terrence Higgins Trust.

I said flippantly, 'Who's Terrence Higgins when he's at home?'

'He's dead,' she said, softly. The pamphlet was about Aids.

Bianca broke down and confessed that in 1990 she had had an affair with a man called Brian Boxer, who in turn confessed to her that in 1979 he'd had an affair

with a bisexual woman called Diane Tripp. I shall ring
the Terrence Higgins Trust Helpline in the morning
and ask for help.

Saturday February 1st

The first twenty-two chapters of *Lo! The Flat Hills of
My Homeland* are now a pile of 197 pages of neat
typescript. I keep picking it up and walking round the
room with it in my arms. I can't afford to get it
photocopied, not at ten pence a page. Who do I know
in London who has access to a photocopier?

Flat 6
Brenda's Patisserie
Old Compton Street
London

Dear John,

I have taken your advice and revised *Lo! The Flat Hills
of My Homeland.* I have also employed the services of a
professional typist and you will be pleased to see that
my manuscript now consists of twenty-two chapters in
typewritten form. I consider that, when completed, *Lo! The
Flat Hills of My Homeland* will be eminently suitable for
being read aloud on the radio, possibly as part of your
Classic Serials series.

As you can see, I have enclosed my MS and entrust it
into your care. However, I still need to make several minor
changes. Would it be too much trouble for you to photocopy

the hundred and ninety-seven pages and send a copy to me at the above address?

Thanking you in advance,

Yours as ever,

Adrian Mole

Tuesday February 4th

I walked to Broadcasting House this morning. As I struggled to push the big metal doors open, a gaggle of autograph hunters rushed towards me. I reached inside my jacket for my felt tip, but before I could extract it, I saw them surrounding Alan Freeman, the aged DJ. I pushed through them and entered the hallowed reception area of the British Broadcasting Corporation, watched by the stern-looking security staff. I walked up to the reception desk and joined the short queue.

In the space of four minutes, I saw famous people galore: Delia Smith, Robert Robinson, Ian Hislop, Bob Geldof, Annie Lennox, Roy Hattersley, etc., etc. Most of them were being seen off the premises by young women called Caroline.

Eventually the blonde receptionist said, 'Can I help you?' And I said, 'Yes. Could you please make sure that Mr John Tydeman receives this parcel? It is most urgent.'

She scribbled something on the jiffy bag which contained my letter and the manuscript of *Lo! The*

Flat Hills of My Homeland and threw it into a wire basket.

I thanked her, turned to go and bumped into Victor Meldrew, who plays the grumpy bloke in *One Foot in the Grave*! I apologized and he said, 'How kind.' He is much taller than he looks on television. When I got back to the room I told Bianca that I had been chatting to Victor Meldrew. I think she was quite impressed.

Wednesday February 5th

We both woke early this morning, but we didn't make love as usual. We had a shower and got dressed in silence. We went downstairs and had croissants and cappuccino in Brenda's Patisserie and listened to the gossip about the demise of the British film industry. Then, at 10.45 a.m., we paid our bill and walked to the clinic in Neal Street. (We forked out one pound, forty pence to the various beggars who met us on the way.)

We were counselled separately by a very empathetic woman called Judith. She pointed out that, should our tests prove positive, it wouldn't necessarily mean that we would develop full-blown Aids. After seeing Judith, we went for a drink in a pub in Carnaby Street to discuss our options:

a) Have the test and know the worst
b) Not have the test and suspect the worst

We decided to sleep on it.

Thursday February 6th

We have both decided to have the test and have pledged to care for each other until the day we die. Whatever the outcome.

Saturday February 8th

Mr Britten, the greengrocer who supplies 'Savages' with fruit and vegetables, came into the kitchen today and told us that he is going out of business next week. He said that Savage owes him seven hundred pounds in unpaid bills. I was outraged, but Mr Britten said defeatedly that Savage is only one of his many bad debtors. He said, 'If the Bank'd give me another two weeks I'd be all right, but the bastards won't.'

I made him a cup of tea and listened to him ranting on about interest charges and Norman Lamont. I think he felt slightly better by the time he left to make his next delivery.

I rang my mother to tell her about my conversation with Victor Meldrew and found that she has also been seeing a counsellor. A debt counsellor. I have been wondering for some time now how she has been paying her mortgage. Now I know. She hasn't. She has received a legal notice from the Building Society, informing her that the house where I spent my childhood is to be repossessed on March 16th. She begged me not to tell the other members of the family. She is hoping that something will turn up to avert disaster.

I didn't tell her that I have got one thousand, one hundred and eleven pounds in the Market Harborough Building Society. But I did say that Bianca and I would come to Leicester tomorrow. She sounded pathetically grateful.

Sunday February 9th

When we got to St Pancras Station, Bianca told me to look up.

'You are looking at one of the largest unsupported arch structures in the whole world,' she said. 'Isn't it beautiful?'

'Quite honestly, Bianca,' I said, 'all I can see is a dirty, scruffy roof covered in pigeon shit.'

'It was stupid of me to ask you to look at something further than your own nose,' she said, and stormed onto the train, leaving me to carry our overnight bags.

I'm always forgetting that Bianca is a qualified engineer. She doesn't look like one and since I've known her, she's only ever worked as a shop assistant and a waitress. She applies for at least two engineering jobs a week, but has yet to be called for an interview. She is considering calling herself 'Brian Dartington' on her cv.

The ticket inspector forgot to punch our three-monthly returns, so our journey to Leicester cost us nothing. But any feelings of happy triumph vanished as we got into the house. My mother was putting on a brave front, but I could tell she was inwardly distraught – at one point, she had one cigarette in her mouth, another in the ashtray and another burning on the edge of the kitchen window sill. I asked her how she'd got into such terrible debt.

She whispered, 'Martin needed the fees to finish his degree course. I borrowed a thousand pounds from a finance company, at an interest rate of twenty-four point seven per cent. Two weeks later, I lost my job with Group Five – somebody grassed on me and told them I was forty-eight.' I asked her to tell me the full extent of her indebtedness. She brought out unpaid bills of every description and colour. I urged her to tell Muffet the true nature of their financial situation, but she became almost hysterical and said, 'No, no, he *must* finish his engineering degree.'

I seem to be surrounded by engineers. Bianca informed my mother that she too was a qualified engineer.

I said jokingly, 'Yes, but she has not built so much as a Lego tower since she left university.'

To my amazement, Bianca took great exception to my harmless joke and left the room, looking tearful.

My mother said, 'You tactless sod!' and followed her into the garden.

I sat at the kitchen table, braced myself, and wrote three cheques: to Fat Eddie's Loan Co. (two hundred and seventy-one pounds); to the Co-op Dairy (thirty-six pounds, forty-nine pence); to Cherry's Newsagent (seventy-four pounds, eighty-one pence). I know it does not solve my mother's housing problem, but at least she can answer her front door now without being hounded by local creditors.

When Martin came back from Grandma's (where he is in the middle of replacing her two-pin sockets with three-pin ones), I introduced him to Bianca. Within seconds, they were bonded. They talked non-stop about St Pancras Station and unsupported arch structures. It is some time since I saw Bianca so animated. They sat next to each other at the dinner table and volunteered to wash and dry afterwards.

I helped Rosie with her English homework essay, 'A Day in the Life of a Dolphin'. I then went into the kitchen and found Bianca and Muffet droning on about the St Pancras Station Hotel and its architect, Sir George Gilbert Scott.

I interrupted them and informed Bianca that I was going to bed. She hardly looked up; just muttered, 'Okay, I'll be up soon.'

The spare bedroom was full of Rosie's hideous, fluorescent My Little Pony models.

Monday February 10th

I have no idea what time Bianca came up last night. She must have got into bed beside me without waking me up. All I know is that Muffet and my mother are not speaking and that I am utterly miserable.

11.30 p.m. Worked on *Chapter Twenty-Three: Conundrum.*

Jake sat in Alma's, the patisserie favoured by the intelligentsia, and scribbled on his A4 pad. Night and day, he worked on his novel. He was already on Chapter Four.

Chapter Four: Rocks
Sparg crept through the lush undergrowth. He knew they were there. He heard them before he saw them. They were grunting about their mutual interest in rocks.

  Sparg parted a yukka plant and they were there in front of him: Moff and Barf, bathed in sunlight, tangled together. Their limbs were entwined in an intimate manner.

  Sparg stifled a jealous grunt and crept back towards Kronk, the settlement of his birth.

Tuesday February 11th

We get our results tomorrow. I should be agonizing and reflecting on mortality, etc. But all I can think about is the way that Muffet looked at Bianca and the way that Bianca looked at Muffet when they said goodbye on Monday morning at Leicester station.

Wednesday February 12th

Judith told us that our tests are negative! We are not HIV positive! We are not going to die of Aids!

However, I feel that I may well die of a broken heart. Bianca has suggested another day trip to Leicester. She claims that she is tired of London. A feeble excuse. How could anyone be tired of London? I am with Dr Johnson on this one.

Thursday February 13th

A letter has arrived from the BBC.

Dear Adrian,

When my secretary handed me your letter and your manuscript of *Lo! The Flat Hills of My Homeland* yet again, I thought I must be hallucinating.

You have more cheek than a Samurai wrestler, more neck than a giraffe. The BBC does not run a free photocopying service. As to your laughable suggestion that your novel be read as one of our classic serials ... The writers of such texts are usually dead, their work having outlived them. I doubt if your work will outlive you. I am returning the manuscript immediately. Owing to an administrative error, a photocopy *was* taken. I am sending this on to you, though with great reluctance. You really must not bother me again.

John Tydeman

Friday February 14th
St Valentine's Day

A disappointingly small card from Bianca. Mine to her was a thing of splendour. Large, padded, expensive, and in a box tied with a ribbon.

Savage is in a clinic for drug and alcohol abuse. Luigi went to see him on Sunday and said that Savage was playing ping-pong with a fifteen-year-old crack addict from Leeds.

Saturday February 15th

Bianca is going to Leicester for the day on Monday, to see my mother. I wish I could go with her, but I am now working a sixteen-hour day, seven days a week. Somebody has to keep my mother out of prison, and I am now the only person in our family who has a proper job.

My duties at 'Savages' now include the preparation of vegetables. It is tedious work, made more difficult by the obsessive attitude of Roberto, the chef. He insists on uniformity of vegetable length and width. I have to keep a tape measure in my apron pocket.

Sunday February 16th

It is now seven days and nights since Bianca and I made love. It is not only the sex I miss. It isn't the sex. It really isn't only the sex. I miss holding her and smelling her hair and stroking her skin. I wish that I could talk to her about how I feel. But I can't, I just can't. I really can't. I've tried, but I just can't. I held her hand in bed tonight, but it didn't count. She was asleep.

Monday February 17th

Before I went to work at 6.30 a.m., I wrote a note and left it propped against the bowl of hyacinths on the table.

Darling Bianca,

Please talk to me about our relationship. I am unable to initiate a discussion. All I can say to you is that I love you. I know something is wrong between us, but I don't know how to address it.

Love, for ever,

Adrian

Bianca was very kind to me early this evening. She assured me that nothing has changed regarding her feelings towards me. But she was talking to me on the telephone from Leicester. She has arranged to stay another day, to help my mother.

When I got home from work at 11.30 p.m., I re-read the note, which was still on the table, and then tore it up and threw it down the lavatory. It took three full flushes before it disappeared completely.

Tuesday February 18th

I was very tired last night, but was unable to sleep, so I got out of bed, got dressed, and went for a walk. Soho never sleeps. It exists for people like me: the lonely, the lovesick, the outsiders. When I got home I read Dostoevsky's *The Humiliated and Insulted*.

Wednesday February 19th

The gods are not exactly smiling on our family. Mrs Bellingham has sacked my father and kicked him out of her bed. She was outraged to find out that my father had been selling her security lights for half price in low-life pubs. He is back living with Grandma. I only know this because Grandma rang me at work, complaining that my mother owes her fifty pounds from last December. Grandma needs the money because she is going to Egypt with Age Concern in June and needs to pay the deposit next week.

I pointed out to Grandma that she has got substantial savings in a high interest bank account. Couldn't she withdraw fifty pounds? Grandma pointed out that the bank requires a month's notice of withdrawal. She said, 'I'm not prepared to lose the interest.'

I casually asked Grandma if she had seen anything of Bianca. She casually answered that she had seen Bianca and Muffet on the top deck of a number twenty-nine bus, heading towards the town. She threw in a few details. They were laughing. Bianca was holding a bunch of freesias (her favourite flowers). And Muffet looked 'happier than I've ever seen him'. There was a twanging noise as she leaned back in her chair by the telephone and said, 'It doesn't take an Einstein to work that one out, does it, lad?'

Thanks, Grandma, Leicester's answer to Miss sodding Marple.

Thursday February 20th

I fear the worst. Bianca is still in Leicester. I received a brochure this morning from an organization called the Naxos Institute. They were offering me a holistic holiday on the Greek island of Naxos, complete with courses in creative writing, dream workshops, finding your voice and stress management. One photograph in the brochure showed happy, tanned holidaymakers scoffing green foodstuffs at long tables under blue skies. Close examination with a magnifying glass showed the foodstuffs to be made up of lettuce and courgettes with a bit of what looked like cheese thrown in. There were bottles of retsina on the tables, vases of flowers and rough-hewn loaves of bread.

Another photograph showed a beach and a pine forest and the bamboo hut accommodation spread over a hillside. It looked truly idyllic. I turned a page and saw that Angela Hacker, the novelist, playwright and television personality, was 'facilitating' the writing course for the first two weeks in April. I have not read her books or seen her plays, but I have seen her on the television programme *Through the Keyhole*. She has certainly got a gracious home, though I remember being struck at the time by the amazing amount of alcohol in evidence. There were bottles in every room. Loyd Grossman made a quip about it at the time, something about 'sauce for the goose'. The studio audience laughed itself stupid.

I closed the brochure with a sigh. Two weeks on Naxos talking about my novel with Angela Hacker would be paradise, but I can't possibly afford it. My Building Society reserves are running low. I'm down to my last thousand.

Saturday February 22nd

Bianca rang the restaurant at lunchtime and said that she would be catching the 7.30 a.m. train from Leicester tomorrow and would be arriving at St Pancras at around 9.00 a.m. Her voice sounded strange. I asked

her if she'd got a sore throat. She replied that she'd
been 'doing a lot of talking'. Every fibre of me longs
for her, especially the bits around my loins.

Sunday February 23rd

I was on the platform when the train came in and saw
Bianca jump onto the platform. I ran towards her,
holding a bunch of daffodils I'd bought from a stall
outside the Underground on Oxford Street. Then, to
my surprise, I saw Martin Muffet step down from the
train, carrying two large suitcases. He put them down
on the platform and put his arm around Bianca's slim
shoulders.

Bianca said, 'I'm sorry, Adrian.'

Muffet said, 'So am I.'

To be quite honest, I didn't know what to say.

I turned away, leaving the two engineers under the
engineering miracle of St Pancras Station and made
my way back to Old Compton Street on foot. I don't
know what happened to the daffodils, but I hadn't got
them when I arrived home.

Monday February 24th

Chapter Twenty-Four: Oblivion
Jake slipped the hose over the exhaust pipe and checked

that it was properly connected. Then he put the other end of the hose through the side window of the car. He took a long, last look at the glorious vista of the Lake District panorama spread beneath him. 'How glorious life is,' he said, aloud, to the wind. All around him the daffodils nodded their agreement. Jake took his portable electric razor from his toiletry bag and proceeded to shave. He had always been vain and he was particularly keen to look good as a corpse. His bristles flew into the wind and became as one with the earth. Jake splashed on Obsession, his favourite after-shave lotion. Then, his toilette completed, he climbed into the car and switched on the engine.

As the fumes filled the inside of the car, Jake ruminated on his life. He had visited four continents and bedded some of the world's most beautiful women. He had recovered the Ashes for England. He had climbed Everest backwards, and found the definitive source of the Nile. Nobody could say that his life had been without interest. But, without Regina, the girl he loved, he did not want to live. As Jake slipped into oblivion, the needle on the petrol gauge turned to 'E'. Which would run out first, Jake's oxygen supply, or Jake's petrol . . .?

Tuesday February 25th

Got the courage up to ring my mother. My father answered. He said that he has moved back to live with my mother 'on a temporary basis' until she has recovered from the immediate shock of the Bianca/

Muffet affair. Apparently, she is too ill to leave her bed and look after Rosie.

He asked how I had taken it.

I said, 'Oh me, I'm fine,' and then big, fat tears rolled down my cheeks and into the electronic workings of the telephone handset. My father kept saying, down the phone, 'There, there, lad. There, there, don't cry, lad,' in a tender voice that I don't remember him using before.

Roberto the chef came and stood at my side and wiped the tears away with his apron. Eventually, after promising to keep in touch, I said goodbye to my father. For years I have thought of him as a feckless fool, but I now see that I have misjudged him.

When I got back to the room, I found that Bianca had taken all her personal belongings, including the photograph of Isambard Kingdom Brunel.

Wednesday February 26th

I went to a place called Ed's Diner at lunchtime today and had a hot dog, fries, a Becks beer and a mug of filter coffee. I asked for a glass for my beer and then noticed that the other men of my age were swigging it from the bottle, so I pushed my glass away surreptitiously and did as they did. I sat at a high stool at the counter in front of a mini-jukebox. Each selection cost five pence. I selected only one record, but I played it three times.

I used to be able to recite the lyric of 'Stand by Me' off by heart. Bianca and I used to sing along with Ben E. King when we cooked Sunday breakfast together. Our percussion instruments included: a box of household matches, a spatula, and a tin of dried lentils.

In Ed's Diner I tried to sing the words under my breath but I couldn't remember a word.

At the end of the song I was in tears. Why couldn't she have stood by me?

A man sitting on the next stool asked if there was anything he could do. I tried to compose myself, but to my absolute horror I began to sob loudly and without restraint. There were tears; there was snot; there were undignified gulpings and heavings of the shoulders. The stranger put his arm around my shoulders and asked, 'Have you had a relationship gone wrong?'

I nodded, then managed to say, in between sobs, 'Finished.'

'Same here,' he said. Then 'My name's Alan.' Alan told me that he was 'devastated' because his partner, Christopher, had fallen for another man. I ordered two more beers and then I told Alan the whole story about Bianca and Martin Muffet. Alan confessed himself to be shocked and was thoughtful enough to enquire as to my mother's feelings. I told him that I'd phoned her last night and that she'd told me that her life was over.

Alan and I have arranged to meet for a drink at

8.00 p.m. tonight. Am I now, like Blanche Dubois, dependent on the kindness of strangers?

Midnight Alan didn't turn up. I sat in the 'Coach and Horses' for over an hour, waiting for him. Perhaps he met another stranger with a more original tragic story.

I miss her. I miss her. I miss her.

Thursday February 27th

Roberto stood over me this evening and made me eat a plate of tagliatelle with hare sauce. He said, 'A woman issa woman, but food issa food.'

Perhaps it has more meaning in the original Italian.

Jake handed the envelope containing the money to the sinister man.

'Quick and clean,' he said. 'They mustn't know what hit them.'

The man grunted and left the Soho drinking den. Jake looked around him, at the tawdry, painted girls, at the bestial faces of the late night drinkers. Was it only yesterday he was in the Lake District attempting suicide? As he rose to his feet, a young prostitute attempted to procure him. He pushed her away irritably, saying, 'Get lost, baby, I've known and lost the only woman I'll ever want.'

He strode out into the vibrant Soho night, his cowboy boots tapping strangely on the murky pavement. I must get them soled and heeled tomorrow, he thought. As he passed down Old Compton Street, he looked up at the window of the flat above Alma's Patisserie. The light was still burning but he knew that by now all human life had been extinguished. He was a murderer by proxy.

Tears poured inside his heart, but his face was as it always was, hard and unforgiving and without God's blessing.

Saturday February 29th

I have informed Mr Andropolosis, the landlord, that I have taken over the tenancy, and paid him a month's rent in advance, so the room is now mine. Thank God for the end of this month. It has surely been the worst since time began.

To complete our catalogue of family misery, Grandma was admitted to hospital during the early hours of this morning with abdominal pains. I rang the hospital this afternoon and was told by the ward sister that Grandma was 'comfortable'. If this is true, then she is the only member of the family who is – the rest of us are in total misery.

Sunday March 1st

I joined my mother, father and Rosie at Grandma's hospital bedside this afternoon. It was the first time I had seen Grandma without her teeth. I was shocked at how *old* she looked.

My mother has lost weight and her eyes looked sore, as though she has been weeping constantly since Muffet upped and left her. After visiting time was over and we were trooping down the ward, my mother said bitterly: 'They're in Hounslow, staying with his brother, Andrew.'

I said, 'I don't want to know, Mum.'

My father said, 'Let it drop, Pauline.'

Rosie said, 'I'm glad he's gone. I hope he never comes back.' She held her hand up and my father took it and steered her through the big double doors at the end of the ward. As we walked alongside the hospital tower blocks, the litter swirled around our feet and I had a premonition of doom.

I almost turned back to say a proper goodbye to Grandma, but I didn't want to keep the others hanging around in the potholed car park, so I didn't. Instead, we went home and had a Marks & Spencer's roast beef dinner each. Mine was quite nice, but it wasn't a patch on the real thing cooked by my grandma. As I was compressing the dirty tin foil trays into the kitchen pedal bin, the telephone rang. It was the hospital, telling us that 'Mrs Edna May Mole passed away at 5.15 p.m.'

I tried to remember where I was *exactly* at 5.15 p.m. I worked out that I was in a BP petrol station, helping my father to check the pressure in his car tyres.

I haven't shed a single tear for her yet. I'm dried up inside. My heart feels like a peach stone.

Monday March 2nd

It is a well-known fact that Grandma and my mother never got on, so nobody was prepared for the positively Mediterranean grief my mother is displaying over her mother-in-law's death: copious tears, breast-beating, etc. This morning she was lamenting, 'I owed her fifty quid' over and over again.

My father continues to astonish me with his maturity. He has dealt with all the death paperwork and haggled over the cost of the funeral with commendable efficiency.

Tuesday March 3rd

At 10.00 p.m. I rang 'Savages' to tell them that I am staying in Leicester for the funeral on Friday afternoon. Roberto said, 'I'm glad you ring, Adrian. Your flat has been called on by burglars.' He made it sound as though burglars had been invited to tea, brought flowers and left a visiting card. There's nothing I can do tonight. The police have employed the services of a locksmith. The new key is at 'Savages'. I feel strangely calm.

Wednesday March 4th

Train to Leicester 8.40 p.m.

They have taken everything, apart from my books, boxer shorts and an old pair of polyester trousers. How they got the bed down the stairs will probably always remain a mystery. The policeman I spoke to on the phone said, in answer to my question about the likelihood of their finding the culprits: 'You know what chance a snowball has in hell? Well, halve that. Then halve it again.' He asked if I had insurance.

I laughed scornfully and said, 'Of course not. This is Adrian Mole you're speaking to.'

I am now a man without possessions.

Thursday March 5th

I went into Grandma's home this morning. Everything was the same as ever. My GCE certificates were still there, framed on the wall. My dead grandad Albert's photograph was on the mantelpiece. The clock was still ticking. Upstairs, the linen lay folded in the cupboard and in the garden the bulbs pushed through the earth. The biscuit barrel was full of fig rolls and her second best slippers stood by her bed. Inside a kitchen cupboard, I found her Yorkshire pudding tin. She had used it for over forty years. Stupid to weep

over a Yorkshire pudding tin, but I did. I then wiped
it dry and replaced it in the cupboard, as she would
have liked.

Friday March 6th
Grandma's Funeral

My mother and father, Rosie and I worked together
as a team today and managed to give Grandma a
good send-off. There was a respectable turnout in the
church, which surprised me, because Grandma didn't
encourage people to call on her. She preferred the
company of Radio Four. She had been known to
turn people away from her doorstep, should they be
inconsiderate enough to call during the Afternoon
Play.

The hymns were 'Amazing Grace' and 'Onward
Christian Soldiers'. Bert Baxter sang out loudly, almost
drowning the others in the congregation. For an
atheist, he certainly enjoys singing in church. As I
watched him, I couldn't help thinking wistfully that it
should have been him who died instead of Grandma.
The vicar said a lot of incredibly stupid things about
Grandma being born into sin and dying in sin.

Anybody who knew Grandma knew that she was
incapable of sin. She couldn't even tell a lie. When I
asked her once if my spots were clearing up (I must
have been about fifteen), she answered, 'No, you've
still got a face like a ladybird's arse.' She occasionally

used such mild profanities, but she was certainly not a sinner.

I don't like to think of her lying under the earth, alone and cold. Still, at least she was never burgled or mugged. She is safe from all that now.

The funeral tea was held at our house. My mother had been up most of the previous night, cleaning and polishing and trying to get the stains out of the lounge carpet.

My father replaced the missing light bulbs and mended the ballcock so that the lavatory flushed properly.

Tania Braithwaite came round to give her commiserations and kindly offered to defrost some vegetarian quiches she had in the freezer. She told us that Pandora had cancelled a lecture and was intending to come to the funeral tea and would be bringing six bottles of Marks & Spencer's champagne with her.

She said, 'Pandora believes in celebrating death. She sees it as a new adventure, as opposed to a rather boring ending.'

Bert Baxter had phoned to ask what time the service started, which reminded my mother that there was no beetroot in the house. So Rosie was given a personal safety alarm and sent round to the corner shop to buy a jar from Mr Patel's shop.

At midnight, I watched my parents spreading a white tablecloth over the dining-room table, which had had its leaves fully extended. As they flapped and adjusted the cloth, one at either end, I had a sudden sense of being a member of the family.

Rosie had arranged some daffodils and freesias nicely in a vase and was praised by everyone. Even the dog behaved itself. When we finally went to bed, the house looked perfect; everything was in its place and we Moles could hold our heads high. Grandma would have been proud of us.

After the funeral service, Rosie and I ran ahead of the other mourners to take the clingfilm off the sandwiches and sausage rolls.

Pandora was waiting outside the house in her car. We filled the bath with cold water and put the bottles of champagne into it to chill.

Pandora looked beautifully severe in a black tailored suit. However, I no longer felt in awe of her, so we were able to talk to each other as friends and equals. She complimented me on how well I was looking and she even praised my clothes. She fingered the lapel of my navy blue unstructured Next suit and said, 'Welcome to the nineties.'

The house soon filled up with mourners and I was kept busy circulating with glasses of champagne on a tray. At first, everyone stood around, not knowing what to say, nervous of enjoying themselves for fear of being thought disrespectful to the dead. Then Pandora broke the ice by proposing a toast to Grandma.

'To Edna Mole,' she said, lifting her glass of champagne high, 'a woman of the highest principles.'

Everyone clinked glasses and swigged back the champagne and it wasn't long before laughter broke out and I was fishing the bottles out of the bath.

My mother rummaged in the sideboard and brought out the photograph albums. I was astonished to see a photograph of my grandma at the age of twenty-four. She looked very dashing, dark-haired, with a lovely figure, and was laughing and pushing a bicycle up a hill. There was a man next to her wearing a flat cap. He had a big moustache and his eyes were crinkled against the sun. It was my grandad. Everybody remarked that I looked like him.

My father took the photograph out of the album and went into the garden and sat on Rosie's swing. After a while, I followed him out. He handed me the photograph and said, 'I'm an orphan, son.'

I put my hand on his shoulder, then went back inside to find that the funeral tea had turned into a party. People were laughing hysterically at the photographs in the album. Me at the seaside, falling off a donkey. Me in a secondhand cub's uniform three sizes too big. Me at six months, lying naked on a half moon-shaped rug in front of a gas fire. Me two days old with my grinning, young-looking parents in the maternity hospital. On the back was written, in my mother's handwriting, 'Our darling baby, two days old'.

There was a photograph I don't remember seeing before. It was my mother and father and my grandma and grandad. They were sitting in deckchairs, watching me, aged about three, playing in the sand. On the back was written: 'Yarmouth, Bank Holiday Monday'.

Rosie said, 'Why aren't I in the photo?'

Bert Baxter said, 'Cos you 'adn't been bleedin' born, that's why.'

At seven o'clock, Ivan Braithwaite offered to escort some of my grandma's elderly neighbours back to their pensioners' bungalows while they and he could still walk.

The rest of us carried on until eleven o'clock. Tania Braithwaite, who has been vegetarian for nine years, cracked and ate a sausage roll and then another.

My mother and father danced together to 'You've Lost That Loving Feeling'. You couldn't have slid a ruler between them.

Pandora and I watched them dancing. She said, 'So they're back together again, are they?'

'I hope so,' I said, looking at Rosie.

As I said before, it was a good send-off.

Monday March 9th

Old Compton Street

I am back in my room with only my books and boxer shorts for company. I have given the trousers away to a young man selling *The Big Issue*. I made a pillow out of my underwear and slept on the floor. I have often wondered what it would be like to be a celibate monk in a bare cell. Now, thanks to burglary and desertion, I know.

I went into 'Savages' to help clean the kitchen. Savage himself was there, released from the alcohol abuse unit and looking fit and athletic and sipping on a glass of mineral water. He commiserated with me on my various losses and said that there was some old furniture in the attic above the restaurant that I could have.

'Just help yourself, kid,' he said.

I can't get used to this new, kind, philanthropic Savage. I keep thinking he must be Savage's long lost twin brother, recently returned from a missionary station in Amazonia.

My room is now furnished with rococo style banquettes and fag-stained *faux* marble tables. Stuff that was obviously thrown upstairs when Savage took over the restaurant. I now sleep on two banquettes pushed together. I have angels at my head and cherubs at my feet. Roberto gave me some cutlery and crockery and kitchen utensils. Most of my fellow workers brought something to work with them this morning, to donate to the Adrian Mole Disaster Fund. I cook on a ring fuelled by a gas canister and I read by a mock chandelier, both donated by Luigi.

Wednesday March 11th

I rang home this morning. My father is still there, living in sin with my mother. My mother told me that Bianca and Muffet are intending to set up an engineering partnership called 'Dartington and Muffet'.

I cannot bear the thought of Muffet's bony fingers touching Bianca's lovely pale skin.

I cannot bear it.

Thursday March 12th

Chapter Twenty-Five: Resurgence
Jake sat down at the *faux* marble table and began to write another chapter of his novel, *Sparg from Kronk*.

Chapter Five: Green Shoots
Sparg missed his woman, Barf. There was a part of him that would never be reconciled to her loss.

It was springtime. Green shoots showed through the earth. Sparg left his hut and went outside. He was glad to be outside, for the hut was damp and the damp was rising fast.

Sparg needed a woman, but the only woman in sight was Krun, his mother. Though her face was wrinkled, her thighs were inviting. But it was forbidden by Kronkian law to take your own mother, even if she agreed.

Sparg walked aimlessly up a small hill and then walked aimlessly down. He was bored. There was firewood to collect, but he was sick of collecting firewood. It did not challenge his intellect. He grunted in despair and wished it were possible to communicate with his fellow Kronkians. It was just his luck, he thought, to be born in prehistoric times.

If only there was *language*, grunted Sparg internally . . .

to be continued

Jake fell back. The intensity of the writing had left him drained and pale. He left his room and walked to Wilde's, his favourite restaurant, where he was greeted by Mario.

'Longa tima noa see, Mr Westmorland.'

'Hi, Mario. My usual table, please, and my usual bottle, well chilled, and I'll have my usual starter, usual main course and usual pudding.'

'And for your aperitif, Mr Westmorland?' purred Mario.

'The usual,' barked Jake.

I've got to finish *Lo! The Flat Hills of My Homeland* soon, but I can't do that until Jake has finished writing *Sparg from Kronk*. I wish he would hurry up.

Friday March 13th

More businesses are closing around us. Every day, the boards go up at shop and restaurant windows. Every night, I pray that 'Savages' stays financially viable. I need my job. I'm aware that I'm being exploited, but at least I have a reason to get up in the morning, unlike three and a half million of my fellow citizens.

Grandma left my father three thousand and ninety pounds in her will, so my mother is not going to have her house repossessed. This is truly joyous news. It means that I won't have to break into my Building Society savings. I couldn't have seen her thrown onto the street. At least, I don't think I could.

Saturday March 14th

I received the following message when I got to work this morning. It was written on the back of a paper napkin. 'Forgot G. Left 500.' Nobody knew what it meant or who had taken the message.

Monday March 16th

Received another brochure from the Naxos Institute. Why are they mailing me so assiduously? Who has put them on to me? I don't know any holistic types. I'm not even a vegetarian and I swear by paracetamol.

I went to the National Gallery today, but it brought back painful memories of B., so I went back to Soho and paid two pounds to watch a fat girl with spots remove her bra and knickers through a peephole. I *watched* her through a peephole. She didn't remove her underclothes through a peephole.

Query: Are there night classes in syntax?

Tuesday March 17th

I ran out of toilet paper last night and reached for the Naxos Institute brochure to help me out of my emergency, when something about Angela Hacker's face made me pause. It seemed to say, 'Come to me, Adrian.' Her face is nothing to write home about, in fact it's nothing to write *anywhere* about.

I put the brochure down and picked up the *Evening Standard* instead. It has far better absorbency qualities.

11.45 p.m. Can't sleep for St Patrick's Day revellers, so have idly filled in the booking form for the first two weeks in April at the Naxos Institute in Greece.

Thursday March 19th

Idly filled in a cheque made out to 'Naxos Institute', but I was only trying out a new pen. I couldn't possibly afford the time off work, or the money.

10.00 p.m. The full message was: 'Forgot to tell you Grandma has left you five hundred pounds, love, Dad.' Luigi, who had been away from the restaurant with food poisoning, returned today and congratulated me on 'Alla money ya got'. Naturally, I looked at him blankly. Confusion abounded for some minutes and then came the glorious realization, which we celebrated with a bottle of corked Frascati.

Saturday March 21st

The newly benign Savage has agreed to give me two weeks' leave (without pay). I posted my booking form this morning and this afternoon I bought some swimming trunks from a shop that was closing down in the Charing Cross Road. I can't wait to feel the warm Aegean sea on my body.

Worked on *Lo!* with Angela Hacker in mind.

Jake opened his manuscript book. The ivory handmade paper looked enticing. He took his Mont Blanc pen in his hand and began to write.

'Sorry, darling,' he said to the glorious example of English womanhood who sprawled opposite him, showing her knickers, 'but the Muse is upon me.'

Then he lowered his handsome head and was at once in Kronk, the home of his hero, Sparg.

Sparg grunted, recognizing the hated form of his father in the darkness. His father grunted back. Sparg threw a pebble from one hand to the other. Why hadn't something been invented to pass the hours of darkness before bed, he wondered. Something like a game such as cards, he wondered. He went back into his hut and pushed the animal skins listlessly around on his bed. He was cold at night without a woman. He determined that he would get up early the next morning and find one and bring her home to Kronk.

Thursday March 26th

I bought a short-sleeved shirt and a pair of Bermuda shorts from a stall in Berwick Street market. I have never worn shorts since reaching adulthood.

A new Adrian Mole is emerging from the ashes.

Savage turned up drunk and disorderly at the restaurant and proceeded to fire Luigi, Roberto and the whole of the kitchen staff apart from me. He said, 'You can stay, Adrian. You're a fucking loser, like me.'

He has promoted me to *Maître d'*, a position I do not want and cannot do.

Luigi and Roberto sat in the kitchen, smoking and talking in Italian. They didn't seem too concerned. Meanwhile, dressed in Luigi's suit, I was forced to fawn over customers, show them to their seats and pretend to be interested in their requirements. Savage sat at the bar, shouting out the biographical details of his customers as they came in. As one respectable-looking middle-aged couple entered, he yelled: 'Well, if it isn't Mr and Mrs Wellington. He's wearing a toupée and she's paid three thousand pounds for those perky looking titties.'

Instead of going straight back out, or thumping him on the side of his drunken head, Mr and Mrs Wellington grinned and allowed me to show them to table number six. Perhaps they are proud of their artificial attributes. As my recently dead grandma would say, 'There's nowt so strange as folk, especially London folk.'

Poor Grandma. She never went to London in her life.

For the past four days, I have been unable to write a word. The thought of Angela Hacker reading my manuscript has totally inhibited me. However, tonight I achieved a breakthrough.

He had writer's block. For over five hours he stared down at the mockingly empty page. His publisher was calling hourly. The printing presses were waiting, but still he could not finish his book. Jake looked out of the window, hoping for inspiration. The New York skyline stretched away into infinity . . .

'Infinity!' shouted Jake, excitedly, and he began to work on his novel, *Sparg from Kronk*.

Sparg had wandered far from Kronk and was standing on a high headland, looking in wonderment at a strange watery mass and a blue line ahead of him. Without knowing it (because there was no language), Sparg was marvelling over the sea and the far distant horizon. Sparg growled and began to descend the headland. He would walk to the far blue line, he thought. It would be something to do. Sparg thought this because there was as yet no swimming ...

Received confirmation from Faxos Institute that I have a place on the Writers' Course. I am terrified.

Friday March 27th

Luigi has been reinstated and I am safely back in the kitchen, thank God. Roberto has been allowing me to watch him at work. For most of my life, I have been denied a proper food education. There was never anything to learn from my mother; she stopped cooking real food soon after reading *The Female Eunuch*. Though, ironically, the author of that seminal tome, Ms Germaine Greer, is a renowned cook and dinner party giver.

Thanks to Roberto's kindness, I can now cook pasta '*al dente*' and make a basic sponge cake and I've almost cracked making watercress soup. I now spring from my double banquettes in the morning, eager to get to work.

Plane tickets arrived today.

A new girl started work as a waitress at 'Savages' this evening. Her name is Jo Jo and she is from Nigeria. She is studying Art at St Martin's. She is taller than anybody else in the restaurant. Her hair is braided with hundreds of tiny beads. She rattles when she walks. Her mother is something big in the Nigerian tractor industry.

Saturday March 28th

Made a *tower* of profiteroles today. Roberto said: 'Congratulations, Adriana! The chocolate icing issa perfection.'

Jo Jo tasted the first one and pronounced it to be 'delectable'. Luigi happened to have his polaroid camera with him, so he photographed me and the tower and Jo Jo. I have pinned the photograph on my wall. I look quite handsome.

Sunday March 29th

I was still in bed at midday when there was a knock on the door. I never have visitors, so I was a little alarmed. I put my ear to the door, but all I could hear was a peculiar rattling noise. I eventually opened the door, but I kept the security chain on. I was delighted to see Jo Jo through the crack.

She smiled at me and said that she was going to the Tate Gallery.

'Do you want to come?' she asked.

I slipped the chain off and invited her in. She walked around the room and commented on how tidy it was.

She stopped at the table where my manuscript lay in its transparent folder and said, 'So this is your book.'

She touched it reverently. 'I would like to read it one day.'

'When it's finished,' I said.

I made her a cup of Nescafé and then excused myself and went into the bathroom to wash and change.

I looked at myself in the washbasin mirror. Something had happened to my face. I no longer looked like John Major.

Jo Jo likes walking, so we walked to the Tate. I was proud to be seen with such a stunning looking woman. I asked her about Nigeria and she spoke about her country with obvious love. She is a Yoruba and comes from Abeokuta.

She asked me about my family and I told her about the tangled web of relationships, the break-ups and the reconciliations.

She laughed and said, 'To work out the relationships in my family, you would need an extremely sophisticated computer.'

I had never been to the Tate, but Jo Jo knew it well. She guided me round and made me look at a few of her favourite paintings – all depicting people, I noticed. We looked at paintings by Paula Rego, Vanessa Bell and Matisse, and a piece of sculpture by Ghisha Koenig called 'The Machine Minders', and then she insisted that we leave before we got bored and our feet started to ache.

As we were going down the steps, Jo Jo asked if I would like to have tea at her flat in Battersea.

I said, 'I'd love to.' We crossed the road and stood at the bus stop, but then, on impulse, I flagged down a black cab and we rode to her flat in style.

She lives on the top floor of a mansion block. Every room is full of her paintings. Many of the paintings are nude self-portraits, in which she has depicted herself in many colours, including green, pink, purple, blue and yellow.

I asked her if she was making a statement about her colour. 'No,' she laughed. 'But I would get bored only using blacks and browns.'

We ate scones and drank Earl Grey tea and talked non-stop: about 'Savages'; Nigerian politics; cats; one of her art teachers, who is going mad; Cecil Parkinson; the price of paint brushes; Vivaldi; our star signs – she is Leo (but on the cusp of Cancer); and her girls' boarding school in Surrey, where she lived from the age of eleven until she got expelled at sixteen for climbing on the roof of the chapel in a protest against the lousy food.

Over a glass of cheap wine, we discussed trees; Matisse; Moscow; Russian politics; our favourite cakes; the use of umbrellas; cabbage; and the Royal Family. She is a republican, she said.

Over a final glass of wine and a plate of bread and cheese, I talked to her about my grandmother, my mother, Pandora, Sharon, Megan, Leonora, Cassandra and Bianca. 'You're carrying a lot of baggage,' Jo Jo said.

We parted at 10.30 p.m. with a friendly handshake. Before she closed the door, I asked how old she was. 'Twenty-four,' she said. 'Goodnight.'

Monday March 30th

I ran out of 'Savages' during my break time and bought Ambre Solaire (Factor 8), espadrilles, sleeveless tee shirts, three more pairs of shorts and sixteen thousand drachmas.

I worked on the book late into the night. I am nervous about Angela Hacker's opinion. Added more descriptive words to *Lo! The Flat Hills of My Homeland* and took out more descriptive words from *Sparg from Kronk*.

Tuesday March 31st

The staff arranged a small *bon voyage* party in the kitchen after the restaurant closed at lunchtime. I was very touched. Roberto cooked kebabs and arranged an authentic Greek salad in my honour. Jo Jo bought two bottles of retsina earlier in the day and we all clinked glasses and swore eternal friendship. Then Savage came in, complaining that Luigi had forgotten to add VAT to somebody's bill, so the party broke up. Jo Jo is good at packing, she said. She offered to come and help me.

I laid my clothes, toiletry bag and manuscript out on my bed before proceeding to pack, and then realized that the burglars had taken my suitcase.

Jo Jo ran to Berwick Street market and bought one of those man-made fibre striped bags, the type that refugees have on the television news. Once I was packed, I debated with Jo Jo on whether or not to take a warm coat with me. She said I ought to, but I decided not to. Instead, I slung a cotton sweater around my shoulders. Everybody has said that Greece is warm in April. My legs look very white at the moment in my shorts, but by the time I return, they will be gloriously tanned.

Spring

Dear Jo Jo,

For the first time in my life, there is nobody to wish me a Happy Birthday. I am now twenty-five years old. Which is a millstone in anybody's life. Do I still qualify to be called a 'Young British Novelist'? I hope so.

Other participants in the Naxos Institute course are swirling around downstairs in the hotel lobby, chatting easily to each other. I fled back into the lift when I saw them, and went up to the roof terrace, but Angela Hacker was up there, smoking a cigarette and looking moodily at the Acropolis in the far distance. She is skinny and dresses in white clothes. She was weighed down by ethnic silver jewellery.

I don't know when the photograph of her in the brochure was taken, but in life she looks at least forty-eight. Obviously past it, sexually and artistically.

I didn't thank you properly for that afternoon in the Tate. I keep thinking about the pictures. I particularly liked those painted by that Portuguese woman, Paula something.

All best wishes,
    Adrian

                        Ferry
                Friday April 3rd

Dear Mum and Dad,

I am writing this on the first ferry, which is taking us to where we catch the second ferry to Naxos. Angela Hacker and most of the twelve members of the writers' group are already in the bar. The majority of them smoke. You would probably get along famously with them, Mum. The other, more holistic, holidaymakers are looking over the side of the ship, taking photographs or swapping aromatherapy recipes. I am keeping to myself. I don't want to lumber myself with a hastily-made 'friend' and spend the next fortnight getting rid of him or her. It has just started to rain. I will have to stop now and go inside.

Love from your son,
    Adrian

                        Ferry
                Friday April 3rd
                    4.00 p.m.

Dear Jo Jo,

There has been torrential rain for the whole of the three-hour crossing. I am wearing my cotton sweater, but am still cold. I now wish I'd followed your advice and brought a coat with me.

Angela Hacker has been falling down in the bar. The sea *is* choppy, but I think her lack of balance is due more to the copious amounts of retsina she is throwing down her neck. My fellow writers have been laughing non-stop since boarding the ferry. Some private joke, no doubt. I have not yet introduced myself to them.

Bamboo Hut Number Six

8.00 p.m.

The wind is whistling through the slats of my hut. Outside, the sky is grey and dotted with storm clouds. Supper was eaten in the open air, under a 'roof' of palm fronds. Not surprisingly, the ratatouille was cold.

I can hear Angela Hacker coughing from here, though her hut is at least two hundred yards further down the rocky hill.

There was a community meeting at eight o'clock, where the permanent staff and the facilitators introduced themselves and their work. The meeting was held in what they call here the 'Magic Ring', which is on the very top of the hill. The Magic Ring is a concrete base, surrounded by a low wall and covered in the usual palm frond and bamboo roof. There is nothing magical looking about it.

I was most concerned to hear Ms Hacker describe her course as 'Writing for Pleasure'. I get no pleasure from writing. Writing is a serious business, like painting.

There is a man here who wears his hair like yours. I saw him on the headland, looking out to sea. From a distance he looked like you. My heart did a backflip.

My hut is next to the hen-coop. A goat has just put its

head inside my hut and a donkey is braying somewhere in the pine woods. If Noah's Ark was washed up on the beach, I wouldn't be surprised.

    Best wishes,
       Adrian

                         Faxos
              Sunday April 5th

Dear Pan,

    You asked me to let you know how the Naxos course was, so I'll tell you about the first day.

    The writers collected on the terrace at 11.15 a.m. I sat upwind, away from the cigarette smoke. At 11.30 a.m. Angela Hacker had still not appeared, so a man called Clive, who had seven boils on his neck, was sent to her hut. She eventually showed up at noon and apologized for having overslept. She then rambled on for an hour and fifteen minutes about 'Truth' and 'Narrative thrust' and 'developing an original voice'.

    At 1.15 p.m. she sprang to her feet and said, 'Okay, that's it for the day. Write a poem including the word "Greece". Be prepared to read it aloud at 11.15 tomorrow morning.' She then headed for the bamboo bar, where she stayed for most of the day. When I'd written my poem, I went in for a cup of tea and heard her talking about your college in Oxford.

    I asked her if she knew you and she said she had met you at Jack Cavendish's house a few times, 'before Jack left his third wife,' she said.

    I said, 'It's a small world.'

'Try not to use clichés, darling,' she said.

She's a strange woman.

All the best from,

Adrian

Faxos

Monday April 6th

Dear Rosie,

I hope you like this postcard of the cheerful donkey. There is something about its daft expression that reminds me of the dog.

I have sent you a poem I was forced to write about Greece. It's time you started to take an interest in cultural matters. There is more to life than Nintendo games.

Love from your brother,

Adrian

Oh Greece, ancient cultured land
You wrap around my heart just like
An old elastic band.
Your hag-like women pensioners
Clad in clothes of black,
Are they unaware of all the services they lack?
Will they be content to watch
The donkey with its load?
Won't they want a vehicle to
Drive along the road?

Faxos
Tuesday April 7th

Dear Baz,

I am here on Naxos with Angela Hacker, whom I understand you know quite well. She and I hit it off immediately
and she has invited me to stay at her place in Gloucestershire
when we get back. I may be able to make the odd weekend,
but I am currently doing research in a restaurant kitchen
in Soho for my next book, *The Chopper,* so will not be able
to stay for a couple of weeks, as she would like.

The reason I am writing is to say that I hope there are
no hard feelings any more over the Sharon Bott affair, because
we are likely to be moving in the same circles soon and I
would rather there were no acrimonious feelings between us.

Congratulations on finally getting to number one!

Cheers,

Your old friend,

Adrian Mole

Faxos
Wednesday April 8th

Dear John Tydeman,

As you cannot fail to see, if you have noticed the postmark, I am on the Greek island of Naxos. I am a member
of a writers' course being facilitated by Angela Hacker (she
sends you her love).

She asked us to write the first scene of a radio play, which
is something I have never attempted to do before.

I thought you might be interested to read what I have
written. I would be more than willing to finish it, if you
thought it had merit.

I shall be back in London at 3.00 p.m. on the 15th April, if you would like to talk to me face to face.

On second thoughts, the 16th would be more convenient for me. I shall probably need to rest after my journey.

Here is how the play opens:

The Cucumber Sandwich
A Play for Radio by Adrian Mole

A room in a wealthy house. A game of tennis can be heard through the french windows. Tea is poured. A spoon rattles in a cup.

LADY ELEANOR: A cucumber sandwich, Edwin?

EDWIN: Don't try to fob me off with your bourgeois ideas of gentility. I know the truth!

LADY ELEANOR (*gasps*): No! Surely not! You don't know the secret I have kept for forty years!

EDWIN (*contemptuously*): Yes, I do. The servant girl, Millie, told me.

A bell rings.

MILLIE: You rang, mum? Sorry to keep you, only I was 'elpin' cook with Master Edwin's twenty-first birthday cake.

LADY ELEANOR: You are dismissed, Millie. You have blabbed my secret.

MILLIE: What secret? Oh! The one about your being born a man?

To be continued

I do not wish to prejudice you in any way, but after I had finished reading this text, there was a stunned silence from my fellow writers. Angela's only comment was, 'You should have spun the secret out until the last scene of the play.'

Good advice, I think.

Anyway, I hope you enjoy *The Cucumber Sandwich.*

Yours,

With best wishes,

Adrian Mole

Faxos

Thursday April 9th

Dear Jo Jo,

The sun has shone for two days now and has turned Naxos into Paradise. The colours are breathtaking: the sea is peacock blue, the grass is peppermint green and the wild flowers are scattered on the hillside like living confetti.

Something has happened to my body. It feels looser, as though it has broken free and is floating.

I have been going to dream workshops at 7.00 a.m. The facilitator is a nice American woman dream therapist called Clara. I told her about a recurring dream I have that I am trying to pick up the last pea on my dinner plate by stabbing it with a fork. Try as I may, I cannot get the prongs of the fork to stab into the flesh of the pea.

For years I have woken up feeling frustrated and hungry after dreaming my pea dream.

Clara advised me to look at the dream from the *pea's*

point of view. I did try hard to do this and, by discussing it with Clara later, I understood that I, Adrian Mole, was the pea and that the fork represented DEATH.

Clara said that my pea dream showed that I am afraid to die.

But who is *looking forward* to death? I don't know anybody who is cock-a-hoop at the prospect.

Clara explained that I am *morbidly* afraid of death.

How do you feel about death, Jo Jo?

I have made friends with the bloke with the beaded plaits like yours. His name is Sean Washington. His mother is Irish; his father is from St Kitts. He is here taking the stress management course, but he hangs out with the writers' group on the bar terrace.

We were both on vegetable chopping duties today and I was complimented by him and others on my expertise. I think I would like to be a chef. I may ask Savage if he'll give me a trial when I get back.

Angela Hacker has forbidden her writers' group to use clichés, but she will not be reading this letter, so I'll sign off by saying:

Wish you were here,
    Adrian

Saturday April 11th

My first fax! It was addressed to 'Adrian Mole, Naxos Institute', and arrived at the travel agent's shop in the town. It was then conveyed to the Naxos Institute by greengrocer's van and delivered to me on the bar terrace by Julian, the handsome bald-headed administrator. It caused a sensation.

Dear Adrian,

Thank you for your letters. I wish I were there with you. It sounds idyllic.

I'm so glad that you feel at ease. When I first saw you in Savage's kitchen, I thought: that man is in *pain*. I wanted to touch you and comfort you there and then, but of course one does not do such a thing – not in England.

I think you have it in your power to become a happy man, providing you can let go of the past. Why not try to live in the present and leave all that baggage behind on Faxos when you return?

I couldn't wait to tell you that I have been offered a shared exhibition of 'Young Contemporaries' in September. Will you come to the opening? Please say you will.

Roberto is complaining that the man Savage has hired to take your place for a fortnight is massacring the vegetables and he now regrets letting you go on holiday.

Everybody at 'Savages' sends their best wishes. Roberto asks if you will bring a bottle of ouzo back for him.

I miss you.

I send you my best wishes as well,

Jo Jo

Hut Number Six
Faxos Institute
Faxos
Sunday April 12th

Dear Jo Jo,

What fantastic news about the exhibition! Of course I will come to the opening. September seems a long way off, though. The spring is so glorious here. I've never seen such colours before.

At our meeting yesterday morning Angela Hacker asked the writers' group to write the first page of a novel.

I wanted to run up the hill to my hut immediately and present her with the whole manuscript of *Lo! The Flat Hills of My Homeland*, but I restrained myself. The book was only a few pages short of completion. Why spoil the ship for a ha'p'orth of tar? (Since being forbidden to use clichés, I find myself using them all the time.)

I worked all day and most of the night on *Lo!* And I think that now the book is finished. This is how it ends:

Jake got up from his computer terminal and paced around his study. He adjusted the painting of a stately African woman that he had recently bought in an exhibition.

He then stared moodily out of the window and watched a child dragging a stick along the ground.

Jake was desperate to finish *Sparg from Kronk*. He could hear the printer banging on his door, demanding the finished manuscript. His publisher had been admitted to hospital the night before with nervous strain, but the ending of his book continued to elude him.

The child outside the window stopped to scratch the stick into the dry earth of drought-hit London.

'Goddit!' shouted Jake, and he leaped into his state-of-the-art typing chair and began to write the end of his book.

Sparg wrestled with Krun, his father, for possession of the stick. He wondered why they were fighting over this particular stick. There were plenty of others lying around.

He looked at his father's old face, now disfigured by anger, and thought: why are we *doing* this? He let go of the stick and allowed his father to take it away.

Sparg sat on the baked earth and thought, if only there was *language*, we wouldn't have to be so damned *physical*.

He poked his finger into the dust. He drew it along. In a few minutes, he had made marks and symbols.

Before the sun had gone down, he had written the first page of his novel. He hoped it wouldn't rain in the night and obliterate his work.

Tomorrow, he would continue his work inside a cave, he thought. What should he call his novel? He grunted to himself and tried out several titles. Finally, he settled on one and hurried to the big cave to scratch it on the wall before he forgot:

A BOOK WITH NO LANGUAGE

Yes, that was it. And he picked up a stick and began to gnaw the end of it into a point.

Jake could hardly wait for the electronic printer to spew out the typewritten page.

'At last,' he jubilated, 'I have finished *Sparg from Kronk*!'

Please let me know what you think, Jo Jo. I really value your opinion.

I gave the completed manuscript to Angela Hacker this morning. She took it from me and groaned, 'Sodding hell. I only asked for one page!' Then she put it into the blue raffia bag that she carries everywhere with her and continued her conversation with Clara about a dream she'd had of being chased by a giant cockroach.

At 11.00 p.m., after spending the evening with my friends, singing on the bar terrace, I got back to my hut to find that the following note had been slipped under my door:

Adrian,

I've skipped through *Lo! The Flat Hills of My Homeland*. I won't waste words. It's typical juvenilia and has no merit at all. *Sparg from Kronk* has been done a million times, dearest boy. But *A Book With No Language* – Sparg's novel – is a truly brilliant concept.

I would like you to come and see me when we get back to London. I'd like to introduce you to my agent, Sir Gordon Giles. I think your originality will appeal to him.

Congratulations! You are a writer.

Angela Hacker

I may be a writer, Jo Jo, but I can't find the words to express my happiness.

My plane gets into Gatwick on Wednesday at 3.00 p.m.

Love from,
  Adrian

Tuesday April 14th

Angela Hacker announced this morning that the writers' group's last meeting was to be held on 'Bare Bum Beach'. My penis shrivelled at the thought. I have never appeared in the nude in public before. 'Bare Bum Beach' is where the extrovert and confident desport themselves. I am neither of these things. However, after three glasses of retsina at lunchtime I found myself slithering over the rocks, heading for the nudist beach.

I was astounded by the ridiculous blue of the sea. The rocks shone pink as I stumbled towards the beach which was the colour of custard. It seemed the most natural thing in the world to shrug my shorts off and embrace the sand. For twelve long years I have worried about the size of my penis. Now, at last, by glancing at my fellow male writers I could see that I am made as other men. I easily fell within the 'normal' range.

At half past six in the evening I turned over and exposed myself to the sun. Nothing terrible happened.

There was no thunderbolt. Men and women did not run away, shrieking in horror at the sight of my full frontal nakedness.

I walked into the sea and swam towards the blood-red sunset. I allowed myself to float and to drift. It was almost dark when I swam back to the beach. I did not use my towel. I let the water dry on my body.

I walked back to the Institute in pale moonlight. I took a short cut through the woods. The floor was covered in pine needle debris, every footstep was a crackling aromatic delight.

I walked ankle deep through a glade of soft grass and wild flowers. Then I smelled honeysuckle and felt a tendril brush across my face. I reached the headland and stood for a moment, looking down at the Institute. The kitchen door was open. Out of it spilled bright light, laughter and the delicious smell of grilling meat.

Wednesday April 15th

10.00 p.m. I saw Jo Jo waiting beyond the barrier. I threw all my baggage down and ran towards her.